ANOTHER TANGO

"I don't hop into bed with every man I'm attracted to, and I don't plan to hop into bed with you. You're wasting your time on me. The night's still young, I'm sure you can find someone else to tango with."

He chuckled, tipping her chin with a curved finger and a familiarity that astonished her. His gaze was slightly admonishing, his smile one-hundred percent lethal. Callie knew it wasn't the sudden jerk of the elevator going up that caused her stomach to drop to her feet.

"I'm surrounded by tall, leggy blondes, tall, leggy brunettes, and tall, leggy redheads. I could have any of them or all of them." Somehow, he managed to say this without conceit. "But they don't even come close to stirring my blood the way you have tonight. What does that tell you?"

"That you're tired of tall, leggy women?" Callie quipped, surprising herself. Her sudden blush betrayed her.

"A bona fide blush," he drawled, sounding truly amazed. "Now, that's something you don't see every day. Who are you? Where have you been all of my life?"

CRITICS RAVE FOR SHERIDON SMYTHE!

MR. COMPLETE

"Sprinkled liberally with laugh-out-loud scenes, and not one but several yummy hunks, this fast-paced story will keep you engrossed to the last page."
—*Romantic Times*

"Humorous and hunk-heaven, Sheridon Smythe spins a delightful tale."
—*Midwest Book Review*

"*Mr. Complete* is absolutely, positively HOT. Sheridon Smythe has written another sexy, hilarious romance that will keep you laughing out loud and have the windows fogging up. From the sexy characters to a definitely unique plot, this book is a Perfect 10 all the way around."
—*Romance Reviews Today*

"This will become many a fan's favorite...it will make you a fan of her hot, steamy, and completely wonderful romances!"
—A Romance Review

HOT NUMBER

"*Hot Number* is a fast-moving story with loads of sexual pressure and plenty of hot scenes....[a] light and humorous tale."
—*RT BOOKclub*

"...An engaging romance... For a thoroughly entertaining read, I recommend *Hot Number*."
—*Romance Reviews Today*

"*Hot Number* moves at a fast pace, and gives us lots of chuckles...a great read that any fan of contemporary romance won't want to miss."
—A Romance Review

COMPLETELY YOURS

SHERIDON SMYTHE

LOVE SPELL NEW YORK CITY

LOVE SPELL®

May 2005

Published by

Dorchester Publishing Co., Inc.
200 Madison Avenue
New York, NY 10016

ISBN 0-505-52613-1

The name "Love Spell" and its logo are trademarks of Dorchester Publishing Co., Inc.

Printed in the United States of America.

Visit us on the web at www.dorchesterpub.com.

This one's for my niece,
Miranda Lee Partee. You're not only
beautiful, you're intelligent, talented, and sweet.
I'm looking forward to watching you turn into
the wonderful woman I know
you'll become. I love you!

A special thanks to the Haverkampf twins for
inspiring the characters Dillon and Wyatt Love.

Prologue

"How was your trip?" Callie Spencer asked, kissing her sister's cheek before taking a seat across from her. The second her butt hit the chair, a waiter arrived with a tall, frosted glass of unsweetened tea, no lemon. Exactly the way she liked it. Callie arched a questioning brow at Fontaine, who blew out a cynical breath.

"That was a perfect example of how my trip went," Fontaine grumbled. "Everyone in Dallas knew I was coming. If I ever discover the little mole who's ratting me out, I'm going to boil him or her alive."

"You think someone in the company is selling us out?" Callie thought the possibility a little ludicrous. *Next Stop* was a travel magazine; they specialized in helping travelers find the best—and avoid the worst—restaurants, hotels, and entertainment across the United States. Callie knew that Fontaine planned to expand their magazine to include exotic locations around the world as soon as their budget allowed.

"What other explanation could there be?" Fontaine countered. She tapped her scarlet nails on the table, revealing her frustration. "Our readers want unbiased, honest critiques, and we can't provide them with that when the establishments I'm targeting get advance warning and put on their best faces."

Callie, who helped design the top-notch travel magazine, sympathized with both sides. She unfolded her napkin and placed it across her lap, searching for a delicate way to voice her opinion without sounding disloyal. "Millions of people depend upon your magazine when they plan their vacations, Fontaine, which gives you enormous power. If you owned an establishment and knew a review could make or break you, wouldn't *you* want to be forewarned?" Now that she thought about it, she could very well imagine someone paying for the information.

Fontaine stuck out her tongue. "Traitor. You're trying to make me feel guilty for telling the truth, but it won't work. I owe my loyalty to my readers, and I'm never unfair." She pushed her menu aside and leaned forward, dropping her voice so that Callie had to lean forward as well. "I've got a brilliant plan, Callie, but I'm going to need your help."

"The last time I heard those words," Callie reminded her dryly, "I spent two weeks twiddling my thumbs, grounded for helping you sneak out of the house to meet your boyfriend."

With an unrepentant grin, Fontaine waved a careless hand. "You have to admit, dressing Mom's seamstress dummy in my pajamas was a brilliant idea."

"I wouldn't exactly call it brilliant, since it didn't fool Mom."

"I think it was the wig. Oh, well, this is different."

Callie shot her a wary glance, but went for the bait. "What have you got in mind?"

With a smug, catlike smile, Fontaine sat back in her chair. "Atlanta's next on my schedule. I'm going to send in a decoy, then fly down afterward to catch them with their pants down."

Although she felt a pang of sympathy for the unsuspecting establishments, Callie had to admit her sister's plan was a good one. "Who's the decoy?"

"You."

"Me?" Callie squeaked out. "Why me?"

"Because it's high time you stopped grieving over pretty boy Lanny and had some fun. This will be the vacation you should have taken last year, and the year before."

"But—"

"No buts. I'm not taking no for an answer, and you'll be helping me out, remember? We're the only people who know you'll be a decoy, so our little informant's reputation will suffer when Atlanta's entrepreneurs find out he gave them false information."

A nervous waiter arrived to take their order. Fontaine wisely waited until he was out of earshot before she continued.

"As my decoy, you'll get the red-carpet treatment. Your only job will be to relax and enjoy yourself. Lanny's taken enough from you, don't you think?"

Callie swallowed painfully. She and Lanny had been divorced for three years, and she still couldn't bear to look at a men's catalog for fear of seeing his handsome face. Since the divorce, she had buried herself in her work, avoiding "pretty boys" in any shape, form, or fashion.

"Do this for yourself, Callie, and for me," Fontaine pleaded persuasively. "Let your hair down—and I mean that literally—and live a little. God, you look like a schoolteacher, and you could have been a model!"

Involuntarily, Callie's hand went to her unattractive, tight ponytail. She started to protest, but knew she would be lying, just as Fontaine would know it. Pushing her glasses back into place, she said with quiet dignity, "I'm not that naive little girl anymore, sis."

Fontaine lifted a challenging brow. "If that's true, then what are you afraid of? And by the way, I've reserved an escort for you from a company called Mr. Complete. The owner agreed to furnish an escort for the three weeks you'll be in Atlanta in exchange for an ad in our magazine." Before Callie could argue, Fontaine rushed on. "I always hire an escort when there's one available. It keeps the hounds at bay."

Callie's mouth went dry. She took a hasty sip of her tea. "H-hounds?"

"Yes, hounds. I've discovered that attractive women traveling alone are like red flags to men." Fontaine laughed at Callie's alarmed expression. "Honey, we have to get you over this dating phobia, and I think hiring an escort is just the ticket. You'll get a chance to test your new wings with a gorgeous hunk who knows how to make a woman feel desirable."

Narrowly avoiding disaster with her tottering tea glass, Callie curled her fingers around it to hold it in place. "Did you say gorgeous? Because if you did, you know how I feel—"

"Callie, Callie. These men are professionals. They won't step out of line, no matter how tempted they are. Trust me on this. I checked out the company thoroughly, and Mr. Complete has a pristine reputation. Your escort will be a perfect gentleman."

"I don't need an escort." Especially a gorgeous escort who got paid to make her feel desirable. Callie shuddered inwardly. The mere thought provoked a panic that was almost nauseating.

"Nonsense. After your makeover and a new wardrobe, you'll be grateful for the buffer." Fontaine's lips curved with mischief. "Don't worry; if you happen to meet someone who interests you, you can tell your escort to get lost. He won't take it personally."

The idea was so ludicrous, Callie couldn't stop an involuntary laugh. It was time to set her sister straight. "First of all, my devious, meddling sister, I'm not interested in a makeover, or a new wardrobe. I'm also not interested in an escort, gorgeous or otherwise. If I do you this favor, I do it on my own terms."

Fontaine's eyes narrowed, warning Callie that she wouldn't give up without a fight. "Have you forgotten, my darling little sister, that you'll be representing *Next Stop*? Do you really want to go to Atlanta looking like a frumpy spinster?"

"That's a cheap shot!" Callie felt her face heat. She glared at Fontaine. It wasn't easy to argue when she knew deep in her heart that Fontaine spoke the brutal truth.

Gentling her tone, Fontaine moved in for the kill. "Have you looked in the mirror lately? I mean, really, really looked at yourself?" She indicated the shapeless dress Callie wore. "I can't tell if you weigh a hundred pounds or two hundred pounds. And your face . . . you haven't worn makeup in ages, or done anything different to your hair. Are you truly happy hiding under a rock, Callie?"

Callie wanted to tell her the truth: that she *was* happy under her safe little rock, but she knew her sister wouldn't understand.

Fontaine had never suffered a broken heart.

Chapter One

"So, do you think Ramon will like it?"

Dillon Love stared at the undulating shark tattooed across the blond giant's butt with a mixture of horror and fascination. He couldn't decide which was more shocking: the animal-print thong the man wore, the tattoo, or the fact that he'd so blithely dropped his drawers in front of him.

Before he could jump-start his brain out of its shocked state, the bare-assed man jerked up his pants and turned to face him.

"It's neat, isn't it? I mean, how can Ramon not believe I love him when he sees his name tattooed in the belly of old Jaws? This should put his silly insecurities to rest, right?" He zipped and buttoned his jeans, grinning like a fool and completely without embarrassment. "I owe you one, man. Your idea was brilliant. Chalk another one up for Dr. Love!"

The way Dillon figured it, he had two choices. He could simply nod and pretend that he knew what Greg was talking about. Or he could embarrass the hell out of the man by telling him he wasn't Wyatt.

It was no contest. The devil in Dillon couldn't resist. He stuck out his hand, and with a wicked grin said to the unsuspecting Greg, "You must be Greg. I'm Dillon, Wyatt's, um, twin brother. I think we've met before, but it was dark and you were drunk."

Greg's jaw dropped. As Dillon struggled to contain his laughter, a red flush rose past the collar of Greg's shirt and suffused his handsome face. Even his ears turned red.

Slowly Greg covered his scarlet face with his hands and spoke between his fingers. "I can't believe I dropped my pants in front of Wyatt's brother. The guys will never let me live it down."

Dillon's laughter bubbled over. He clasped his chest and gasped for breath. "Don't worry . . . I won't tell . . . a soul!"

The escort looked so hopeful Dillon thrust out his hand again to offer the shake Greg had been too embarrassed to see the first time around. "I swear. Let's shake on it."

With an aw-shucks grin that immediately endeared him to Dillon—on a manly level, of course—he clasped Dillon's hand and popped two of Dillon's knuckles with the strength of his grip.

"I completely forgot Luke and Lydia were leaving for their honeymoon and you were coming in to take Luke's place!" Still clutching Dillon's hand in a crushing grip, he leaned closer, peering into Dillon's face. He let out a disbelieving whistle. "Man, if it wasn't for the eye color, I'd say you and Wyatt were identical."

"We *are* identical," Dillon tugged his hand out of

7

danger, resisting the urge to massage his aching knuckles. "Wyatt wears colored contacts. He's blind as a bat without them."

"Really?" Greg's wicked grin was infectious. "Son of a gun! Ramon and I had a bet that he wore contacts."

"I take it Ramon's the lucky guy floating in the belly of your shark?" Dillon leaned back and clasped his hands behind his head, relaxing.

"Yeah, Ramon's my man," Greg said, blushing again. "He's having these weird dreams about finding me with someone else. It's making him paranoid and me crazy."

Dillon's lips twitched. "I think the tattoo should do it."

"Really? You're not just saying that?"

"If I were Ramon—" He stopped short, biting the inside of his cheek. He'd just discovered it was impossible to think "gay" when you were one hundred percent straight. "Let me put it this way: if Ramon doesn't like it, he's a fool."

Greg flopped into a chair and ran a hand through his blond hair, looking relieved. "If he doesn't like it . . . I'm going to smack him. Son of a bitchin' tattoo hurt like the devil." His face brightened. "Hey, you're almost as good with this Dr. Love thing as Wyatt is. Maybe it's in your genes. Now I owe *you* one. Anything I can do for you?"

"Well . . . as a matter of fact, there is." He spread his hands to encompass the messy desk. "I could use a few tips. The only thing Luke said to me just before he handed me the keys was, 'Don't worry; running this place is a piece of cake.'"

For the next two full minutes, Dillon had to sit patiently while Greg collapsed into helpless laughter. Underneath, a trickle of unease began to skitter along his nerve endings. Greg wasn't just chuckling; he was nearly falling out of his chair laughing. Tears were rolling down the big guy's face. And Dillon didn't think he was faking it.

That was the really scary part.

"You . . . you . . ." Greg pointed a finger at him, then hugged himself as another spasm of laughter shook his giant body. Finally he sucked in great gulps of air, wiped his eyes, and tried to keep a straight face. "I'm sorry. That's the best laugh I've had in a week or more. He really said that? Those exact words? In front of Lydia, and she didn't crack up?"

"Yes," Dillon said dryly. "And no, Lydia didn't laugh, but she did smile. Now that I think about it, Luke was grinning, too. Damn."

"You've been had, my friend. Running this place will make your nightclub seem like a walk in the park."

"Wonderful. Spill, please." Dillon crossed his arms and braced himself.

"Well, for starters, have you met the infamous secretary?"

"Briefly, at Luke and Lydra's wedding party. Mrs. Scuttle, right?"

"You can't use that tone."

Dillon felt a jolt of alarm. "What tone? Was I using a tone?"

"Yes, you were." Greg looked grim. "You have to say her name reverently."

"Reverently?"

"Yes, reverently. And loudly enough for her to hear you. Otherwise she'll think you're calling her something else, and that wouldn't be good."

"Quick with her tongue, is she?"

"No. Life would be so much simpler and safer if she used her tongue as a weapon." He paused a beat, as if allowing the anticipation—and in Dillon's case, terror—to build. "She'll throw something at you."

"You're pulling my leg, right? Luke would have mentioned something like that to me—"

"No, no, he wouldn't have." Greg gave his head an emphatic shake. "She terrifies him, but he's too macho to admit it."

Dillon swallowed slowly. "Terrified?"

"Terrified," Greg confirmed. "There are three basic rules you need to remember when you're around Mrs. Scuttle. Don't contradict her, no matter what she says. Don't mention computers, faxes, or scanners. And never, ever approach her if she's napping."

"She naps at work?"

"She's seventy-nine years old, Dillon. She's lucky she's not taking a permanent nap."

"If she's that old, why is she working?"

"Okay, that would be number four. Never ask her that."

"What happens if I approach her when she's napping?"

"She bites. She nearly bit Jet's hand off when he tried to see if she was still breathing."

Confused, Dillon couldn't resist. "If she's that terrifying to be around, why does Luke keep her on?"

Greg didn't hesitate. "That one's easy. She's great at her job, she's loyal, and we all love her to pieces."

Dillon scratched his head and gave up. "Anything else? Any other Mrs. Scuttles I should know about?"

"No, she's one of a kind," Greg said without a twitch of his lips. He shrugged. "I don't know. Oh, yeah, you might want to know that sometimes Luke babysits Ivan's four-year-old, Joey, while he's working out in the gym."

Quickly putting a face to the name, Dillon swallowed hard and managed a flippant laugh. "What could be so daunting about a four-year-old?"

"You—" Greg snapped his mouth closed. "Never mind. Mainly, just be there for us; carry your beeper and your cell phone at all times. Be the boss, the troubleshooter, our friend, our shrink. . . ." He spread his hands. "You're the man." He rose and walked to the door. He glanced back over his shoulder to add, "Oh, you might want to get a gun before Mrs. Scuttle comes back. For protection." His sudden, wicked grin revealed dazzling white teeth. "Just kidding. Holler if you need me. You've got my number."

After Greg had gone, Dillon soaked up the blessed silence for a moment, ignoring the insistent, hysterical voice screaming at him to abandon ship. He'd agreed to take over for Luke for three weeks, and come hell or Mrs. Scuttle armed with a paperweight, he was going to fulfill his promise.

He sighed, leaned back, and closed his eyes. It was never quiet at his nightclub, no matter what time of day, and he'd been hoping for a break from the constant noise. Plus, this arrangement would give Wyatt an opportunity to take on more responsibility at the club, in addition to his part-time job working as an escort for Mr. Complete.

Eager to get started, he opened the thick schedule book to begin the task of rearranging Wyatt's appointments so that he was free to manage the club while Dillon managed Mr. Complete. Mrs. Scuttle wouldn't be back from vacation until the following Thursday, so Dillon was in charge of the whole enchilada until she returned.

Troubleshooter, object dodger, babysitter, shrink, shark expert—he could swing it, if only to prove to

11

Luke that he hadn't pulled the proverbial wool over Dillon's eyes. His friend would find out that payback was a bitch.

Dillon smiled at the dozens of sticky notes filled with Luke's reminders and suggestions placed sporadically throughout the appointment book. The man was thorough, Dillon mused, turning the pages in search of Wyatt's appointments.

A sheet of company stationery stuck between the pages caught his attention. He recognized Luke's handwriting, but it was the contents that gave him pause. It was a reminder to Mrs. Scuttle not to charge Callie Spencer for escort services during her three-week stay in Atlanta, explaining that the travel magazine, *Next Stop*, promised a full-page glossy ad in its year-end review issue in exchange for escort services rendered.

Next Stop.

Dillon cursed beneath his breath. Just the mention of the travel magazine that had nearly ruined him last year was enough to make him seethe with renewed anger. The bad review had cost him thousands of dollars. In the end, he'd been forced to rename the club and sink another ten grand into remodeling.

He was still paying off that loan, dammit.

He was tempted to call Luke a traitor, until he remembered that he hadn't known Luke at the time.

No, Luke hadn't known about the disaster, and Dillon had been too humiliated to confide in him. That humiliation returned to haunt him each time he saw a copy of the glossy travel magazine, or heard the magazine mentioned, which was far too often for Dillon's peace of mind.

The small, previously unknown magazine had

grown into a household name in record time, making it doubly dangerous for unsuspecting restaurants, nightclubs, and hotels that weren't up to *Next Stop*'s impossibly high standards.

Dillon thumped a frustrated fist onto the desktop. What gave a person the right to make or break a business? Nobody should be in possession of that kind of power, he reasoned.

Rubbing the sudden ache between his eyes, he read the rest of the note, seeing that Luke had assigned Jet to be Callie Spencer's escort, leaving him a long list of dos and don'ts. His gaze narrowed as his mind began to turn down a devious path.

Callie Spencer might have the power in her impossible-to-please hands, but he had a bit of ammunition of his own.

He knew she was coming to Atlanta.

He could warn everyone that might possibly be on her hit list.

And he could escort her himself, charm the pants off her—literally, if he had to. It wasn't as if Callie Spencer would be paying him—Dillon wasn't even on Luke's payroll—so Luke's steadfast rule of no intimacy between client and escort wouldn't exactly apply in this particular case.

Dillon wasn't conceited. He knew women were drawn to him, just as they were drawn to his brother. In fact, as a nightclub owner, he had become a damned expert at fending off women, to the point that he'd become cynical and jaded.

It would be a challenge and a refreshing change to woo a woman, especially when the end results would help so many of his fellow businessmen. He'd have to throw himself into the task 110 percent in order to distract her from her job, Dillon mused, because he wasn't foolish enough to think she'd be easy. Any woman who chose such a nasty job had to be not only tough, but resistant to outside influence. Cold and calculating. Career driven. In all probability, a controlling, tight-lipped, immaculately groomed middle-aged judge wannabe.

Yes . . . definitely a challenge.

With a righteous gleam in his eyes, Dillon reached for the phone.

He froze, his fingers hovering over the buttons. Slowly he slid his gaze sideways to get a full view of the whisker-twitching creature staring back at him from the desktop with beady little black eyes.

The black-and-white rat balanced effortlessly on his hind legs. His nose twitched, sending the black whiskers vibrating.

"Easy, fella," Dillon heard himself say in a shamefully squeaky voice. "You're a pet, right? You've got to be a pet. Please tell me you're a pet."

The phone rang. The rat jerked, and Dillon thought he saw a flash of razor-sharp teeth. Using his little finger, he jabbed quickly at the speaker button. Sweat popped out on his brow and upper lip.

"Dillon? You there?"

It was Greg. Dillon kept his eye on the rat as he said, "Yeah." He was afraid to move his lips too much, afraid he might entice the rat.

"I forgot to tell you . . . Joey lost Bingo in the office last Tuesday. If we don't find him before Mrs. Scuttle comes back . . . well, think like Stephen King on that one, my friend."

"Bingo," Dillon managed through clenched teeth.

14

"Rat?" At the moment, Mrs. Scuttle was the lesser of the two evils.

"Yeah, he's a rat. Black and white, about two pounds. Big sucker."

Dillon wanted to ask if he was a biter, but he didn't want to give Bingo any ideas. "Uh, suppose Bingo was sitting on my desk right now. Got any ideas on how to catch him?"

"Yeah. Luke put a block of cheese in his left-hand drawer, hoping to lure Bingo inside. If you get him there, just close the drawer and call Ivan. Good luck."

The line went dead, but not before he heard Greg chuckling. Dillon carefully jabbed at the speaker button a second time, hanging up. Very slowly he retracted his hand until he thought it was safe from those sharp, pointed teeth. Moving cautiously, he opened the left-hand drawer.

Sure enough, there was indeed a block of dried cheddar cheese lying smack dab in the center of a glossy copy of *Next Stop*. Dillon suppressed a wince at the sight of the magazine from hell, looked at Bingo, saw his nose start twitching furiously, and decided it would be prudent to sit tight and see what developed.

Bingo dropped to all fours, leaned over the desk, and peered inside at the cheese, then fell onto it as if he hadn't eaten in days.

Dillon slammed the door hard enough to move the desk. He covered his sweating face with his hands and groaned. "Piece of cake, my ass." After a calming moment, he inched the drawer open enough to see the gleam of Bingo's eyes. "By the way, that magazine you're standing on is your toilet, buddy."

Chapter Two

The dress was too red.

Too red, too short, and too much. Once upon a time wearing red had made Callie feel sexy. Now it made her feel exposed.

She was seated at a small table for two in the elegant hotel bar, enjoying an after-dinner drink to complement the excellent grilled salmon she'd eaten in the hotel restaurant. So far she didn't have one single complaint about the staff, the hotel, or the food. But then, she wasn't the expert; Fontaine was. Fontaine had always told her she was too easy to please.

Well, Callie had to admit that her sister was smart—and usually right—but she'd been wrong about the hounds. She'd been in Atlanta more than eight hours. Dined alone, walked alone along the well-lit streets outside the hotel, and now sat in a hotel bar alone, and nobody had approached her. Canceling her escort for the night had been the smart thing to do, she told herself for the fifth time. She would never have been able to relax and enjoy herself if she'd been with a man . . . especially a paid escort who would undoubtably lie through his teeth to her all night long and remind her of someone she'd rather forget.

"Excuse me . . . haven't we met before?"

Startled, Callie nearly spilled wine down the front of her too-red, too-short dress. She clutched the stem and looked up. The man who'd spoken the worn-out cliché in a deep, disturbing voice flashed a wicked smile at her. Her breath caught in her throat.

A hound. An extremely good-looking hound. On a hound scale of one to ten, he was definitely an eight. Possibly a nine.

"Just kidding. But seriously, if I had met you before, I most certainly wouldn't have forgotten."

When she continued to stare at him blankly, he flashed her that bone-melting smile again, his blue eyes glinting with a devilish light that made her heart skip a dangerous beat.

"Just kidding . . . again." He glanced at her nearly empty glass. "Can I buy you another glass of wine?"

Callie finally found her voice. "I don't think—"

"No strings attached, I swear. I got dumped tonight, so I'm feeling a little blue."

Dumped? This gorgeous hunk got dumped? Callie might be naive, but she wasn't stupid. No woman in her right mind—well, *she* might be an exception—would dump a man like this man without a damned good reason.

So it was another line, a hook, a ploy to gain her sympathy . . . for what?

To Callie's surprise—and alarm—she found herself slightly curious. "Um, go ahead. Have a seat, but I can buy my own drink, thank you." How long had it been since she'd flirted? Had a man come on to her? And *was* he coming on to her? Or was she overdramatizing?

"Ah," he said as he pulled out the dainty little metal chair and sat across from her. "Independent."

She heard herself say with admirable flippancy, "Aren't all women these days?"

He surprised her again by frowning, looking thoughtful. Finally he shook his head. "You're probably going to think I'm crazy, but I think deep down a woman wants to be pampered and spoiled." His blue eyes clashed with hers. "Maybe even dominated, if it's subtle enough."

The sudden flare of sexual heat that sparked between them had Callie swallowing nervously. It was one thing to think about flirting with a strange man, quite another to have thoughts of going to bed with him. *Maybe that's what you need.* The reckless, stunning thought slammed into her. She felt her eyes go wide with the realization. Revealing heat crept into her face. Who would have thought a rather brutal analysis, a simple makeover, a new wardrobe, and a trip to Atlanta would turn her into a slut, panting after the first man to make a move?

Panting? Was she panting? Alarmed, Callie checked her breathing, deciding it wasn't exactly panting. Breathing fast. *Yes, that's it.* She was breathing fast. She'd had two glasses of wine, and everyone knew that alcohol thinned the blood.

Lowered inhibitions.

Numbed a mind to danger.

Besides, the man was a hunk, even hunkier than her ex. He made Lanny the underwear model look like Peter Pan. The realization should have had alarm bells clanging in her head by now. Flirting with him would be like taunting fate, and she never believed that old adage about fighting fire with fire. Except . . . now that she thought about it, it did have its merits.

Or maybe that was the wine talking.

The bartender himself delivered their drinks—another white wine for her, and a frosted bottle of imported beer for her new friend. She watched him curl his long, slender fingers around the bottle and found herself imagining those fingers stroking her, teasing her.

A quiver flashed low in her belly. She tipped her wineglass and downed half the contents. They reached for a napkin simultaneously, bumping fingers. A hot jolt shot through her hand and into her arm. She jumped to her feet, causing the metal chair to rock precariously behind her.

Now she *was* panting. What the hell was wrong with her? Had the bartender put something in her drink? A female version of Viagra or something?

The stranger rose with her, looking genuinely concerned . . . and as bewildered as she felt. Was it possible, she wondered, that he felt the same intense connection? Or was she having some sort of weird sexual breakdown? Was there such a thing? She'd gone three years without sex, without even kissing another man. She supposed anything was possible.

"You're pale. Are you sick?"

Sick? Damned right she was sick. And if she wasn't, she should be. Panting after a . . . a gorgeous hunk of a man who had the gall to talk about intimate things like domination with a complete stranger.

With hands that visibly shook, she snagged her purse from the chair and fumbled inside for her credit card. She couldn't look at him, didn't dare. "Um, I'm not feeling well, so I think I'll make it an early night." A quick, darting glance before she added lamely, "Jet lag."

"Right. Let me at least walk you to your room."

His apparent concern warmed her in places that hadn't been warmed in a long time. She shook her head, heading for the bar to pay her tab, praying he wouldn't follow.

Hoping that he would.

The bartender took her card and swiped it, then handed it back. Callie knew the instant *he* came to stand beside her. She tried to ignore him as she quickly signed the credit slip the bartender slid her way.

"I insist," the handsome stranger said softly, taking her elbow in a firm grip. "I may not know you, but my mother would have my hide if I let you go off to your room without an escort, especially with you feeling ill."

Callie tried, and failed, to imagine this man fearing anyone. *Dominating.* Yes, he definitely exuded dominance. And why did the very idea make her quiver inside?

She spun on her heel and brushed past him, trying to ignore the fact that he followed. Maybe she couldn't stop him from playing out his gentlemanly charade, but she didn't have to acknowledge him.

"Slow down."

Or talk to him. She jabbed the elevator button and clutched her purse, staring straight ahead.

"Was it something I said?"

Or maybe something he didn't say? They'd hardly spoken, yet she felt as if someone had rubbed her from head to toe—taking special care with her elbow where his fingers had touched—with that erotic warming lotion they discreetly advertised in the backs of magazines. *Maybe I'm having a hot flash*, she thought. She was thirty, and although she knew it was rare, she also

COMPLETELY YOURS

knew it wasn't impossible to be experiencing early menopause.

The thought made her suck in a sharp, pained gasp. She wanted children, and a homely husband who loved only her.

She did *not* want to have wild, dominating sex with a perfect stranger, even if he did make her bones melt and her skin burn.

Callie took a deep breath, willing the elevator doors to slide open. Okay, maybe she did want to have sex with him, but that didn't mean she'd be foolish or reckless enough to do it. And yes, maybe it *was* what she needed—she was certain Fontaine would agree—but that didn't mean she would do it.

Besides, the man hadn't actually suggested they have sex.

She flinched as his big hand landed softly on her back. He might as well have held that hand under an open flame before he touched her.

"You look positively flushed. Are you having a bad reaction to the wine, you think?"

No. I'm having a bad reaction to you. Fortunately the doors slid open, saving her from having to answer. She hurried inside, turning to face him, forcing a smile to her stiff, overheated face. "I'm fine, really. Good night."

He shoved his hand over the elevator door, stopping it. His gaze searched her face slowly, thoroughly, with the intensity of a painter contemplating his new subject.

Callie saw the exact moment he realized she wasn't ill, but aroused. She saw it in the sudden flare of his nostrils, and in the brief flash of primitive male satisfaction in his eyes.

With a muffled moan, she closed her own eyes, too embarrassed to face him. She stood there, trembling,

21

clutching her purse and wishing she'd kept that date with her escort. If she hadn't been so hell-bent on thwarting her sister, she would be saying good night to a professional who knew not to invade her very private, very jumpy space.

She heard the elevator doors swish closed, and wanted very badly to open one eye and see if he'd stayed on the other side.

Then she felt his warm breath on her neck, and knew that she was doomed.

"I'm just as confused as you are," he whispered, nuzzling her exposed neck so lightly she wasn't certain she didn't imagine it. "But whatever is happening between us . . . don't you think we owe it to ourselves to see it through?"

Another line, even if it was delivered with convincing sincerity.

Callie was no longer that naive, silly, blind girl she had once been. She took a deep breath and opened her eyes.

He was standing slightly to the side and behind her. She could feel the brush of his dinner jacket against the thin silk of her dress. Still feel his warm breath on her neck. But she did not have to look into his chiseled face and risk drowning in those gorgeous blue eyes.

"Believe it or not, I don't normally do this type of thing."

She chose—in the name of safety and sanity—not to believe him.

"And I don't think you're the type of woman who normally reacts this way, either."

At least he'd gotten *that* right! Oh, had he ever. She licked her lips and said with a huskiness she couldn't hide, "We should just . . . just forget about it."

"Chicken."

That softly spoken erotic challenge shivered over her. She tightened her fingers on her purse straps as if it were a lifesaving device and tried to conjure up an image of her lying, cheating ex-husband. Whenever she felt a moment's weakness, that usually did the trick.

But what swam before her eyes was the square-cut jaw, blue, blue eyes, and honey-blond hair of her elevator companion. She focused on the sexy dimple in the middle of his chin, realizing that she had to face him and stand up for herself.

To hell with her wild, insane-acting libido. She would *not* give in to it.

Hoisting her chin, she said with as much coolness as she could muster, "I don't hop into bed with every man I'm attracted to, and I don't plan to hop into bed with you. You're wasting your time on me. The night's still young; I'm sure you can find someone else to tango with."

He chuckled, tipping her chin with a curved finger and a familiarity that astonished her. His gaze was slightly admonishing, his smile one hundred percent lethal. Callie knew it wasn't the sudden jerk of the elevator going up that caused her stomach to drop to her feet.

"I'm surrounded by tall, leggy blondes, tall, leggy brunettes, and tall, leggy redheads. I could have any of them or all of them." Somehow he managed to say this without conceit. "But they don't even come close to stirring my blood the way you have tonight. What does that tell you?"

"That you're tired of tall, leggy women?" Callie quipped, surprising herself. Her sudden blush betrayed her.

"A bona fide blush," he drawled, sounding truly amazed. "Now, that's something you don't see every day. Who are you? Where have you been all of my life?" He filtered his hand into her hair and tried to tug her close. Bold and erotic. A dangerous mix.

Callie pooled her resources—panic, pride, and prudence—and held back. She seriously doubted she'd survive a kiss from this Romeo of men. She feared she would literally burst into flames and become one of those phenomena people talked about.

His gaze was on her mouth as he murmured, "An honest-to-God girl next door."

His soft, husky words washed over her like an arctic tidal wave.

He couldn't have known, but Lanny had said the same exact thing to her right before he proposed. He'd wanted an earthy, innocent wife, a woman who would stay home and have his babies while he . . . while he . . .

The elevator ground to a halt. The doors slid open with a whoosh. Callie literally shoved him aside and ran for her life.

Dillon stared after the fleeing woman, absorbing the shock of the effect she'd had on him.

Still had, in fact, if the pounding of his pulse and the tightness in his groin were any indication. What was it about the mystery woman that stirred his blood when countless other women—women more beautiful—left him cold? Was it her soft, husky voice with its intriguing tremors, or was it her huge, dark blue eyes, eyes that had filled with an erotic mixture of lust, panic, and embarrassment?

The hot attraction between them had been undeniable, yet she had reacted as if he'd offered to pay her for an exclusive lap dance in front of her mother.

He stuck his hands in his pockets and chuckled ruefully. It was a shame he had a more pressing agenda, because he'd enjoy nothing better than to pursue her and see what developed. He pressed the button to summon the elevator, wondering who she was and how long she was staying in Atlanta.

Too damned bad he had to charm the cobra, Callie Spencer, over the next few weeks. If she was as tough as Dillon suspected, he'd have little time for play.

The elevator doors slid open soundlessly. Dillon stepped inside, inhaling the mystery woman's lingering fragrance. He pushed the button labeled "lobby." Closing his eyes, he summoned up an image of her flushed, startled face when she realized he'd joined her in the elevator.

Fascinating . . .

He had to know more, had to find out her name. There were some things in life, Dillon decided as he stepped from the elevator and strode into the bar, that a man just had to do.

The bartender looked up as Dillon approached the bar. Dillon slid a twenty across the counter, capturing the man's undivided attention. "The name of the mystery woman?"

"I can't give out that information, sir." The bartender didn't pretend not to know what he was talking about.

Without blinking, Dillon switched out the twenty with a hundred dollar bill. "Her name?" he prompted.

Eyeing him warily, the bartender said, "You could be an ax murderer, for all I know. I don't want that on my conscience." He hesitated, then added, "I've got three girls of my own."

"And I've got a little sister." Dillon took out his billfold, withdrew his driver's license, and slid the card to him across the gleaming counter. "Make a copy of

25

that. If her body pops up in a Dumpster somewhere, you can clear your conscience by giving this information to the cops." He wasn't being sarcastic. He actually admired the man for his caution. As a nightclub owner, he'd been known to intervene on more than one occasion when a regular got drunk and recklessly decided she would leave the bar with a stranger.

Nine times out of ten—although they were never happy with him at the time—they came back and thanked him the next day. Once he'd gotten flowers and a thank-you note.

To Dillon's silent amusement and approval, the bartender took his license and disappeared into a tiny office located behind the bar. When he reappeared, he went to the cash register, opened it, and lifted the tray. He brought Dillon his license and the credit slip she'd signed and slid them across the counter to him. When the bartender's hand came away, the hundred-dollar bill was gone.

Dillon smiled at him, his pulse picking up speed as he turned the credit slip around.

His heart stuttered.

He blinked and read the name again, hoping to high heaven his eyes were playing nasty tricks on him.

They weren't.

His groan was loud enough to draw the attention of several patrons, not to mention the bartender, who was watching him with one lifted brow.

Callie Spencer. Obviously not a middle-aged, workaholic ballbuster, although the ballbuster part was still iffy.

"Something wrong?" the bartender asked.

Dillon bared his teeth. "You have no idea."

Chapter Three

Wyatt spewed root beer across the previously clean counter.

Stone-faced, Dillon patiently waited for his twin to stop laughing. He had a few splatters of root beer on his forearms and hands, but for the moment he ignored them.

Dillon's patience began to wear thin as Wyatt held his stomach and continued to laugh.

It was several hours before opening, so they were alone in the nightclub. Dillon had called Wyatt and asked his brother to meet him there, and now he was regretting that rash decision.

He should have known Wyatt would get a kick out of his blunder.

Wiping at his streaming eyes, Wyatt managed to gasp out, "So you acted like a randy goat, totally unaware that this woman was . . . was . . ." He went off again, the force of his mirth bending him double. "And now you want me to . . . to . . . Oh, this is too much! You have *got* to tell Mom!"

"Unlike you," Dillon said through gritted teeth, "I don't feel comfortable sharing the details of my sex life with our mother."

"But Mom would get a kick out of this one. You know how she loves a good laugh."

"No, thanks. I'll pass." Dillon grabbed a towel from the bar and wiped at his arms. He shot his twin a baleful look. "This affects you, too, now that you're part owner," he said, cheered when the reminder quickly sobered Wyatt. "Need I remind you what the last bad review cost the nightclub—and my wallet? If we get another bad one, you can kiss your plans to expand the dining area good-bye."

Wyatt straightened at that. "Wait a minute! It can't be that bad!"

"It is. It *could* be." And after last night, Dillon thought morosely, it most probably would be.

"And you honestly think your plan will work?" Wyatt rescued the bar towel Dillon had been twisting and slung it over his broad shoulder. "I get the apology part, but I don't see how my standing in for you is going to help."

Dillon put a hand over his mouth so that his response was muffled. "I don't trust myself around her just yet."

"Huh?"

"I said, since you'll be you pretending to be me, you won't scare her the way I did last night. After a couple of dates with you, she'll relax. Then I can take over and work my charm."

Wyatt's eyes narrowed slightly. "Are you saying I can't be charming?"

Stifling an impatient sigh, Dillon said, "Of course you can be charming. You work for an escort service, for

Pete's sake! I'm saying you can be charming without . . . without . . ."

"Acting like a randy goat?" Wyatt supplied helpfully. His cheeks bulged with the attempt to contain his laughter.

Dillon scowled, although he couldn't deny the accusation. He *had* acted like a randy goat, which was why he didn't trust himself around Callie until he was certain she wouldn't be gazing at him with that open, erotic, innocent lust. Just the memory drove him mad.

"What if she reacts to me like she did to you?"

"She won't." Dillon didn't care if his growled statement came out sounding like a threat.

"What if she does?" Wyatt persisted, mainly, Dillon thought, to irritate him.

"What if I put my fist down your throat?"

"Whenever you're feeling lucky."

"Go to hell."

"Ladies first."

They stared at each other just as they had from the time they both became aware of each other at the age of four months. Dillon was confident Wyatt would blink first; his contacts no longer allowed a very lengthy stare-down.

Which reminded him. "You'll have to change your contact lenses. I'm pretty certain she noticed the color of my eyes." His groin tightened at the memory. That wasn't all she'd noticed, he thought with a surge of male satisfaction and a hearty dose of anticipation.

"Dammit, Dillon!" Wyatt threw the towel onto the counter. "You want me to go in blind? I'll have to wear my old contacts, and I'm not exaggerating when I say they are *old*."

"Don't you have glasses? I seemed to remember seeing you in them a time or two."

"I look like a nerd. I will not wear glasses. I'd rather be blind."

That suited Dillon, since it meant he wouldn't have to worry about Wyatt ogling Callie. "Whatever. Are you in? I'll owe you one."

"Damned right you will. Big-time."

"Sheesh, Wyatt. It's not like you don't do this sort of thing for a living."

"Exactly my point. I'm on vacation from Mr. Complete, remember? I don't have to shave if I don't want to. I don't have to worry about clipping my nails, or getting dirt beneath them, or smelling good." He waved a hand at his worn jeans and faded T-shirt. "I can dress like a bum, and—"

"Mercy!" Dillon cried, holding up his hand in surrender. "I get it, I get it. I will owe you big-time, little brother."

"Born five stinkin' minutes after you," Wyatt grumbled good-naturedly. "You gotta make a big deal out of it. And not only that, you give me the nightclub for three weeks; then you take it away."

"Three dates. Three lousy dates with a beautiful woman. Should be a refreshing change."

"Bite me. I go out with plenty of beautiful women. Two dates."

"Three."

"Let's flip for it." Without waiting for an answer, Wyatt dug a quarter out of the tight pocket of his jeans. He flipped it in the air and clamped his hand over it when it landed on his arm. "Call it."

"Heads."

Wyatt lifted his hand and peered at the coin. "Bastard."

Dillon grinned. "Sore loser." The beeper Luke had given him began to vibrate against his leg. He pulled it out, frowning at the number. Wyatt took it, glanced at it, then handed it back. Dillon didn't miss the suspicious gleam in his eye, either.

"That would be Ivan paging you."

Ivan. Joey. Big rat named Bingo. Dillon suppressed a shudder at the memory. "Wonder what he wants? I don't think he's on the schedule for tonight."

His twin shrugged. "Only one way to find out." He handed Dillon the portable phone and turned to wipe out the bar glasses with a clean towel.

Telling himself he had nothing to be nervous about—and that the gleam in Wyatt's eye was just an immature attempt to shake him up—he dialed the number from the pager.

Ivan answered the phone on the first ring. He sounded out of breath. "Thank God you called, Dillon."

Although Dillon didn't know Ivan well, he'd gotten acquainted with him during the numerous occasions when Ivan came into the nightclub with a client, or brought his wife in for an occasional night out.

"What can I help you with, Ivan?"

"Do you know anything about plumbing?" Ivan asked breathlessly.

Plumbing? Dillon frowned at the phone. Was this a joke? Deciding to play along, he said cautiously, "A little. I replaced a sink once in Mom's upstairs bathroom."

"Good enough. Can you come over and help me with a little problem?"

"Ah . . . what problem would that be, Ivan?" Dillon waited for the punch line, certain it was coming. It would probably be something disgusting about bowel movements, or—

"Joey flushed his turtle down the toilet."

Not a punch line . . . at least not one that Dillon was familiar with. "Um, I'm sorry to hear that, but I don't know how I could help."

"It's stuck in the sewer pipe under the house. I can hear it scratching. The last babysitter let Joey watch this horror flick where an alligator gets flushed into the sewer system and grows into a giant killing machine. He wanted to see if it would work with the turtle." He paused a beat to let that sink in before adding, "I'm going to need an extra pair of hands when I go under the house and take the pipe apart."

Dillon stared blankly at Wyatt, who shot him an innocent smile. Covering the mouthpiece with his hand, Dillon asked his twin, "Would Luke help Ivan with his plumbing?"

"In a heartbeat."

Glaring at his brother, Dillon said into the phone, "Give me twenty minutes to change into some old clothes." After he'd hung up, he handed the phone to a far too innocent-looking Wyatt. "He's *your* buddy. Why don't you go?"

"Hey, I'm not the one who replaced the sink in Mom's upstairs bathroom."

"Why doesn't he call a plumber?" Dillon asked, unable to mask his irritation.

"Do you know what a plumber charges these days? Ivan's got two kids and a mortgage." Wyatt popped the cap from another root beer and slugged it back. He set the bottle on the counter with a thud and said with a straight face, "Besides, Ivan's had trouble getting a plumber after the last, um, incident."

Groaning would only entertain his rascally brother, Dillon thought, and managed to swallow it. "Care to fill me in?"

Wyatt cast him a pitying look. "You don't want to know, brother. You really don't want to know."

For once in his life, Dillon heeded his warning.

Feeling foolishly guilty, Callie reached into the zippered pocket of her big suitcase where Fontaine had failed to look and withdrew the smuggled dress. It was one of her favorites, a comfortable, shapeless number that helped her feel invisible.

She faced the full-length mirror and held the dress against her body. The muddy green color gave her tan a yellowish cast, and the ankle length completely hid her newly waxed legs as well as her shape.

In this dress, she would look like her old self. Invisible. Plain. Possibly thin, possibly fat. With her hair drawn into a tight ponytail and her face free of makeup, she would be . . . safe.

She had to do something. If she was indeed having some sort of weird sexual breakdown from three years of abstinence, then she could protect herself by slipping into her old skin.

This way, even if she couldn't control her own libido, it was unlikely she would attract a man like the one she'd met last night.

A shiver snaked down her spine. She clutched the dress, staring at the frightened girl in the mirror. Deliberately, she recalled her sister's harsh assessment. *Lanny not only broke your heart, he broke your spirit, and for that he should be tortured.*

But her spirit wasn't broken. She'd discovered that last night in the company of a gorgeous stranger.

And tonight she would be in the company of another gorgeous stranger, one whose work ethic would prevent him from provoking her starving libido with flaming looks and sexy innuendoes, if her sister could be believed. In fact, according to Fontaine she could strip naked and throw herself at her escort and he wouldn't take the offering.

Callie had to admit the thought was rather . . . liberating. If she was to climb out of this three-year slump, who better to practice on than a paid escort? It would be like having her very own robot.

Before her courage deserted her, Callie rolled up the dress and shoved it back into the hidden pocket. She sat down at the vanity. Her hands trembled slightly as she began to apply her makeup. When she'd finished, she brushed her hair until it shone and left it framing her face.

She slipped into a black, slinky strapless dress that felt like satin against her skin. Sexy black two-inch-high sandals and a tiny black purse completed her ensemble.

When she saw the seductive stranger in the mirror, her stomach took a sharp dive. Fear made her knees quiver. What was she doing? Was she truly ready for this 180 degree change? What if she ran into *him?* She might as well strap on a sign that said, "Take me."

"You're going to be with a professional escort," she reminded herself out loud. "There is no big, bad hound waiting to pounce on you the moment you open the door."

Someone knocked. She jumped, and so did her heart. Right into her throat.

34

Her escort had arrived.

Taking a deep, fortifying breath, she forced her wobbly legs to take her to the door.

He stood with his back to her, apparently unaware that she had opened the door. She cleared her throat.

He turned.

She gasped and took a hasty step in shocked retreat.

He stared at her, his jaw hanging as they locked incredulous gazes. Finally, he groaned in genuine embarrassment. "Tell me you're not the client? Please?"

She swallowed hard, but her voice came out husky anyway. "Are . . . are you saying that you're my . . . my escort?"

He groaned again. "Yes, and I swear that I had no idea who you were last night. I mean, I don't usually drink that much—"

"You were drunk?" Callie's thinking was too fuddled to dwell on why she felt insulted by the confession.

"God, this is so embarrassing. I wouldn't blame you if you called and reported me to the boss. I deserve to be fired." He shot her a beseeching, sheepish look that jolted her out of her shock. "But if you can give me another chance, I swear I'll make it up to you."

When he reached out and grabbed her hand, Callie instinctively braced herself.

Nothing happened.

No jolt of electricity. No hum of awareness. No sudden panic. Not a single sign of what she'd felt last night when this man had touched her. In fact, last night his smoldering look alone had sent her into a tailspin of confusion and desire.

But he was looking at her now, and he . . . "You've . . . you've got one brown eye and one blue eye!" she blurted out.

His quick, boyish smile evoked sympathy . . . and nothing more.

"Well, yeah. I lost one of my contacts. If I look at you like this"—he closed one eye and peered at her—"then I can see you clearly." He switched eyes. "But if I look at you like this, then you're kinda fuzzy."

"Fuzzy," she repeated faintly. He was squinting, which should have made him look silly. It didn't. Despite her strange lack of reaction, he was still the most gorgeous man she'd ever seen.

"But don't worry; I can still see that you are beautiful." He raised her hand and brought his lips down.

Callie tried to tug her hand free, certain her body would suddenly remember and the touch of his lips would start that shameless panting again. Maybe she really was having a breakdown, and this sudden numbness was part of it. Maybe blowing hot and cold was part of it, which meant she'd have to be on her guard for a sudden heat wave.

He kept her hand and kissed it.

His lips were cool. Belatedly she realized that his hand was cool as well, whereas last night it had felt like a branding iron on her back.

"Dillon Love, at your service. Oops." He gave a little laugh. "Maybe I shouldn't say that. At Your Service is the name of our competitor."

His last name was Love? Was he joking? Callie wondered, finally successful in retrieving her hand. Were the escorts like prostitutes, adopting catchy, provocative names?

She surprised herself by asking, "Is Love really your last name?"

He chuckled ruefully. "I'm afraid so. I lost count of the

black eyes I collected during my school years because of that name. We begged Mom to have it legally changed."

"We?"

"Oh, um, my brother, Wyatt, and myself. Little sister loved it. So, is all forgiven? I'll understand if you decide to get a replacement."

Callie was tempted. Boy, was she tempted. Could she trust herself around Dillon Love for the next several hours or more? And what if she couldn't? What if she *did* have another meltdown? He knew that she was a client now. Work ethics would prevent him from taking advantage of her in her weakened state, according to Fontaine.

She would be taking a risk . . . but taking risks was something she had avoided the past three years. If she was going to start living life again, then she had to start somewhere.

Why not with a blond, gorgeous, charming escort?

Offering him a weak smile, she said, "Why don't we just forget last night ever happened, and start over?" The relieved sigh he blew out caused her stomach to clench in dismay. She ignored the traitorous organ.

"Thank you." His smile was warm and grateful. "I knew you were an angel."

If he thought she was an angel after last night, Callie mused as she retrieved her lacy wrap from the bed, then what did he think of really bad girls? Hopefully, she wouldn't have to find out.

Inhaling a ragged breath, she curled her fingers around the rock-hard biceps of her escort and allowed him to lead her.

Chapter Four

Wyatt was going to enjoy being an uncle. He found himself smiling at the thought, and the perfect woman sitting across from him caught him in the act.

"Happy thoughts?"

If she only knew, Wyatt thought, trying hard to keep his smile from turning into a wicked grin. It had taken him an hour to get her to relax; he didn't want any setbacks. "Definitely happy thoughts. I think my brother's in love, and I was just thinking about how much I'm looking forward to becoming an uncle."

Her smile was wistful. "He's going to be a father?"

Wyatt nearly choked on a mouthful of lobster. "Um, no. I was jumping the gun. He's not exactly married yet."

"Oh." She lifted a dark, amused brow. "You really *are* jumping the gun, aren't you? Have they set a date?"

Dillon was right: he really did have a big mouth. "No, but I don't think it will be long now."

"Love at first sight?"

"Oh, yeah." Wyatt chuckled. "I'm not even sure my brother knows it yet." It was going to be so much fun watching Dillon struggle to pull Cupid's arrow out of his ass.

"This is your older brother?"

Wyatt resisted the immature urge to lie. "Yeah. How about you? Do you have any siblings?" A sister, maybe, who was as perfect as she was?

"Fontaine. She's also a workaholic, so I don't think I'm going to be an aunt anytime soon."

Nope. Just a mother, Wyatt thought gleefully. "Are your parents still living?"

She shook her head, those huge eyes suddenly filled with shadows. "No. We lost them in a car accident seven years ago."

"That must have been tough."

"It was. How about you?"

"Mom's still alive and kicking. My father died of a heart attack when I was in high school. Mom put us through college, so my brother and I are returning the favor. She's going to be a teacher."

"I'm sorry about your father."

"Me, too." Wyatt swallowed a lump in his throat. Callie was not only going to make an excellent wife and mother; she was going to be a great sister-in-law, too. Hoping to lighten the mood, he asked, "How long have you worked for *Next Stop*?"

"About three years. My sister owns the magazine. I work in the design department."

Very carefully, Wyatt laid his fork aside, striving to keep his expression neutral. "I thought you were here to critique Atlanta's hot spots."

"Oh. Yeah. That."

Wyatt eyed the darkening of her cheeks with extreme interest. He was getting the strong impression that she was lying. But why? "You're not here as a reviewer?"

"Yes, yes. I am." She took a roll from the breadbasket and made a big show of buttering it, effectively avoiding his curious gaze.

She was a lousy liar, Wyatt observed. More to the point, why would she lie? It didn't make sense. Lying and saying that she *wasn't* a reviewer he could understand. According to Dillon, reviewers were sneaky, conniving, heartless people who lived to surprise unsuspecting businesses.

Determined to dig until he got to the bottom of this mystery, Wyatt turned up the charm a notch or two. "I hope you don't mind my candor, but you're a beautiful woman, Callie. I can't believe some lucky guy hasn't snatched you up." He glanced up in time to catch the stark pain that suddenly flashed in her eyes.

He was dumbfounded.

The flush he'd seen earlier returned. Her chin angled out and up. "Some lucky guy did. Unfortunately, he didn't consider himself very lucky. I divorced him three years ago."

The lobster turned cold on his plate as Wyatt wrestled with a surprising surge of anger. "He hurt you." It was a statement of fact. Wyatt knew this as surely as he knew that Dillon would someday marry this woman.

"Not physically," Callie said. Her gaze dropped to her plate.

She looked so vulnerable Wyatt wanted to find the bastard who had hurt her and beat him to a pulp. If *he* felt that way, how would Dillon react when he found out?

"I'm sorry. I don't know why I told you something so personal."

"I was a priest in another life." Wyatt waited a beat. He was relieved when he saw her lips twitching. He pretended to be offended. "What, you can't picture me as a priest?"

"No."

"Hey, don't try to spare my feelings."

They both laughed, and the tension that had sprung up between them eased. As curious as Wyatt was to know more about her marriage, he knew when to back off. Apparently it was still a very painful subject. That explained the air of vulnerability surrounding her.

Not a weakness, but the result of a deep, deep hurt.

Dillon would have to handle her very carefully. She would spook easily. In fact, Wyatt was fairly certain Dillon had spooked her plenty last night, if her horrified expression when she'd opened the door was any indication.

The conversation turned to photography, something Wyatt had an interest in. By the time dinner was over, Wyatt was very certain of two things.

He would definitely mention to Dillon that Callie had been in a bad marriage and was as skittish around men as a saddle-shy filly, but he was *not* going to tell Dillon his suspicions about Callie's reason for being in Atlanta.

Wyatt chuckled inwardly, imagining Dillon's face after weeks of wooing Callie, only to discover she wasn't the threat he thought she was.

Dillon would kill him.

Oh, yes. Life was sweet!

She'd made it.

Callie stared at the closed door where her gorgeous escort had been standing just moments ago. She checked

her watch. Three hours and fifteen minutes in his surprisingly pleasant and relaxing company, and she hadn't
transformed into a panting, wild-eyed tramp.

Either she was cured, or last night had been a fig-
ment of her imagination. Possibly hallucinations
brought on by . . . jet lag? She supposed anything was
possible.

But to go from raging lust to not even a smidgen of
attraction?

"I've got to be going nuts," Callie mumbled. She
slung her evening wrap over the back of a chair and
slipped out of her shoes. Her laptop lay open on the
hotel desk, the screen saver a slide-show collection of
her favorite photos. She padded in her bare feet to the
computer.

Fontaine had sent three e-mail letters, each demanding to know why she hadn't responded to the first
dozen or so. She wanted details. Was she having fun?
Was she having wild sex with anyone? Was she hiding
in her room, and if she was, was Callie prepared to
have Fontaine fly down and drag her into the real
world?

Because she knew that Fontaine was fully capable of
carrying out her threat, Callie sat at the desk and answered. Yes, she was having fun. No, she wasn't having
wild sex, and no, she wasn't hiding in her room.

With amazing ease, Callie found herself telling
Fontaine about her evening with Dillon. He was funny
and charming . . . witty and silly. Yes, he was drop-dead
gorgeous, and Callie planned to use him again and
again.

Callie frowned. She hit the backspace button to
erase the words *use him again and again*. She was making him sound like some kind of sex slave, and wouldn't

Fontaine just love that? If her sister thought she was actually having sex with a man, Callie wouldn't put it past Fontaine to fly up just to document the historic event.

Finally Callie typed in, *plan to request his services again.* She sent the e-mail, then began to count slowly to one hundred as she dressed for bed. If she knew her sister . . .

The hotel phone rang before Callie reached fifty.

"You went out with a man," Fontaine said before Callie could say hello.

"What if you'd gotten the wrong room?"

Fontaine chuckled. "Then someone would have been shocked by my question. You didn't hyperventilate or throw up on him or anything?"

Hyperventilate. Callie twisted the phone cord around her finger. *Hyperventilate* could be another word for panting, she thought, recalling how she'd reacted to Dillon last night.

"Oh, my God. You threw up on him?"

Suppressing an exasperated sigh, Callie said, "No, I did not throw up on my escort."

"You hyperventilated?"

"Tonight? No, I didn't." Last night didn't count. Something had been wrong with the wine or her brain or something. Whatever happened had been a fluke. She'd felt nothing tonight. He could have been her brother, or a cousin. "Sorry to disappoint you, sis."

"You're not disappointing me, and you know it." Fontaine exhaled noisily. "In fact, I'm close to hyperventilating myself at the thought of you going out with a man for the first time in years."

"An escort. I believe there's a difference." A big difference, Callie thought, according to her libido. Was that the clue? Was she not attracted to him tonight because she knew that he was being paid to be attentive?

Last night he could have been a nameless one-night stand.

Her pulse quickened at the thought.

"Okay, so he's an escort, but you admitted that he was gorgeous, and you didn't freak out on him, right?"

"Right. I had a really good time, so will you relax?"

"I'm trying. Are you wearing the clothes we bought you?"

"You mean the ones that make me feel like a high-priced hooker? Yes."

"And the shoes?"

"You mean the ones that pinch my toes? Of course." Callie's lips twitched. "You really should get married and settle down, have your own kids."

"I just want you to be okay, Callie. Is that so wrong?"

Tears stung Callie's eyes at Fontaine's sincere tone. She blinked rapidly. "No, it's not wrong." She hesitated, then added softly, "I'm going to be okay, sis. I promise."

"I'll believe that after you have sex again."

Callie laughed while the tears still swam in her eyes. "You sound like a man, Fontaine. Sex is not the answer to everything."

"The hell it isn't," Fontaine argued. "You'll see."

"Good night, Fontaine."

"Good night, darling sister. Be bad. Be very bad."

After she hung up, Callie glanced around the hotel room, still chuckling over Fontaine's parting words. Maybe, she speculated, if the Dillon of last night were with her, she would be very bad.

But he wasn't, and the hotel bed looked big and lonely.

* * *

44

"Have you had a tetanus shot in the last five years?" Wyatt asked Dillon, reaching for his bandage-wrapped finger.

Dillon held it out of reach. It was throbbing like the devil from being banged and smashed all evening while helping Lou at the bar. The last thing he needed or wanted was Wyatt poking it. His mother had done enough of that to last him a lifetime after she had pried the turtle's jaws open and liberated his finger.

According to Ivan and his distraught wife, they'd never seen the turtle with his mouth open in the year they'd had him as a pet. Apparently the turtle's traumatic encounter with the sewer pipe had brought out the beast in him; Dillon had pulled the turtle out of the pipe while it was still attached to his finger.

"Forget the finger," Dillon snapped. "Tell me more about Callie Spencer."

Wyatt shrugged. "There isn't much more to tell. She was a great dinner partner, and not half-bad at kissing, either."

"Do you have a death wish?" Dillon asked silkily.

"Not particularly." Wyatt pointed to the bandaged finger, tongue in cheek. "Do *you?* Come on, bro. You know I would never poach on your preserve."

"She's not my anything. I just don't want my little brother getting his heart stomped into the ground by that man-eating, cold-blooded woman." Never mind that he didn't really believe she fit that description.

"How many times do I have to tell you? She's harmless, Dillon. Completely harmless. You've met her, nearly jumped her bones in the elevator. She seem like a man-eater to you?" When Dillon merely lifted a brow, Wyatt punched him in the arm. "Not *that* kind of man-eater, you idiot. The heartbreaking kind."

"Don't let her fragile looks deceive you. Remember why she's in Atlanta."

"So that's it? You're just going to forget that you nearly went into a seizure when you met her?" Wyatt slapped his forehead in exaggerated surprise. "Oh, I forgot. You do that every time you see a woman, right? So it's not a big deal."

"Maybe it is a big deal," Dillon admitted. "But I can't let lust stand in the way of our future. We've got a mom and a baby sister to put through college, remember?"

"You're going through with your original plan?"

Dillon ignored the censure in his softhearted brother's voice. "Yes. When the reviews are in, then I'll deal with the lust thing."

"Love," Wyatt corrected.

"Lust." Dillon glared at him. "You might be my twin, but you can't read my mind."

"We'll see. We'll just see."

"Yes, we will. Did you tell me everything?" When Wyatt didn't immediately answer, Dillon narrowed his eyes on his brother's guarded expression. "Wyatt?"

"Um, yeah. I told you everything that you need to know."

Then why, Dillon wondered, did he get the feeling Wyatt was holding back on him?

When the hotel phone rang, Callie was jerked out of a pleasant, if strange dream about lobster fishing in a country stream with Dillon.

They had both been naked, with the exception of their fishing hats, which had been shaped like funky lamp shades.

She felt for the phone in the dark, knocked it from

the nightstand, then fell out of bed when she tried to grab it on the way down.

It was some moments before she could get the receiving end to her mouth. She hoped her groggy "hello?" made Fontaine feel terrible for waking her.

But it wasn't Fontaine who answered with a husky chuckle.

It was Dillon.

"Callie? Don't tell me I woke you?"

The strange shiver that crept down her spine at the sound of his voice was nothing more than an aftereffect of the dream she'd been having, Callie told herself. "Um, okay. I won't tell you."

"I did. I'm sorry. I'll let you get back to sleep."

Hastily she said, "That's okay. I'm awake now. Did you want something?"

The insinuating silence that followed made Callie's pulse start to pound. What was going on? Why was she reacting this way to Dillon? This time she couldn't blame it on the wine; she had stuck to water all night.

"I just wanted to tell you that I had a great time tonight."

He was calling her at . . . Callie glanced at the glowing alarm clock beside her bed. Okay, so midnight wasn't really that late. "Me, too. Is this . . . would this be what you would call a polite follow-up call?"

His low chuckle made her nipples pucker. Alarmed, Callie climbed onto the bed and dived under the covers. She was starting to pant, too. *Oh, God.* What was wrong with her? This was Dillon. She had just spent nearly four hours in his company without so much as a twinge of arousal.

"No, this call isn't part of the package, Callie."

47

Callie. She couldn't remember Dillon saying her name with such . . . seductiveness. A growling purr that made her toes curl.

"I just wanted to hear your voice . . . again. I'll let you get back to sleep. Good night."

"Good night."

The phone fell from her numb fingers. When she realized that she couldn't breathe, she flung the covers from her face and blew out a hot, frustrated breath. This was ridiculous!

She turned on the lamp beside her bed and stared at the ceiling, waiting for her pounding heart to get back to a normal rhythm. She'd never been so confused in her life! Was she or was she not attracted to Dillon Love? And if she was, what should she do about it? She knew what Fontaine would say . . . and the thought made her blush.

But Dillon Love was a paid escort. She knew sleeping with a client would be a big no-no. Maybe something that would get him fired.

Callie glanced at her hard nipples poking up under the sheet. Dillon didn't seem like the type to let a few rules stop him from getting what he wanted.

What *she* wanted, too.

She could no longer deny it.

In the darkened living room of his apartment, Dillon replaced the receiver and leaned back in the chair, letting the air from the vent overhead cool his overheated skin. Just talking to Callie Spencer had left him aching and hot. Knowing she was in bed, that he had awakened her . . . pure fantasy in the making.

He tried to think of another time he'd felt this way about a woman. High school, maybe? And even then it had taken more than the sound of a girl's voice to get him in this condition.

It wasn't just lust, although he wasn't ready to admit that to Wyatt. He had his pride, and if Callie Spencer turned out to be the black widow spider he suspected her to be, then nobody would have to know he'd been a fool.

He had three days to get himself under control.

What if he couldn't? What if his body continued to act like a hormonal teenager's?

Wyatt believed she was petrified of men because she'd been hurt. What if she wasn't pulling Wyatt's leg? It would explain why she had bolted like a frightened rabbit from the elevator.

If that were the case . . . he would have to find a way to control his libido around her. He wanted to woo her, not send her running.

An unhappy Callie would equal a death sentence for Atlanta.

Chapter Five

Sunday was the only day Dillon closed the Love Nest.

It was also the only day of the week Dillon's mom, Mary, insisted they share a meal. Dillon's sister, Isabelle, was away at Michigan State, but Wyatt and Dillon were seated in their customary chairs, anticipating the lasagne they'd been smelling since they arrived.

Mary was a petite woman with short blond hair that had just begun to turn gray at the temples. Her sons had inherited their blazing blue eyes from her, as well as her energetic personality, big heart, and shrewd mind.

Not much got past Mary, Dillon mused a little uncomfortably, stealing a questioning glance at Wyatt, who shrugged to let him know he hadn't said a word about the plotting that was afoot.

When Mary came out of the kitchen carrying a steaming lasagne in an aluminum foil pan, both men simply gaped.

She set it in the middle of the table and stood back, hands on hips. "Don't look at me like that. It's a good brand and tastes fine. I've got a test tomorrow and a lot of studying to do."

Dillon swallowed his disappointment. There was nothing in this world like his mother's homemade lasagne, but he knew she'd been studying hard. "You should have told us, Mom. We could have gotten something at home or ordered takeout."

Without responding, Mary went into the kitchen and returned with a big bowl of salad and a plate of garlic bread. She sat down before she answered, looking from one to the other. "Then I wouldn't get to find out what's going on with you two."

Never failing to be amazed at her intuition, Dillon stalled for time. He helped himself to a plate of salad, wincing as he bumped his sore finger against the bowl. *Damned turtle.* "What makes you think something is going on?"

His mother sent him a chiding look. "Because I gave birth to you two, remember? After eighteen long, agonizing hours. Besides, you're worried about something, and your brother"—she pointed a scolding fork at Wyatt— "is tickled pink about whatever it is that you're worried about. In my book on raising twins, that usually means trouble." With her knife and fork poised, she looked from one to the other. "Now, who's going to spill it?"

Knowing his evil twin was bursting at the seams, he waved a piece of garlic toast in his direction. "Go for it, *little* brother. You know you're dying to."

With barely suppressed glee, Wyatt filled his mother in from the beginning, when Dillon had first found out *Next Stop* was sending a reviewer to Atlanta.

Dillon focused on enjoying his meal—which wasn't half-bad, considering. Periodically he shot Wyatt a warning scowl, yearning for the old days when he and his brother could go at it until one of them cried uncle.

Wyatt was enjoying the telling far, far too much for Dillon's taste, especially the part where Dillon made a fool of himself when meeting Callie for the first time. He sighed fatalistically when his mother burst into unrestrained laughter. She tried to cut it short for Dillon's sake, but Dillon could see that she was having trouble regaining control.

"I'm sorry, Dillon," she said, using the napkin in her lap to wipe the mirthful tears from her face. "But what are the odds of your having a romantic run-in with the very woman you're out to seduce and con? I mean, I'm with Wyatt. I think it was destiny or fate that threw you together."

Leave it to his mom, Dillon thought, to turn an explosive, lustful interlude into a romantic encounter. "Mom," Dillon began patiently. "The magazine this woman works for nearly destroyed me last year. Would *you* trust her?"

"Maybe this reviewer is different."

His mother would look for good in the devil himself, Dillon mused wryly. "Okay. I didn't want it to come to this, but you leave me no choice. Your favorite steakhouse with the huge salad bar? *Next Stop* gave it a seventy-five."

Mary gasped. "Not the Angus Feedlot?"

Dillon nodded gravely. He hated to give his mother bad news, but a man had to do what a man had to do. "They nearly went under after the magazine published the bad review."

"I can't believe it!"

Scooping up a huge forkful of lasagne, Dillon shot Wyatt a smug look just before he took a bite. The sappy fool wasn't looking so tickled now. After chewing and swallowing, Dillon asked his mother, "Have you ever gotten bad service at the Feedlot?"

"No!"

"Bad food?"

"Never."

"You should go to *Next Stop*'s Web site and read the review. You might change your mind about eating there."

"I wouldn't believe a stranger over my own eyes and taste buds!"

"A lot of people did," Dillon told his shocked mother grimly. "That's why Callie Spencer needs to be stopped."

"And you're going to do that . . . how?" his mother queried.

Dillon reached for another slice of garlic toast, not comfortable enough with what he was about to say to be looking at his mother when he said it. "I'm going to charm the pants off of her."

"Figuratively speaking?"

"Literally, if I have to."

Wyatt's laugh sounded choked. "What a chore, huh, bro? Seducing a hot babe you're going to have kids with someday. Man, I am so glad I don't have your life."

"Shut up, Wyatt. You don't know what you're talking about."

"Sure I do. Mom, would you witness this bet?"

She sighed. "Do I have a choice? If I had a nickel for every bet you boys have made over the years, I could pay my own way through college."

"If I'm right about you and Callie Spencer, then you have to clean out Mom's garage. If I'm wrong, I clean it."

"Oh, I love this bet," Mary said, rubbing her hands together. "I win either way."

Wyatt waited until the restroom was clear before he dialed Dillon's cell number.

A harassed-sounding Dillon answered. "Yeah?"

Background music blared in Wyatt's ear, and he heard the bartender, Lou, yelling at someone to get off the bar. Yep. It was happy hour at the Love Nest. He wished he were there. "Dillon, it's Wyatt. I'm in trouble. I need you to come to the Lynwood Steak House on South Street. Use the back door, and go to the rest-room and wait for me."

"Are you insane?" Dillon shouted. "I'm not only helping Tyler with his lines for an audition tomorrow, but there's also a convention in town. This place is packed!"

"Why isn't Tyler's wife helping him?"

"I asked the same question. He said that his kids keep interrupting them."

Since Tyler had four kids, Wyatt could believe it. A crowded bar at happy hour was probably the lesser of two evils. "Tell Tyler it's a code red." And please God, Wyatt prayed fervently, let Tyler realize it was for real.

"What the hell is a code red?"

"Just tell him. He'll understand. In fact, get him to cover for you. He's tended bar before." Or was that Collin? Wyatt glanced impatiently at his watch. Sweat popped out on his brow. "Look, Dillon, I wouldn't ask you if it wasn't important."

"Can you at least tell me what it's about?"

"Something's wrong with Callie." And it wasn't some-thing Dr. Love could fix, or something his brother would *want* Dr. Love fixing. Of that Wyatt was one hundred percent certain.

There was a satisfying hint of panic in Dillon's voice as he barked out, "What's wrong with her? Is she sick?"

"Not exactly." Wyatt hesitated. There wasn't much he couldn't talk to his twin about, but this was awkward. He searched for a comfortable analogy. "Um, remember that prime rib Mom cooked one Easter Sunday? You actually started drooling when she set it on the table. Just from one corner, though, and you did manage to catch it before it reached your shirt."

"This is about food?" Dillon shouted.

Wincing, Wyatt held the phone an inch from his ear. "No, it's about Callie Spencer."

"Wyatt . . . if you don't spit it out, so help me, I'll—"

"She's staring at me the way you stared at that prime rib," Wyatt blurted out. A drop of sweat landed on the back of his hand. He grabbed a paper towel and began blotting his forehead. "I don't know what happened. She's been like this since I picked her up at the hotel. If I didn't know better, I'd think you—"

"Hell."

Wyatt ground his teeth at his brother's expletive. "Why do I get the distinct feeling you have forgotten to tell me something?"

"I called her late Saturday night."

"Why?"

"Because I wanted to hear her voice."

"You are so dead."

"Hey," Dillon protested, "all I did was tell her I had a good time, and good night."

"Well, she's acting as if you two had a little phone sex and you left her hanging, bro." Wyatt blotted his upper lip and blew out a frustrated breath. "This doesn't feel right. I think it's time you stepped in."

"I can't."

"Chicken."

"No, I mean I literally can't. Two of the waitresses quit tonight."

"You're kidding."

"No, I'm not. When I showed the girls their new uniforms, Angie and Debra quit. They said they couldn't afford to lose tips, not even for the three weeks they'd have to wear them."

Wyatt rubbed his sweaty temples. "Weren't they the ones who were bitching about the short shorts and halter tops?"

"Yeah. Go figure. Listen, Wyatt. I've got an idea."

"Pray tell."

"You're sick."

"Hey!" Wyatt exclaimed, misunderstanding. "It's not *my* fault my future sister-in-law is drooling over me!"

Dillon huffed a laugh. "No, not *that* kind of sick. *Sick* sick. Bellyache. Migraine. You get the picture?"

"I get it." In fact, it wasn't the only picture Wyatt was getting. He grinned as a little harmless revenge began to take shape in his mind. "Okay, I'll take care of it, but this is the last date with the lust monster."

"Hey, watch your mouth."

"Bite me."

Wyatt was smiling when he pocketed his cell phone. He started whistling as he left the bathroom. It was so sweet of Dillon to give him such brilliant ideas.

Sweet, indeed.

"You're allergic to red meat?" Callie cast a guilty glance at her steak-and-shrimp plate. She had badgered him into trying a bite of her delicious filet mignon—which she had cut with her fork—just moments before he had hastily excused himself and disappeared into the men's bathroom. "Why didn't you tell me?"

Wyatt shrugged, looking boyishly embarrassed. "Well, my allergy specialist tells me I should try it occasionally just to see if I still have the same reaction. It's like . . . I turn into a different person when I eat red meat. My mother calls it the 'Dr. Jekyll and Mr. Hyde syndrome.' "

Callie felt the bottom drop out of her stomach. She laid her fork and knife aside. "How long does this reaction take . . . after you've eaten red meat?"

"Oh, a couple of hours. Sometimes longer, sometimes sooner." He was beginning to look anxious. "Why do you ask?"

She licked her lips, resigning herself to the inevitable. "Saturday night you ordered Swedish meatballs as an appetizer." She watched, hopelessly, as he frowned in thought. Suddenly his brow cleared.

"Yeah, I did. But they were made with pork, weren't they?"

She shook her head. "No. I'm pretty certain it was beef." Taking a deep breath, she asked, "You don't remember calling me afterward, do you?"

His eyes—both blue tonight—widened in shock. "I called you? After I dropped you off at your room?" With a groan, he splayed his fingers over his face and peeked at her between them. "Did I say anything offensive?"

"No. You just . . . sounded different." Like someone else. A different Dillon Love, one who made her pant and act like a sex-starved nympho. She had known the moment she opened the door tonight that the maddening inner switch to her libido had once again turned itself off. Determined to find the key, she had focused on the first night they'd met, and had been doing a fairly good job of turning herself back on until her escort had disappeared into the men's room.

Now, once again, the power to her circuit board had been cut.

Dillon had blamed his odd behavior on a food allergy. What was *her* excuse?

Dillon's voice was positively menacing as he shouted at Wyatt. "You told Callie I was allergic to *red meat*? Do you realize I'm going to be spending a hell of a lot of time with Callie over the next three weeks?"

"Boss! We're outta Jack Daniel's!" Lou shouted from the bar. "And you need to get this woman *off my bar!*"

Lou's angry shout reminded Dillon of another grievance he had with his twin. "By the way," he yelled over the live band and the laughing, screaming crowd, "Tyler does *not* know how to tend bar, you dolt! Half these people are falling-down drunk thanks to *you*, so I hope you're prepared for a long night of playing taxicab."

"Well, I . . ." Wyatt stumbled back as a leggy blond with glassy eyes and a goofy grin thrust her way between them. She was attempting to balance a tray of longnecks and walk at the same time, and doing a surprisingly good job of it. "Hey, I thought you said that Debra quit!"

"She did, and then she came back. So did Angie. They just made a little detour to the competition across town first to talk things over." Dillon gave his head an impatient shake. With Debra weaving her way through the crowd and out of the way, he moved closer. His head was pounding from all the shouting he'd had to do. "Don't change the subject—"

"Boss!"

It was Lou again. Dillon muttered a nasty curse and shoved his way to the bar. Unceremoniously, he grabbed the drunken, dancing waitress around the waist and tipped her over his shoulder. Stomping back to Wyatt, he ignored the wriggling woman and continued berating his innocent-looking brother. "I'm convinced God put you on this earth to make my life a living hell."

Wyatt spread his hands in a helpless gesture that didn't fool Dillon. "Hey, I was just trying to help, bro! *Your* woman was about to eat me alive."

"You could have told her something else. Now I'm going to have to eat rabbit food for the next three weeks, thanks to you."

"There's always chicken and pork."

"I think I'll kill you right now," Dillon said with deceptive calm. Instead he dumped Angie into Wyatt's arms. "Take her into the office and get some coffee in her. She's damned lucky I don't fire her ass on the spot." He glowered at Wyatt before adding, "And yours."

"You can't fire me. I'm part owner now, remember? And I still don't see why you're so mad." Ignoring Angie's clumsy attempt to kiss him, Wyatt followed Dillon to the bar.

It wasn't often Dillon wanted a drink, but at that moment he was tempted to bring the draft spigot to his mouth and let it fly. Not only had two of his waitresses decided to play hooky, but there was also a convention in town that he hadn't been aware of. Added to that, Tyler had been serving straight Jack Daniel's in place of a variety of mixed drinks.

Behind him, Wyatt shouted, "I think we should close the bar! Everyone's had enough anyway. Let them dance it off, offer free coffee and Cokes."

It was a brilliant idea, one Dillon regretted not thinking of an hour ago—before Eddie Palmer got down on one knee and asked Brooke Lancaster to marry him—right in front of his seething wife.

They'd be lucky to finish the night without someone slapping a lawsuit on them.

Reluctantly, Dillon turned to look at his brother. His expression softened. "I just might have to let you live after all, little brother."

Wyatt flashed him a wicked smile just as Angie's searching tongue found his ear.

His shocked expression made Dillon burst out laughing. "Dump her in the office and let Tyler take care of her. Let's take a break."

"Tyler's still here?"

"In my office, studying his lines with some guy he met in the restroom."

"You locked the safe?"

Dillon scowled at him. "Do I look like an idiot?"

"Well—"

"Shut up."

"Bite me."

"Go to hell."

"Ladies first."

They stared each other down, but not for long. Dillon was too exhausted. He slung his arm around his brother's shoulders and led him to the far wall.

It was the only place in the joint that looked safe.

Chapter Six

Was it possible to get a therapist on short notice in a strange town?

Callie didn't know, but she was becoming convinced that she needed one.

Hot.

Cold.

Hot again.

Cold again.

And with the same guy.

She was definitely prime shrink material. In fact, after tonight she figured she could bypass the therapy and go directly into a climate-controlled padded room.

After Dillon called last Saturday night, she had lain in bed, dazed and confused. An hour later she had come to one terrifying conclusion: she was going to have to jump Dillon's bones to see which way the wind *really* blew in regard to her erratic libido.

Did she want him, or did she not?

Even more baffling were Dillon's actions tonight, at

least until he'd confessed to a strange allergy to red meat.

Callie propped her arms behind her head, frowning at the memory. She was lying on her hotel bed still fully dressed, trying to fit the pieces of the puzzle together. Did she believe Dillon about the food allergy? She had no reason to think he'd lie, but then she didn't really know him, either. For all she knew he was a compulsive liar, like Lanny had been.

Or maybe he wasn't attracted to her at all, and this was his way of saving her the embarrassment of coming right out and telling her. Callie felt her face heat at the possibility. How totally humiliating would that be?

She sat up so fast it made her dizzy. She wanted a drink. Maybe two, or three. The restless feeling inside her seemed to be growing, as if Dillon Love—the Dillon she had met the first night—had awakened a sexual monster and now there was no stopping it. It needed satisfaction.

"Sexual monster?" Callie laughed out loud, and even to her own ears, the sound was rusty. "You have definitely lost it, my girl, if you think you've turned into a sexual anything. Get a life."

Get a life.

Wasn't that was she was supposed to be doing? Getting a life? Or more specifically, getting *her* life back? Regaining her self-confidence . . . laughing more . . . having sex again?

So what was she doing sitting in a hotel room pondering her own insanity?

It was a damned good question, Callie decided, slipping into her high heels. If Prince Love couldn't commit now that he had awakened Sleeping Beauty from her sexual slumber, then maybe she should visit another castle or two. Check out the body armor.

Surely Dillon Love wasn't the only prince in this kingdom?

Right?

"Of course," Callie said staunchly. She smoothed her hair and headed for the door, snatching up her little purse along the way. Her stride felt strong. Confident. Determined.

In fact, she told herself as she opened the door and stepped into the hall, there were probably better princes, ones who weren't so . . . unsettling. Men who didn't make her feel so . . . *dominated*.

Her knees quivered once. Twice. She shored them up and walked to the elevator. Stabbed the button.

The elevator doors slid open. The hotel manager, coming out of the elevator with his head down, nearly ran into her. When he looked up and saw her face, his eyes widened in obvious recognition.

"I'm so sorry. I didn't see you, Ms. Spencer! Can I get you something? Room service? A masseuse?"

Callie veered from her determined course long enough to realize that Fontaine had been right: someone was definitely ratting them out to the local businesses.

Then she did what she thought any smart, red-blooded woman would do when faced with a brown-nosing hotel manager.

She took advantage of the situation.

"As a matter of fact, I need a cab and the name of a casual club where I might, um, get a drink and maybe mingle with some people my own age."

Before Callie could finish her request, the hotel manager had whipped out his cell phone and called her a cab. He tucked it back into his pocket and punched the elevator button with the swift expertise of a born manager.

On the way down, he rattled off a list of nightclubs in the area, most of which Callie recognized from the list Fontaine had given her. One in particular caught her attention.

"The Love Nest?" she repeated, amused at the title. Fate, perhaps? An omen? "Singles bar?"

The manager pursed his lips. "Not exclusively, no. It used to be called Country Train. I think it changed hands or something."

Well, Callie thought wryly, the name of the club hadn't improved with the changing of hands. The owner, in her opinion, was definitely in need of a good PR person. Fontaine would knock off ten points for the ridiculous name alone.

Maybe if she ran into the owner, she would give him some free advice.

"Your cab should be right outside," the hotel manager informed her as the elevator doors slid open to reveal the hotel foyer. "Good night, Ms. Spencer."

"Good night, and thanks." Definitely an upscale hotel, she decided as she headed for the waiting cab. After giving the cabbie her destination, she settled against the seat and let out a slow, shaky sigh.

She couldn't believe that she was going out on the town alone, where any number of hounds could be lurking. Her sister wouldn't believe it either, Callie thought, and found herself smiling at the thought of Fontaine's shocked expression.

Callie Spencer, once the blissfully naive wife of an underwear model.

How many calls had she gotten once everyone

found out she knew about Lanny's infidelities? Half a dozen? A dozen? So many she had lost count. So many that she had disconnected her answering machine and had stopped answering the phone.

She'd caught Lanny red-handed, with his fancy underwear down around his skinny ankles. She didn't have to know from so-called well-meaning friends about all the other humiliating times he'd dropped his infamous underwear for other women.

Once had been enough to break her heart clean in two.

Everyone had assumed Callie would do as millions of other divorcees did: cry, see a therapist, get mad, and get over it.

But she hadn't. She had taken a vacation from real life, immersed herself in work, and ignored the person she had once been to the point that she had nearly forgotten who that person was.

"This is it, Ms. Spencer. No charge. Charlie said to put it on his tab."

Callie paused with one foot on the pavement. "Charlie?"

"The hotel manager, ma'am."

"Oh. Right." Which would also explain how the cabdriver knew her name. "Tell him I said thanks."

"Sure thing, ma'am."

The cab drove away, and Callie had to physically restrain herself from calling it back. Now that she was standing at the front entrance of the Love Nest, the courage that had stiffened her spine seemed to have deserted her.

What was she thinking? She couldn't go inside, dressed to kill, and mingle as if she did this sort of thing all the time.

She hadn't even *kissed* a man in three years.

Hadn't flirted. Hadn't held an intimate conversation with a man.

Well, with the exception of Dillon her first night in Atlanta, and what had she done? She had run as fast as her toned, tanned, and waxed legs would carry her.

Now she was thinking of walking back into the fire, like a glutton for punishment.

Callie decided she hated that whiny note in her subconscious voice. She straightened her spine—again—and proceeded to the door. She knew she looked her best. Fontaine had made certain of that. Sexy. Sophisticated. Available.

Unfortunately, she'd feel safer if she looked her worst.

The vibrations from the live band pounded through her, mocking her pounding heart. She reached for the door and it swung inward, startling her. A laughing couple came stumbling out, wrapped up in each other and oblivious to her presence.

The sight caused her heart to clench hard enough to make her gasp. She wanted that again. She missed that kind of intimacy, even if it hadn't been real.

"Your ID?" a voice shouted right into her ear.

She turned from watching the couple to find a tall, heavily muscled man with a gray-streaked mustache regarding her expectantly. Hastily she fished out her driver's license, watching as it disappeared into his big hand. He held up a small penlight to confirm her birth date, nodded, then handed it back. The band was playing an impressive cover of Bob Seger's oldie but goody, "Old Time Rock and Roll."

He leaned forward and yelled, "You meetin' anyone?"

Doubting he'd hear her if she tried to speak, she simply shook her head.

"You have any trouble with anyone, you let me

know." He folded his beefy arms over his chest, offering her a friendly smile while at the same time emphasizing his muscles. "The name's Fish."

She mouthed the word *thanks* and moved slowly into the crowd, searching for a table, preferably in a dark corner where she wouldn't be noticed. At least she had the comfort of a man like Fish at her back, she thought, swallowing a nervous giggle.

Weaving her way through the packed crowd, Callie caught a glimpse of an empty table against the wall. Relieved, she headed for it with the single-minded purpose of a linebacker.

Just as she was beginning to see daylight, she saw him. Dillon.

He was standing against the wall behind the targeted table, talking to another guy . . . Callie's eyes went wide. She stood frozen as people jostled around her.

It was Dillon . . . talking to Dillon.

She blinked. Then blinked again.

Still Dillon . . . talking to Dillon.

They were dressed differently, but there wasn't any doubt they were twins. The Dillon on the right still wore the casual tux he'd worn to the restaurant with her.

The other Dillon wore faded jeans, scuffed boots, and a dark blue button-up shirt. His shirtsleeves were shoved to his elbows, and his ankles were crossed where he leaned against the wall. Perspiration had darkened his hair at his forehead and temples.

Callie's astounded gaze landed on the open neck of his shirt. Dark curls peeped out from a tanned, rock-hard chest, also glistening with sweat. Her heart did a crazy flipflop. On the heels of this phenomenon, a liquid heat flooded her belly.

Her legs immediately tried to fold.

She grabbed the first body she could to hold herself upright.

"Hey! You okay, little darlin'?"

Looking up into the flushed, smiling face of her human anchor, she managed to nod. Hastily she uncurled her fingers from his arms and straightened again. She muttered an apology, but she was fairly certain nothing came out.

When she was reasonably certain her legs would support her again, she looked at the Dillon on the right, the one she'd dined with tonight.

The one who had told her he was allergic to red meat. The one who couldn't seem to get away from her fast enough. The very one who had left her at her hotel room door with the fabricated excuse that he was beginning to feel a little strange.

He laughed at something the other Dillon said, his white teeth flashing, his handsome face creased in a big smile. His Adam's apple bobbed along the strong column of his throat as he said something back. She doubted there was a woman alive who wouldn't agree that he was drop-dead gorgeous.

Callie watched and waited. Nothing happened. Her legs were regaining their strength, and her heart was slowing to a normal rhythm, as if she were staring at a blank wall instead of *Playgirl* material.

She deliberately switched her bug-eyed gaze to the Dillon on the left. The one in the butt-hugging jeans. The one whose piercing blue gaze seemed to have X-ray vision when he looked at her.

Her heart reversed direction, her pulse scrambling to keep up.

Her mouth went bone dry.

All the blood in her head seemed to drain south,

leaving her light-headed, as if she'd downed a couple of glasses of wine on an empty stomach.

She wasn't crazy. There were two of them.

But only one sent her libido into a tailspin and her heart into shock.

"Care if I join you?"

Callie glared up at the man who dared to approach her table in the hotel bar. Her fingers tightened around the stem of her third glass of wine. She had a pleasant buzz going on, but it was a far cry from the oblivion she sought.

"Get lost," she growled at him, hunkering over her wine like a witch over a boiling cauldron of lizard eyes. "Hound *dogs*, all of them," she muttered beneath her breath.

"So-rry!" the man said before stomping away, muttering his own indistinguishable comment.

How humiliating. She'd been the brunt of a childish prank played by twin hunks. Was that what they had been laughing about at the club when she'd spotted them against the wall? Having fun at *her* expense?

When she thought of how long it could have gone on . . . she had to grit her teeth to keep from cursing a blue streak.

She was a fool. A stupid, naive fool.

Her first night in Atlanta she had met the first Dillon. After that, it had been his twin, whatever his name was. On the phone, Dillon again. Tonight at the restaurant, the nameless twin.

Beavis and Butthead.

"Would you care for more wine, Ms. Spencer?"

Callie looked at the bartender, sighed, and sat back in her chair to give him access to her empty wineglass.

"Hit me again, Roy. Thanks." When you were on a first-name basis with the bartender, what did it mean? That you were a loser?

For certain she was a sucker. Her face burned at the memory of them laughing and talking together.

Allergic to red meat . . . in a pig's eye! Or would that be a cow's eye?

She tapped her fingers on the table. Why had they switched after that first night in the elevator? *He* had pursued *her*, hadn't he? Sure, she had been rather obviously interested . . . okay, obviously aroused by his flirting and talk of domination, but she hadn't run after him.

She had run *from* him.

Callie sat up straight. Was that it? He thought he had frightened her, so he had sent his twin in to soothe the nervous filly? Get her to relax . . . before he moved in again? She laughed out loud and didn't care who heard her or noticed or thought she might be crazy.

Her eyes rolled heavenward. It was her first time back in the jungle in three years. Why couldn't she have had a normal romantic encounter with a man? Was it just too much to ask after three years of abstinence, not to mention the heartache Lanny had caused?

Whatever their reasons for the switch, her pride was stinging. Hell, not just her pride . . . her ego, something she thought she'd lost when Lanny broke her heart.

By her fourth glass of wine, Callie had gone over the last five days thoroughly, beginning with her arrival Thursday night and meeting Dillon in the hotel bar. The attraction between them had been real; of that she was certain. At least on her part, and she could think of no reason he would pretend to be attracted to her.

Surprised and frightened by her reaction, she had tried to get away from him. He had pursued her to the elevator, working his charm and making her breathless and even more panicky.

Before she had bolted from the elevator, he had realized she was just as attracted to him as he claimed to be to her. She had seen it in his eyes, witnessed the dawning of realization and the supreme male satisfaction that had followed.

Callie shivered in remembrance. What a rush it had been to find herself feeling desire again.

Okay, *lust*. It was definitely hard-core lust for Dillon Love. The first Dillon Love. The second Dillon she had felt nothing for, which had been nearly as scary as the lust she'd felt for the first.

All this thinking was making her head swim. Or was it the wine?

What should she do? Call Mr. Complete tomorrow and ask for a different escort and just put the whole humiliating experience behind her?

That was exactly what the old Callie would do. The timid, naive Callie, the one who was convinced she'd never feel alive again. That Callie would just forget the entire embarrassing episode, even the amazing part about panting for Dillon Love.

After all, the most important fact was that she *could* still feel desire for a man. Now that she knew, she could start dating. Go to singles bars. Meet other men.

Sweat popped out on Callie's brow at the thought. Okay, so maybe she'd start slow. Pretend her washer was broken and hang out at the Laundromat.

Or . . . she could exact a little revenge and keep seeing the devious twin hunks, maybe fry a few of *their* circuits with some harmless pranks. Tit for tat and all that. How long would it take for the real Dillon to move in? Did they both work for Mr. Complete? What was the real reason they were playing their childish game with her? Was it possible the hot attraction that had sizzled the air between them had frightened Dillon as well? Oh, that would be rich! And not fair. She didn't have a twin to send in *her* place.

A tipsy giggle escaped Callie. She smothered another one with her hand, deciding she'd keep her vacation interesting . . . stick with the Dillon twins and find out their motive for fooling her. Maybe she'd get what she really wanted in the end: to have wild sex with the first Dillon. Maybe she'd do her own little personal review on him.

She couldn't deny that her life had certainly changed when she'd met him. Them. Dillon and Dillon of the Dillon twins. Sneaky little devils.

Callie hiccuped and drained her wineglass, grinning. The Dillon twins were about to find out that payback was definitely a bitch.

In her case, it was a bitch wearing a silver sequined miniskirt, a deceptively demure black silk blouse—Fontaine's words, not hers—and three-inch high heels that were pinching the absolute hell out of her toes.

Chapter Seven

He was five minutes late.

That was because he had been standing outside Callie's hotel room for the past six minutes, trying to remember another time in his life when he'd been this nervous over a woman.

Dillon straightened his cuffs again and tugged at his tuxedo jacket for the tenth time. "For God's sake, she's just a woman," he muttered, lifting his fist to knock on the door.

He let it fall without touching as doubts assailed him anew. What if he couldn't control himself, like the first time? What if he came on too strong and she bolted again? He couldn't let that happen. Too much hinged on his ability to play it cool, to seduce and woo and charm Callie Spencer, all without letting his libido rule his head.

Sleeping with her, Dillon had decided in the wee hours of the morning, wasn't a good idea. If he slept with her, the situation could get sticky. What if it didn't work out? What if it was just lust on his part, as he'd tried to convince Wyatt? The last thing he wanted to happen was for Callie Spencer to leave Atlanta with bad memories.

Hell hath no fury like a travel reviewer scorned.

Great. Dillon swore softly as he realized the enormity of his mistake. A wiser man would have stayed out of the picture. He should have sent one of the seasoned escorts in his place, someone with lots of style and charm, like Greg or Collin. Greg was gay and Collin was happily married. In fact, Ivan, Jet, and Tyler were also happily married, therefore safe and nonthreatening.

But no, he had to give in to temptation, dance close to the fire until he scorched himself *and* the other businesses in Atlanta, all because he couldn't resist Callie Spencer.

He was a real peach. Atlanta's golden boy.

He would be drawn and quartered in the town square.

Unless he could convince himself that Callie was no different from the single women who hit on him night after night at the club. Women who made no bones about looking for a good time.

The door in front of him opened abruptly. Callie Spencer looked startled to find him in the hall. Then a slow, welcoming smile curved her full, sensuous lips.

"Dillon! I was just about to start beating on doors to get help with this stubborn zipper." She whirled around and pulled her satiny hair aside, presenting the luscious, *bare* curve of her back. "Would you, please?"

She had a dimple in the middle of her back. A cute, touch-me-with-your-tongue dimple.

Dillon's great-grandfather had once told him about an ornery mule that had kicked him in the groin and laid him low for a week. As Dillon's mouth went bone-dry, he had a strong feeling he knew exactly how his great-grandfather had felt.

His hands visibly trembled as he reached for the zipper pull. It was tiny, so it was impossible to grasp it without brushing his fingers against her skin.

And absolutely impossible for his fingers not to linger.

"Hmm," Callie murmured in a sexy, intoxicating voice. "Your fingers are warm."

Stifling a husky groan, Dillon forced himself to finish the task quicker than he would have liked. The white dress was a simple little number that outlined every luscious curve, every tempting line.

With his eyes nearly closed in bliss, Dillon was inhaling her mysterious fragrance when she turned back around and grasped his hands in hers. He jerked his eyes open. Panic shot through him.

She beamed at him. "I decided I'm going to take your advice," she announced, squeezing his fingers. A hot flood of pure desire weakened his knees at her simple touch.

The search for moisture was futile, Dillon realized as he struggled to speak. "My . . . my advice?" What had Wyatt said? It was terrifying not to know, because with Wyatt, it could be anything.

Which intensified Dillon's terror.

She shot him a coy glance from beneath her thick, dark lashes. "Come on, Dillon! Don't you remember? When I told you about my divorce, you suggested I put an end to this dry spell and start dating again."

To Dillon's amazement, she dropped his hands and leaned in to elbow him in the ribs.

Buddy style.

"You were absolutely right, you know, so if I give you the sign tonight, you'll know to get lost."

Dillon had to clear his throat twice before he found his voice. "The . . . sign?"

With a puzzled little frown, she nodded. "Yes, the sign. Don't tell me that you've forgotten?" She laughed and elbowed him again before she reached for her wrap and purse on the table next to the door. "You really should stay away from red meat, Dillon."

Taking his arm, she led him through the door and locked it behind her. They were in the elevator going down before Dillon realized she hadn't told him what "sign" he was supposed to be looking for.

Wyatt was so dead.

Inside the elevator, Callie kept her arm snug in his so that Dillon couldn't have put space between them even if he'd had the willpower.

Which he didn't.

"I've always had a fantasy about making love in an elevator," Callie said, giving his tense arm a hefty squeeze. "How about you?"

"Yeah," Dillon managed to croak out. He might have been extremely flattered if not for the strong suspicion that she wasn't talking about doing it with him.

"God," she said with a lusty sigh that made Dillon's groin tighten even further. "It's just so wonderful to be with a man I can say anything to. It's almost as if you were gay."

Dillon managed to turn his choked gasp into a cough. When he caught his breath again, he said, "He . . . I didn't tell you that I was gay, did I?" Her sudden burst of laughter did funny things to his insides.

"Of course not!"

He looked down to find her gazing up at him with a

definite gleam of mischief in her eye. Since when did mischief turn into another word for blow-me-away erotic?

"I haven't forgotten the first night we met, Dillon. Unless you thought I was a man, you're not gay." Another lusty, wistful sigh stirred his senses. "Too bad it was the liquor talking . . . for both of us. Wouldn't that have been just *awful* if we'd had sex?"

Yeah, Dillon thought, clenching his jaw, *just friggin' awful*. Especially for his mother, who was soon going to be mourning her dead son . . . Wyatt.

"I mean, these past few dates have made me realize how awkward that would have been. I would have had to pick another escort, and I wouldn't have had the opportunity to make a special friend like you."

Friends. Dillon tried to be silent when he ground his teeth. *Hell.* Apparently his plan had worked *too* well. What happened to the wild-eyed, panting woman who had bowled him over that first night? Was it possible for anyone to turn off that kind of physical attraction?

And if it was, why couldn't *he* do it?

Because the gut-clenching arousal he'd felt that first night hadn't waned for him. He was as hard as a rock and as randy as a sailor too long at sea.

He wanted to throw aside his civilized veneer and back Callie up against the elevator wall, press his hard body into hers from breast to knee. He wanted to run his hot hands over her bare, sexy legs . . . edge his fingers along the damp elastic of her panties until he found—

"Thank God, here's our floor." She tugged him forward. "It was getting hot in the elevator, don't you think? Must be something wrong with the vent."

There was a venting problem, all right, Dillon

thought, but it had nothing to do with the elevator and everything to do with the tight fit of his trousers.

"Mmm, oh, God, this is good! Charlie knows his restaurants."

With barely controlled violence, Dillon watched her bring a dainty bite of juicy, medium-rare streak to her moist lips. Those luscious lips opened, then closed around the meat. She closed her eyes and moaned as if the food were orgasmic.

For Dillon, watching her, it almost was.

She opened her eyes, peering at him from beneath half-lowered lids. "I hope I'm not tempting you. Am I?"

"No," Dillon snapped just before he stuffed a man-sized bite of lettuce into his mouth. He chewed as if he were attempting to murder his food. Less than one hour in her company and he was seriously tempted to strip naked, crawl into the men's room sink, and douse himself with cold water.

"So . . . how's your, um, personal problem coming along?"

Her question startled Dillon into dropping his napkin. When he leaned over to retrieve it, he saw that she'd taken off one of her shoes and was rubbing one foot sensuously against the other.

A little foreplay to go along with the orgasmic food.

He had a vivid, erotic image of her transferring that talented little foot to his crotch. A dribble of cold sweat trickled down his spine. When he sat up, he eyed a champagne bucket of ice at a nearby table with longing.

"Dillon? Are you okay? You've been acting a little strange since you picked me up tonight. Is it . . . did you strike out again last night? Is there anything I can do to help?"

Oh, there was plenty she could do, Dillon thought as he snatched up his napkin and slammed it into his lap so hard he winced, but he didn't think Callie Spencer would be doing it in his lifetime. And what the hell did she mean, "strike out again last night"? Too bad he couldn't ask, since he was supposed to know what she was talking about. This would teach him to launch a plan before thinking it through. Now he was paying the price.

Stalling for time, he took a drink of the root beer Callie had ordered for him . . . courtesy of Wyatt, of course. He hated the stuff. "Um, no, I didn't strike out. In fact, I hit a home run." There. That should cover—

"You're kidding!" Callie shrieked joyously, drawing every eye in the dining room. "That's wonderful news!"

To Dillon's horror, she jumped up and hurried around the table to where he sat in stunned silence. She wrapped her arms around him and yanked his head to her breast, squeezing the breath out of him.

Of course, he'd already lost his breath the moment his nose disappeared into her cleavage.

"See," she murmured consolingly next to his ear. "I told you that the moment you stopped thinking about your mother, your problem would disappear."

Her outrageous comment set his ears on fire. Dillon hadn't felt so embarrassed since his mother had found a battered *Playboy* beneath his mattress.

When she finished torturing him, she returned to her seat, seemingly oblivious to the commotion she had caused.

Dillon stared at the beaming woman sitting across from him, at a loss for words. But he had no trouble thinking of the many and varied ways he was going to kill . . . his . . . brother. He'd thought Wyatt had matured over the years, put his boyhood pranks behind him. It was one of the reasons he'd decided to invite his twin into the nightclub business.

Obviously he was wrong. Wyatt wasn't ready for anything but an early grave. Dillon pushed his acute disappointment aside and searched for a quick way to change the subject, since he didn't think the floor was going to magically open up and swallow him.

He was saved by the vibration of his cell phone against his thigh.

Relief weakened his knees as he dug it out. "Excuse me," he said as he pressed a button and put it to his flaming ear. "Dillon here."

"Dillon. It's Greg."

Dillon tensed at Greg's urgent whisper. "Yes?"

"I need your help."

Relief turned to dismay. With a fatalistic sigh, Dillon said, "I'm listening." What would it be tonight? A clogged drain? A tarantula hunt?

"I'm being stalked," Greg whispered.

Oh. Nothing as difficult as a flushed turtle or a frantic actor in need of a leading lady to help him rehearse. Just a little stalking problem that apparently Luke had forgotten to tell him about.

His gaze met Callie's. He read the question in her gleaming eyes, watched her take a sip of her wine . . . saw how the wine made her full lips glisten. Imagined his tongue wiping away the moisture—

"Dillon?"

"Um, yeah, yeah." Dillon cleared his throat and forced his gaze to a safer place. Like his bowl of rabbit food. If the sight of it didn't kill his libido, nothing could. "I'm here. Have you called the police?"

Greg's shocked gasp carried clearly through the phone. "Call the police on my own boyfriend? I don't *think* so! Are you drunk?"

Dillon wiped a frustrated hand over his bristly jaw and sighed. God, how he wished he *were* drunk. "I wasn't aware that you were talking about Ramon when you mentioned a stalker." Then he asked the obvious question. "Why is Ramon stalking you?"

"Have you forgotten who you paired me with tonight?" Greg asked with a hint of accusation. "Only the richest *gay* guy in Atlanta!"

Belatedly, Dillon made the connection. Greg and Julian Santos. Santos had requested an escort to accompany him to a gay birthday bash his friends and family were holding in his honor. At the time it had made perfect sense for Dillon to schedule Greg as his escort.

Obviously a big mistake. "I'm sorry, Greg. I didn't realize it would cause problems for you in your personal life." He paused a beat. "After all, it is your job, right?"

"Yeah, yeah, it's my job, but I told you about Ramon's dreams and how jealous he's been lately . . . which brings me back to the pressing present, boss. I repeat, Ramon is stalking us. He causes trouble, Santos files a complaint, I could lose my job."

Across the table, Callie slipped the last bite of her steak into her lovely mouth.

Beneath the table, Dillon clenched his thighs together. "Um, how can I help, Greg?"

"I need you to distract Ramon. We're about to leave the restaurant to finish the party at Santos's house. I don't think Ramon knows where he lives, so if we could leave without Ramon seeing us, I think he'll give up."

"How, pray tell, do you propose I distract Ramon?" God knew *he* needed distracting, Dillon thought, frowning as Callie pulled out a pen from her purse and scribbled something on her napkin.

She held it up for him to read.

Seconds later, before her request fully registered, Dillon felt her bare foot against his thigh. He nearly dropped the phone. Another inch higher and she would have discovered another "special friend."

According to her quaint little sign, Callie wanted one of his wonderful foot rubs. It seemed she had a cramp in her toes from the shoes.

Wyatt was so very, very dead. *If* he lived long enough to kill him.

It was definitely an iffy question. Bracing himself for the impact, Dillon slowly curled his fingers around her toes and began what he hoped was a wonderful foot massage. It was wonderful for him, anyway.

Mind-blowing, in fact.

"I don't know," Greg was saying. "You're the boss. I know you'll think of something." He rattled off the address before adding, "We're leaving in half an hour. Don't let me down."

Dillon slipped his phone into his jacket pocket. He continued to rub her toes, inching back in his chair as his erection lengthened alarmingly. "I've got to help a friend," he said, gently easing her foot from his leg and certain disaster. "I'm sorry, but I guess I'll have to cut the night short."

And spend the rest of it in a cold shower—after he took care of Ramon.

"Can't I come?" Callie asked with a pouty smile that kicked another inch into his arousal. "I won't be any trouble, I promise."

"It might get sticky," he warned.

She shrugged. "Anything has to be better than being alone in that hotel room, and maybe I can help."

Dillon's brow shot up. "You want to help when you don't even know what it's about?"

"I'm not deaf, Dillon. We're going to distract Ramon, who is Greg's boyfriend, who is stalking Greg, so Greg and his client can leave without Ramon following them."

"You got all that from listening to my end of the conversation?" Dillon was impressed. "Sharp as well as beautiful," he murmured. To his delight, Callie blushed.

"So I can come?"

"Sure." Anything, Dillon thought as he signaled the waiter for their bill, to keep her from uttering that provocative statement again. "Just don't blame me when you end up with a turtle hanging from your finger." He glanced at her just in time to catch her puzzled look, and laughed. "Never mind. It's a long story."

Chapter Eight

She'd made some bad judgment calls in her life—who hadn't? But tonight Callie decided she had taken the cake.

What was she thinking when she decided to take on Dillon Love and extract a little revenge? Sure, her plan seemed to be working—if the beads of sweat across his forehead and upper lip were any indication—but in her impulsive anger to launch her seductive game, she had forgotten her own inability to stay cool around Dillon.

She was hotter than a rocket inside a Coke bottle on a hot summer's night.

Beside her in the close confines of his Jeep, Dillon cut the motor and pointed to a late-model SUV. The vehicle might have been dark green or black. "That's him."

"How do you know?" Would he notice how breathless she sounded?

There was a thread of amusement in his tone as he said, "The license plate says, 'Ramon loves Greg.'"

"Oh." She bit her lip. "Won't he know you?"

Dillon hesitated. "He might. I've met him socially a couple of times."

"If he recognizes you, won't he suspect something?"

He looked at her, his penetrating gaze sending a flash of fire into her belly. The man not only had a killer smile; his look was lethal. How many women had succumbed to that smile? How many hearts had he broken?

Thank God the only thing Dillon seemed to stir in her was a powerful lust. As if that weren't hard enough to resist.

"I think you've missed your calling, Detective Spencer," Dillon drawled. "Because you're absolutely right. Do you have any suggestions? My brain seems to have taken a vacation tonight."

She knew exactly how he felt. It was hard to think straight when he was looking at her as if he could gobble her right up. Callie licked her dry lips and pulled her gaze from the magnetic force of his. She stared at the SUV parked in front of them. If she didn't get out of the vehicle soon, she was afraid she was going to do something she would woefully regret.

Like crawl across the console, straddle him, and demand he satisfy her six ways to Sunday.

"Um, we could pretend to have a big fight, and I could run to him and beg him for a ride back to the hotel." Therefore defusing *both* situations.

"We'd have to be very convincing," Dillon said, his voice curiously husky.

Callie's voice matched his. She struggled to breathe without panting. "I'm . . . sure we could be. After all, Greg is depending on us."

"Yes, he is. We should probably get out of the Jeep so Ramon can see and hear us when we start fighting."

"Maybe lean against it as we embrace." Callie did

her best to ignore the frantic leap of anticipation her suggestion caused.

"I could kiss you," Dillon said softly.

"And I could slap you, then scream at you and tell you that I never want to see you again."

"Just to be convincing."

"Yes . . . just to be convincing." And maybe convince herself that was exactly what she needed to *really* do. Dillon Love was out of her league, even if it was just lust between them. He not only messed with her breathing pattern; he screwed up her rational thinking, and that couldn't be a good thing.

Right?

"You ready?"

Now that was a loaded question if Callie had ever heard one. She took a deep breath and let it out very slowly, giving herself time to get over the temptation to blurt out the truth: that she was more than ready. "Um, ready if you are."

They both opened their doors at the same time. Callie knew enough about her body's reaction to Dillon Love by now to anticipate her wobbly legs when she tried to stand. She balanced herself against the door until she felt steady enough to walk around to the driver's side, where Dillon waited.

To kiss her. Dillon was going to kiss her, and she wanted him to very badly. Her first kiss in three years. Would she remember *how* to kiss?

She had exactly five seconds to panic over the thought before she reached Dillon. He snatched her against the hard length of his body, his arms tight around her, his erection like an open flame against her belly.

He was hotter than a furnace. She melted against him with a little moan of surrender, lifting her face to his. He bent to her mouth, nuzzled her lips, breathed softly against them. Moaned her name.

He was trembling.

She was shaking.

Who in the hell were they trying to fool? Not themselves, and probably not anyone watching, Callie thought.

Their lips met, and the world around Callie faded until she could hear the thundering of their hearts. She opened her mouth to him, and his tongue shot inside, teasing her, tasting her. Her legs tried to collapse. Dillon held her tight, lifting her up along his body until his throbbing erection fit snugly into the hollow between her legs.

A match to her passion-soaked torch.

Callie stiffened in shock, stunned to find herself hovering on the brink of an orgasm. She gripped his arms and tried frantically to pull away. How had that happened? How could she possibly be on the verge of . . . *screaming* with pleasure over a little kiss? They were standing in a public road! Never mind that it was dark.

She did the only thing she could to save herself the embarrassment of a public orgasm.

She slapped Dillon, just as they had planned.

He jerked his head back in shock. She was close enough to see his pupils expand, then contract as he stared at her in dazed confusion.

Panting like a dog in heat, she pushed at his chest. She knew she sounded far more panicky than was necessary for the scene, but she couldn't help it. "Let me go!" she cried, hoping he didn't realize how much she meant it. "You . . . you bastard! Let go of me!"

He dropped his arms abruptly, and she stumbled back

several steps before finding her legs. She raced to the driver's side door of the SUV and pounded on the glass.

The handsome guy behind the wheel stared back at her with a frown of concern. Yes, she thought, struggling for breath, he'd obviously seen their shadows merging in his rearview mirror, and had heard the ensuing fight.

She hitched a breath and stood back as Ramon opened the door and stepped out. All six-foot-four of him. She had to tilt her head back to look at him.

"What's going on?" he asked, slanting a frown at Dillon, who was nearly indistinguishable in the dark, before turning back to Callie. "Did this guy hurt you?"

It was so far from the truth that Callie had to swallow a laugh. "No, he just . . . We had a fight. I need a ride home."

Ramon wasn't convinced. "You look pretty shaken to me."

Oh, she was. She was *very* shaken. To prove it, she put a trembling hand to her throbbing mouth. "No. I'm . . . we . . ." Her jaw dropped as Ramon cut her off with a menacing curse.

"Get in the car. I'll take care of this creep."

Before she could think, Ramon closed the distance to Dillon in three long strides, slammed him against the Jeep, and socked him in the jaw with his fist. Her unsuspecting rescuer stood back, breathing hard.

It all happened in a matter of seconds.

The shadowy figure that was Dillon grabbed his jaw, apparently too stunned to move.

"That'll teach you to manhandle a lady," Ramon snarled. Without a backward glance, he strode back to Callie. "Get in. I'll give you a ride home, sweetie. No need to put up with that creep any longer than you have to."

Callie glanced at Dillon, caught his furtive wave, and hastily went around to the passenger door. She got inside and buckled her seat belt, forcing herself to remain facing the windshield.

She couldn't look at Dillon again. If she did, their plan would be blown to hell and back, because her chest was already hurting with the effort it took to hold back laughter.

Ramon got in behind the wheel and slammed the door. He shot her a concerned glance. "Are you sure you're okay?" When she nodded, he started the engine and peeled onto the road. "I should have beaten him to a pulp," he said. "My old man used to knock my mother around, and I was too little to do anything about it."

So that explained his explosive reaction, Callie thought, her amusement fading abruptly. "I'm sorry," she said. "But it wasn't necessary to hit him. He was just . . . just kissing me." Rocking her world. Setting her body on fire. Reminding her of what she had been missing.

Arousing her to the point of terror . . . and a long-anticipated orgasm.

"Don't apologize for him," Ramon growled harshly. "I know his type. By the way, I'm Ramon Scott."

"Callie Spencer. I'm staying at the Regency Hotel."

"You're not from around here?" He hit the brakes at a red light, throwing Callie against her seat belt. "So did you just meet that creep or something? He seemed familiar, but I couldn't really get a good look at him in the dark. What's his name?"

"Um, it doesn't matter," Callie said hastily. "In fact, I don't think I even caught his name. He was just giving me a ride home from, um, some nightclub."

Ramon's look was chastising. "You really should be

careful. That guy might have taken advantage of you if I hadn't been there."

"You're probably right," Callie murmured. In fact, she was certain of it.

And she would have let him.

Cold showers supposedly worked for men.

Callie twisted the cold water knob full blast and stepped back. She pealed the damp dress from her clammy body and let it fall to the black-and-white tiled floor.

Her rueful chuckle echoed in the small hotel bathroom. If someone had told her that she would someday be trying to cool her lust under a cold shower spray, she would have laughed herself silly. Not Callie Spencer, mouse among women.

But here she was, her body humming with unfulfilled lust, her heart still pounding with excitement and need. Her lips still throbbing from that possessive, dominating kiss.

Dillon Love had done that to her. Forced her to feel again. Need again. Want again. Be alive again.

If she could get past the terror of getting hurt again, she would likely have the time of her life with Dillon. A purely lustful, give-and-take affair that might wash away the loneliness and self-imposed isolation of the last three years and leave her feeling confident and ready to take on the world again.

Other women did it. Why shouldn't she? She was no longer that naive, pitiful woman who walked around in an old-fashioned fog of love, marriage, children, and happily ever after.

Callie stuck her toe beneath the frigid spray, yelped in shock, and yanked it back out.

If wasn't as if she no longer believed in love, or finding Mr. Right. She did still believe it could happen. In the meantime she wanted to enjoy life, live it to the fullest. She was through hiding her light under a bushel . . . slinking around trying to remain invisible so that she would never have to feel that god-awful pain of betrayal again.

From now on she was going to take a leaf from an old episode of *Sex and the City* and treat sex the way a lot of men did: have a good time, then walk away before things got sticky. Since most men *did* seem to feel the same way, Callie didn't see how it could be a problem.

Yes, she owed Dillon for turning her on—no pun intended—to life again, despite the fact that he had tricked her by sending in his twin to cool her off. And she was fairly certain that was what he'd been doing, although she had yet to figure out his motive.

Callie drew a deep breath, pulled the shower curtain aside, and planted her entire, throbbing body beneath the cold spray. The water chilled her overheated body, but it couldn't wash the burn of Dillon's kiss from her memory.

She should get mad more often, she mused, turning to let the cold water cascade over her neck and shoulders. Anger had given her the courage to act the tease with Dillon, although her courage had played out near the end. She had forgotten how potent Dillon's burning look could be, and his kiss had literally blown her away.

Fontaine would turn cartwheels if she knew, although Callie wasn't certain she would approve of Dillon. *Get out there and play ball!* her sister would shout.

With a coach like Dillon, how could Callie resist?

Chapter Nine

There was only one thing stopping Dillon from getting physical with his immature, not-so-funny twin.

Well . . . make that three things: Lou behind the bar, Fish stacking chairs, and Dillon's still-throbbing jaw.

Dillon gingerly adjusted the Ziploc bag of ice against his jaw and continued to glare at Wyatt, who was wisely keeping out of swinging distance. "What, pray tell, would give her the impression I had a problem between the sheets, if you didn't tell her?"

Wyatt spread innocent hands wide. "I swear, Dillon! I didn't tell her that. I admit that it sounds like something I would pull, but I know how important this woman is to you."

"She's important to all of us," Dillon corrected caustically, not ready to admit just how important she was becoming to *him* personally. "And what about Dr. Love advising her to get out and start dating again? Please don't insult me by telling me *that* wasn't your work, either. It had your stink all over it."

Frowning in thought, Wyatt finally shook his head.

"You're absolutely right: that sounds like something Dr. Love would say, too, but I don't think I did for the simple reason that I didn't know she *hadn't* been dating. She told me she's been divorced for three years. She didn't say anything about going underground. I would remember that, bro." He leaned forward as much as he dared, peering at Dillon's swelling jaw. "Man, I can't believe Ramon hit you! From the way Greg talks, Ramon's a big harmless teddy bear."

"Yeah, a real teddy bear," Dillon drawled. "Don't change the subject. What about the foot massages?"

This time Wyatt held up both hands, looking horrified. "No way, bro! You couldn't pay me good money to touch your woman's toes!"

"She's not my woman."

"Oh, really?" Wyatt folded his arms and lifted a sarcastic brow. "Is that why I'm having to keep this table between us so you can't tear my head off, because Callie Spencer *isn't* your woman?" He turned the chair in front of him upside down on the table and leaned his arms against it, staring at Dillon through narrowed eyes. "There's really only one explanation for all of this, Dillon, because the Callie you met tonight isn't the Callie I've gotten to know. The Callie I know is too jumpy and gun-shy to even *think* about letting a man zip her up, and I still can't wrap my mind around the fact that she asked for a foot rub, in public, no less."

Dillon slowly lowered the ice pack. "And your theory is . . . ?"

"She knows about us," Wyatt declared, reaching for another chair and upending it on the table. "That has to be it. She knows and she's pissed and she turned the tables on us."

"How could she know? Almost the only time we've

been together lately is when we're here at the night-club." Wyatt's theory made sense, but Dillon still wasn't convinced he hadn't come up with the idea to save his own sorry hide.

"Callie Spencer isn't a dummy," Wyatt pointed out needlessly.

Fish, who had been stacking chairs close by, jerked around at the sound of her name. "Callie Spencer? Cute little number with dark hair and blue eyes? California driver's license?"

A finger of dread traced a cold line down Dillon's spine. There was only one reason he could think of that Fish would know Callie.

She'd been to the club. Fish rarely forgot a face or a name.

"When?" Dillon asked without elaborating.

"Last night, right after you stopped serving booze. You two were holding up the back wall. She stayed for about ten minutes, then left in a hurry. She looked upset."

Dillon met Wyatt's dismayed gaze. "She saw us. Damn." When Wyatt started chuckling helplessly, Dillon closed his eyes and let out an aggravated sigh. He might have known his brother would find it funny.

Wyatt's chuckles soon turned into belly-rolling laughter. He pointed at Dillon. "She got to you, bro! She had you so flustered you didn't know if you were me or you!"

Scowling at him, Dillon said, "Believe me, that was never in question."

"Oh, man!" Wyatt wiped at his streaming eyes, still chuckling. "I really like this one, Dillon."

Beside Wyatt, Fish was grinning. "I really like her too, boss."

"Sounds like a keeper!" Lou called from the bar.

"Yeah, well." Dillon glowered at all of them with equal ferocity. "We'll see how you all feel about her when you read her review in *Next Stop* . . . while you're filling out papers for your unemployment wages."

Dillon took his ice pack, a fresh beer, and his aching jaw into the small office he and Wyatt now shared. He needed to think, and he couldn't do that with Wyatt's irritating laughter ringing in his ears.

He shut the door and took a seat behind the cluttered desk. Now Callie's taunting made sense.

The only bright spot was that she'd stayed only ten minutes, hopefully not long enough to really notice the place. Not that Dillon was ashamed of his establishment, but he knew how critical others could be. Most of his patrons were low- to middle-class citizens looking to relax and have a good time. What had the last reviewer called his nightclub? Redneck heaven, or something equally derogatory.

His lips twisted into a grimace. What his nightclub lacked in class, it made up for in heart, something the reviewer had failed to mention. He doubted she'd stayed long enough at the bar to notice how Lou greeted people by name and asked after their kids, or to see that his waitresses, more often than not, knew what the regulars were going to order. She probably hadn't noticed the far wall by the pool table, the one that was covered with baby pictures stapled, pinned, and taped there by proud parents, grandparents, aunts, and uncles. And okay, yes, by daddies who weren't always certain they were the fathers.

No, what she had mostly likely noticed was . . .

Dillon groaned and beat his fist on the desk. In the excitement, he'd forgotten last night's fiasco. His waitresses had quit, gotten drunk at another club, then returned to spill drink orders and dance on the bar. And his customers . . . God, his customers. They had been rowdier than usual due to Tyler's ineptness and generosity with Jack Daniel's.

He put his hands gingerly over his face and moaned, remembering Todd Hamilton, the son of a prominent politician who had been coaxed into the club by a few locals, whirling on the dance floor with several feet of toilet tissue flying out behind him. By the time his giggling girlfriend got him to stop, everyone in the place had been howling with laughter.

How much had Callie seen? He had to get her back after he had a chance to clean the place up a little. He had new, more conservative uniforms for the waitresses, and casual suits for Lou and Fish. His cook had promised to add a few fancy dishes to the menu, too.

He hadn't been ready for her, dammit!

And now it might be too late for damage control.

Unless . . . unless he could come up with a damned good reason for switching on her.

When Luke's cell phone began to vibrate inside his jacket pocket, Dillon was struck with a brilliant idea. He pulled it out, saw that it was Greg, and pushed the button. "Greg, I'm glad you called. I've got a code red. I repeat, I've got a code red. Can you come to the club?" When his request was met with stunned silence, Dillon grinned.

Apparently it hadn't occurred to any of the escorts that *he* might have a code red.

"What's up?" Greg finally asked a little warily.

"I'll tell you when you get here." Dillon disconnected, scrolled through the list of numbers, and pushed "Send." A groggy Tyler answered on the second ring.

"This had better be good. You probably woke the baby."

"It's Dillon. I've got a code red. I need you at the club in thirty minutes."

He didn't wait for questions or excuses. He dialed the next number, his grin widening. By the time he'd called the last escort, he was chuckling openly. This was really fun!

Wyatt stuck his head in the door. "I heard you laughing. Have you lost it, bro?"

"No, I haven't. Don't turn out the outside lights just yet. Your coworkers are on their way. We're about to have a meeting. I've got a code red."

"You can't have a code red," Wyatt blurted out. "I mean, it's just . . ." When he realized that Dillon was waiting patiently for an explanation, he shook his head and pulled the door hastily shut.

Dillon rubbed his hands together gleefully. If his suspicions were right and there wasn't actually a code red, there was now. And unless the escorts were willing to come clean and admit he was the butt of a group joke, he'd have them all here within a short time.

If two heads were better than one . . . then just under a dozen had to be foolproof.

By tomorrow he should have the perfect excuse to offer Callie.

Dillon's bar resembled an audition for the Chippendales.

The escorts of Mr. Complete lounged on bar stools and sprawled in chairs. A couple of them wore pajama bottoms and T-shirts, and Greg was dressed in spandex running shorts and a faded sweatshirt.

Tyler smothered a yawn, and it spread through the entire group.

The newest member of the group, Will Tallfeather, a Native American with shoulder-length black hair and pitch-black eyes, was the only one in a tux, having dropped his client off moments before answering Dillon's call to arms.

Will shucked his jacket, loosened his bow tie, and gratefully took the frosted root beer Lou offered him. Fish was busy pouring coffee and taking drink orders, but Dillon wanted everyone's attention, so he waited until his staff finished serving and took their seats.

Collin, who was pushing forty but looked thirty, ran a hand over his five-o'clock shadow and eyed Dillon with sleepy eyes. "Let's get the show on the road, Dill. It's freaking two in the morning."

"At least you're not going to have kids bouncing on your chest in about three hours," Tyler grumbled.

"I heard that," Ivan said, lifting his Coke in Tyler's direction.

With a leering grin, Collin said, "No, but with any luck I'll have a tall, curvy blonde bouncing on my chest instead."

A wave of groans and good-natured curses swept over the crowd. A sixteen-year marriage to a gorgeous cover model made Collin the envy of his coworkers, and he loved to rub it in.

"Tell us, Collin," Jet taunted, "are those babies real?"

Collin shot him a huge grin. "Damn straight, they're real."

"What about yours?" Greg joked. "Are *they* real?"

Dillon couldn't resist laughing when Collin swept his shirt off and began to make his pectoral muscles dance. He was beginning to understand why his twin had developed an attachment to the "boys." They were all good-natured, loyal men.

Now Dillon was anxious to test their problem-solving skills. He stepped up to the bar and raised his hand to get their attention.

The crowd fell instantly silent. Belatedly Dillon realized they were staring at his discolored jaw, and more than a few of them looked angry.

"What the hell happened to you?" Ivan demanded, standing so fast his chair went crashing to the floor. His fists clenched, defining his impressive muscles.

"Yeah, what happened?"

"Did someone jump you?"

"Did you see who it was?"

"Just give us a name, boss."

A huge lump formed in Dillon's throat as the bristling men came forward to examine his jaw. They looked positively menacing. He glanced questioningly at Wyatt, who was shaking with silent laughter.

But Wyatt's eyes were gleaming with pride, Dillon saw.

Dillon wasn't exactly comfortable with the sappy warmth that filled his heart at the sight of these muscled men looking so bristly and upset over *him*. He cleared his throat just to make absolutely certain he didn't embarrass himself by sounding husky. "Um, it was an accident."

"Well," Greg said in a growling voice, "we'll make sure it's an 'accident' when we beat the crap out of whoever did this."

Ivan puffed out his chest. "That can definitely be arranged, Dill."

Dill. He couldn't remember anyone ever calling him Dill. Not even his mother.

"You should have told us you were having trouble," Collin said. He swung an accusing look at Wyatt, who hastily sobered. "Where were *you* when this happened?"

"Um, tending bar." Wyatt glanced at Greg. "You'd better tell them, bro, before they start knocking on doors and punching people out."

Although Ramon wasn't exactly Dillon's favorite person at the moment, he was beginning to feel a little bit sorry for him. "Greg, you'd better sit down," Dillon told him. When a puzzled Greg resumed his seat, Dillon took a deep breath. "Our little plan to distract Ramon sort of backfired."

"Our?" Greg repeated.

"I'll explain about Callie in a moment. She was with me when you called with the SOS. It was actually her idea to get into a fight so she could run to Ramon for protection and get him to take her home."

"Oh, man," Greg breathed, turning pale. "Tell me you didn't hit her."

Dillon couldn't prevent the flush that crept into his face. "Of course not! *She* hit *me* after I kissed her. It was the plan." Although he doubted either of them had planned to get so carried away with that scorching kiss.

Jet folded his beefy arms. "We're listening."

"It's pretty simple. Ramon thought I was manhandling her, so he hit me."

There was a round of collective gasps. Yep, Dillon thought with an inward smile, they were definitely surprised. So much for Ramon's big, fluffy teddy bear image.

Greg shot out of his chair like a cannon. "You're shitting me," he burst out. "Ramon catches flies with his bare hands and throws them outside." He flushed when several eyebrows rose in amusement. "I was just trying to make a point, that's all. I'm sorry, Dill. I really am."

Dill again. Dillon cleared his throat and resisted the urge to rub his aching jaw. "I'm sure that Ramon just got the wrong idea, Greg. I'll live." He leaned against the bar and put his arms on the counter. "Let's move to the real reason why I got you out of bed with a code red." Dillon wasn't surprised when none of the guys looked him in the eye. He suppressed a grin. Quickly he outlined the situation for them, leaving out the intimate details, of course.

By the time he finished, everyone with the exception of Will was either grinning, chuckling, or outright laughing.

Dillon's fingers itched to grab the draft nozzle from beneath the counter and spray their ornery mugs. Instead he held on to his patience until the laughter died to a low rumble. He focused on Will, who had the barest hint of a smile in his dark eyes. "Will, what do you think? Now that we suspect she knows about the switch, how would you handle it?"

Will appeared to be contemplating the question. Slowly he said, "I would tell her the truth."

"The truth?" Dillon frowned. "You mean tell her my plans to butter her up before she sees this place?"

"No." Will stared at Dillon, unblinking. "Tell her the *other* truth, that you used Wyatt like a wet blanket to dampen the flames of the fire *you* started."

There was a short silence before the room erupted into loud, braying laughter. Will, Dillon noted sourly, was now laughing as hard as the others. Like a good sport, Dillon rode it out for a few moments before he reached beneath the counter for the spray nozzle. He deliberately pointed it in their general direction.

One by one, they sobered. Or at least struggled to.

"Now maybe we can get down to business," he said softly. "Would anyone care to make a *serious* suggestion?" When Ivan held up his hand, Dillon pointed the nozzle in his direction, warning him.

He turned his palm toward Dillon, a helpless chuckle escaping. "Hold on! I'm serious when I say that I agree with Will. You're safer sticking to the truth. It's flattering to her, for one thing, and if she truly feels the same way, she should understand."

As Dillon looked from one escort to the other, they all nodded their agreement. Had he really called them out in the middle of the night only to have his dilemma settled so quickly and easily? He cast a wary glance around the room again, this time more slowly, looking into their eyes and searching for signs of mockery or jest.

Either they were damned good at hiding it, or they were utterly serious. Finally, he conceded to their unanimous vote. "Okay, so I tell her the truth. What happens then?"

Grinning, Lou poked Tyler in the ribs. "If you don't know the answer to that one, Dillon, then you need to go back to the schoolroom."

Collin spewed coffee before he managed to clamp a hand over his mouth. He swallowed hard, maintaining a straight face with extreme effort. "What's really busting your balls, Dillon?"

Dillon ground his teeth, asking himself for the tenth time why he felt the need to keep humiliating himself. But he'd gone this far. . . . "Let's say the attraction is mutual, and we do end up in the sack, and afterward the relationship goes sour? She may be one woman, but she could pack quite a punch against the city of Atlanta." *And I don't want that on my conscience*, Dillon wanted to shout.

Will reached for his jacket and pulled it on over his broad shoulders. "Looks like you've got a big decision to make," he said as he strode to the door.

"And that's a decision only *you* can make," Ivan added, following Will.

Dismayed, Dillon watched as they all began to leave, including his traitor twin.

Tyler shot him a pitying look over his shoulder. "Wouldn't want to be in your shoes, bro. No way. Glad I'm married."

"Amen to that," Collin breathed, waving to Dillon.

Jet stopped at the bar to set his empty coffee cup down and give Dillon a piece of advice. "No relationship worth keeping is gonna be easy," he warned. "Cameron and I went through hell before we realized we loved each other."

"I'm not—" Dillon clenched his jaw. What was the point? *Worthless bunch of brats.* "Who said anything about love?"

With a wink, Jet clapped him on the shoulder. "That's right, buddy. Keep denying it until the end. But when it bites you on the ass, don't say I didn't warn you."

After the door closed on the last man, there was no one left to hear Dillon's long and colorful string of curses.

Chapter Ten

When Dillon heard voices behind Mrs. Scuttle's closed office door as he veered toward Luke's desk, he paused to double-check his watch calendar.

No, he didn't have the date wrong. It was ten A.M. on Wednesday morning. Mrs. Scuttle wasn't supposed to be back from her vacation until Thursday. And whom was she talking to? He didn't have any appointments this morning, that he recalled. But then, he *had* been burning the candle at both ends lately, so he supposed he could have forgotten.

Gathering his courage—and trying to remember Greg's dire warnings about the infamous secretary—he knocked lightly on her office door.

"Come in," a sweet, elderly voice called out.

Feeling ridiculously nervous, Dillon opened the door. "I just wanted to welcome you back from—" The rest of his greeting got stuck in his throat as his astounded gaze landed on Callie sitting in the chair in front of Mrs. Scuttle's desk.

She turned around, flashing him a warm smile that

matched the warmth of her sunny yellow dress. With her dark hair piled carelessly on top of her head and a heavy camera slung around her slim neck, she might have been a tourist who had wandered in from the sidewalk.

But Dillon, for one, knew better.

As far as he knew, Mrs. Scuttle did not.

Tamping down panic, Dillon assessed the situation. Would Callie be smiling so warmly if the secretary had spilled the beans about his nightclub business? He didn't think so. At least, he prayed it wasn't so.

Thank God he'd won the battle with his exhausted body this morning and hadn't slept that extra hour. Sweat broke out on his upper lip as he thought of how catastrophic that would have been.

"Good morning, Dillon. Mrs. Scuttle was just telling me what an excellent job you've done filling in for your boss while he's on his honeymoon."

"She . . . she did?" he croaked. He attempted to clear the frog from his throat, stepping into the office. "I'm glad to see that I . . . measure up to her high standards." He caught the slight rising of Mrs. Scuttle's brows above the huge owlish eyes magnified by her thick lenses and hastily added, "But I'm relieved that she's back. This place goes to the dogs when she's gone."

Or the rats, rather.

He was relieved to see the thin line of Mrs. Scuttle's mouth soften into a pleased smile. So far, so good. "I wish you'd let me know that you were returning a day early. I would have swung by the bakery and picked up one of those cheese pastries you like so much."

"Ah . . . Luke trained you well," Mrs. Scuttle said, preening. She pointed to a pastry-filled saucer on her desk. "Since I decided to surprise you by comin' back a day early, I stopped to get my own pastry. I'm so happy to be back, I'm not even gonna to fuss about the fact that someone's been eatin' raisins at my desk. I'll just stick 'em on top of my Danish so they don't go to waste."

Dillon started to relax until her words sank in. He froze, staring at the secretary in growing horror as she slowly transferred the scattering of raisin-shaped pellets one by one onto her pastry.

Not raisins . . . but rat droppings left by a runaway, two-pound black-and-white rat named Bingo.

His legs went weak. He grabbed the doorjamb for support, his brain scrambling for ways to keep the elderly lady from eating the rat turds without telling her the truth: that a rat had been practically living in her office while she was gone. How had he gotten to this point? he wondered, giving his head a dazed shake.

He focused on Mrs. Scuttle just as she lifted the Danish to her mouth. "No!" he shouted. She froze with the pastry inches away from her pink-painted lips, blinking at him with her owlish eyes. Oh, God, what could he say? "I . . . I need that pastry," he blurted out frantically. "My blood sugar has dropped. I'm feeling weak and dizzy." Which was true, the last part anyway. "If you'll just give me that one, I'll get you another as soon as I stabilize." He clutched the doorjamb and held his breath to see if Mrs. Scuttle would swallow his lie.

She must have thought he looked the part of a diabetic on the verge of collapsing, because she rose and shuffled as fast as her little seventy-nine-year-old legs would carry her around the desk to hand him the Danish.

She blinked at him in concern. "Luke should have

told me about your condition," she scolded, using her hand to urge his own toward his mouth with the Danish. "That way I could have kept an eye on you and made sure you took your insulin shots. I've got a good friend who has to take them all the time, and sometimes I have to help her. It's not easy reaching your own butt when you get to be our age."

Dillon resisted the forward motion of his hand as much as he dared. He could feel Callie watching the scene, her concern almost palpable. Yet another lie he would have to explain.

And he would, the moment he figured out how to avoid eating the rat-turd-infested Danish.

"You might have to help me here," Mrs. Scuttle said to Callie, grunting with the effort to push his hand forward. "I think he's going into diabetic shock. We might have to force this into his mouth."

"Just say the word," Callie said with earnest concern.

There was only one thing to do, Dillon realized, forcing his hand to start shaking violently.

He dropped the Danish onto the carpet. Before the secretary could bend her arthritic knees to pick it up, Dillon beat her to it. He hastily brushed off the rat raisins, muttered a short prayer, and stuffed the entire Danish into his mouth before Mrs. Scuttle could see what he had done.

Around a mouthful of cheese Danish, he said, "It's working. I can feel it working." He struggled not to gag.

Mrs. Scuttle slapped the back of her hand into his chest, making him grunt in surprise. "Don't talk with your mouth full, boy! Didn't your mama teach you better? Speaking of your mother . . . she called earlier. We had ourselves a nice chat."

Her smile made Dillon's blood run cold. He nearly

choked as he tried to swallow the Danish so he could cut her off before she said something he might regret.

"Yes, it's been an interesting morning. Made me glad I came back a day early." This time there was a definite glint of pure mischief in her eyes as she stared up at him. "First the phone call from your mother, then a visit from Ms. Callie here. She told me you two had already met, seeing as how you're her escort and all."

Dillon froze as Mrs. Scuttle reached up to touch his shadowed jaw where Ramon had socked him.

"Ms. Callie here told me what happened." Her chuckled sounded ancient. "Can't believe that big ol' baby hit you. Did you know that Ramon won't even kill a pesky fly? He catches it and lets it back outside." She shook her head. "As if it won't just turn around and fly right back inside."

Shuffling over to her desk, she said to Callie, "You shoulda took a picture of that. It ain't every day an old woman saves a man's life, you know. It's a shame, though, about the Danish. I had a cravin' for raisins. Must be low on iron or something. Hate taking the supplements, though. They constipate me." She made it to her chair and flopped down, heaving a sigh. "Now, if you two don't mind, it's time for my morning power nap. Dillon, wake me in thirty minutes, will you? I've got a lot of work to catch up on."

Before Dillon could fully realize what had happened, he and Callie were standing on the other side of the closed door, wondering how the hell they got there.

Callie lifted a skeptical brow. "You're not really diabetic, are you?"

"No." The temperature between them jumped from cool to blazing in three seconds flat as he slowly looked her over. His brow shot upward, matching her expression. "You're not really a tourist, are you?"

She nodded. "Today I am. I was walking along the sidewalk, taking pictures, when I noticed the sign out front. I couldn't resist popping in to say hi." She reached up and touched the corner of his lips. "You've got some icing right there."

Dillon sucked in a sharp breath at her touch. "As long as it's not a raisin," he murmured huskily, slowly drawing her near. He wanted to kiss her. Slow and easy. Hard and thrusting.

He wasn't picky.

Her gaze was on his mouth as she whispered, "So what was that all about? Why didn't you want her to eat the Danish?"

"Oh, you caught that one, did you?" Dillon chuckled. "Trust me, you don't really want to know."

"Yes, I do."

He tugged her another inch closer, until her camera bit into his chest. Damned piece of interfering equipment. "I promise you that you don't . . . want . . . to . . . know." Now he was staring at her mouth, just as she was staring at his. She wore a clear gloss today that made her lips look wet and delectable. "Have lunch with me."

"It's only ten thirty."

"Have brunch with me."

Her lips tilted. "You just ate a Danish. Are you sure you're hungry?"

The comment reminded Dillon that he really needed to brush his teeth, maybe even rinse with disinfectant or bleach or something.

And he didn't want to kiss Callie until that happened.

Well, he *wanted* to, but he shouldn't. If he kissed her

and she pried the information out of him about the Danish, he suspected she wouldn't thank him. "Then let's go for a walk in the park. I've got to explain something to you."

Her gaze lifted, locked on his eyes. "Something good, or something bad?"

"That depends."

"On what?"

"On a lot of things."

"Let me guess. Your favorite genre is mystery."

Dillon grinned wickedly. "Wrong. My favorite genre is action."

"No fair. I don't think action is a genre. It mostly applies to movies."

Dropping his hands to her hips, Dillon pulled her against him. "Wanna bet?" He was gratified by her sharp gasp. Gratified enough to let her pull away to a safer distance.

"Let's go, then, before Mrs. Scuttle catches us and makes us stand in the corner for misbehaving."

"Ahu . . . I've got to do something before we go. Wait for me here."

"Another mystery?"

Shaking his head, Dillon headed for the bathroom, where he kept a toilet supply kit under the sink. "Trust me, Callie," he threw at her over his shoulder. "You really, really don't want to know."

They walked along the busy sidewalk until they came to a small park tucked between a bank and a hotel. The park was practically hidden behind a high brick fence covered in ivy.

"The guidebook doesn't mention this park," Callie observed, admiring the overhanging trees and the blossom-littered path. She took several pictures, wishing she'd brought along more film. It was a very romantic setting.

"It's a well-kept secret," Dillon said. "Locals have to have some place they can go without running into camera-toting tourists." He shot her a naughty grin. "Present company excluded."

"I'm not a tourist; I'm a reviewer, remember?" She was glad he had his back to her so that he couldn't see her blush over the lie.

"It's the same, isn't it? Tourists and reviewers alike see only the surface of the city. They never reach down into the heart of it and find out what makes it tick. They don't realize that it's constantly changing, while somehow remaining the same." He paused at a blossom-covered bench and gently brushed it clean with his hand. "Have you ever had bad service or bad food at a restaurant, and then gone back two weeks later and experienced the exact opposite?"

Callie took her time considering his question as she settled on the bench beside Dillon. She had almost gotten used to the fierce pounding of her heart when she was near him.

But she didn't think she would ever get used to her knee-jerk reaction to his touch.

She had that reaction now as he picked up her hand and threaded his fingers through hers. Forcing herself to concentrate, she said, "I think I know what you mean. Restaurants, nightclubs, hotels . . . they're only as good as their staff, and any establishment can have a bad day or even a bad week when new employees are learning the ropes."

"Exactly." He looked at her, his blue, blue eyes crystal clear and earnest in the bright morning sunshine.

"Do you, personally, judge a business on the merits of your first and only visit?"

He was asking the wrong person, Callie thought, because she was absurdly—according to Fontaine—easy to please. But he didn't *know* he was asking the wrong person, and she couldn't tell him the truth. She couldn't risk blowing her cover as a reviewer and disappointing Fontaine just because she was deeply attracted to Dillon.

"Was that a tough question?" Dillon prompted, his gaze intent on her face.

So Callie did the only thing she could do. She attempted to put herself in Fontaine's shoes and answer the question as she imagined Fontaine would answer it. "I think it would depend on how much time I have, and whether my instincts were telling me I should give the business another chance. Is this the big mystery you wanted to talk to me about?" Because if it wasn't, Callie really wanted to change the subject. She wasn't comfortable lying about her reason for being in Atlanta, even if it was for a good cause.

He brought her hand to his lips, sending tiny shock waves skipping along her arm.

"No, it isn't. I wanted to tell you a story about a man and a woman who met by chance in a hotel bar. The attraction between them was instant and powerful, so powerful the man made a fool of himself and scared the woman away."

A tremor shot through Callie. She felt every muscle in her body grow still.

"The randy goat—"

"Randy goat?"

Dillon's smile was boyishly rueful. "The randy goat being me. Anyway, the man was so intrigued with the

112

mystery woman, he bribed the bartender into giving him her name."

"How much?" Callie asked, struggling not to smile.

"A hundred-dollar bill and a copy of my driver's license in case I turned out to be the mad slasher."

"Oh." Callie was dumbfounded. She didn't know what to think, so she fell silent again.

"Imagine the randy goat's surprise when he discovered the very woman who had made him forget his own name—and his manners—was the woman he was to escort around town for the next three weeks. Not only was his work ethic compromised, but he was deeply afraid she'd never forgive him for nearly ravishing her in the elevator."

Her bones liquefied at the reminder. She tried to take slow, even breaths, but it was no use. She was starting to pant again. Shameful. Ridiculous.

Amazing.

His hand tightened on hers as if he feared she might try to run. "So, not thinking rationally, he sent his twin brother in to smooth the troubled waters, not only for the sake of his job, but because he wanted a chance to get to know this mystery woman."

She didn't pretend to be shocked. She knew by the way he was staring at her that he knew that she knew.

"Now the foolish, randy goat has seen the error of his ways, and wonders how he can get his mystery woman to forgive him for pulling a childish switcheroo."

Callie let him squirm as she absorbed his story. Not only did he sound sincere, but he hadn't tried to lie his way out of it. *What's not to admire in a man who can admit he's wrong?* she thought.

But now that the jig was up, where did that leave them? It was a dynamite question, and one Callie wasn't certain she wanted to ask. She didn't know if she was ready to give in to her irrational, insane desire for this man, but she also didn't know if she could continue using him as an escort if she *didn't* get to jump his bones.

What a dilemma!

Stalling for time, Callie asked, "What's your twin's name?"

"Wyatt."

Wyatt. Now she could stop calling him the other Dillon—the one who *didn't* turn her bones to mush. "He's sweet."

Dillon flashed her a wicked smile. "Now, *that's* what I wanted to hear. Sweet is okay. Charming is okay. Anything else means I'll have to take him out." His smile grew crooked. "You nearly gave me a heart attack when you asked for that foot rub."

"Good." Callie felt like laughing, and she didn't know why. She'd never felt more confused in her life, and she knew she should be angry. "Because you had *me* thinking I was going through early menopause, flashing hot, then cold, then hot again."

His smile slipped a little. "You really weren't attracted to Wyatt? Not even a little bit?"

The mischief maker in her let him stew a moment before she said, "Nope, not even a little, which is really weird, considering you two look exactly alike."

"You wanna know something about me that nobody else—except my mother and Wyatt—knows?"

When Callie nodded, he took her hand and slipped it inside his shirt, between the buttons. Hot, hard flesh rippled beneath her fingers. She had to bite her tongue to keep from groaning. What was he doing to her? When would the torture stop?

"There. Feel that little indentation?"

Callie forced her befuddled mind to focus. "Yes, I feel it." And a whole lot more. In fact, she wanted to rip his shirt off and lick every inch of his chest with her tongue.

The realization shocked her.

Dillon's gaze heated as if he could read her every erotic thought. His voice was a husky burn to her senses as he said, "When we were seven, we found a stash of bottle rockets in the neighbor's shed. Wyatt got me on the first try."

"You were shooting them at each other?"

He chuckled at her shocked expression. "You don't have any brothers, do you?"

She shook her head. "Just a sister, Fontaine, and I can't imagine her doing anything so dangerous." Beneath her trembling fingers, she could feel his heart thundering. She suspected she wasn't the only one skirting around the real issue.

"How about you, Callie? Have you ever done anything . . . dangerous?"

"I don't think I've ever wanted to . . . before."

"And now?"

Licking her lips, she reluctantly withdrew her hand. "I don't know. I'd hate to ask you to jeopardize your job just for . . . for . . ."

"Mind-blowing sex?" he suggested with a wicked grin. When she blushed, he chuckled. He sobered abruptly. "But you have a point. I can't see myself putting the company's reputation on the line." His gaze lingered on her mouth, his voice dropping to a thick whisper. "On the other hand, I don't know if I can be around you every night without taking you to bed."

It was impossible to look at him without getting breathless, but it would probably be a good idea to slow things down a little. "We . . . we could try to be good, at least until you're no longer my escort. Then, if we still feel the same way . . ."

Dillon's brows rose in admiration. "Not a bad idea. I could schedule a vacation and join you later in California."

"Sounds like a plan to me." And the best part, Callie thought, was the fact that she would still get to see Dillon every day. On impulse, she said, "We could help each other by saying something totally unsexy when we're getting, um, overheated."

"Good thinking. Let's try it out, because if you don't stop looking at me that way, I'm going to explode right here in front of God and everybody."

Callie quickly looked at the ground, biting her lip to keep from smiling as she said, "Mrs. Scuttle . . . naked."

He groaned, then burst out laughing. "Hey, I think this might just work!"

Yes, Callie thought, watching the sexy column of his throat as he laughed. *But for how long?*

Chapter Eleven

"Mmmm. I'm so glad you talked me into this," Callie said from her facedown position on the massage table. "You have such great ideas."

Dillon, lying on another massage table not more than two feet away, tried his best not to respond to the sheer pleasure in her voice.

It didn't work. "Damn," he said. "I was just thinking about asking Mrs. Scuttle if she needed her toenails trimmed."

Callie turned her face in his direction, a slow, wicked smile curving her beautiful lips. "Really? What did I say?"

"It wasn't *what* you said." Dillon found himself wishing perversely that the rather small towel covering her would slip a little farther south. "It's *how* you said it, as if you were talking about something you might be doing in the bedroom." He saw the quick, embarrassed glance she cast over her shoulder at the masseuse, and chuckled.

"Dillon!" she hissed. "They have ears, you know."

His own masseuse slapped him soundly on his bottom, making him yelp in surprise. He didn't take offense; the masseuse was not only a personal friend, she was Lydia's partner in Lydia's Affordable Spa, Casey Winters.

Casey suddenly filled his vision, hands on hips, her very pregnant belly inches from his nose. He was startled to realize he could see her stomach moving.

"We not only have ears, we have *feelings*," Casey said with an injured sniff. "I haven't had sex in three weeks because *she* won't stop moving for the five minutes it takes, and Brett freaks out."

"Definitely more information than we needed to know," Dillon said dryly. He gave in to the urge to reach out and place his hand over her undulating stomach. With a sense of awe, he felt the baby kick his palm. Once. Twice. Then the baby pushed slowly against it as if she sensed his marvel and wanted to show off.

Dillon panicked and jerked back his hand.

"Oh, me, too! Me, too!" In her excitement, Callie raised herself onto her elbows, giving Dillon a scorching view of her lovely breasts.

"Dirty diapers!" Dillon all but shouted. "Spit-up. Cheese Danish topped with rat turds!"

Belatedly, Callie hastily lowered her upper body to the table again.

"Sheesh," Casey said, casting him a baleful glance as she obliged Callie and presented her stomach. "You don't have to keep reminding me. I know what's in store."

"No," Callie began, her face lit with wonder as she cautiously placed her palm against Casey's protruding stomach. "He doesn't mean—"

"Don't," Dillon warned. "If you tell her, everyone will know by sundown, and I'll never hear the end of it."

The dirty look Casey shot Dillon should have been enough to obliterate the memory of Callie's perky bare breasts. "For your info," Casey said, "I don't have a big mouth. Now spill. It's not nice to keep a pregnant woman in suspense. Especially one who has access to hot oil."

Since Callie had gotten them into this mess, Dillon decided she could do the explaining. With a smug smile, he turned his face away and pretended to doze.

The little devil did her best to distract Casey. Unfortunately, the only person she succeeded in distracting was Dillon.

"Wow," she breathed. "That feels so neat! Are you excited? Have you picked out a name? Do you have the nursery ready?"

The obvious yearning in her voice caused Dillon's heart to contract in a curious way. Callie Spencer wanted babies.

Casey sounded sly as she said, "I'll answer your questions if you'll answer mine. Why was Dillon shouting about dirty diapers and rat turds?"

With his face in hiding, Dillon grinned and waited.

"Well, um, you see, it's sort of this game we invented to distract each other when we started thinking about, um, sex."

Dillon didn't have to be looking to know that Casey's eyebrows had disappeared beneath her bangs, and that Callie was blushing furiously. In fact, if he turned his head, he'd probably see that she was blushing all over her gorgeous body.

"Man-eating turtles," he muttered to himself, without much success.

"Oh," Casey said, clearly dumbfounded.

He easily imagined he could hear the wheels turning in her head.

"I wonder if it would work for me?" Casey mused out loud.

When her cool hands suddenly landed on his back, Dillon jumped.

"That's what you get," she said righteously, "for calling me a bigmouth."

Casey began to knead with a vengeance, reminding Dillon why Lydia's Affordable Spa was so popular. It felt heavenly. The only thing better would be *Callie's* hands on his butt—er, back.

"Are you coming to the barbecue Saturday at Ivan's house?" Casey asked.

Stifling a moan, Dillon muttered, "It's not a barbecue. It's more like a barn raising, only with a tree house instead of a barn. Ivan's building one for Joey." And no, he wasn't going, not in this lifetime.

"Oh, so that's why Ivan asked Brett to bring a hammer and nails. Still, I can't believe you're not going. I mean, just because you're in for the short haul—"

Dillon cleared his throat loudly to remind Casey of the phone conversation they'd had before he booked the works for Callie and himself. Fortunately, she remembered before she blew his cover.

"Um, I mean, you never know when *you're* going to need *their* help building a tree house or something."

She would have to evoke the guilt, Dillon mused, by reminding him that the escorts had already helped him. Telling the truth *had* worked with Callie. He shifted into a more comfortable position, thinking ruefully that it might have worked *too* well.

Recklessly, he seized on the first excuse he could think of. "I'm scheduled to escort Callie."

"I would *love* to meet the other guys," Callie piped up, much to Dillon's dismay. "A barbecue sounds like fun."

Dillon groaned. "Bet my shorts one of us will regret it."

"You're on. My shorts against yours," Callie said, then added fervently, "Melted gum stuck to the bottom of my shoe."

He could no more resist the taunt than he could resist Callie. "What? Was it something I said?"

Being married to an underwear model meant Callie was no stranger to beautiful men, but the escorts of Mr. Complete were a different breed altogether, she soon discovered.

Like models, their smiles were dazzling, their physiques impressive, their manners around women and children impeccable.

But that was where the similarities with Lanny ended.

These were real men with unique jobs. They sweated, they cursed—when they thought their women couldn't hear them—they laughed, they cried, and they got dirty.

Callie sat in a daze on the cluttered patio with the other women and watched the men, including Casey's husband, Brett, build the biggest, ugliest tree house she'd ever seen.

Sharing a Kool-Aid pitcher filled with weak margaritas with a well-known supermodel, a popular singer, three ordinary housewives, and her rescuer, Ramon,

Callie couldn't remember a time when she'd felt so relaxed and happy.

Of course, the gorgeous toddler sleeping on her lap might have had a bit to do with her feeling of contentment. Carrigan, with her dark curls, chocolate-colored eyes, and rosy cheeks, had wrapped herself around Callie's heart from the moment Callie walked into the sprawling, cluttered, fabulous family home of Ivan and Diane.

Joey, Ivan's four-year-old son, had launched himself at Dillon screaming, "Uncle Dill! Uncle Dill!" Callie smiled at the fond memory of Dillon's terror-stricken face as he'd had no choice but to the catch the flying missile.

When Joey proceeded to wrap his little arms around Dillon's neck and rain kisses upon his astounded face, she had watched his expression turn from terror to a bewildered mixture of pride and embarrassment.

Diane hadn't let her curiosity over the reunion simmer for long. After introducing Callie to everyone, Diane had given her a blow-by-blow account of the turtle rescue before the first pitcher of margaritas was made. Dillon, apparently, was a hero in Joey's eyes. Another mystery was solved as well when Diane casually mentioned that Dillon had also found Joey's pet rat, Bingo, after Bingo had been lost in the offices of Mr. Complete for several days.

"Oh . . . my . . . God," Callie had muttered, capturing the attention of everyone within earshot—which, thank goodness, did not include any of the men, with the exception of Ramon, who was manning the barbecue grill.

"What?" Diane demanded, her curiosity apparently aroused by Callie's expression.

Callie hadn't known whether to laugh or gag as she retold the story about Mrs. Scuttle's cheese Danish and the "raisins"—which Callie now suspected were *not* raisins.

The howling, screaming laughter that had followed had earned more than one suspicious, wary look from the men too far away to have heard what was said. Even Tyler's three older children, Cameron's son Byron, and Joey had stopped their play long enough to glance curiously in the women's direction.

Now, two hours later, Callie felt as if she'd known them for years instead of hours.

"Here, let me take her. It's almost time to eat."

Callie gave a start and glanced up into Diane's smiling face. She tried to lift the arm that cradled Carrigan's head to help Diane, but found it wouldn't obey her commands. Diane laughed at her startled expression, gathering the sleeping child into her arms with a groan and a grunt.

"Don't worry; the feeling will return in an hour or two."

An hour or two? Surely she jested. Callie tried again to lift her arm. It lay against her side like an alien object. With a rueful laugh, she resigned herself to eating with her left hand until her arm decided to come back to life. So much for helping the other women set up the long picnic table for the barbecue.

Sighing her contentment, she kicked back in the lounger and looked for Dillon among the crowd of working men. Apparently he'd disappeared into the big oak tree, for he was nowhere to be seen.

Callie shaded her eyes, catching sight of Wyatt standing at the foot of the tree with Ivan, Collin, Greg, and Will. How had she ever thought he and Dillon were identical? She could easily identify them now. Wyatt was always laughing, whereas Dillon was more conservative, although he certainly possessed a sense of humor.

Suddenly there was a shout from the tree, followed by a mad scrambling of falling leaves and flailing limbs. The men around the tree backed away as Will came tumbling to the ground, followed by Brett and Jet. They all began to run in the direction of the patio, shouting and waving their arms. Ivan scooped up two children along the way, and Greg gathered the other two into his massive arms. Byron, being the oldest, was sprinting ahead on his own.

Frowning, Callie got to her feet, her heart pounding in alarm. What were they shouting about? And where was Dillon?

"Get in the house!" Ivan bellowed, in the lead. "Get in the house! Hornets! Hornets!"

Casey let out a squeal as Ramon scooped her up and bounded across the patio into the house. The other women followed, yelling and screaming. Ivan hit the patio at a dead run, followed by Jet. Jet tried to grab Callie's arm and drag her along, but she pulled away.

Where was Dillon? Her heart was beating a sharp tattoo against her chest.

And then she saw him. He dropped from the tree and hit the ground running. He waved his arms and shouted at her.

"Get in the house, Callie!"

She was alone on the patio, with a crowd screaming at her from the patio doors and Dillon running at her, still shouting. A dark cloud swarmed behind Dillon, just inches from his head. She saw him swat at the air. He cursed a blue streak and increased his speed.

It was Ramon who saved her, scooping her up as he had Casey and running back inside with her. He stepped aside just as Dillon came sailing across the threshold, then deftly hooked the sliding door with his foot and pulled it closed.

The crowd fell silent as the horde of angry hornets flew against the glass patio doors. *Thump, thump, thump.*

"My God," Diane whispered in a shaky voice. She pulled Joey against her legs in a tight embrace. "If they hadn't found that nest . . ."

But Callie scarcely heard her.

She was looking at Dillon, who didn't look like Dillon at all.

"Tobacco mixed with saliva."

"An aspirin."

"I heard Crisco is good for stings."

"How about meat tenderizer?"

"Gramma always dabbed my stings with ammonia. Worked every time."

"What about a Bounce fabric softener sheet?"

"Hey! I got that e-mail, too. Is that before or after you use the sheet in the dryer?"

"Baking soda works, too."

"So does mud. Just straight mud."

"Grandpa peed on—"

"No." Amanda, Tyler's wife, stepped to the front of the crowd that had gathered around Dillon. "Ice is best. I took some nursing classes when I first got out of high school, and ice is definitely best. Are you certain you aren't allergic, Dill?"

Dillon shook his burning head. He felt a little nauseous, but that was because he'd straddled a tree branch on the way down. He just wanted to stick his head in a bucket of ice water and end his misery.

Beside him, Wyatt ended his phone call and placed an encouraging hand onto his shoulder, unwittingly hitting a hornet sting. "Mom says that if you've got more than six stings, you should probably go to the emergency room."

His twin then proceeded to count his stings, despite Dillon's attempts to swat him away as if he were one of those pesky hornets. Dillon caught Callie's worried eye and gestured her over. When she reached him, he grabbed her hand and pulled her in close so that he could whisper in her ear.

"Do not, I repeat, do *not* let any of these maniacs pee on me."

She pulled back to eye level, giving him a faint smile. "I won't. I promise."

Amanda handed Callie two Ziploc bags of ice, then passed the rest out to Wyatt and Diane. Callie placed one bag on Dillon's forehead, covering two stings with one bag, and placed the other bag on top of his hand—right below the fading pink wound the turtle had left.

He winced as Diane settled a cold bag against his neck. Despite his considerable pain, he couldn't resist ogling Callie's cleavage as she leaned forward to adjust the bag on his forehead. "I just had to add a decorative chimney to the roof so that it would resemble a real house," he muttered, hoping to get his mind out of the gutter by remembering how many brain cells he lacked. "And to do that, I just had to clear a few more branches out of the way."

"If you hadn't," Diane said with a hint of terror lingering in her voice, "Joey would have angered them sooner or later, and they would have gotten him. He can't run as fast as you, and he's never been stung, so we don't know if he's allergic."

"Why do *you* always get to be the hero?" Wyatt joked.

"Because I'm always the one getting bitten, stung, or punched," Dillon said dryly.

"Don't forget the rat—"

Dillon looked up just in time to see Cameron clamp a hand over Casey's wayward mouth. His eyes narrowed on Callie's suspiciously red face, but he couldn't get her to look at him.

Which could mean only one thing.

The women—and Ramon, if his shaking shoulders were any indication—knew about the rat-turd Danish.

Was nothing sacred? he wondered, already plotting his revenge on his delectable date. Oh, it would be sweet. He had no doubt about that.

And then Dillon remembered something even sweeter: he'd won the bet.

Callie owed him her shorts.

He glanced at his watch and saw that the night was still young. Sure, they'd made an agreement not to have sex, but they hadn't banned foreplay.

As Callie leaned forward again, Dillon's gaze clashed with hers.

He was amazed the ice didn't melt instantly from the heat they generated with just one look.

Hairy legs, she mouthed.

An angry horde of stinging hornets, he mouthed back.

She smiled.

He chuckled.

Chapter Twelve

"I'll be moving to a different hotel tomorrow," Callie told Dillon as she waited nervously for him to unlock his apartment door. She was already regretting her impulsive decision to say yes to his offer of a nightcap. How could they possibly keep things under control in such an intimate setting? As much as she wanted him, she didn't want him doing anything he'd regret in the morning.

"And how did you rate the hotel, if you don't mind my asking?"

Was it her imagination, or had his voice chilled a few degrees?

He swung the door open, and she followed him in, deciding she was being overly sensitive. "I have no complaints," she said, keeping it vague. The apartment was surprisingly neat and homey, the shelves above the fireplace filled with trophies and pictures, the walls covered in prints and more family pictures. Not her idea of your ordinary bachelor pad. She expected a coffee table cluttered with empty pizza boxes and bare walls.

Dillon seemed to read her mind. "Mom insisted that if we weren't going to live with her, then we had to take some of our junk with us."

"She sounds like a practical woman."

"She's great. You'd like her."

"I'm sure I would, if she's anything like your friends."

She jumped when Dillon suddenly swung around to face her. He slid his hands around her waist and pulled her close, his voice deepening.

"And me? Do you like me?"

"I think you know the answer to that, Dillon." She gingerly touched the welts on his forehead, her pulse rate spiking. "Does it still hurt?"

His chuckle was rueful. "If you're trying to distract me, it's not working, not while I'm this close to you. Not even if I had a *hundred* bee stings."

"Someone has to be sensible," she said breathlessly.

"Not me. I'm injured."

She smiled against his mouth. "You rat!"

"No!" Dillon feigned horror. "Call me anything but that!"

"Tease?" Her breathing grew erratic. His teeth nipped her bottom lip, making her gasp and press her lower body closer. Two weeks felt like a lifetime away. But she had to admit it was definitely something to look forward to.

"Mmm. I love it when you talk dirty."

Liquid heat pooled between her legs. "Maybe we shouldn't talk at all," she suggested, grabbing his head and pulling his mouth shamelessly to hers.

Sheridon Smythe

The kiss deepened, igniting little campfires in strategic places all over her body. When she felt his hands at the waistband of her shorts, she pulled away. "What are you doing?"

"Claiming what is rightfully mine," he murmured seductively, continuing to unbutton and unzip her shorts. "You lost the bet, remember?"

"Oh, my shorts." She struggled to suck more air into her lungs. "But that will leave me in my . . . panties."

"I'll give them back to you before we leave," he offered magnanimously.

"Probably not a good idea."

"Okay, I won't give them back to you."

She bit his lip playfully. He retaliated by pushing her shorts slowly over her hips. "I meant it's probably not a good idea to take them off," she said breathlessly.

"What's the worst that can happen?"

Callie could have told him, but saying it would be like saying the opposite of their turnoff words, and she was hot enough, thank you. Besides, it was too late. Her shorts hit the floor. Like a good nymphomaniac, she stepped out of them.

She shrieked when he picked her up and hoisted her legs around his waist. "What . . . what are you doing now?"

He grinned at her, his eyes smoky, filled with lustful intent. "You sure ask a lot of questions. But since it *is* your body I'm carting off, I guess I should tell you that I'm taking you to the kitchen . . . counter."

Gulping in air, Callie clung to his neck and tried not to think about his erection pulsing against the core of her. Desperately, she drummed up turnoff words. "Maggots. Moldy pizza. Dirty socks."

130

He snorted and kept going. "You scare easily. Dirty socks? Houston, we might have a problem."

She buried her face in his neck as he lowered her butt to the counter. "I'm sorry that I don't have your life experiences."

His chuckle bathed her neck in warmth. "Yeah, you're so jealous."

Before she could think of a snappy comeback, he was kissing her senseless again . . . and doing some sneaky maneuvering with his hands and her panties. It was dark in the kitchen, and Callie liked it that way.

Three years was a long time. She needed slow and easy.

Dark and dirty.

As she danced with his feisty tongue and thought what a wonderful kisser he was, Dillon hooked his forefingers beneath the elastic of her panty legs and slowly slid his fingers forward . . . and down. She could feel liquid anticipation pooling between her legs.

His fingers paused on either side, standing sentry to her throbbing center.

Callie thought she might die if he didn't touch her, and she was fairly certain she would explode if he did.

To her complete and utter disappointment, he slowly removed his hands, sliding them upward along her taut belly beneath her T-shirt. He rested them just below her aching breasts.

"Tease," Callie hissed out, closing her teeth over the taut cord on his neck. She bit him lightly, loving the salty taste of his skin.

"You're supposed to be the sensible one," he whispered gruffly. "I'm delirious from bee stings and can't be held accountable for my actions."

He closed his hands over her breasts, and she gasped and arched her back. Dear God, had it ever felt so good with Lanny? She couldn't remember. In fact, she couldn't remember sitting on their kitchen counter for any reason. Lanny had been picky about those things.

Cookie jars went on the kitchen counter. Butts did not.

But here she was, with her butt on the cool Formica and her back against a cabinet, poking holes in Dillon's hands with her rock-hard nipples. She could feel every callus, every valley, every line in his hands outlined against her burning flesh.

And she couldn't think of a single, solitary turnoff word to save her life.

Or her, er, virtue.

Her fingers crept down along his belly to that hard bulge in his jean shorts. She just wanted to touch him. Feel it. See for herself if it would scorch her fingers, like she suspected it would.

"Baby, that's not a good idea."

Her fingers froze at his raw whisper. *Rats*. He'd caught her trying to dip her hand in the cookie jar. Deciding she'd better come clean—for both their sakes—she confessed, "Well, I don't think it was a good idea to give me the job of being the sensible one, and don't give me that song and dance about a few measly bee stings. *I'm* the one who hasn't had sex in three years."

She literally felt the shock hum through him. He froze with his thumbs pressed against her nipples. Groaning, Callie buried her flaming face against his neck. Why had she blurted that out? She knew some men avoided virgins. Was a three-year abstinence a similar turnoff for men?

Had she blown her chance of getting partially laid, dammit?

"I'm sorry," she mumbled.

"No, it's not that," he said in a strangled voice. "It's . . . the thought of how tight you must be. I almost lost it." He moaned, closed his eyes tight, and began to mumble.

Callie drew back to watch his taut, beautiful face. She couldn't understand anything he said, but she knew what he was doing. He was trying to regain control by thinking about false teeth and bunions.

She was looking at Dillon when the overhead light came on, nearly blinding her. Over Dillon's shoulder, she caught sight of a woman framed in the kitchen doorway. The woman rubbed a fist over first one eye, then the other, as if she couldn't believe what she was seeing. She blinked several times; then her eyes went wide.

Callie shrieked.

The woman screamed.

What the . . . ? Dillon's eyes flew open, locking on Callie's stunned face. He whipped his head around just as the light clicked back off. He'd only caught a glimpse of the woman, but it was all he needed.

"Okay," his mother said calmly. "This is slightly more embarrassing than finding a *Playboy* magazine beneath your mattress, but we got over that, and we'll get over this."

"Mom." Dillon slowly removed his hands from Callie's T-shirt, so very glad his mother had turned the light back off. "What are you doing here?"

"Sorry, kiddo. I tried to call, but I didn't get an answer. What am I doing here? I'm here checking on you, my first-born son. It isn't everyday you get attacked by killer hornets." She cleared her throat. "But, um, apparently you're okay."

133

He heard a shuffling noise before she spoke again, as if she'd turned away, then decided she wasn't finished. Flip-flops, he thought. She was wearing flip-flops. Probably those hideous blue ones with the big yellow plastic sunflowers on top. Normally his mother was a chic dresser, but she had a thing for ugly flip-flops.

"I was up all night studying, so I fell asleep on your bed waiting for you to come in. Now I'm going to go back there and lie down again. We can all forget this happened, and you can come in and find me there and act all surprised, okay?"

His mother was embarrassed, Dillon realized. Just as embarrassed as he was, but probably not as embarrassed as Callie must be. Since he couldn't think of a better plan, he said, "Okay, Mom. You do that. And Mom? Will you make the bed while you're in there, and pick up my dirty socks? I'll explain why later."

"Very funny, wise guy, and I already made your bed. As for your dirty socks . . . you can't see which finger I'm holding up, but I'm sure you can guess which one."

A short, startled laugh burst from Dillon. "Mom!"

"Sorry." She didn't sound a bit sorry. Just weary and amused. "Must be all those sassy college kids I'm hanging out with these days. You're lucky I'm not using that four-letter word they keeping throwing around.

"After I go back to your room, please tell your lady friend with the nice legs that I'm not judgmental and that I'm looking forward to meeting her. In fact, tell her that I know exactly how she feels. My dad caught me skinny-dipping in the neighbor's pool with a boy when I was fourteen. I couldn't sit down for a week. Not because he whipped me, but because I slid off the side of the concrete pool when I saw him coming and skinned my butt."

"Okay, Mom." Dillon smothered a laugh. His mother was definitely exhausted, and would undoubtably regret her confession in the morning. "I'll tell her, but since she's sitting right here, I'm sure she heard you."

"But I'm not really here. I'm lying on your *freshly* made bed, snoring my head off. I haven't seen or heard anything that I've just seen and heard."

"Sleep deprivation," Dillon whispered, nuzzling Callie's ear.

"I heard that," his mother said. "And you're probably right."

"Do you want me to fix a pot of coffee?" Dillon asked. Since his mother couldn't see him and it didn't appear she was going to leave anytime soon, he started to sneak a feel beneath Callie's T-shirt.

Callie slapped his hand away, sounding frantic as she whispered, "Are you out of your mind?"

Maybe he was, because for the first time in his life, he wasn't glad to see his mother.

"That's sounds great," his mom said. "But it's already ready to go. Just turn it on. Gonna go now. See you in a few minutes. Oh, just in case I really do fall back to sleep before you come in there and pretend to wake me, wake me for real. I really want to take a look at those bee stings . . . and meet Callie."

Dillon felt Callie stiffen in his arms. *Uh-oh.* "Sh-she probably heard about you from Wyatt. He was born with the biggest mouth in Georgia." He didn't relax until *she* relaxed, thinking that Wyatt certainly came by his big mouth honestly. But at least his mother had a good excuse: sleep deprivation.

In a pained whisper, Callie said, "She must think I'm a fool for not catching on sooner."

"As a matter of fact, she can tell you a dozen stories about getting fooled herself."

"Give me a preview."

"Well, like the time I got a D on my report card, and Mom grounded me. I gave Wyatt my allowance and agreed to take the trash out for a month if he would take my place so I could go swimming with Sheila Reynolds."

"How old were you?"

"Twelve, I think."

"And your mom never found out?"

Chuckling at the memory, Dillon said, "Oh, yeah, she knows. Last year for Mother's Day, Wyatt and I got together and confessed to all our sins on paper. We put it in her card."

"That's terrible!"

Dillon waited a beat, then added, "And we put the card inside a brand-new Nissan Ultima. Hunter green, her favorite color."

"V-6 engine?"

He nodded gravely. "Six CD player." In the dark, the most he could see was her lips curving, but he suspected her eyes were laughing, too. Something hot and wild and a little tender bloomed in his heart. He saw her cock her head, and knew that the dark curtain of her hair would be brushing her right shoulder.

"Factory tint?"

"Of course."

"Leather or cloth?"

"Leather. Tan, with power seats and windows."

"Sold!" She curled her arms around his neck, leaned in, and nibbled his earlobe. "We should find my, um, shorts, and go wake your mother. I can't wait to hear all the nitty-gritty stuff about you and Wyatt."

"Didn't you hear enough today?"

She pulled back, and he could hear the frown in her voice. "Strangely enough, not much was said about you beyond the critter rescue stories. Everyone kept changing the subject, as if they were afraid they'd blurt out the wrong thing or something." She scooted closer and tightened her legs around his waist. "Maybe she can fill in the blanks for me. Why don't you carry me to the living room? I'm not sure my legs will hold me after that scare."

Scare? Dillon almost called her on that little fib, but he was distracted by the feel of her hot core pressed against his erection. He claimed her mouth in a long, hot kiss, until she began to whimper. Then he released her. His voice was rough as he said, "You are so very bad." She did that cute head-cocking thing again.

"Am I? I don't think anyone's ever said that about me."

"You're pulling my leg."

"Which one?"

"The—" Dillon narrowed his eyes. "You're being bad again, aren't you? If my mother wasn't here . . ."

Her lips brushed his as she whispered, "Promises, promises."

"You're just being cocky because we now have some-one sensible in the next room." To retaliate, he hoisted her up and turned with her, making absolutely certain she came in contact with his erection to the fullest extent.

He was rewarded by the sharp gasping noises she made with each step he took. *Ha*, he thought as sweat broke out on his forehead and upper lip, *now who's cocky?*

Spunky.

It was the first word that came to Callie's mind after

Mary Love drank her first cup of coffee. With her short blond hair, crystal blue eyes, and petite figure, Mrs. Love hardly looked like Dillon's mother. Not that Dillon was old, just that Mary seemed so young.

"You must have been a child bride," Callie said as she sipped her coffee and ignored Dillon, who was leaning against the wall behind his mother's chair, scorching Callie with hungry, shameless looks.

Mary's eyes twinkled. "Honestly, I don't like to talk about the adoption in front of them."

Callie laughed at Dillon's startled look. When he made rabbit ears behind his mother's head, she proved that all mothers had eyes in the back of their heads.

"I had you; I can take you out. Don't forget that, Dillon Thomas Love!" She turned in her chair just in time to catch Dillon glowering at her for revealing his dreaded middle name.

Yanking him around to stand beside her, she began to inspect the hornet stings as if he were a boy of six instead of a six-foot grown man. "Do they still hurt?"

"Do bears crap in the woods?"

She boxed his ears, making him yelp and Callie double over with laughter. Dillon's mother was far funnier than any sitcom mother *she'd* ever seen! Pair her with the hilarious secretary at Mr. Complete and they could have their own show, she thought, wiping at her eyes.

"The questions aren't that difficult, son. Just answer them, please."

A more subdued Dillon answered. "Okay, okay. Yes, they still hurt, but I can handle the pain."

"Wyatt said something about nausea."

"Mom, could you honestly understand Wyatt over all that cruel laughing he was doing?"

Her lips tilted in a rueful smile. "You have a point,

138

Dillon. Your brother is certainly a character." She pushed on a bee sting, making Dillon yelp. "I thought you said they didn't hurt?"

"I didn't say they didn't hurt; I said that I could handle the pain."

Mary rolled her eyes in Callie's direction. "Just as I suspected. The worst injury was to his pride. He's never run from anything in his life, so I bet that *did* hurt." She checked out the fading bruise on his jaw, then carefully inspected the wound on his finger. She sighed and shook her head. "Good thing you're grown, son. If you were still a child with all these injuries, people would think you were being abused."

"I *am* being abused," Dillon muttered darkly. "By jealous boyfriends, psychotic turtles, and killer hornets."

Propping her hands on her hips, the little woman glared up at her son. "How do you keep getting yourself into these scrapes?"

Dillon's jaw dropped. "Me?" he squeaked. "You're blaming all of this on *me?*"

Callie held her aching side and kept a hand over her mouth as she shook with silent laughter. Through her streaming eyes, she saw Mary take her seat again. She winked at Callie and grinned.

"There, darlin'. We women have to stick together. Do you think that just about makes up for the dirty switcheroo they pulled on you?"

"Wait a minute," Dillon objected. "You don't even know Callie, and you're taking up for her over your own son?"

Mary nodded happily. "Yep."

"Unbelievable," he muttered, but Callie saw that his lips were twitching. "What about Wyatt? Did he get into trouble?"

Leisurely stirring her coffee, Mary looked up at Dillon. "Next time you see him, ask him to show you his socks, or even his boxers. I helped him with his wash, and I swear I didn't know my hot-pink bra was in there." She shrugged and shot Callie another naughty wink. "Well, I *sorta* knew, but I wasn't a hundred percent certain the color would run. Sleep deprivation and all that."

Chuckling, Callie took a sip of her coffee just as Mary did the same. They exchanged a look of mutual affection and approval.

"Wait a minute," Dillon said, his eyes narrowed on his smug-looking mother. "What are *you* doing with a hot-pink bra?"

Both women spewed coffee onto the table.

Chapter Thirteen

"Sissy glasses," Lou said with open disgust when Wyatt unpacked the first dozen from the box and lined them up on the bar. "They won't last a week around this joint."

Wyatt agreed the glasses weren't very strong, but they were definitely classier than the heavy boot-shaped mugs they'd been using. "A week's all they need to last," Wyatt said in defense of his twin. "Dillon has his shorts in a tangle about Callie seeing this place all spiffed up, so it's our job to get it done."

"I don't understand. If she's as crazy about him as you say she is, then why do we have to waste all this time and money showing her that we're something we're not?"

He had a good point, Wyatt mused. He'd have an even better point if he knew that Wyatt suspected Callie wasn't a real reviewer. But Wyatt was having too much fun watching his brother bust his balls to win Callie over to share that little secret with Dillon. Besides, he liked Callie. She'd been through a lot, and she deserved to have a man convincing her she was the only woman in the world, especially when that man really was falling in love with her. Wyatt chuckled to himself, then jumped when a hand landed on his shoulder. He looked into Dillon's suspicious eyes, thinking for one horrified moment that he'd been thinking out loud.

"I think Mom's seeing someone," Dillon said.

To Wyatt's mystification, his twin then proceeded to squat at his feet and lift up his jeans to look at his . . . legs? Socks? Check for a hidden weapon? "What the hell are you doing, bro?"

"Your socks are pink," Dillon informed him grimly, as if Wyatt couldn't see for himself.

"I know. Mom helped me catch up on my laundry, since I've been working the club, and she said she accidentally mixed it with something of hers. Obviously something pink." Self-consciously, Wyatt shoved down his jeans over the embarrassing pink sock. "Lower your voice, Dillon, and chill. I plan to replace them when I get the time." Dillon straightened and looked at him so intently, Wyatt's heart began to pound. "What is it?"

"That something pink was our mother's *hot-pink* bra."

"Now, why would Mom have a pink . . . Holy smoke!" Wyatt's face revealed his shock. "The late nights . . ."

"The frozen, store-bought casseroles," Dillon supplied grimly.

Wyatt nodded. "And the mix-up in the laundry. That's not like Mom to make that kind of mistake."

"That wasn't a mistake. That was to pay you back for

the switcheroo we pulled on Callie. That's how I found out about the pink bra."

"What? Mom's taking up for Callie, and she doesn't even know her?" Another shock. Wyatt clutched his hand to his chest. How many could a guy take in one day?

"Um, she's met her. Mom was waiting in my apartment last night when I brought Callie home with me from the barbecue. She fell asleep on my bed."

"Who, Callie?"

"No, Mom. Said she'd been up studying all night."

In fascination, Wyatt watched his twin's face slowly fill with color. Then he knew—as he sometimes did, being a twin—what had happened. He let out a low whistle. "Oh, man. You were making out with Callie and Mom caught you."

Dillon glowered at him. "You've talked to Mom this morning, haven't you?"

"Nope. The entire story was practically written all over your lusting, guilty face, and you just confirmed it. My God, she didn't actually catch you *doing* it, did she?"

"No, she did not. We—wait a minute. I didn't come here to talk about me. I came to tell you that I think Mom's seeing someone."

Wyatt bit the inside of his cheek, giving the possibility some serious thought. "I agree that Mom's owning a hot-pink bra is kind of freaky, but I don't think that necessarily means she's seeing anyone."

"We don't live with her anymore. She could have a horde of men living with her and we wouldn't know it."

"A horde of . . . men?" Wyatt's brow rose. The bee stings on Dillon's forehead were mere red bumps now, but he wondered if they might have done more damage than they had originally thought.

"It was just an expression," Dillon said through gritted teeth. "Look, I thought you'd be concerned, too."

"I am! I mean, I would be if she's really seeing someone. Not that I don't think she deserves to meet a decent guy."

"Bingo. It's *who* she might be seeing that concerns me. She's going to college, for Pete's sake. Are you following me, little brother?"

He was. Sort of. "Are you trying to imply that you think our mother might have a *boy toy?*"

"God, you're slow. You must have bumped your head one too many times on my butt inside the womb."

"Bite me."

"You probably did that, too, because I've still got teeth marks on my—Wait a minute! We're getting off the subject. I want you to follow Mom tonight. She said something about going to a friend's house to study."

"You want me to stalk our own mother?" Wyatt gave in to the urge to feel Dillon's forehead. His brother jerked out of reach and shot him a dirty look.

"It's not stalking. You're just seeing that she arrives safely wherever it is she's going. She's looked out for us all our lives. There's no harm in returning the favor."

"Somehow," Wyatt said dryly, "I don't think Mom would agree."

"If she's seeing someone, and it's not someone she should be ashamed of, why would she not tell us she was seeing someone?"

Wyatt cocked a brow. "Think back over the last ten minutes of our conversation. Do you still have to ask that question? Obviously one of her twins is a psychotic, overprotective—"

"Get a life, Wyatt," Dillon snapped.

"I can't. I'm too busy stalking our mother. Now tell me again, why me and not you?"

"I have a date with Callie."

"Oh. So she can help you distract a jealous boyfriend, and go with you to a barbecue–slash–tree house raising–slash–piss-off-the-hornets party, but she can't go Mom stalking with you?"

Something warm glowed briefly in Dillon's eyes. "You haven't seen them together, or you'd know why I can't let her in on this. It's like they were best friends in another lifetime or something."

"Well, then why don't you just ask Callie to talk to Mom, see if she can get her to spill the beans?"

"You just don't get it, do you?" Dillon blew out an exasperated sigh. "Even if Mom *did* confide in Callie, Callie wouldn't tell me. Callie's a very loyal person."

Another shock. Wyatt clamped a hand to his heart. "Is it *that* bad?"

Grim-faced, Dillon nodded.

Of course, Wyatt had meant something else entirely, but he knew Dillon was too distracted to notice. "Well, hell. I guess one of us needs to check it out, and that one of us is going to be me. You've got yourself a stalker." Dillon looked relieved. Wyatt clapped him on the back. Dillon had always taken life too seriously. He needed to loosen up.

Maybe Callie would fill that order.

"So," Wyatt asked, "where are you two going tonight?" He stifled a grin as his brother's eyes suddenly glazed over. Dillon had it bad, he thought. Really bad. And he didn't have a clue.

"Callie made reservations at a little Italian place called Marie's. I don't think I've ever been there. Have you?"

The little devil on Wyatt's shoulder seldom let Wyatt miss an opportunity to make Dillon's life more exciting . . . or more miserable. "Yeah," Wyatt lied. "In fact, I know one of the managers. I'll do the honors of alerting him, if you want."

"Great. That would be great." With that settled, Dillon picked up one of the new glasses from the bar. He frowned at it. "Sissy glasses," he muttered. "We'd better get a good review out of this."

Wyatt met Lou's gaze. They both burst out laughing.

"Great atmosphere!"

"What?" Dillon had to shout back at Callie, because he could barely hear himself or her over the loud, abusive argument going on in the kitchen of Marie's Italian restaurant.

Practically everyone in the restaurant had stopped talking to listen in on the fight. A few customers looked embarrassed. Some were obviously amused, like Callie, and about a third were craning their heads in the direction of the kitchen like seasoned eavesdroppers.

Dillon was about two seconds away from settling it himself. They had been waiting for their salad for more than half an hour, along with the bottle of white wine he'd ordered. His impatience had long since turned to frustration and dismay. How could he expect Callie to give the restaurant a good review after this fiasco?

Trying to be subtle, Dillon signaled a passing waiter.

"Hold your horses!" the waiter snarled. "I've only got two hands!"

As Callie smothered a snicker, Dillon glowered. "I hope he isn't expecting a tip."

"They must be shorthanded," Callie said. "From the sound of that argument, their chef walked out."

146

But Dillon wasn't in a forgiving mood. Callie didn't know that Wyatt had given the restaurant fair warning that she would be here tonight. How could they blow it like this?

A plump girl who couldn't have been more than sixteen paused at their table to slap down a breadbasket filled with bread sticks. Dillon grabbed her sleeve before she could move away.

"We're supposed to have salads before our meal, and white wine," he informed her with barely concealed impatience. "Would you please tell our waiter—"

The girl jerked herself free. "I don't speak English," she said in perfect English before moving on.

"I don't believe this," Dillon muttered, reaching for a bread stick.

It was cold.

Callie took one and attempted to break it in two.

They both put the bread sticks back into the basket and looked at each other. Callie's lips were twitching. Dillon scowled. What was so funny about the lousy service and terrible food? Was she happy knowing she could bomb the restaurant with a clear conscience?

Everything that he'd learned about Callie Spencer told him otherwise. The Callie Spencer he knew would not revel in someone else's misery.

But what about the Callie he didn't know? The reviewer?

When Dillon saw their waiter approaching the table, he relaxed slightly. Now maybe the service would improve, and they'd get to eat.

The waiter was frowning. "I'm sorry. You'll have to order something else. We're out of pasta."

"You're *out* of pasta?" Dillon echoed in disbelief. "But this is an Italian restaurant! You can't be *out* of pasta! That would be like KFC saying they were out of chicken."

"I'm sorry, sir, but our chef walked out, and he's the only one who knows how to make it."

Dillon almost choked. Was the waiter insane? Telling his customers that the chef had walked would be paramount to Dillon announcing to his customers that the bartender had quit. It just wasn't done. Before Dillon could give the waiter some advice he obviously needed, Callie spoke.

She sounded calm and sympathetic as she said to the waiter, "We'll have whatever is easiest to prepare." Flashing a dumbfounded Dillon a bright smile, she added, "Everyone can have a bad night, don't you agree, Dillon?" When the waiter left, she glanced around at the full house. "If the service was always this bad, the restaurant wouldn't be so crowded. Relax, will you? Try to imagine how the manager must feel right about now. I feel sorry for him or her."

With extreme effort, Dillon bit his tongue. If Callie could be sympathetic and understanding, why couldn't he? *She* was the reviewer. *She* was the one with the power to put Marie out of business, or force her to clean up her act so that the next customer would have a better experience.

Hmm. Dillon drummed his fingers on the table, not much caring for the direction of his thoughts. Was that how the last reviewer had felt about his nightclub? Had the reviewer caught him on a bad night? God knew he had his share of bad nights, and his waitresses—not to mention his cook—definitely had their share of off nights. Even Lou, who was fairly amenable most of the time, had blown his stack a time or two.

Just as Dillon had hinted to Callie in the park, one

unpleasant experience didn't necessarily constitute a bad business. Realizing what a hypocrite he was being, Dillon made an effort to adopt Callie's patience and understanding, when what he really wanted to do was grab a rock-hard bread stick, find the manager, and bonk him over the head with it.

He was with a beautiful, sexy woman whose very presence in Atlanta kept him awake at nights. Why was he sweating the small stuff? He should be concentrating on the important things in life . . . such as how he was going to resist making love to Callie. In covering the truth, he had allowed her to believe it was because he didn't want to compromise his work ethic. Not only had she seemed to approve; she also appeared to agree with him. If she knew the real reason—that he was playing her in the name of Atlanta tourism—he had a very bad feeling she wouldn't understand or approve at all.

If she knew . . . she might have a problem believing that his plan had backfired, that he'd fallen in lust with her and was enjoying the seduction far more than he had expected.

"Dillon? I was thinking we might stop in at the Love Nest and have a couple of drinks after dinner. From what I heard the short time I was there, the place had a decent band."

If Dillon had been drinking the wine that the waiter had never delivered, he would have choked on it at her suggestion. Instead he choked on the tepid water the harassed waiter had sloshed into their glasses after they were seated.

She waited until he caught his breath before she said, "Was it something I said? I thought since you and Wyatt were there and appeared to be having a good time, it must be a happening place."

Caught in the throes of panic, Dillon searched for a believable excuse. She couldn't see his nightclub yet—he wasn't ready—and when he *was* ready, he couldn't be with her. He'd be ratted out within moments of entering the door by one of his regulars. He'd planned to fake an illness and send her with another escort while *he* hid out in the kitchen and made certain everything ran smoothly.

By the time he got around to speaking, Callie was eyeing him with faint suspicion. "Oh, it's a great nightclub, all right," Dillon said quickly as he got to his feet to implement his hasty plan. "Um, will you excuse me for a moment?"

Just as he started to turn from the table, their waiter came charging at them with their salads. The man was still scowling, and Dillon quickly discovered that his attitude hadn't changed.

"The wine's coming," he snapped, practically dropping the salads onto the table. An unpeeled—and from the looks of it, unwashed—radish bounced from one of the bowls and went rolling to the floor. The waiter kicked at it viciously. "And hopefully within the next decade, you'll get the rest of your food."

Momentarily speechless, Dillon stared down at the salad. Or he *supposed* it was a salad, if one could call a few wilted leaves of lettuce and a slice of tomato a salad. No dressing, no croutons, and not a pepper mill in sight.

"Hurry back," Callie told Dillon brightly. She picked up her knife and fork and started sawing on her half-green tomato, missing the dirty, threatening look Dillon shot the waiter before the coward darted away.

The men's restroom, at least, Dillon found relatively clean and quiet. He locked himself inside a stall and pulled out his cell phone. He closed his eyes and tried to remember who was working, and who wasn't.

Tyler. He'd asked for the night off because his wife had some type of party to attend and Tyler had to babysit his four kids. Dillon let out a shaky sigh of relief. Tyler was an actor, and he had kids. If anyone could invent a convincing catastrophe that required Dillon's help, it would be Tyler.

He called him as the man in the next stall finished his business and left. Tyler answered on the fourth ring.

Before he ever said hello, Tyler could be heard yelling. "Bradley Tyler! If you hit your sister again, you will go to bed *before* pizza, and I am *not* kidding!"

Belatedly, Dillon jerked the phone from his ear to save his eardrum. He cautiously brought it back. "Excuse me?"

"Hello?" Tyler dropped his voice to a tolerable level and sounded astonishingly cheerful. "Dillon? Sorry about that. Bradley threw an empty plastic milk jug at his sister because she drank the last of the milk—after he'd called it. I don't think he hurt her, but she screamed bloody murder anyway. What's up?"

It was a moment before Dillon answered, because he was thinking about what his mother had undoubtedly gone through raising three rowdy kids without much help from his dad. Maybe he'd buy her a new patio set.

"Dillon? You there?"

"Yes. I'm here. At the restaurant, with Callie. She wants to go to the Love Nest when we leave this godforsaken place."

"So . . . what's the problem?"

Had Tyler heard anything Dillon had told him that night he'd called the guys together? Dillon wondered, swallowing his exasperation. "She can't go to the Love Nest because it's not ready, and she can't go with me because I own the place and she doesn't know it . . . remember?"

"Oh, yeah. I gotcha." Tyler sounded pleased that he'd remembered. "How can I help?"

"I need you to call me back in twenty minutes with a code red."

"But I don't have a code red."

Dillon slowly beat his forehead against the stall door. He suspected Tyler was being deliberately obtuse. "I know you don't, Tyler. I need you to *invent* one so that I'll have an excuse not to take Callie to the Love Nest."

"Oh." Then, as realization dawned, he said again, "Ohhhh. I get it. Twenty minutes?"

"Twenty minutes."

"I should be able to think of something by then. You can count on me, boss."

"Good." *Thank God.* Dillon hung up and left the restroom, plowing into a woman heading in the direction of the women's restroom across the hall. Instinctively, he caught her shoulders before she could bounce back and possibly fall from the impact.

"I'm so sorry!" she wailed, her red-rimmed eyes filling with tears. She thrust a crumpled handkerchief to her nose and blew loudly.

"No harm done," Dillon said, and started to step around her.

Then he caught the name tag pinned to her navy blue suit. She was the manager, he realized, not surprised that she was crying. She probably suspected she wouldn't have a job when the news of this night's fiasco got back to the owner.

"Is there something I can do to help?" he asked, without much hope there *was* something he could do. The night was pretty much a bust for her, he figured.

She wiped her nose again and looked at him, her expression miserable. She shook her head. "Unless you know how to make pasta, or meatballs, or a dozen of the other dishes only Franco knew how to make, then no, you can't help me."

"Franco was your chef?" Dillon guessed without much effort. It wasn't as if the entire restaurant hadn't heard the argument.

She sniffed, and her watery eyes took on a sudden fierceness that impressed Dillon. If anyone could save the day, he thought, it would be this woman.

Unfortunately, he didn't see how she *could*, with her chef gone and most of her customers running out of patience. . . .

"*Was* our chef," she said with loathing. "When Marie found out that our restaurant was going to be reviewed by *Next Stop*, she fired our regular chef, Marco, and hired Franco, which turned out to be a big mistake. He was nothing but a conceited, hot-tempered, egotistical, controlling, narrow-minded"— she paused to suck in a quick breath—"jackass who was supposed to be the best Italian cook in Georgia."

Her passionate description made Dillon's lips twitch. Prudence held back his smile as he said, "Why did he quit?"

"Why did he quit? He quit because one of our customers—a regular—suggested he'd put too much sugar in his sauce." She swiped at her eyes and straightened her spine. "It was true, too. I tasted it, and it was too sweet."

"So you told him," Dillon guessed.

"Yes, I told him. I told him very nicely, and do you know what he did? He took the entire pan of lasagne and dumped it in the garbage!"

Dillon winced. He could definitely relate. "What about the kitchen help?"

She shook her head, her eyes clouding again. "All new. Marie went into a frenzy of hiring and firing last week when she found out the *Next Stop* reviewer was in town. The new employees are good workers, but Franco guarded his recipes like a miser guards his gold." With a snort, she added, "As if any of them were *worth* guarding."

Thinking quickly, Dillon asked, "Do you sell gift certificates?"

"Yes, yes, we do."

"Are you open to suggestions?"

"Are you kidding?" Her eyes lit with hope. "I'd kiss your feet if I weren't happily married."

"It's the thought that counts," Dillon said with a grin. "Here's my suggestion. Go around—you personally—to all of your customers and pass out gift certificates good for a free dinner on a return visit, and explain to them what happened. Well, the bare facts, anyway. They'll appreciate your honesty."

The woman nearly danced in place. "That's a great idea. I'll have to check with Marie first, but I think she'll go for it, especially after I tell her what happened."

"If she's a wise woman, she will."

Beaming, the manager took his hand and pumped it. "I'm so glad I ran into you in the hall. You saved my life. With any luck, we'll get Marco back before the reviewer blows through, if he hasn't already."

Dillon kept his face impassive. The poor manager had been through enough without finding out that the reviewer she feared wasn't a he, but a she, and she was sitting in the dining room eating wilted lettuce and green tomatoes.

It wasn't until he headed back to join Callie that Dillon realized the manager had said Marie had known about the intended review *last week*.

It not only meant that someone else had known Callie was coming to Atlanta; it also meant that Wyatt had failed to call as he'd promised. He really needed to talk to his mother about taking out life insurance on his brother, Dillon mused darkly.

Because he was really going to kill him someday.

Chapter Fourteen

"What's he doing now?"

Callie smiled at the faint terror in Dillon's voice. "He's chewing on his fingers."

"How long have we been driving?"

She consulted her watch. "Thirty-two minutes."

"Are you absolutely certain he's buckled into that contraption?"

"Yes. I checked it three times." A little dryness tinged her voice as she added, "He's only six months old, Dillon. He can't unfasten a car seat restrainer belt."

"Does he look sleepy?"

She studied the baby's big blue eyes, wishing—for Dillon's sake—that she had better news. "Not a bit. His eyes are big round saucers."

"Why?" Dillon asked quickly, sounding panicked. "Is my driving scaring him?"

This time Callie couldn't resist laughing outright. "No, Dillon, your driving is not scaring little Ben. Just like Tyler said, as long as the vehicle is moving, he's happy."

"I still don't get it," Dillon muttered, easing to a stop at a red light as if he were transporting nitroglycerin. "What's riding in a car got to do with teething?"

"When babies are in pain, motion soothes them." Callie glanced at the hard set of Dillon's jaw and sighed, wishing he'd relax. She reached out to touch his shoulder. He jumped and swerved the wheel. Prudently, Callie pretended not to notice. "It's really wonderful of you to help Tyler and Amanda out this way." She meant it. When Tyler had called him at the restaurant, Dillon hadn't hesitated to help. What she'd felt for him at that moment had nothing to do with lust, but she had quickly pushed her warm fuzzies to the back of her mind. That was dangerous thinking.

Dillon shot her a grim look. "Yeah, well. I didn't know this was what he had in mind, or I would have told him no. I'm sorry you keep getting dragged into these bizarre situations."

"I'm not. I love babies." *And I love being with you*, she thought but wisely didn't say. "We can go to the Love Nest another night."

"I guess you're right." He darted her a quick, grateful glance. "What's he doing now?"

"I think he's wondering why the Jeep has stopped." She realized her mistake when the light turned green and Dillon squealed his tires taking off, pinning her to the seat.

"What's he doing *now?*"

Definitely panicked, Callie thought, smiling inwardly. "He's chewing on his fingers again."

"Maybe we should take him home," Dillon suggested hopefully. "Maybe he's missing his daddy."

Callie felt sorry for him, but a promise was a promise, and she knew he'd regret it if he broke it. "We told Tyler we'd drive around until Ben was sound asleep."

"What if he *doesn't* go to sleep?" He asked the question as if it were the most terrifying thing he could imagine.

"Tyler assures us that he will." Because she couldn't resist, Callie asked, "Have you always been this terrified of kids?"

"He's not a kid; he's a baby."

Evasive tactics. *Transparent* evasive tactics, she corrected. "Joey's not a baby, and you were terrified of him."

He must have realized he was caught, for he said reluctantly, "I haven't been around kids *or* babies much."

"What about your baby sister?"

"She was for torturing, not tending."

"So you haven't worked for Mr. Complete long?" It would stand to reason, she thought, that he would have been accustomed to Tyler's and Ivan's children if he'd known them long. They were a close-knit group, almost like family.

"Um, no, not long." Quickly, as if he were hoping she'd drop her line of questioning, he asked, "What's he doing now?"

Callie frowned, wondering why Dillon didn't want to talk about his past. She knew the present Dillon, and she had gotten a sketchy outline about his childhood thanks to his mother, but almost nothing about the years after his graduation and before Mr. Complete. If they were eventually going to sleep together, then she felt they should get to know each other better.

Sleep together. A thrill shot through her. Remembering the baby, Callie hastily said, "His face is turning red, and he's grunting. I think maybe he's filling up his diaper."

The Jeep swerved again. Dillon shot her an incredulous look. "Filling up his diaper? With *what?*"

She blinked innocently at him. "Baby poop, Dillon. Just a little baby poop." Pointing through the windshield at a well-lit area ahead, she said, "If you'll pull into that convenience store parking lot, I'll change him."

"In my Jeep?"

Dillon pulled into the parking lot a bit too fast for comfort, and Callie wondered if she should offer to drive. She unclipped her seat belt and shot him an amused, dry look. "Well, I guess I could put him on the concrete to change him, but it might be a little uncomfortable."

Instead of answering, Dillon unclipped his own seat belt and shot out of the Jeep as if he'd been propelled by a giant spring. "I need coffee. Do you want anything?"

Callie smothered her laughter. "I wouldn't mind a bottle of springwater, if they have it."

"I'll get it." He started inside, but stopped after a few feet and turned back to her. His expression was a mixture of chagrin and bemusement. "Um, about how long will it take?"

"How long will what take?" Callie asked innocently as she pulled out a disposable diaper and a box of baby wipes from the diaper bag Tyler had given them. When Dillon glowered at her, she laughed and gave in. "About five minutes, unless it's really messy. I think Amanda's breast-feeding, so it could be . . ."

She was talking to thin air; Dillon had disappeared at the speed of light.

* * *

"You've got to call me and tell us to bring the baby home," Dillon demanded the moment Tyler answered the phone. He was standing behind the snack rack, peering over the top through the storefront window at his Jeep. He caught flashes of Callie's perky bottom as she bent to her task through the open back door.

"No can do, boss. Once you start driving, you can't stop until Ben falls asleep."

Tyler still sounded absurdly cheerful—and why wouldn't he? Dillon thought murderously. The rat was watching a movie with his three older children, while *he* drove endlessly around town wondering how he would be able to live with himself if he wrecked the car with Ben inside.

He ducked down as Callie turned from the Jeep to walk the short distance to the trash can with the dirty diaper. When he found himself whispering, he thought about murder again. "Why can't we stop?"

"Because Ben will raise hell, that's why. Trust me; I know from experience. Now that you've started driving him around, you have to wait until he falls asleep."

Dillon forced a smile as the store clerk walked by, eyeing him with a great deal of suspicion. Apparently he wasn't accustomed to customers hiding out behind snack racks and whispering into cell phones. "You're an actor. I thought you'd be more creative," he told Tyler, hating the whiny note in his voice.

"I wasn't aware you didn't like kids," Tyler said, sounding hurt.

Grinding his teeth, Dillon said, "I *do* like kids. I just . . . just . . ."

"Don't like babies?"

"No! That's not it." Dillon muttered a curse and got

a dirty look from the store clerk, who was hovering nearby under the pretense of stocking sodas in a cooler. Because he didn't want to admit his fear to Tyler, he lied, "I don't want Callie getting any ideas."

"From the sound of it, she won't have any illusions by the time you bring Ben home."

"You are not funny."

"I wasn't trying to be."

Realizing the conversation was getting him nowhere, Dillon changed the subject. "Is Amanda home?"

"Yes, she is, and she agrees that you can't bring Ben home until he goes to sleep. He would keep us up all night screaming, poor guy."

Desperately, Dillon said, "You don't even know me that well. Do you always trust strangers with your children?"

"Insulting me won't work, Dillon. You're Wyatt's brother, and I trust Wyatt. You called me for help. I helped you. Good luck. Oh, if Ben starts screaming and loses his breath, blow in his face, especially if his lips start turning blue."

The line went dead.

As Dillon added Luke to his hit list for getting him into this mess, he caught a motion from the corner of his eye. He looked through the storefront window to see Callie waving at him frantically from the Jeep.

His heart made a giant leap into his throat. He dropped his cell phone, accidentally kicked it as he made a grab for it, and sent it sliding across the slick floor. It bumped against the clerk's foot and came to rest.

Mumbling an apology, Dillon snatched it up and ran from the store, imagining all sorts of horrors.

"Hey!" the clerk shouted after him. "Wait!"

But Dillon ignored him. He didn't have time for

chitchat. The moment he cleared the door, he heard the baby screaming. His heart thundered. What if Ben's lips turned blue? What if he stopped breathing, and blowing in his face didn't work?

"Get in!" Callie shouted when he reached her. "Hurry and drive."

He bounded around to the driver's side and threw himself inside, tossing Callie's bottled water into her lap. His hands were shaking as he jabbed the keys into the ignition and started the engine.

The moment he put the Jeep in motion, Ben stopped screaming.

Dillon was terrified to look back. In a croak, he asked Callie, "What's he doing? Is he breathing?"

"Of course he's breathing," she said, looking at him strangely. "We're moving again, so he stopped crying."

He blew out a sigh of relief, adjusting the rearview mirror to see for himself that Ben was indeed still conscious.

What he saw made him curse a blue streak: flashing lights, and now that he was paying attention, he could hear sirens, too.

As he pulled over, he made several dismaying realizations in quick succession; he wasn't in his seat belt, and Callie wasn't in hers; he was doing a fast fifty in a thirty-five zone, and because of the bright streetlights, he'd forgotten to turn on his headlights.

Could the night get any worse?

Dillon was reaching into his back pocket for his wallet when a sharp rapping sound on the window made him freeze.

"Keep your hands on the wheel, sir," a stern voice ordered. "Open the door and get out nice and slow."

"You've got to be kidding me," Dillon muttered,

casting an equally bewildered Callie a can-you-believe-this look.

In the backseat, Ben began to whimper.

It was enough to throw Dillon into action. He opened the door and stepped out. The cop was young, possibly early twenties, and he looked deadly serious. After muttering a fervent prayer that—Dillon peered at his name tag—Officer Gorden had kids, he rushed into an explanation. "Look, Officer, I'm sorry that I was speeding. Ben's teething, and when I stopped to let Callie change him, he started screaming. I was so intent on getting the Jeep into motion that I didn't notice I hadn't turned on my headlights, or even how fast I was going." Dillon tried a you-know-how-it-is smile, but Officer Gorden remained grim faced. "You know how kids are, right?"

"As a matter of fact, I do," Gorden said, but his eyes narrowed ominously.

Dillon felt a chill travel down his spine. It was becoming obvious that the cop's *knowing* wasn't necessarily a good thing. "Then you understand how I could have been distracted—"

"What I understand, sir," Gorden clipped out in a stern voice that would have been almost comical in one so young if not for the uniform, "is that you were speeding with an infant in the car, which means you were endangering your child. Driving without your lights on could also be construed as endangerment."

When Dillon started to sputter, Gorden held up his hand, warning him to keep quiet.

"But what really gripes me is the fact that you seem to think you can just take what you want without paying for it." The cop's face had slowly turned an ugly shade of red. He stepped closer to Dillon, which put him almost nose-to-nose—if Gorden hadn't been roughly four inches shorter. "Is this *vehicle* yours, sir? Or did you just take it, too?"

Gaping at him, Dillon finally found his tongue. "Of course it's my Jeep. I've got my registration forms in the glove compartment." He frowned. "I think there's been some mistake. I didn't get gas at the station, if that's what you're implying I took."

Officer Gorden used his nightstick to shoulder Dillon aside. He also used it to point at Callie. "Do you have a receipt for that bottle of water?" he asked with a smugness that told Dillon he already knew the answer.

With a groan, Dillon slapped his forehead. He'd been holding the bottled water when Callie had gestured from the Jeep, sending him into a panic. The clerk had followed him from the store, shouting something at him, but he had ignored him.

Now Dillon realized why the clerk had been shouting.

He hadn't paid for the water.

But he hadn't *stolen* it—he'd just forgotten to pay for it!

From the backseat, Ben let out a warning cry. Dillon knew it was just a matter of moments before Ben let loose with ear-splitting screams. It would serve the cocky cop right, Dillon was thinking righteously when Callie spoke up for the first time.

"Let me try to explain," she told Dillon. She flashed the officer a sweet, embarrassed smile, and Dillon felt a surge of hope. If anyone could soften this overly zealous policeman, it would be Callie.

"I'm Callie Spencer, and this is Dillon Love. We're riding Ben around for a good friend of ours, until he goes to sleep."

Gorden pointed his nightstick at Dillon. "This isn't your husband?"

"No," Callie said, "But—"

He leveled the nightstick at the backseat, where Ben was working up an impressive head of steam. The baby's face had turned beet red, and his arms were swinging as if he were boxing. "And that isn't your baby?"

"No, but—"

"Can I get you to step out of the vehicle, ma'am, and join Mr. *Love* here? And bring the stolen merchandise with you."

Callie blinked at the bottled water in her lap, then looked at the officer as if he'd lost his ever-loving mind. Dillon wholeheartedly agreed with her. He felt as if they had been thrust into a sequel to the zany comedy *Super Troopers*.

"Ma'am?" Gorden prompted in a tough voice that would have done the producer of *Walking Tall* proud.

When she'd gotten out and joined Dillon, he removed his handcuffs and cuffed Dillon and Callie together. Then he reached inside the Jeep and snatched the keys from the ignition.

"Don't even think about running," he warned.

With a disbelieving laugh, Callie said, "If this is a joke, it's a good one, but if it isn't, you're going to feel really stupid. Dillon is my escort—"

Dillon groaned.

Officer Gorden froze, his eyes narrowing on Dillon's face. "Escort? He's an *escort?*" Shaking his head, he walked back to his patrol car, leaned in, and grabbed the mike, pulling it through the open window. His voice was laced with importance and thick with disgust as he spoke into the mike. "I have a possible robbery—"

Robbery? Dillon closed his eyes and sighed. Could a person go to jail for accidentally stealing water?

"—a possible kidnapping—"

Now wait a damned minute—

"—and a probable prostitution charge on one Dillon Love, male, Caucasian, about six-feet, with blond hair and blue eyes. Can you run a check for me?"

He was dreaming, Dillon thought. Because this couldn't be happening. Out loud he said, "You should get my wallet out of my back pocket. If they have my Social Security number, we could get this over with quicker."

Inside the Jeep, the volume of Ben's cries began to rise.

"What's your hurry?" Gorden demanded, striding back to them.

Dillon's temper sparked. "We have someone waiting across the state line to buy this baby—Oof!" He lost his breath as Callie elbowed him in the ribs.

"What he really meant to say," she said hastily, "is that Ben is getting hungry. There's a bottle in the diaper bag in the back."

Gorden studied them for a suspicious moment before taking out his keys and unlocking the cuffs. "Get the baby and his things," he ordered Callie. "We're all going to take a ride down to the station." He turned Dillon around and cuffed his hands behind him.

Completely out of patience now, Dillon glared at him over his shoulder. "I hope you're prepared to get the hell sued out of you for false arrest," he growled as the cop took his elbow and led him to the waiting patrol car.

Holding up the bottled water, Gorden asked, "Did you pay for this?"

"No," Dillon snapped, "but I didn't steal it, either. I just forgot to pay for the damned thing!"

"Tell it to the judge," Gorden said. "I'm sure he's never heard *that* one before."

Chapter Fifteen

Wedged between Wyatt and Tyler on a hard bench in the police station, Callie waited for Mary Love and Casey's lawyer husband, Brett, to arrive and spring Dillon out of jail.

The accessory-to-kidnapping charges against her had been dropped after Tyler and Amanda arrived to claim Ben and confirm their story. Dillon was still being held with pending charges of stealing a bottle of water from the convenience store, endangering a minor, and soliciting sex.

Amanda had left with a very unhappy Ben and her three other sleepy children to continue driving around in the hope the poor teething baby would exhaust himself and go to sleep. Occasionally Callie would catch Wyatt's twinkling eye and have to look away before her own lips started twitching.

It wasn't really funny, she told herself sternly. Dillon would be emotionally scarred for life after this fiasco, as if he weren't already frightened to death of children. She could only imagine how guilty he must be feeling, having to call Tyler and inform him that he was in jail and Ben was two steps away from becoming a ward of the state.

Although . . . Tyler hadn't looked all that alarmed when she met with him in the waiting room after they released her. In fact, more than once Callie thought she'd caught *his* lips twitching as if he were holding back a smile.

She was having a difficult time understanding. His friend and coworker had been arrested and charged with kidnapping, robbery, prostitution, and reckless endangerment of a minor. None of the charges were true. How could he find it funny, especially in light of the fact that Dillon had been doing Tyler a favor?

Spotting Mary and Brett coming through the glass security doors, Callie jumped to her feet. She let out a sigh of relief and went to meet them halfway. Thank God *Mary* didn't seem to find the situation amusing! In fact, she looked alarmed enough to concern Callie.

Mary grabbed Callie's hands and began asking questions, ignoring Wyatt and Tyler for the time being. "Kidnapping?"

"We were driving Tyler's baby around trying to get him to sleep," Callie explained.

"Robbery?"

"We stopped at a convenience store so I could change Ben. Dillon went inside to get coffee and bottled water, and Ben started crying. I signaled him through the window and he panicked. He forgot he was holding the bottle of water." Mary nodded as if that made perfect sense to her, much to Callie's relief. She made a mental note to pump Mary when they were alone for more information about Dillon's apparent fear of kids.

Mary squeezed her hands. "Child endangerment?"

Callie grimaced. This one would be tough. "Dillon *was* speeding, and he *had* forgotten to turn on his lights, but Ben was never in danger." Mary would have only Callie's word, but Callie put sincere conviction behind her explanation.

"I think I get the prostitution charge," Mary said dryly. "Either you or Dillon must have mentioned that he was an escort."

Wincing, Callie said, "That would be me."

"Narrow-minded bigots," Mary muttered. She turned abruptly to Brett, who had been listening intently. "Can you handle this?"

Without hesitation, he nodded, looking very much the lawyer in a suit and tie. He edged closer to Callie, keeping his voice low. "In regards to the prostitution charge . . . I'll have to get a signed statement from you stating you and Dillon haven't had sex."

Aware of Mary's unabashed interest, Callie flushed to the roots of her hair. "That won't be a problem," she whispered.

A commotion at the door caught Callie's attention. She gaped as their arresting officer appeared with Mrs. Scuttle, who was attempting to kick him with her sensible shoes. He was literally dancing to protect his shins while holding on to her elbow.

"Stop it!" Officer Gorden yelled.

Before Callie could blink, Wyatt, Tyler, and Brett were surrounding the cop, bristling openly.

"What the hell do you think you're doing?" Wyatt demanded.

Tyler glared at Gorden and took Mrs. Scuttle by her other arm as if he were prepared to play tug-of-war with her. "Get your hands off her."

Brett, more sensible, but no less fierce, towered over Gorden. "Why are you manhandling this woman?"

Officer Gorden kept dancing as he explained, "I caught her spitting on my patrol car! *Spitting* on it! That's destruction of property—"

"Bullshit," Brett said softly. "I'm a lawyer. You can't arrest someone for spitting, you fool. Let go of her immediately before *we* charge *you* with police brutality." To emphasize his threat, he pointed to the security cameras documenting the scene.

Callie held her breath as Gorden lost his bluster and began to look uncertain.

"She can't go around spitting on cars," he stated with less heat. But he released her arm and stepped nimbly out of reach of her flying shoes. "Must be a full moon," he muttered as he stomped away. "Bunch of crazies—"

"I'll full moon *you*!" Mrs. Scuttle bawled, and launched her sizable purse at the officer's unsuspecting head.

Wyatt leaped into the air like an all-star and caught the purse before it could reach its target. Callie couldn't deny that she was disappointed. It would have been worth a night in jail to see the cop decked by Mrs. Scuttle's purse after what he'd put them through.

"How did she know?" Tyler asked as Mary attempted to calm Mrs. Scuttle.

Brett answered. "Mary had to call her to get my number. She's very protective of her 'boys.'"

"Yes, she is." Callie felt all warm inside watching Mary calm the secretary, who had been getting a little harmless revenge by spitting on a police car.

Tyler chuckled. "Luke was in jail once. The cop at the desk made the mistake of taunting him about his occupation. Mrs. Scuttle had the cop hunkering in fear behind the desk for twenty minutes. He was half her age and had a gun. *She* had a paperweight."

"That was before I joined the agency," Wyatt said wistfully. He handed a slightly mollified Mrs. Scuttle her purse.

Callie looked from one to the other, frowning. "Luke's the boss, right? And Dillon's filling that position while he's gone. Is it a curse or something to be in that position?"

Wyatt looked at Tyler. They both burst out laughing.

But they didn't laugh long. Mary glared Wyatt into abrupt silence. When Tyler kept on laughing, Mrs. Scuttle calmly opened her purse, withdrew what appeared to be a heavy tube of ointment, and chucked it at his head.

The laughter stopped.

Three long hours later, Callie sat with Dillon in a back booth at Joker's Bar and Grill, drinking a huge frozen banana daiquiri and sharing a platter of beer-battered popcorn shrimp with her jailbird escort. His blond hair was a little ruffled, and he looked tired, his eyes drooping in a sexy way.

Callie had never seen him look more appealing.

She tried to keep a straight face as she dipped a shrimp in cocktail sauce and popped it into his mouth. The tip of his tongue flicked over her finger, and she swallowed a gasp. "So, now that you've got a record, what do you intend to do with your life?"

He bared his teeth. "Very funny, Ms. Accessory to Kidnapping." He fed her a shrimp, and she tried to bite his finger. "Never bite the hand that feeds you," he chided.

"Dillon . . . what did you do before you went to work for Mr. Complete?"

He paused with his hand on the bottle of beer, then brought the bottle to his mouth and drank.

Callie had to stifle a shamelessly contented sigh as she watched the strong column of his throat move. She could stare at him for hours, she thought suddenly. But in the end, staring wouldn't be enough. It astonished her to realize that if Dillon were a prostitute, she would seriously consider paying him for sex. She'd bet her untouched divorce settlement he'd be worth every penny.

"I was a gigolo," Dillon said, startling her.

When she looked into his laughing eyes, she grinned and relaxed. He hadn't read her mind, of course. It was just an amazing coincidence.

Dipping a shrimp in sauce, she slipped it between her lips, then proceeded to slowly lick her fingers, hoping she looked naughty. When she glanced at him, she found his gaze riveted on her mouth. "In that case, I've got a divorce settlement I'm dying to waste."

He caught her hand, brought her fingers to his mouth, and sucked each one until she was breathless and aching. "I would love to be your gigolo . . . but the truth is, I went into business for myself after college. I bought a small pizza parlor."

"Really?"

"Really."

"What happened?" He kept her hand, and Callie let him.

He shrugged. "It paid the bills, but it wasn't enough. I eventually sold it."

"Then you went to work for Mr. Complete?"

"No. After I sold the pizza parlor, Wyatt and I formed a rock band."

Callie's mouth dropped. "No kidding? I'll bet Mary loved that."

Dillon lifted a smug brow. "She did. She was our manager. It was her way of making sure we didn't turn to drugs and drink." His smile was tinged with nostalgia. "We were pretty good. We played in local clubs and occasionally for school dances."

"What instrument did you play?"

"Guess."

"Drums." When his brow shot up again, this time in surprise, Callie grinned. "Just a lucky guess. You've got good rhythm." Their gazes locked. Heat flared between them. When her nipples began to pucker, she folded her arms on the table in front of her breasts, hoping to hide her telltale reaction. He reached out and curled his hands over her arms, the tips of his fingers brushing the thrust of her breasts.

His knowing look made her blush. "You're driving me crazy," he said in a low, sex-roughened voice. With a groan he pushed back against the booth and ran a hand through his hair. "Let's talk about you. What did *you* do before you went to work for the magazine?"

Callie had to take a deep, steadying breath before she spoke. "I was married, as you already know. Before that I was a photographer for a small modeling agency. That's how I met Lanny."

"Wyatt got the impression you were hurt."

She couldn't look at Dillon as she attempted to be flippant. "Doesn't everyone when they get divorced?"

"He was an idiot," Dillon said harshly.

She looked at him in surprise. "Thanks. In fact, thanks for . . . waking me up, so to speak. I was impossibly bitter and ugly, and you helped me realize that my life wasn't over, that I still had life left in me."

173

"You could never be ugly. You couldn't convince me of that in a million years."

"I don't mean physically." Although she felt as if she had been physically unattractive. "I mean ugly on the inside." Her voice dropped to a whisper. "I think I made everyone else suffer because I was so miserable." She looked up to find him frowning at her. She laughed to lighten the moment. "I sound like a drama queen. Let's talk about something that doesn't weigh a ton. How's your headache?"

Dillon rubbed his jaw. "Better, thanks. Sorry to cheat you out of going to the Love Nest *again*."

"I'm glad," she said, and meant it. "I think we needed to talk, don't you?"

"Yeah." His gaze heated as it slid slowly over her. "We seem to get distracted easily."

She shivered, wondering how she was going to survive the next two weeks without making a complete fool of herself. "So what's on the agenda for tomorrow? We should probably target public places where we . . . where we—"

"Can't make out?" Dillon teased. He pressed his knee against hers beneath the table. "As disappointed as I am to hear you say that, I suspect you're right."

"Meanwhile . . . wanna go back to my hotel and fool around?" Callie batted her eyelashes at him, and laughed when he growled. "My new hotel has a Jacuzzi in the room. We could wear our bathing suits, but it's *your* turn to be the sensible one."

"Rats."

"Moldy Cool Whip."

"No," Dillon said, laughing. "I mean, rats that I have to be sensible. Moldy Cool Whip?"

"Yeah. I hate opening something from the fridge

that I've forgotten about and find that green stuff all over it. It grosses me out."

"More than dirty socks?"

"Yes, more."

He slapped a relieved hand to his chest. "Thank God. I've been seriously stressing over the dirty-sock thing. I went on a sock hunt, and now my hamper is full of dirty socks, so don't look in there."

Callie's heart began to beat faster. "Are we going to your apartment?"

He held out his hand, his grin wicked and full of promise. "Yes. To get my swimming trunks."

She swallowed hard and took his hand.

Dillon did not have the look of a sensible man.

Chapter Sixteen

The Jacuzzi was huge.

Callie's bathing suit was not.

With his chest feeling very tight, Dillon watched Callie as she eased shyly out of the hotel bathroom and raced toward the Jacuzzi.

He moved at the speed of light, tackling her before she reached it, taking her giggling, squirming, panting form down to the plush carpet until he got her beneath him.

They were both breathing heavily. Callie was still giggling, as if she couldn't stop, a happy, abandoned sound that filled him with joy. He stared down into her flushed, laughing face and felt something stab at his heart.

It wasn't lust, although lust was certainly present.

"You call that a bathing suit?" he asked her gruffly.

Huffing, she tried to look down between them, but they were sealed tight from the waist down.

And Dillon liked it that way.

"You call *those* swimming trunks?" she countered breathlessly. "Because I call that thing a Band-Aid."

Dillon lifted a warning brow. "Are you insulting my manhood?" Her spontaneous laughter poured over him like warm honey. He felt his Band-Aid slipping. If she didn't stop squirming . . .

She stopped, her eyes suddenly wide and not so innocent. "A supersize Band-Aid," she whispered with an erotic quaver in her voice. "Okay, they're swimming trunks . . . very large swimming trunks, to cover a very large—"

He had to kiss her to shut her up before she said something he couldn't ignore. With earth-shattering heat, she kissed him back, open-mouthed with a lot of tongue, the way Dillon liked it. It was as if she could read his mind, anticipate his every fantasy.

Beneath him, he felt her legs begin to spread. He held his breath and closed his eyes, waiting and wanting to feel his erection cradled in the sizzling heat of her.

Apparently coming to her senses, she hastily clamped her legs together and pushed at his chest. There was a flicker of panic in her eyes, but Dillon instinctively knew it wasn't because she feared him.

She feared losing control, doing what they weren't supposed to do, because it was against his work ethic.

"To hell with ethics," he murmured, and leaned to capture her moist, hungry mouth again.

But she kept her arm locked between them. "We . . . we should get in the Jacuzzi," she panted. "Before we scorch the carpet."

At least she was honest and aware of impending danger, Dillon mused ruefully. He gave her one last chance before he relented and let her up. "Do you really believe you'll be safe in the Jacuzzi?" he asked, his voice a rough whisper. He was fully aroused now, stretching the bikini trunks to their limit, throbbing against her like a drumbeat. Was that the rhythm she spoke of?

The thought made him suck in a sharp breath and mutter, "Cold spinach."

She blinked. "You hate spinach?"

"No." He chuckled, reluctantly easing away from her delicious, delectable body. "I just couldn't think of anything else. My mind is a blank. No, that's not true. My mind is on one track tonight."

"Mine, too," she confessed, rolling away from him and standing.

His hot gaze traveled up her long, slim legs, paused on her gently rounded hips, then skipped up to the thrusting breasts her bikini top hardly covered.

Her nipples were erect, and she was still breathing hard.

Good. At least he wasn't alone in this torture. He watched her step up to the Jacuzzi, loving her heart-shaped bottom and firm thighs.

Which led him to the erotic image of her clutching him with those firm thighs, thrashing beneath him—

"Buttermilk," he said.

She turned to smile over her shoulder at him, and looked incredibly sexy doing it. "Now there's one we agree on." She swung a leg over the side of the tub and tested the water.

Dillon swallowed hard and focused on her face.

"When I was little," she said, sinking down into the water until the only thing he could see was her head and shoulders, "my uncle Tim thought it would be funny to put buttermilk in my sippy cup."

"That's not funny," Dillon said, and meant it.

She laughed. "No, it wasn't, but Uncle Tim thought it was, and so did everyone else in the room. When I wouldn't drink milk after that, my mother didn't think it was so funny."

Dillon rose and slowly approached the Jacuzzi, wondering how in hell he was going to get in that thing and not make love to her. "Did you ever drink milk again?"

"No." She stared at his bulging erection, and Dillon saw her swallow. Her voice got hoarse. "I mean, I know it's not going to taste like buttermilk, but I guess I can't get it out of my head."

"I know exactly what you mean." Dillon wasn't talking about buttermilk, and they both knew it. He got into the Jacuzzi and sank into the warm water, keeping his distance . . . for the moment. The thrusting jet streams came at him from all directions, doing little to take his mind off of sex with Callie. "Come over here and kiss me," he ordered.

She shook her head. Her eyes were a dark, smoky blue. "I can't."

"Why?" The question hung in the air. Dillon found that he couldn't wait to hear her answer.

"Because . . . you said I was driving you crazy. Well, you drive me crazy, too." She pulled her knees up and wrapped her arms around her legs, looking suddenly pensive. "After Lanny, I totally swore off gorgeous men."

Dillon would have been lying if he told her he wasn't flattered. He'd also be lying to himself if he denied that hearing her ex's name made him jealous. He wanted—badly—to wipe that scum from her memory, and he knew just how to do it.

Only he couldn't do it . . . yet.

Life *sucked*.

His eyes narrowed speculatively on her flushed, pensive face. There were ways, he mused, to make her forget about Lanny and her self-imposed vow to stay away from gorgeous men without breaking the rules completely. Not that he gave a shit about the rules anyway, since he wasn't getting paid and she wasn't paying. But she *believed* he was getting paid by the agency.

"If I promise to be the sensible one, will you come to me?" Holding his breath, he watched the struggle on her face, saw the yearning mixed with caution as the two impulses battled it out. His heart kicked into overdrive as she unfolded her legs and floated across the water.

Trusting him.

He let out a sigh, his arms catching her around the waist and turning her around so that she lay with her back against his chest, her butt snuggled firmly against his groin.

Their position was part of his rapidly forming plan.

Her blissful sigh echoed his as she laid her head against his shoulder. "I can't think of a single place I'd rather be right now," she murmured, then stiffened, as if she feared she'd said something wrong.

Dillon chuckled. "Relax. It wasn't a marriage proposal, and I agree with you. There isn't anywhere else I'd rather be, either."

"I really want to feel you inside me, Dillon," she whispered with an ache in her voice. "So much, sometimes I think I'm gonna die."

Feeling alarmingly humbled and incredibly turned on, Dillon breathed, "Wow," and tightened his arms around her waist. Then he slid his hands up, cupping her breasts. She moaned and arched against him, pushing her rear further into his groin and making *him* groan. He brushed his thumbs across her hard nipples, and she lifted her arms up and back and wrapped them around his neck.

Her legs fell open, and Dillon suspected she wasn't even aware of the sensual, impossible-to-resist invitation. He was breathing hard and fast in her ear, his heart thundering with anticipation as he slid one hand along her taut belly, inching toward her center. He'd made love to dozens of women, but never had he anticipated the feel of one the way he did now.

Her bikini bottoms were tight, but the ties that held them at the hips were easy work for Dillon, even one-handed. Before she realized what had happened, they were floating away and Dillon was reaching for paradise.

He found her swollen nub in the pulsing water, brushing his thumb lightly over the folds. She arched again and cried out in surprise, then looked down in bewilderment at the water.

"What . . . what happened to my bottoms?" she whispered in a husky croak.

But Dillon was pleased to realize that she didn't sound all that concerned. "They melted away," he whispered in her ear. He took her earlobe between his teeth and nibbled gently, distracting her from his true mission. "You were so hot, they simply melted away. I'll buy you a new pair."

Her head fell back in surrender. "Okay," she purred, then shocked Dillon by reaching her hand behind her and dipping into his trunks to curl her fingers around his rock-hard erection. "But if you get to play, then I get to *finally* touch you, too." She sighed, tightening her grip, then slowly, torturously, stroking his erection with her hand. "Mmm. You're so big and hard. If we stay in this position, we can stay sensible, right?"

Dillon paused with his finger inches from her tight opening, wondering if she were truly so naive that she really didn't know how easily he could lift her up and impale her on his shaft, driving deep and sending them skyrocketing into oblivion.

The way his heart was pounding, he wasn't entirely certain that move would be healthy.

As he clenched his jaw against the incredible feel of her hot little hand on him, stroking him, he slowly shifted their almost weightless bodies around until they faced one of the powerful jet streams.

Then he moved closer, his fingers spreading her petals until the thrusting water hit her core full force.

She bucked and gasped, sounding shocked as she said, "What are you doing?"

"Not having intercourse," he whispered in a voice meant to soothe and seduce. He was shameless in his quest to bring her pleasure, to wipe out Lanny's memory and remind her that she was a beautiful, desirable woman.

"Bill Clinton tried that," she panted, squeezing him so tightly he nearly came on the spot. "It didn't work."

"Do you want me to stop?" he asked, knowing that he couldn't—she couldn't. Before she could think about answering, he slipped three fingers inside her, pushing deep, satisfied when she bucked again and cried out. She wasn't there yet . . . but he sensed that she was close. With the jet stream pounding gently against her swollen nub and his fingers buried deep in her incredible tightness, he knew it was just a matter of minutes.

He couldn't wait, had never looked forward to something so much in his life.

She thrashed restlessly on top of him, causing him to grit his teeth to keep from exploding. Her hand was clenching around him, unclenching, then clenching again.

"I want . . . I want you inside of me," she begged shamelessly, and tried to turn her body around.

Dillon held her tight, using every ounce of willpower that he possessed to hold her in position. If she turned, he knew he'd be lost. "No," he growled, hating himself for saying it and loving her for reminding him why life was so freaking awesome. He pushed them closer to the jet stream, feeling her take in a huge breath and hold it.

She let it out in a rush of breathless, erotic words that nearly sent him over the edge again. "I won't come without you, Dillon. I won't!"

"You will, baby. You will." He moved his fingers in and out, slowly, erotically, swiping his thumb back and forth across her swollen bud to intensify the jet stream's relentless, incredible massage.

"I . . . will . . . not!" she hissed through gritted teeth, her chest heaving.

But Dillon was far more stubborn than she knew. "Come for me, baby," he coaxed persuasively, gratified when her hips began to jerk in time with his fingers. "Imagine me thrusting deep inside you. God, you're so tight, so incredibly tight. I can feel you grasping me, sucking me inside you." He caught his breath as her hand tightened around him again and began to stroke him in rhythm to his fingers thrusting in and out. "The jet stream's pulsing against you . . . imagine it's my tongue thrusting out to taste you over and over again, because that's exactly what I plan to do to you next—"

"Dillon!"

It was a cry, a plea, and a threat all rolled into one heart-pounding syllable. "That's it, Callie. You're going to make me so happy when you—"

He froze as her inner muscles tightened to an unbelievable degree around his fingers. She arched her back and hung there, suspended, in shock, her hand clamped around his thick erection so tightly he had no trouble using *his* imagination.

When her deep spasms began to close around his fingers, Dillon came with her, an unbelievable journey of pleasure that he never would have imagined he could have outside a woman's body.

The aftershocks went on forever as they floated in the water, the jet streams moving them gently to and fro. Finally, when Dillon was certain his heart wasn't going to burst through his chest, he turned her so that she lay cradled in his arms. He'd never minded the cuddling most women seemed to love and expect afterward, but this time he found himself actually reveling in it. Callie was an armful of beautiful, passionate woman, and he took full advantage of the opportunity to hold her.

When their breathing had finally returned to normal, Callie lifted her head and looked at him, her eyes still smoky with lingering desire and fulfillment.

His chest swelled just thinking that he'd put that look in her eyes. If pride was a sin, then he was a sinner—big-time.

"The voters," she informed him in a comical, lofty tone, "did not agree with Bill Clinton."

Dillon chuckled and tapped her on her cute little

nose with his finger. "We're not in politics, so we can make our own rules."

She studied him for a long, intense moment. Finally she leaned down and kissed him softly on the lips. "Thank you," she murmured, "for being sensible. I don't remember the last time sensible felt so good."

"My pleasure," Dillon said, pulling her down for a long, leisurely kiss. His heart took up an odd, slightly alarming beat. When he pulled back, her eyes were soft and sexy. "We'd better get out of here," he said, growing hard again. "Before I stop being sensible."

She pushed up and away, tossing her wet hair over her shoulder and looking stunningly beautiful. "You're the president," she said, stepping out of the Jacuzzi and leaving him clinging to the sides, laughing helplessly.

"Dear God," Callie muttered, lying spread-eagled on her bed after Dillon left. Who would have thought an orgasm could leave a body so weak? She barely had the strength to hold her head up, let alone walk. If this was how she reacted when they *didn't* have sex, what would she be like after they did?

But she honestly couldn't say that they hadn't had sex, she thought, blushing all over again. Nothing that felt so good could be called anything but. Still, if believing otherwise helped Dillon deal with his conscience, who was she to argue?

She grinned into her pillow. No, she definitely didn't want to argue.

The phone on the nightstand buzzed. Callie frowned, glancing at the time. One o'clock in the morning. It had to be Dillon, she decided, lifting her heavy arm to answer it. Probably calling to torment her with a little nonintercourse phone sex.

He was inventive, no doubt about it.

"Hello," she purred into the phone seductively. "Calling for seconds?"

"We will definitely come back to this subject," Fontaine said, sounding startled and highly curious. "In the meantime, I'm calling to let you know that I broke my ankle."

Callie leaped to her knees, discovering she really *could* move. "What? What happened?"

"It's a silly story. I was walking to the parking garage after leaving work today, and the heel of my shoe sank into a crack in the concrete. It was a clean break, both my heel *and* my ankle. I'm just now getting back from the emergency room after an interminable wait, X-rays, and a cast."

"Why didn't you call me? I could have come home!"

"That's exactly why I *didn't* call you," Fontaine said dryly. "There's nothing you can do about it. I'm stuck at home for the next six weeks, maybe more. Thank God for Faith and her unfailing energy."

An image of Fontaine's assistant, Faith, came to Callie's mind, and she had to agree. Faith was one of a kind: bright, loyal, hardworking, and great with people. Callie had no doubt the magazine would be in good hands while Fontaine recovered.

"I still think I should cut this vacation short and come home," Callie said, worrying her bottom lip. "You'll be bored to tears."

"As a matter of fact, I plan on working a lot from home. I can catch up on my soap operas, too. You know you can not watch them for years, and still figure out what's going on."

Callie smiled. "Yeah, it's true. But what are you going to do about the Atlanta review?"

"Ah. That's where *you* come in. You're going to have to do them for real, Callie. So much for my plan to catch people unawares."

Panic made her voice high as Callie said, "I can't write reviews!" Had Fontaine lost her mind? Had she forgotten the many times she'd teased Callie about what a lousy reviewer she would make because she was so easy to please?

"You can do it," Fontaine said. "I know you can. You've just got to be tough. Think like me. Be impartial. I'll be helping you, too, from here. The main thing is to give me a detailed outline of the establishment's highlights—the ups and downs—and send it to me. Then I'll transform it into a review. You're basically going to be my five senses."

"I don't know, Fontaine." Callie flopped onto her back and stared at the ceiling. She'd never wanted to do what Fontaine did because it seemed too judgmental.

"Think of it this way," Fontaine said. "You've hinted that you think I'm too critical. Here's your chance to tell it from a different perspective."

When she thought of it that way, Callie had to admit the idea was appealing. Not that she had much choice in the matter. She couldn't let Fontaine down in her time of need, and she was already in Atlanta, going to all the popular places that Fontaine would have gone.

"Okay," Callie said slowly. "But I'm not going to say something bad about a place just to even things out. If I feel that it's batting a thousand, then that's what I'm going to say." *And this hotel*, Callie decided, remembering the Jacuzzi and its surprising uses, *is definitely batting a thousand*.

"I never doubted it, sis. Now, back to the beginning of our rather strange conversation. Was it my pain medicine making me hallucinate, or did you think I was a man calling? And what was this about seconds?"

Since Callie now knew Fontaine wouldn't be hopping on the next plane when she told her about Dillon, she spilled the beans. Well, almost all of it. Callie didn't tell her about her wild, satisfying experience with Dillon in the Jacuzzi, although her sister probably would have been ecstatic to hear it.

Unless, of course, Fontaine disapproved of Dillon's unprofessional actions, and felt compelled to report him to the escort service.

Because Callie couldn't be sure, she decided to leave out the juicy parts of their relationship. She was mildly surprised to find there was a lot to tell that didn't involve kissing, touching, and lots of foreplay.

Funny, bizarre stories about Dillon Love and his penchant for being in the wrong place at the right time.

By the time Callie hung up the phone, it was three in the morning, and she had made Fontaine laugh so hard she'd gotten the hiccups.

Chapter Seventeen

At ten the next morning, Wyatt was in the large store-room separating the dozen or so boxes of mirrored tiles from the liquor boxes when Dillon joined him. His twin had ordered the mirrors, planning to turn the entire east wall of the nightclub into one gigantic mirror in the hopes of impressing Callie. Wyatt wished Dillon would calm down about the review; he was beginning to feel entirely too guilty for not telling his brother that he was wasting his money and *their* time, because if Callie was a reviewer, then *he* was Wyatt Earp.

"Did you follow Mom?" Dillon asked, hoisting a box of mirrors up in his arms and waiting for Wyatt to do the same.

So much for hoping Dillon had forgotten, Wyatt groaned to himself. He picked up one of the boxes and walked ahead of Dillon out of the storeroom. When they reached the wall they intended to revamp, they set the boxes down and headed back for more.

They were in the storeroom again before Wyatt

dropped the bomb. "You were right. Mom's seeing a man."

Dillon grew still. "Go on," he said. "There's obviously more, and from the look of your expression, I'm not going to like it."

Knowing there was no way out of it, Wyatt put his hands on his hips, bracing himself for the storm. "She went to a duplex in Walnut Grove."

"I know the subdivision. Did you get an address?"

Wyatt hesitated. The part he dreaded was coming. "Yeah. I've been out that way before. It's where Will lives."

Dillon's jaw dropped. "*Our* Will? Will Tallfeather?"

Knowing exactly how he felt, Wyatt gave a miserable nod. "It was definitely his house. I saw him greet Mom at the door." His twin's expression was a mixture of shock and disbelief.

"But . . . but he's *our* age, isn't he?"

He doubted it would help, but Wyatt said it anyway. "Actually, I think he's a couple of years older."

"Oh," Dillon drawled sarcastically. "That's such a relief. For a minute there I thought Mom was robbing the cradle." He cussed and shook his head. "What is she thinking? And what the hell does Will want with our mom?"

It happened before Wyatt could heed the voice of caution: his brow shot upward.

Dillon saw it, growled, and went for his throat. Wyatt blocked the attack and jumped back out of reach. They glared at each other.

"Do not," Dillon snarled, "ever think of Mom and sex at the same time. She's fifty years old, for Pete's sake!"

Wyatt pointed at Dillon's groin. "You gonna unscrew that thing and put it away when *you* turn fifty?" he challenged. "You're being ridiculous, Dillon. Mom has every right to a healthy—"

"Don't say it!"

"—*love* life," Wyatt concluded. "She deserves a chance to be happy."

"She *is* happy, and she's got a career ahead of her."

"You're being selfish."

"I'm *not* being selfish! I just don't want her to get hurt."

His twin was sincerely freaked out, Wyatt thought, softening at Dillon's pained expression. "Look, bro. Mom loved Dad, but he's been gone a long time. I think she stayed single because she didn't want us ever to think she was trying to replace him. Now we're grown adults." *Or one of us is,* Wyatt corrected silently. "Do you honestly want her to be alone for the rest of her life?"

Dillon hesitated, then shook his head. "No, I don't, but . . . *Will?* Why couldn't she meet someone her own age?"

Wyatt shrugged. He picked up a box of mirrors and hefted it onto his shoulder. "I don't know. Maybe he loves her."

"What if he *thinks* he does, and what if one day he wakes up and realizes that she's seventeen years older than he is? What happens then?" Dillon grabbed a box as if it weighed nothing and followed Wyatt from the storeroom. "I'll tell you what happens. Mom gets her heart broken and Will Tallfeather ends up in a body bag."

"Sheesh," Wyatt muttered. "We just found out she was seeing Will, and you've got him walking out on her and you killing him for doing it." Slamming the box down onto the floor, Wyatt hoped he'd broken a few of the ridiculous mirrors.

Dillon thrust out a belligerent chin. "I can't believe you're not upset about this."

"I'm concerned, but not angry. Frankly, Dillon, I don't think it's our business."

"She's our *mother!* Of course it's our business."

"Our business to be upset and concerned, but not our business to interfere."

"Meaning you aren't even going to confront Will about this?" Dillon sounded disbelieving and more than a little disgusted with him. "If you won't, I will."

"Don't."

"Are you asking, or are you ordering?" Dillon asked softly.

"Asking." Wyatt sighed, daring to add, "I know you won't like hearing this, but I think it needs to be said. This could be just a . . . hot flash or something."

"Hot flash refers to something that happens to women going through menopause," Dillon said, still in that dangerously soft voice Wyatt knew well. "So if you meant something else, I dare you to say it."

"Oh, grow up!" Wyatt had run out of patience with his twin. He stomped past him. "I'm not going to fight with you about whether our mother is having sex or not. In fact, I don't like thinking about it any more than you do, so why don't we just forget it?"

But Dillon was relentless, as usual. Close on Wyatt's heels, he growled, "She's ashamed of it. If she wasn't, she wouldn't be sneaking around."

"That doesn't mean she's ashamed," Wyatt pointed out impatiently. "It means she's aware that you're a psycho. I just hope she remembers that the only thing identical about us is our looks."

"Go to hell."

Wyatt jerked open the storeroom door. "Now that's tempting, bro. If I went to hell, I wouldn't have to spend the day hanging mirrors on a perfectly good wall so that you can trick Callie into believing we run some kind of classy establishment."

"There's nothing wrong with a little class."

"And there's nothing wrong with a good, down-home, comfortable nightclub where people can let their hair down without having to look at themselves doing it in a mirror."

"You don't understand," Dillon said.

"I guess I don't." Wyatt paused in the process of reaching for another box. He bit back a smug grin, realizing he had managed to get Dillon's mind off the fact that their mother was seeing a much younger man. Turning his back so that Dillon wouldn't see his expression, he said, "Why don't you try explaining it to me again?"

To Wyatt's relief, Dillon took the bait, hook, line, and sinker.

"I can't believe this place was almost demolished," Callie said, admiring the Fox Theater's opulent, historic interior. "Thank God the citizens of Atlanta woke up before it was too late, and rescued it." Beside her, Dillon placed his hand in the middle of her back as he guided her to the gift shop inside the theater.

She shivered, knowing that if she looked at him, she'd get distracted all over again, just as she had when he'd picked her up at the hotel. He was wearing a gray suit and a silver-striped tie, and he looked impossibly gorgeous.

The amazing part to Callie was that he didn't seem

to realize every woman within a hundred-yard radius was either drooling or shooting daggers of envy at Callie.

Unfortunately, she was no stranger to jealous, drooling women; Lanny had reveled in similar attention. But to be fair, Callie didn't think Dillon even noticed. If he did, he was doing a great job of hiding the fact.

Dillon leaned toward her, speaking low in her ear. "Did I tell you that I think that dress you're wearing should be outlawed?"

Blushing despite her attempt not to, she said flippantly, "This old thing?" But she was pleased with his compliment. The deceptively demure dress, an antique white with inlaid peals at the collar and hem, was one of the few dresses *she* had picked out during the forced shopping spree with Fontaine.

She hadn't noticed how sheer it was until she'd slipped it on minutes before Dillon arrived. As a result, she hadn't been able to wear any undergarments with it, much to her dismay and Dillon's apparent delight.

Of course, he'd noticed right away, his eyes going dark and smoky, making her breathless and achy before she had a chance to draw a breath and say hello.

Hoping to distract them both before it became apparent she was getting aroused, Callie picked up a miniature replica of the Fox Theater. She was thinking it would make an excellent paperweight for Fontaine's office. "Are you sure watching the Atlanta Ballet isn't going to bore you to tears?" she asked Dillon, who had stopped to study a painting by a local artist.

He came closer before he said, "I'm going to be too busy wondering if you're naked beneath that dress to be bored."

Callie nearly dropped the paperweight. Belatedly,

she realized her mistake in wearing the dress; it hid absolutely nothing from Dillon, including her reaction to his provocative comment. She tried to laugh. "Well, I guess I should keep you guessing, then."

Dillon moved so close his jacket brushed her erect nipples.

She sucked in a tiny, betraying gasp, and he rewarded her with a wicked smile. His hot gaze flicked over her, leaving a trail of fire in its wake.

"When we leave here," he suggested softly, "let's get a bottle of wine and go to my apartment."

"We . . . we have reservations for dinner," she said faintly. Breathlessly. It was so difficult to remember that she now had another purpose for being in Atlanta.

"We could work up an appetite, then order in pizza."

Shamelessly weakened by his persuasive voice, she was on the verge of agreeing when she heard a woman call out his name. Callie was looking at Dillon, so she saw the alarm that flared in his eyes before he shuttered his gaze to hide it.

They both turned to watch a tall, leggy brunette sashay in their direction. Behind her, a man several inches shorter struggled to keep up. He was wearing an off-the-rack suit that looked too large for his slim shoulders.

"Dillon! It *is* you! I never took you for a theater man. Are you still—"

"Shawna," Dillon cut in. "This is Callie Spencer."

As Callie took the limp hand the woman offered, she knew instinctively that Shawna and Dillon had been lovers. There was an unmistakable air of familiarity in the way the woman looked at Dillon that made the bottom drop out of her stomach. She told herself that she was being silly. Of course Dillon would have old girlfriends. It was ridiculously naive of her to think otherwise.

The realization didn't, however, lessen the sickening sensation in her stomach.

"It's been a while, Shawna," Dillon said, sliding a possessive arm around Callie's waist, as if he sensed her discomfort. "Nice to see you again. Hate to run, but I think the show's about to start."

When he propelled her forward, Callie didn't resist. She wanted to get away from the woman as much as Dillon apparently did, although she did wonder at his motives. Was he afraid the brunette would say too much about their past relationship? Or was Dillon truly being a gentleman?

The moment they were out of earshot, Dillon took her hand in his. "Are you okay?"

"Why shouldn't I be?" It was on the tip of Callie's tongue to add, *You're my escort, not my boyfriend.* Sometimes she forgot, and then she was rudely reminded. From the corner of her eye, she saw Dillon grimace.

"Shawna is talkative. If we hadn't gotten away from her, we would have missed half the show."

Because she couldn't resist, Callie asked, "Is she one of those tall, leggy brunettes you told me about the first time we met?" To her surprise and mystification, he flushed.

"Do you have to remind me of what an ass I was?" he countered, slanting her a rueful smile. "You bring out the devil in me."

"Oh, so it's *my* fault!" She laughed. The knot in her stomach began to ease. A man like Dillon would have had women, probably lots of them. He couldn't wipe out his past just to please her. Besides, the only thing they had going was an incredible lust for each other.

She didn't own him, and he didn't own her. Dillon, for all his surprisingly wonderful qualities, wasn't her type—at least, not for the long haul. She wanted a man she could trust to be completely hers. With a man like Dillon, the temptation to stray would always be there.

Inside the beautiful auditorium they found their seats. Dillon put his arm around her shoulders, and took her hand in his.

Callie stared down at their entwined hands, daring to dream that just for now, Dillon *was* all hers.

"Have I told you how sexy you look tonight?" Dillon whispered roughly in her ear.

She smiled up at him, praying the lights were dim enough to hide the sheen of tears standing in her eyes. "Buttermilk," she said.

Mischief gleamed in his eyes. "Was it something I said?"

Dillon unlocked the door to his apartment with complete confidence.

He knew there wasn't a dirty sock in sight. In fact, there wasn't a dirty sock in the entire apartment. He had bagged them and stuck them in the back of his Jeep, planning to wash them at the first opportunity.

The only thing left to do was make certain his mother wasn't playing the part of Goldilocks again.

After checking his bedroom, Dillon rejoined Callie in the living room. He dug in his pocket and extracted a quarter. "Call it," he said.

She shot him a puzzled, amused look. "At the risk of regretting my blind trust in you, I call it tails."

Dillon flipped the quarter, caught it in the air, and slapped it against his arm. He lifted his hand and held his arm out for her to see. "Heads. You lose."

"I'm almost afraid to ask. What do I lose?"

The throaty sound of her voice made his pulse leap with anticipation. God, she was sexy. "You have to be the sensible one tonight."

Her eyes widened in alarm. "Oh, no. No way." She held up a hand and let out a shaky laugh. "I think we proved last night that *you're* the sensible one."

When he took a step in her direction, she took a step back. Her breath came out in sexy little pants. Dillon couldn't get over how little it took for her to turn him on.

"Wait! Dillon . . . the moment you start kissing me, I can't think straight. So you see, I'm not the one to be sensible. You're much better at it than I am. You . . . you can stay in control. I don't think I can."

"Control?" Dillon slowly approached her until her back was against the door and she could go no farther. He braced an arm on either side of her, pinning her in. For a brief, erotic moment, he nuzzled her soft lips. He drew back slightly and looked into her passion-glazed eyes. "No, baby," he whispered. "I'm not in control." He drew a finger between her breasts, heard her moan, and had to swallow one of his own. "If you knew just how badly I want to be inside you . . . you'd laugh at the notion that I was in control." He slid one thin strap from her shoulder, baring her breast to his hungry gaze. Touching his finger to his mouth, he wet it, then touched it to her rigid nipple. It hardened further beneath his caress. "I love the way you respond to me. I love the way you sound as if you can't breathe around me."

"I can't," she admitted breathlessly, her gaze locked on his.

He lowered his mouth to her nipple, flicking his

tongue back and forth, then slowly suckling her. When he lifted his head, her eyes had closed and her head was thrown back in ecstasy.

"Tell me what you want me to do to you," he ordered in a rough whisper. "Tell me what turns you on."

"*You* do," she gasped without hesitation. "Everything . . . you do turns me on."

Although flattered by her confession, Dillon wasn't satisfied. "Everyone has fantasies. Tell me one of yours."

She shook her head, keeping her eyes closed.

He studied her flushed cheeks with extreme interest. So she *did* have a fantasy, but she wasn't talking.

Which meant he'd have to find out for himself.

Lucky him.

"This dress is driving me insane," he rasped out. Sliding the other strap from her shoulder, he used the flats of his hands to draw it down her body, using his mouth and tongue to ignite a fiery path along her breasts and belly.

He dropped to his knees as her dress puddled around her ankles.

As he had suspected, she was completely naked beneath the dress.

When she buried a frantic hand in his hair and tugged, he paused and looked up at her.

"What are you doing?" she asked.

His gaze burned into hers. "Drawing my own conclusions." And then he buried his face in her dark curls and blew out a hot breath against her core.

She jumped and grabbed his hair again, trying to dodge his insistent mouth. "Wait!"

He paused again, lifting a questioning brow. She was breathing hard and fast, her eyes nearly black with desire. "Are you ready to talk?"

"Y-yes. Just . . . just stop doing that."

"You don't like it?" He knew better, but he would go along with the game.

She nodded, keeping her hand tangled in his hair as if she feared he'd ignore her wishes. "I like it *too* much. That's . . . that's the problem."

Dillon slowly rose, feigning bewilderment. "How is liking it too much a problem?"

She blushed deeply. "Because it isn't . . . isn't fair that I . . . that you . . ." She looked down. Her eyes widened on the bulge in his pants; then she jerked her gaze back to his face.

"Baby," Dillon said softly, taking her hand and placing it on his rock-hard erection, "if you think for one minute that I'm not enjoying this, then think again. Last night was incredible for both of us."

If it was possible, her eyes widened even further. "You mean you—"

"Yes, I did. I thought you knew."

The knock at the door couldn't have come at a more inconvenient time.

Callie shrieked and leaped into his arms, then hastily bent down to grab her dress as if she thought whoever it was could see that she was naked.

Watching her streaking to the bathroom with her sexy dress clutched in her hand, Dillon sighed and checked the peephole to see whom he had to get rid of as quickly as possible.

Wyatt.

Why was he not surprised? Dillon was convinced his brother had taken a 101 class in college on how to make your twin miserable.

He opened the door and barked out, "What the hell do you want?"

Wyatt blinked at his exasperated tone. "We've got a code red down at the club."

"Lower your voice!" Dillon hissed, jerking his head in the direction of his bathroom. "Callie's here."

Actually listening for a change, Wyatt looked past him, then back at Dillon. He looked grim. "I need you to come back to the . . . come back with me."

"Can't you and the guys handle it?"

"I think you'll want to see this for yourself, and bring Callie. She's good with kids, isn't she?"

The mention of kids triggered Dillon's panic button. "Kids? This has something to do with kids?" His gaze narrowed suspiciously. "Is this another plot to humiliate me? Because I'm on to you guys." He glanced over his shoulder to make certain Callie hadn't come out of the bathroom. "And you know I can't bring Callie to the club, Wyatt."

"What I need to show you is around back, so it will be safe to bring her. I'll meet you there."

Dillon closed the door and leaned against it, staring at the closed bathroom door with longing and regret. "Son of a bitch," he muttered, pushing away from the door to go tell Callie the bad news.

Whatever the emergency, it had to be bad to put Wyatt in such a serious mood. For Wyatt's sake, it had better be, Dillon grumbled to himself.

Because he was almost certain Callie had been on the verge of sharing one of her fantasies with him.

Chapter Eighteen

Music spilled out from the open back door of the Love Nest, where Wyatt waited with Fish—the bouncer Callie recognized from her short visit inside last week—and another older man Wyatt introduced simply as Lou.

When Callie and Dillon reached them, Wyatt took Dillon's arm and led the group to the edge of the building. He pointed to a large industrial-size Dumpster situated at the back of the building-in-progress next door. The streetlight between the two buildings was just bright enough to show Callie that the Dumpster looked new and unused.

"The crying came from there," Wyatt told them. "I was taking out the . . . I was helping Fish, like I sometimes do to, um, help pay my tab, when I heard it."

"Maybe it was a cat," Dillon said. "Sometimes they can sound like a baby crying."

Callie wondered if anyone else had picked up on the hint of panic in Dillon's tone. He very definitely didn't want it to be a baby. Well, for once they were in agreement. She shuddered, refusing to think of how or why a baby would be in the Dumpster.

"It wasn't a cat," Wyatt said with conviction. "It was a baby, and he sounded hungry."

"Well," Callie said when it appeared the men were too petrified to move, "someone's gotta go see." She took three steps in the direction of the Dumpster before Dillon caught her arm.

"Whoa, there. It could be someone up to no good, hoping to lure some *gullible* fool close to rob them."

"Then we'll all go." Callie was too polite to scoff at Dillon's desperate comment. She knew it had been panic-driven, and vowed once again to find out at a later date why he was so frightened of children. In the meantime, they had to investigate.

Hooking one arm in Dillon's and the other in Wyatt's, she hauled them toward the Dumpster. Fish and Lou followed, flanking their sides. They all reached the Dumpster at the same time.

Five pairs of hands reached for the heavy metal lid as if it were the coffin of a vampire. Callie was surprised at how easy it was to lift with all that muscle behind it. With a glance at Dillon's pale, dread-filled expression, she peered over the edge of the Dumpster to look inside.

She gasped. Dillon stiffened beside her, then reluctantly leaned forward to look. She heard the rustling of the others as they all peered inside.

Callie blinked several times, convinced she must be hallucinating. She could have been peering into someone's living room—from the roof, that is. There was a lamp perched on an end table; and a futon sofa pushed against the back wall of the Dumpster, the cushion punctured in several places, allowing the stuffing to seep out. A battered, three-legged coffee table dominated the center of the "room," the top littered with take-out boxes and left-over food.

In a daze they pushed the lid completely back, allowing the streetlight to shine into the dark corners of the Dumpster, revealing a pallet of blankets and pillows.

She was the first to spot them. There was a boy of nine or ten, holding a baby on his hip. The baby seemed to be around twelve or thirteen months of age. Sitting partially hidden behind the boy and the baby was another child of around three or four. With a mass of blond curls, it was hard to tell if it was a boy or a girl.

There was no mistaking the stark fear in the faces that stared back at them.

"Dear God," Callie breathed as the realization hit her full force. These kids were *living* in the Dumpster. With a baby and no plumbing. They had furniture and a lamp, but no electricity. No refrigerator for the baby's milk. It was enough to boggle the mind.

"See," Wyatt whispered, but there was no victory in his voice. Only horror and concern. "I told you that it wasn't a cat."

Dillon looked at Wyatt, his eyes a curious, burning black in the dim light. "Wyatt, I swear, if this is a setup—"

Before Callie could finish reeling from the fury in his tone, Wyatt snarled right back at him with equal fury. "What kind of sicko do you take me for? Get over yourself."

"Shh!" Callie glared them into silence. She focused on the oldest of the children, keeping her voice soft and reassuring. "Do you have a name? That's a beautiful baby you've got there. Is it your sister?" Callie had no inkling of the sex of the baby; she was guessing, hoping to draw him into a conversation.

After a long moment of silence, Wyatt said, "I don't think he's going to talk, Callie. He looks pretty frightened."

"I'd be frightened, too," Callie muttered low enough so the boy wouldn't hear, "if I lived in a Dumpster."

"Beside a nightclub," Lou added grimly. "All that noise—"

"—would drown out the baby's cries," Dillon concluded softly, surprising Callie. He was staring at the baby as if mesmerized. "We should call the police."

"We can't do that yet!" Callie burst out, staring at Dillon. "What if they were being abused or something? Then we call the police, the police take them back home . . . we should find out why they ran away."

"I agree," Fish said, his voice suspiciously gruff. "Poor kids are bound to have a reason for living like this."

Still hopeful the older boy would talk to her, Callie turned a pleading gaze on him. "We want to help you. Can you at least tell us your mother's name?"

"*I'm* their mother!" a shrill voice said from behind them.

The voice didn't sound old enough to be anyone's mother, Callie thought, turning with the rest of her group to face the teenage girl. She was clutching an aluminum baseball bat as if she knew exactly how to swing it and wouldn't hesitate to do it.

The girl's eyes were huge with fear, but the tough set of her jaw and her defensive stance told Callie she was ready to try to fight all of them if necessary. Stifling a surge of pity that Callie suspected the girl wouldn't appreciate, she took quick stock of the girl's designer jeans and expensive tennis shoes.

Not the tattered, mismatched clothes of a homeless person, or even the cheap clothes of someone who might have been living from paycheck to paycheck.

Trying to keep the group within her wary vision, the girl swayed with the bat as if she were about to swing for a home run. "Just get out of here and leave us alone," she said harshly. "We're not bothering anyone. They're not even using this Dumpster yet. We'll be long gone before they do."

Lou took a tiny step forward. When she raised the bat in warning, he stopped. "Hold on a minute, girl. We don't mean you any harm."

Jerking her head in the direction of the nightclub, the girl said, "You came out of there, didn't you?" Her lip curled. "You're drunk. You're probably *all* drunk! Just leave us alone!" She hoisted the bat higher.

Sensing the girl was on the verge of hysteria, Callie shot Lou a warning look. The truth was that Lou did look sort of scruffy, with his unshaven face and uncombed hair. She suspected it didn't help that he was wearing a T-shirt with the logo of a name-brand beer across the front in big, drunken black letters, and that he *smelled* strongly of beer and whiskey.

"We're not drunk," Callie said firmly, yet gently, praying she was speaking for the whole group. "We're concerned, and we want to help you and your . . . family. It can't be comfortable living in there in the daytime. You could have heatstroke, or you could all dehydrate." There were a dozen other horrible repercussions she could think of, but she wanted the girl's trust, not to put her on the defensive any more than she already was.

The girl stopped moving back and forth with the bat, but she didn't lower it. Grudgingly, she said, "We don't stay in it during the day. We hang out at the Laundro-mat and pretend to wash clothes. I'm not stupid."

"Nobody thinks you're stupid. In fact, we all think you're pretty brave." To Callie's relief, the men quickly added their praises.

"You got a lot of gumption," Lou said.

Wyatt nodded. "You must be smart, too."

"Wish *I* had a sister like you," Fish said shrewdly.

When Dillon didn't say anything, Callie subtly prodded him with her elbow.

He cleared his throat, but his voice was still hoarse with shock as he said, "I'm not sure I could have been so brave if I were in your place."

Tense moments ticked by. Behind them, Callie could hear the other kids stirring restlessly inside the Dump-ster. The baby whimpered, but was quickly hushed by one of the older kids.

Callie saw a little of the tension ease from the girl's face. She held her breath and waited.

But the girl apparently had second thoughts about trusting them. She thrust her chin up again. "You can't call the police. We can't go back."

"Go back where?" Wyatt asked quickly—too quickly, and too obviously.

"I told you—I'm not stupid."

"Well, you can't stay here," Dillon said, startling Callie with the harshness of his tone. "You can't keep a baby and two young kids in a Dumpster behind a nightclub, for Pete's sake."

Before Callie could hush him, she saw the girl's eyes go even wider. Just as Callie realized the girl wasn't looking at her, but *behind* her, Callie heard a loud thunk.

Dillon let out a curse, grabbed the back of his head, then slumped to the ground.

From the Dumpster, Callie heard the trembling, yet proud voice of the boy call out, "I got one of them, Gina! But I had to break your lamp. Are you mad at me?"

"Dillon!" Callie dropped to her knees beside Dillon, frantically searching his head for blood.

She found none, but there was no doubt he was out cold. She groaned.

When Dillon opened his eyes and saw stars, it took him a moment to realize they really *were* stars.

He was lying on the ground, looking at the sky. He could hear music, and people arguing.

A baby began to cry, its plaintive wail nearly drowning out the voices.

A baby! Remembering, Dillon sat up so fast the world spun around him. He gingerly fingered the tender bump on his head, wincing when he found it. Slowly he focused on the impossible scene before him.

Fish and Lou held the struggling teenager between them, dodging her wildly kicking feet and not always succeeding, if their grunts and curses were any indication.

Callie and Wyatt were arguing, and the boy he suspected of hitting him had climbed out of the Dumpster with the baby and the younger child. The younger child clutched the boy's pant leg, hiding behind him.

For the first time Dillon noticed how well dressed they all were. Not at all what he would have expected from a family living in a Dumpster. What was going on? What was their story?

He tried to concentrate on the argument, but it wasn't easy. The baby was crying in earnest now, reaching chubby arms in the teenager's direction.

"How can we earn her trust if you don't let her go?"

Callie stood with her hands on her hips, bristling at his twin.

With his arms folded, Wyatt held his ground. "Earn *her* trust? She tried to take my head off with the baseball bat! Another second and I would have been stretched out on the ground with Dillon."

Which was exactly where he should be, Dillon thought darkly, for dragging him into yet another bizarre situation where *he* got hurt.

"She wouldn't have hit you," Callie said, only to have her assurance shot to hell by the teenager's shriek of fury.

"Yes, I would have! I'll take all of you out if I have to! We're not going back to that place! You don't know them; they hate us!"

The teenager's histrionics might have stumped a lesser woman, Dillon mused, rubbing his aching head. But not Callie. Smiling gently at the girl, she said to Wyatt, "She's upset. She doesn't know what she's saying. Let her go so that I can talk to her."

"No." Wyatt shook his head to emphasize his stand. "Trust me on this one, Callie. As long as she thinks we're going to turn her in, she's dangerous."

Deciding it was time to enter the ring—again—Dillon started to get to his feet. He was halfway there when his gaze clashed with the boy's, who stood not more than a few feet away. The boy clutched the crying baby and pressed himself against the Dumpster, pinning the younger child behind him.

Dillon had never before witnessed such unadulterated terror in a child's eyes. The realization that the terror was because of *him* made Dillon physically sick to his stomach. The kid thought he was mad. Mad enough . . . to . . . what? *Hit* him?

Softly, Dillon told him, "I swear that I wouldn't harm a hair on your head, kid. Okay?" The conviction in Dillon's voice must have shone through in his eyes, for the boy swallowed visibly, then nodded. Dillon's heart shuddered. A huge lump tried to block his voice, but he managed to get around it without sounding too much like a sobbing woman. "What's your name?"

After a slight hesitation, the boy said, "Matt."

"Well, Matt. I'm Dillon." He took a deep breath, wondering if the bump on his head was maybe worse than he thought. Why else would he be about to say what he was about to say? "Why don't you let me hold the baby? She looks heavy." There. He'd said it, and now there was no taking it back.

The boy stumbled forward and gave Dillon the baby. Dillon prayed his own panic didn't show as he took the baby. "What's her name?"

"Adrienne."

"Adrienne," Dillon repeated, carefully turning the baby around until he could look into her tearstained face. To his astonishment—and secret delight—the baby stopped crying abruptly, staring at him with big brown eyes. Settling her cautiously against his chest, he nodded at the madness still going on behind him. "Why don't you go over there and try to calm your sister down? See if she wants to go for pizza. Tell her we promise not to do anything until we hear your story."

"Okay." He grabbed the hand of the younger child and plowed into the fray.

Anticipating their shock, Dillon turned with the baby. He was nervous about holding her, but he figured as long as her little hands were anchored in his hair, there wasn't any chance of dropping her. Never mind that she gripped a handful of hair close to the throbbing lump on his head. He could handle the pain as long as she wasn't crying.

"You can't hold on to her indefinitely," Callie was saying when Matt walked up to her and touched her arm. "Just a minute," she told him absently, then froze as she realized who it was.

Dillon found himself chuckling at her flabbergasted expression, and was delighted when Adrienne responded by chuckling with him. She clapped her chubby hands against his cheeks and bussed him a good one right on his surprised mouth, then grinned to reveal four shiny upper teeth and two lower ones.

He laughed out loud, so engrossed in playing with Adrienne that it was several minutes before he realized everyone was staring at him.

Even Gina had stopped struggling.

Too late, Dillon went back to scowling. "Close your mouths," he growled, feeling the heat creep into his face. "You're drawing flies."

"She doesn't like men," Gina blurted out, sounding bewildered.

"He's nice," Matt said, as if that explained everything. "He wants to buy us pizza."

Callie slowly closed her gaping mouth. "You want to take them out for *pizza?*"

Self-preservation kicked in; Dillon deepened his scowl. "They look like they could use a good hot meal."

Despite the bad lighting and the distance, Dillon could see Callie's eyes narrowing.

"Are you feeling dizzy? Maybe a little disoriented? Forgetful? Do you need me to refresh your memory of what happened last night? Kidnapping charges—"

"She's right, Dillon," Wyatt said. "These kids are—"

"Hungry," Dillon cut in firmly. "And I promised them pizza. Matt, you and, ah . . ."

"Caleb," Matt supplied.

"You and Caleb can ride with my brother, Wyatt. Gina, you and the baby can ride with Callie and me."

"Are you and him twins?" Matt asked, sounding awed as he looked from Wyatt to Dillon, then back again.

"Unfortunately," Wyatt mumbled. "Come on, kid. Bring your brother and come with me."

"Wait!" Gina cried, digging in her heels and sounding panicked. "We can't be separated."

Callie smiled at her and held out her hand. "You can trust us, Gina."

Gina eyed Callie's hand for a long, tense moment. She finally took it and allowed Callie to lead her to Dillon and Adrienne. When they reached them, she held out her arms for the baby.

Adrienne batted her hands away and clung to Dillon.

The huge lump Dillon had managed to swallow returned.

Chapter Nineteen

Most women had a general idea of when they fell in love.

Callie knew the exact moment.

They had been at the pizza joint less than an hour, and in the last fifteen minutes she had struggled against the urge to cry as she watched Gina and her siblings ravenously consume the better part of two large pepperoni pizzas.

She looked at Dillon to see if he was feeling the same silent horror that she was feeling. Instead she was caught and held mesmerized by the sight Dillon made with Adrienne on his lap.

Adrienne had refused a high chair. Had, in fact, made it verbally known loudly and clearly that she wouldn't be separated from her new friend Dillon, not even for a second.

Time seemed to freeze as Callie stared at him. He had pizza sauce on his cheek, chin, and nose. A string of cheese hung from his hair, and several tufts of hair stuck up in sticky spikes where Adrienne had missed when she tried to feed him her pizza, which she did often and not very successfully.

The oddest, most endearing part was that Dillon didn't seem to mind. In fact, Callie thought as the shock of realizing she loved him seeped into her heart, he was actually smiling as if he *enjoyed* being fed by a clumsy one-year-old who could scarcely feed herself, much less someone sitting behind her.

She loved him.

Not just lust. Not just infatuation.

She had fallen in love with Dillon Love, her escort. A man who could never go unnoticed by other women, not even with pizza sauce smeared all over his face and his hair a sticky mess.

A gorgeous man who would forever be tempted by beautiful women.

Lord help her.

He caught her watching him, completely oblivious to the way he looked. His blond brow rose questioningly. "Was it something I said?"

Callie felt as if someone had punched her in the stomach. Swallowing panic, she asked in a croak, "What . . . what do you mean?"

"The way you're looking at me." He darted a quick glance at Gina and Matt as if making certain they weren't listening. "You've got that look. You know . . . *that* look that makes me want to think of what goes through a sewer pipe."

Thank God, Callie thought, wondering if her chest was going to explode. He'd mistaken her look for one of lust instead of . . . love.

"Mom looked at Donny that way," Matt observed in a tone way too serious for his age. "That's why we let her marry him."

Gina shoved him, glaring. "Shut up, you little punk. I told you to just keep your mouth closed."

Matt looked comically innocent. "Hey! I gotta open my mouth to eat, don't I?"

When Gina's eyes narrowed, Callie hastily intervened. "Please . . . don't fight. Gina, will you tell us what happened? Why are you and your siblings living in a Dumpster?"

"What's a sibling?" Matt asked, and got another shove from his sister.

"It means brother or sister," Dillon informed him. Apparently Adrienne thought he was asking for a bite, and she shoved a piece of pizza crust into his open mouth, for once hitting her target. Despite the fact that the baby had drooled and gnawed on the crust before feeding it to him, Dillon dutifully chewed.

Callie fell deeper in love. She sighed and shook her head, forcing herself to concentrate on Gina and her story. "We want to help you, but we need to know where your parents are."

Gina dropped the pizza in her hand as if she'd suddenly lost her appetite. She kept her gaze down. There was pain in her voice, and anger as well. "Mom's dead. She died last week with our stepfather, Donny. They went to one of their fancy parties, and Donny was drunk. They crashed into a tree on the way home."

"I'm so sorry," Callie whispered, blinking away the burning tears in her eyes. She suspected Gina was near the breaking point, and had probably been holding herself together for her siblings. Callie knew she needed to grieve, but a pizza parlor wasn't the place. "What about family? Grandmother? An uncle, maybe?"

Shaking her head, Gina shot a quick, tear-filled gaze

at Callie before staring at her plate again. "The only family Mom had was Aunt LaVonda. I mailed her a letter, but she hasn't called. We don't have her number, and she's unlisted. I found her address in Mom's purse, but I don't even know if she still lives there."

"You've been living in a Dumpster," Callie pointed out gently. "How can she call you?"

"I gave her the number of the pay phone at the Laundromat," Gina said with quiet pride. "I told you, I'm not stupid." To cover her embarrassment, Gina grabbed a slice of pizza and put it on Caleb's plate. "Eat," she told him in that bossy, big-sister voice Callie knew well.

"What about your stepfather's family?" Callie asked, struggling to keep the pity from her expression.

Gina sat back and looked at Callie, her mouth a taut line of bitterness and anger. "They hate us. They never liked us, and we knew it, but Mom said to give them a chance, that we would grow on them because we were good kids." She took her fork and stabbed her pizza, her actions speaking louder than words. "I heard them talking . . . after the funeral. Nobody wanted us. They were planning on calling Social Services." For a long, heart-wrenching moment, her gaze lingered on Dillon and Adrienne.

Callie saw Gina's eyes soften, and knew that she loved her siblings with all of her heart.

"They didn't even want Adrienne," Gina said. "And she's just a baby."

Confused, Callie frowned. "Adrienne doesn't belong to your stepfather?"

"Mom said she does, but *they* never believed it. They said . . . the day I heard them talking about us . . . that Mom lied to get Donny to marry her because he had

216

money, and she was trailer trash and had a string of bastards she needed help taking care of."

The gasp of outrage escaped before Callie could contain it. "That's an awful thing to say!"

Gina shrugged as if it didn't matter, when it obviously did. "It's true, mostly. Mom was married to my dad, but she wasn't married when she had Matt or Caleb."

"That doesn't make her a bad person," Dillon said softly. "Maybe gullible, but not bad."

Callie saw the beginnings of hero worship in the look Gina cast Dillon. Maybe it wasn't a bad thing, if it meant that Gina was capable of believing in the goodness of others again.

"I plan to major in psychology," Gina said with obvious pride. "I think Mom had a dependent personality, but she loved us."

"Of course she did," Callie murmured, because she didn't know what else to say. "I'm sure that if she'd had any idea that she was . . . well, she would have made sure there was someone who would take care of you."

"Aunt LaVonda would, if she knew." Gina took a sip of her Coke, put another slice of pizza on Matt's plate, and sat back in her chair again. "She's going to call. I know she will." She stared defiantly at Dillon, then Callie. "I'll be eighteen in two weeks. If Aunt LaVonda doesn't call, or doesn't want to take us, then I plan to ask a judge for custody of Matt, Caleb, and Adrienne."

It was a noble plan, one that made tears spring to Callie's eyes again, but it was full of holes. She couldn't help pointing them out, for Gina's sake. "How will you support them? And you talked about going to college. How can you go to school if you're working to support a family?"

There was fierce determination in Gina's eyes as she said, "I don't know, but I'll figure it out. Mama said I was a great problem-solver. When we . . . when we didn't have money for food or rent, I would think of ways to make money."

Callie didn't want to dwell too deeply on the implications of Gina's statements. Instead, she said, "In the meantime, where will you stay? Because . . ." She hesitated, then took the plunge: "Because there's no way Dillon and I can live with ourselves if we let you go back to that Dumpster." On the other hand, she didn't want Dillon returning to jail for kidnapping.

"She won't have to," Dillon said, surprising Callie. "I know where you and your siblings can stay until . . . for a few days, to give your aunt time to call you."

"Dillon," Callie began as delicately as she could. "You can't let them stay—"

"Not with me," he said with a half smile. "It's a temporary home for the homeless called Hope House, founded by a friend of mine. We might have to fudge a little about Gina's age, but I think it's for a good cause, don't you? She just needs a few days to give her aunt time to call."

How could she resist with him giving her that I'm-all-yours look? Callie wasn't immune, no matter how much she wished she were. Wetting her dry lips, she asked the logical question, "How will she know if her aunt calls if she's staying there? Her aunt has the number of the Laundromatt."

His brows rose. "I have a lot of friends who owe me favors. We can make certain that someone is at the Laundromatt to answer the pay phone during the day. In fact, I have a lot of *dirty* socks to wash, so I can take the first shift."

As Dillon smiled at the kids and the kids stared back at him as if he were their savior, Callie closed her eyes and groaned to herself.

That's it, she thought, *I'm toast*.

Something was wrong.

Dillon knew it the moment he touched Callie's elbow helping her into his Jeep. She flinched away from him.

Callie Spencer didn't flinch when he touched her.

She groaned, or moaned, or started to pant, or looked at him as if she wanted to straddle him and yell, "Hi-ho, Silver!"

Whatever was wrong, he intended to find out. But first he had to get the orphans to Hope House, and figure out a way to slip out from Adrienne's death grip on his neck.

After his third attempt to pry Adrienne's arms away, Dillon gave up. "I'll just sit in the back with the baby," he told Callie as if it were his choice. "You can drive."

Squashed in the backseat between Gina and Matt, Dillon tried his best to elicit the teen's help. "Maybe you could talk to her," he suggested. "She was attached to you before she was attached to me. I saw her reaching out her arms for you back at the bar."

There was definite mischief gleaming in the worldly eyes that met his. "She didn't like men before she met you," Gina said. "This is a breakthrough, and I'm not gonna mess with that. Think of it this way: you're saving Adrienne hours of shrink time later on in life."

She was far too smart for her own good, Dillon thought with reluctant amusement. But he still had a problem. "What happens when we get to Hope House and she won't let go?" Because no way could he leave her screaming and crying for him. After what Adrienne had already been through, he'd rather take a bullet.

"You'll have to rock her to sleep," Gina informed him. "That's what Mama always did, and what I've had to do since Mama died."

Well, if that wasn't enough information to shut him up, nothing was, Dillon mused with a pang of sympathy. He stared at the back of Callie's head, suspecting she was getting far too much enjoyment out of his awkward situation. "Take the next exit, then turn left at the light," he told her, willing her to look in the rearview mirror so that he could promise retribution with his eyes.

She kept her eyes glued to the road as she said, "Let's just hope Super Trooper isn't on duty tonight. He'd have a field day with you holding that baby without proper restraint."

"What's a super trooper?" Matt wanted to know.

As Dillon looked down at Matt, he saw Caleb staring solemnly back at him from his position by the door. For the first time that night, he realized that he hadn't heard the child speak one word. "It's a really dumb cop," Dillon told Matt. Then he turned to Gina and asked in a low voice, "What's wrong with Caleb? Why doesn't he talk?"

The teenager frowned. "He hasn't said a word since Mama's funeral. From what I've read, it's not unusual."

"We should get him to a counselor," Dillon whispered, his voice rough with emotion.

"Yeah, we should." And then Gina's chin angled skyward in a position that was fast becoming familiar to Dillon. "Don't worry; I'll take care of him."

"I have no doubt that you will." He lifted Adrienne higher to ease the tightness of her arms around his neck. The poor little thing was choking him. "I don't have a doubt in my mind, Gina."

"Good," she said in a shaky, I'm-barely-holding-on voice. "Because I mean it."

Dillon suspected Gina had been taking care of her siblings for longer than a week, but he held his tongue. It was obvious she loved her mother, however gullible and weak the woman might have been, and would tolerate no slander against her. What *he'd* like to do was get his hands on the in-laws, and shake a little kindness into them. How could they be so brutal, so callous? These kids had lost their mother.

When his jaw started to ache, he forced himself to relax. He could tell by the sudden weight against his chest that Adrienne had fallen asleep. Very gently he tried to ease her from him, but she immediately tightened her hold, whimpering.

He melted like a chocolate bar left on the dashboard of a car in the heat of summer. Time enough to make the separation, he decided, when they reached Hope House. With any luck Ruth, a volunteer Dillon knew to be great with children, would be on call to help Adrienne make the transition.

Callie had never felt more alive and awake in her life.

It was two A.M., and they were in Dillon's apartment after leaving Gina and her siblings at Hope House in the capable hands of Ruth Martin, a middle-aged woman whom Callie had liked on sight.

The last thirty minutes before leaving Hope House, Callie had stood in the doorway of Gina's new room, watching Dillon rock Adrienne to sleep in an old, obviously well-used rocking chair.

It was hard to believe he was the same man who had freaked over driving Ben around.

Curiosity about the man she now knew she loved

burned inside her. She wanted to know everything about him, from the tiniest confession to the biggest reason he lived and breathed every day.

She wanted to know badly enough to push his hand away when he reached for the strap of her infamous dress. Which was definitely saying something, since she wanted him so badly she could taste him.

Taking a sip of the white wine he'd poured, she eyed him speculatively over the rim. "You were petrified of Ben. Why?"

He covered his surprise instantly, but his disappointment at her rejection took a bit longer to hide. "You seem to know an awful lot about babies and kids. Why?"

"I'll tell you if you'll tell me."

"You first."

She smiled. "I don't *think* so. I asked you first."

With a fatalistic sigh, he leaned against the kitchen counter and folded his arms. But the heat in his eyes belied his relaxed position. "You're not going to be satisfied until I give you a reason, are you?"

"You're absolutely right." Just to make things interesting, Callie folded an arm under her breast, hiking the sheer dress even higher. An inch more and there wouldn't have been any need to *wear* a dress. Her shamelessness constantly surprised her.

His gaze dropped, scorched her exposed thighs, then jerked upward to her face. His eyes smoldered with a heat that drew the air from her lungs.

He was wicked. Downright dangerous.

Lethal.

"Okay," he said, deliberately staring at her mouth.

Callie had to resist the urge to lick her lips. He knew exactly what he was doing to her, and she *knew* that *he* knew it. *The rat.* Bracing herself, she thought of every horrible, disgusting thing she could think of.

She managed to keep her cool . . . barely. "I'm waiting," she said, tapping her foot.

"Fine, but I should warn you, it's not a funny story."

"Life isn't always funny," she said softly, thinking of Gina and her siblings. "Sometimes it's brutal and unfair."

"You got that right." Dillon's eyes darkened. The smile faded from his sensual mouth. "Although Wyatt and I are twins, we didn't always share the same friends. In fact, we usually couldn't *stand* each other's friends."

"Jealousy?"

Dillon shrugged. "Probably. One summer when I was about thirteen, I had this friend named Patrick. He and his parents had moved into the neighborhood at the beginning of the summer, and his mom had just had a baby, a girl, Patrick's only sibling. Just from hearing his parents talk, I knew they thought they'd never have another child after Patrick, so they were delirious about the baby."

Callie took a sip of her wine. She had a terrible feeling that she was going to need its numbing effect. "And Patrick?" she asked. "How did he feel about his new sister?"

"He loved her." Dillon grimaced. "Oh, he tried to act like he didn't, that she was just a nuisance, but I could tell that he adored her, just like his parents. At the time my baby sister, Isabelle, was about five. She was not only spoiled rotten; she was a pest. I remember feeling smug, knowing that someday Patrick's sister would be getting into *his* stuff and making him miserable.

223

"Anyway, one Friday night I slept over at Patrick's house, which I did pretty often. We pitched a tent in his backyard and stayed up most of the night talking and looking at *Hustler* magazines that Patrick had filched from the basement. The previous home owner had left them in an old suitcase that nobody had noticed. Patrick's mother woke us up around ten the next morning, and cooked us blueberry pancakes." Dillon's smile was both wistful and sad. "Funny how you remember little things like that. The syrup was blueberry, too. I think I ate a dozen of them, enough to give me a bellyache.

"As we were finishing breakfast, his mother asked Patrick if he'd keep an eye on the baby while she went shopping. The baby was down for her morning nap, and she didn't expect her to awaken for at least two hours. She had baby monitors in almost every room of the house, so it was easy to hear her when she cried.

"Patrick moaned and groaned, like a normal teenager, but in the end he said that he would. After making him promise he would check on his sister every thirty minutes, even if he didn't hear her, his mother left and Patrick and I went into the den to play Nintendo. I think it was Double Dragon. Anyway, we were kicking butt with the gangsters and time got away from us. We didn't remember the baby until we heard his mom's car door slam outside."

Dillon stared into his untouched wine. Callie could see his throat working, as if he were struggling to get the words out. Her heart began to hammer, but it had nothing to do with desire.

She knew where this was going, and now she wished she hadn't asked.

"Patrick asked me to go check on the baby while he

got rid of our milk glasses. His mother had a strict rule against eating or drinking in the living room. I raced upstairs to the nursery, remembering at the last moment to creep into the room." Dillon's eyes glittered as he looked at her. "I guess I saw Mom do it a hundred times when Isabelle was little, put her hand on her chest to make sure she was breathing. It was just a reflex action, or instinct, whatever you want to call it. If I hadn't done that . . . then I wouldn't have known right then. I wouldn't have been the one to find her."

"Oh, God." Callie bit the inside of her cheek to hold back a sob. She tasted the salt of tears on her mouth, and realized that she was crying. "SIDS?"

"Yeah." His voice was rough with emotion. "That's what they said. Nobody touched her. Nobody dropped her. She didn't even have a blanket over her. She just . . . stopped breathing."

She wiped at her face, but more tears came rolling down. "There was nothing you or Patrick could have done to stop it. You know that, don't you?"

He nodded. "I do now. But back then . . . Patrick was worse than I was about it. I don't know if he ever stopped blaming himself, even when his parents sent him to a grief counselor and she told him that he couldn't have done anything to prevent what happened."

"Well." Callie let out a shaky sigh. "I guess that explains why you're so freaked out when you're around kids."

One edge of his mouth tilted in a rueful grin. "Yeah, that explains it. I think I believed that if they could die for no reason, then they must be really fragile. Poor Mom. She had to sleep with Isabelle for the next six months. I refused to go to sleep unless Isabelle was in bed with her, even though she assured me that the risk of a child dying of SIDS drastically decreases after the age of two."

He grabbed the wine bottle and refilled her glass, a glint of wickedness returning to his eyes as the horror of his story began to fade. "So. What's *your* story? How come you know so much about kids?"

Callie wiped her face and smiled tremulously. She moved closer, his sharp intake of breath thrilling her. "I babysat a lot when I was a teenager."

He looked comically disappointed. "That's it? I give you the horror story of my life, and all you give me is *babysitting?*"

Laughing, she set her wineglass down and grabbed his tie, pulling him to her. Beneath her fingers, she felt the roughness of dried pizza sauce on his tie. "Let's see if I can make it up to you." She deliberately ran her tongue slowly over her lips, making him growl in frustration. "How about a shower?"

His brow rose. "Are you hinting that I need one?"

Dropping her voice to a sultry whisper, Callie said, "No. I'm hinting that we take one . . . together."

"Hell, yes! You did lose the bet, didn't you?" he asked hopefully. "You get to be the sensible one."

She sighed. "If I must." Leading him by his pizza sauce–encrusted tie, she tugged him in the direction of the bathroom.

Chapter Twenty

"Close your eyes," Callie ordered as she stood before Dillon in the bathroom. "I want to undress you."

Dillon groaned, but obeyed.

She started with his tuxedo jacket, rolling it from his broad shoulders, her breasts brushing his chest as she leaned forward to slip it from his arms.

His hands shot to her waist, but she firmly took them and pressed them to his sides again.

"No touching."

"No fair," he growled huskily. "You get to touch, but I don't?"

"I'm being sensible, so I'm calling the shots." Maybe it didn't sound fair, but that was the way Callie wanted it to be for the moment. The two-way touching too easily got out of control.

She finished removing his jacket, carefully folding it and setting it on the edge of the sink. His tie was next. Savoring the domestic feel of the simple act, she worked the knot loose and slowly slid his tie from his neck. She added it to the jacket, then went to work on the buttons of his shirt.

By the third button, she was beginning to pant.

"You're getting hot," Dillon whispered in a pleased voice.

"You think?" Her attempt at sarcasm fell short of the mark as her breath came out all fluttery and breathless. She glanced down at the bulge in his pants and smiled. "Looks like I'm not the only one." When he remained silent, she chuckled, going for the fourth button, then the fifth, and finally the sixth.

Holding her breath, she opened his shirt and pushed it from his shoulders. Dillon's arms and chest were hard, lean, and taut. He had the wiry, tough body of a man who loved physical activity, his waist narrow, with a ribbed, rock-hard belly and slim hips. His pants rode low and tempting on those hips, as if the slightest tug of her hands would send them sliding over his hips and down his hard, muscled thighs.

She could have tested her theory, but she wanted to prolong her sensual journey by slipping the button free and drawing the zipper slowly along its track.

Now it was *his* turn to hold his breath, as she let hers out in a slow, shaky stream of anticipation and need. Her eyes went wide when she realized he wasn't wearing any underwear.

He sprang free, thick and proud and shameless.

Her legs went weak. She took another deep, useless breath and pushed his pants over his tight buttocks so that they fell to his ankles.

He was beautiful.

In a half-pleading, aching voice, he said, "I would really, really like to open my eyes and watch you watching me."

"No!" she said more sharply than she intended. Dillon had a way of looking at her that turned her brain to mush. She couldn't risk it, not if she intended to carry out her wicked plan. Lowering the commode lid, she gave him a light push. "Sit down so that I can finish what I started."

He sat, his breath coming in quick, harsh bursts. She turned around and lifted one foot up to remove his shoe, then his sock. She did the same to the other leg, then pulled his pants free and tossed them onto the pile.

"*Now* is it my turn?"

She was tempted. Oh, was she tempted. But she knew that if she gave in, they'd never make it into the shower, and her plans involved lots of soap and hot water.

"No. Just keep your eyes closed and *don't touch me.*"

"Yes, mistress," he growled.

Ignoring his frustration-filled remark, she pulled the shower curtain aside and turned on the shower, adjusting the knobs until she got the temperature she wanted. She suspected Dillon wasn't accustomed to giving up control. With any luck, his first time would be painless and pleasurable.

"You can get into the shower now," she instructed, standing aside.

He disobeyed her and opened his eyes. His pupils were dilated, making his eyes look dark and smoky and sinfully sexy. "What about you? One good turns deserves another. . . ."

Mustering her willpower, Callie shook her head. "Not this time, Dillon. Just trust me, okay?"

He arched a wicked brow. "Trust you? Am I dreaming, or did you really just strip me naked? I didn't have to be watching to feel your eyes eating me alive, baby."

Since she was practically drooling, denying it would be pointless. Her voice was ragged and ridiculously weak as she commanded, "Get in the shower."

To Callie's relief, he stepped into the shower. She yanked the shower curtain closed, and in one quick move, pulled the little slip of a dress over her head. Taking a deep breath, she joined Dillon beneath the hot shower spray. When she reached around him for the soap, he sucked in a sharp breath, then muttered a curse that made her cheeks flame.

"Can you give me a hint? Because the anticipation is killing me."

Callie, feeling ludicrously shy, kept her eyes on his chest as she worked the bar of soap between her hands, forming a rich lather. "Let me show you. Just relax."

"Huh! Fat chance of *that* happening," Dillon growled teasingly, allowing her to turn him around so that his back was to her.

She began with his back, lathering every inch of his taut skin, sliding her hands down his buttocks, lingering, then back up again. Beneath her fingertips, his muscles clenched and quivered at her touch. His reaction made her bolder, more confident.

By the time she turned him around to face her, his jaw was clenched tight, and his eyes were nearly black with desire and barely suppressed control. Callie felt her lips twitch as she scolded, "You don't look relaxed, Dillon."

The softness of his voice belied his tense expression. "That's because I'm not, Callie, as I'm almost certain you're aware of. Why don't you give *me* the soap?"

"Nope." Callie laughed as she soaped her hands again and began to lather his shoulders and chest, drawing her nails lightly over his skin, lingering on his rigid nipples. "My turn to be sensible, remember?"

He groaned and braced his arms against the wall of the shower, unwittingly forcing her to move lower with the soap. "You call this . . . this *torture* being sensible?"

She stopped to look at him, lifting one brow in a wordless reminder of how sensible *he'd* been in the Jacuzzi. "You said it yourself. One good turn deserves another."

And then she dropped to her knees, closing both hands around his erection. As he hissed and braced himself, she worked her hands slowly up, then down, cupping his sac, squeezing, torturing, taunting. Reluctantly, she left him long enough to soap his powerful thighs, legs, and feet. "Rinse off," she instructed, remaining on her knees before him. After shooting her a look filled with the promise of retribution, he obeyed.

Anticipation burst like fireworks inside her. *He doesn't know,* she thought. He didn't know what she had planned for him.

She was waiting for him when he turned back around. Boldly holding his gaze this time, she curled a hand around his erection and brought it to her mouth. He was hard and incredibly huge, yet his skin felt like satin against her lips and tongue. She hesitated, watching him closely, recalling Lanny's rather callous remarks about her clumsy technique.

With her confidence shaken, it had been the first and last time she had attempted to bring him pleasure this way.

But as she watched Dillon fight for control, she realized, rather shockingly, that she was ravenous for the taste and feel of him, whereas with Lanny it had been

231

something she had attempted for *his* pleasure, not her own. Her newly discovered love for Dillon made the act feel natural, wildly erotic.

Satisfying beyond her wildest dreams.

She hadn't known a woman could feel so much pleasure *giving* pleasure to the man she loved. She took him deeper, finding a rhythm that had Dillon throwing back his head and howling like a wild beast.

As she watched him, the last self-imposed barrier came crashing down. She was raw, exposed, vulnerable.

And loving it.

Shuddering from the aftermath of his explosion, Dillon pulled Callie to her feet and crushed her against his heaving chest. The passionate, beyond-sexy woman in his arms had a way of humbling him to the point of unmanly tears.

It wasn't what she had done that humbled him; it was what she had sacrificed to give to him.

In the moments before he'd closed his eyes in ecstasy, he'd recognized the raw vulnerability in her eyes, followed by the dawning joy she'd found in loving him so thoroughly with her talented mouth.

The combination had caused an adrenaline rush like no other, intensifying his pleasure to an almost painful degree.

Callie had given him the gift of her trust, and he was most definitely humbled . . . as well as weak-kneed and sapped of strength and satiated to the point of giddiness.

Praying his legs would hold him, Dillon gathered her into his arms and stepped out of the shower. He didn't care about the dripping water or her halfhearted protests. Locking his mouth on hers, he carried her to his bed and gently laid her down.

He began to worship at her feet, and slowly work his way up. Dillon was a man who liked to keep his promises. . . .

Dillon hummed on his way to work the next day. He hummed as he entered the building and made for Luke's office. In fact, he was still humming when Mrs. Scuttle came out of her office and socked him in the jaw with a box of paper clips.

Stunned, he stared at the paper clips scattered all over his desk and the floor around his chair. His hammering heart belied his calm voice as he looked at the obviously deranged secretary. He felt thirteen again, right down to his embarrassingly squeaky voice as he asked, "What did I do?"

Mrs. Scuttle blinked rapidly. Dillon lost count after fifty before she bawled out, "Shame on you, Dillon Love! Shame, shame, shame!"

A guilty flush crept up Dillon's neck. Sure, he'd left a very sleepy, very satiated Callie in his bed, but how would Mrs. Scuttle know such a thing? Unless she had planted a homing device on Callie that day she came to the office, Dillon couldn't imagine how she *could* know.

Swallowing hard, he tried to keep the guilt from coloring his voice as he said, "Why don't you calm down and have a seat? Tell me what's bothering you. I'm sure as two mature adults, we can—" Too late, he saw the second box of paper clips in her hand. He tried to duck, but they bounced off his head and splattered against the wall behind him.

"Just because Luke broke the rules and ended up

hitched, that doesn't mean you can waltz in here and do the same!" she screeched, pointing an accusing finger in his direction.

She *did* know! Dillon's jaw dropped. He stuttered out, "How did you . . . ?"

The secretary slapped a hand to her hip and blinked at him with eyes that looked even bigger than normal. Bigger and madder.

"How do I know?" she demanded, looking around as if searching for something else to launch at him. "I know because her sister called this morning, looking for her."

"Callie?" Dillon asked, still confused.

Mrs. Scuttle toed off her shoe, bent down with remarkable ease for a woman her age, grabbed it up, and chucked it at his head.

Dillon ducked in the nick of time, inhaling the medicinal smell of Odor Eaters as the shoe went flying over his head to join the paper clips.

"Yes, Callie, you . . . you *tomcat!* Her sister was frantic, had been trying to call her at the hotel all night, but she never answered."

With an uneven gait—since she was missing one of her shoes—she stalked closer to his desk, and Dillon had to grip the edges to keep himself from bolting. Sweat popped out on his brow as he realized the numerous items on his desk that were now within the deranged woman's reach. A stapler, a cup filled with pens and sharp pencils; there was an empty coffee mug, several paperweights, a few odds and ends, and a lethal-looking letter opener that he knew he would never leave out in the open again.

She leaned forward, freezing him in place. Even at her angriest, his mother had never induced this type of terror. Maybe because he suspected Mrs. Scuttle was completely insane.

"Fontaine *knows* you're escorting her sister while she's here, so there was no sense trying to lie for you, mister."

Dillon couldn't be certain, but he suspected Mrs. Scuttle's calling him "mister" was not a good sign. Out of sheer desperation, he tried to bluff his way out of it. "Just because I'm her escort doesn't mean she was with me all night." There. He hadn't exactly lied, he had just tried to make a logical point that Callie *could* have been with someone else.

"Is that right?" Mrs. Scuttle said in a deceptively sweet voice. She grabbed a coaster from his desk and threw it—Frisbee style—at his chest. It stung, but Dillon managed to keep from flinching. "Don't you lie to me, Dillon Love. I saw the way you two looked at each other. Ms. Fontaine didn't sound too happy about that kind of shenanigans. She seems a little worried about what kind of man you might be, compromising your work ethic by sleeping with your client. She said that if you hurt her little sister, then she'd put this business so far under it would never see the light of day again."

"Maybe someone needs to remind Fontaine that her sister is a consenting adult," Dillon dared to suggest. He stiffened as the secretary reached for a paperweight. He didn't let out his breath until she let her arm fall again, apparently realizing she could actually do some serious damage with the object. Thank God she had *some* control over her temper.

"She might be a consenting adult, but she's also a client, and *you* decided to play escort for devious rea-

Sheridon Smythe

sons of your own. When a paid escort sleeps with a client, the law calls it prostitution."

Dillon had no control over the flush that slowly crept into his neck and face. "I'm not getting paid," he pointed out. He didn't think the little Bill Clinton game he and Callie were playing would wash with the secretary.

Mrs. Scuttle banged her fist on his desk and shouted, "Do you think that's gonna matter after it's all said and done? It's the company's reputation that's at stake here, not your gosh-darn morals, and not your gosh-darn nightclub!"

He was suddenly struck with the ludicrous notion that Mrs. Scuttle was wearing a disguise. She was seventy-nine years old, yet her mind was razor sharp, and she had the lungs of a football coach.

Not to mention the throwing arm of a major-league pitcher.

"You will not escort Callie Spencer again, you hear?"

Was she actually calming down? Very quickly, Dillon nodded. "Yes, ma'am, I hear you." For a long, squirming moment, Mrs. Scuttle glared at him with her big owlish eyes.

"I'll assign someone else to her," she said, definitely with less heat. "And after you finish up helping Luke"—her derisive snort made Dillon flush again— "you can court Callie Spencer till the cows come home." When he didn't answer, she bawled out so suddenly it made Dillon jump, "Are you listening, son?"

"Yes, ma'am!"

"Because if you aren't," she threatened, "I've got a thing or two back on my desk that I could use to knock the wax from your ears."

"No, no. I'm fine." Dillon wiggled a desperate finger

236

in his ear and flashed her a goofy grin. "See? No wax there. I hear you perfectly well. Loud and clear." As had half of Atlanta, Dillon suspected, but didn't say.

He didn't relax until the door to Mrs. Scuttle's office had slammed shut. The sonic boom alone would have disintegrated any remaining wax in his ears. He blew out a sigh and allowed himself to relax.

Eventually a smile tugged at the corners of his mouth. For all her ferocity and missile launching, he couldn't fault Mrs. Scuttle's loyalty to Luke and the company. He would heed her warning. He even felt a little shame about risking Mr. Complete's reputation.

But the secretary had said he couldn't *escort* Callie.

She had mentioned nothing about Dillon seeing Callie on his own time.

Chapter Twenty-one

Callie had just stepped out of the shower when her hotel phone jangled.

She grabbed a towel and sat on the side of the bed to answer it. "Hello?" she asked breathlessly, half expecting it to be Dillon calling with a heated reminder about their fantastic night.

There was a telling silence before Fontaine said, "My God. You've had sex!"

Blushing furiously and fully prepared to deny it, Callie flopped back onto her pillows. "Hello, Fontaine. How's your ankle?"

"My ankle is broken and it hurts like hell. You've had sex. Deny it. I dare you."

"Okay, I'm denying it. I have not had sexual intercourse." Callie smothered a laugh with her hand. If she knew Fontaine, her sister would catch on fairly quickly. "And even if I had," Callie continued, "I thought you'd be happy. Delirious. Jumping for joy. Your mousy little sister has once again joined the land of the living." And that was a major understatement, Callie thought, blushing all over again.

"I *am* happy . . . It's who you're not having intercourse with that concerns me. He's a paid escort, Callie. If he's risking the company's reputation by *not* having intercourse with you, then chances are good that he's *not* having intercourse with his other clients. I'm worried about his motives."

Callie's stomach took a sickening nosedive. Leave it to her sister to point out what she had been too blind to even consider. Still, loving Dillon the way she did, she felt compelled to defend him. "Maybe you're wrong. Maybe he's never been this tempted before. Is that too difficult for you to believe?"

Fontaine sucked in a sharp breath. "My God, Callie. Are you saying you think he loves you?"

"No!" Callie gripped the phone and closed her eyes tightly, trying to figure out how she was going to extract herself from the mess she'd made in the last few moments. She should have anticipated how Fontaine would react to her relationship with Dillon. Fontaine wanted her to be happy. On the other hand, she was deathly afraid—as Callie had been—that someone like Lanny would come along and stomp on her little sister's heart again.

And in Fontaine's eyes, Dillon was someone like Lanny.

"Look," Fontaine said in her most gentle, I-care-what-happens-to-you voice. "When I called the office at Mr. Complete—"

"*What?*" Callie shot upright, her heart hammering against her rib cage so furiously it hurt. "Oh, God. Tell me that you didn't!"

"I did!" Fontaine shot back, clearly on the defensive now. "When I couldn't get you at the hotel, I got worried."

Through gritted teeth, Callie said, "I could have been sleeping."

"Um, I knew that you weren't," Fontaine admitted reluctantly. "I frightened the manager into checking your room."

Callie groaned and slapped a hand to her forehead.

"That was at five this morning," Fontaine continued. "So I knew by then that you hadn't come in. It doesn't take a rocket scientist to figure it out from there."

"Thanks, Fontaine," Callie said, letting her fury show. "Your unwarranted concern has probably cost Dillon his job."

"Rules are rules. If he broke them, then he should be prepared to pay the consequences."

"Says who?"

"Says your sister!"

"Okay." Callie forced herself to remain outwardly calm; inside she was beginning to boil. "As *your* sister, I have the right to ask you to stay out of my business. You wanted me out of my shell. Well, I'm out of it, and having a blast. Stop being a hypocrite and just be happy for me."

"And if you get hurt?"

Ignoring the way her heart clenched at the probability, Callie said firmly, "Then I get hurt. Some things are worth the risk. You might consider that before you dump another great guy because you're afraid of commitment."

Callie hung up the phone while her sister was still sputtering. It was time Fontaine concentrated on her own insecurities, insecurities she probably thought Callie didn't know about.

A knock at the door had Callie scrambling for the thick cotton terry robe the hotel provided. As she passed the mirror on the way to the door, she saw that her cheeks were still flushed with anger, and her eyes were dark with worry.

She opened the door to find Dillon on the threshold, right on time. The moment their gazes met, desire flared hot and wild between them. How could that be? Callie wondered rather dazedly.

"I'm not dressed," she said faintly, stating the obvious.

His unhurried gaze drifted slowly over her. A faint smile curved his sensuous mouth. "I'll wait in the hall."

"Fontaine?" Callie asked with a fatalistic sigh.

He shook his head, a hint of mischief in his eyes. "Mrs. Scuttle, two boxes of paper clips, and one size-seven nurse's shoe. I'm afraid I can't escort you anymore." Before Callie could express her disappointment, he added, "But she didn't say I couldn't see you on my own time."

"I'm sorry. Thank God you didn't get fired." She felt her nipples pucker beneath the robe, and wondered how they could possibly find the energy. "Does this mean we're still on for today?"

"I should say so. It doesn't have anything to do with Mr. Complete, so I think we're in the clear." His voice deepened. "Now, unless you want to spend the day in bed, I suggest you shut the door, lock it, and get dressed."

With a squeal of feigned fright, Callie did just that.

"Are you certain I could pass for a lawyer?" Callie asked Dillon for the third time.

They were standing on a porch in front of a three-story house in a neighborhood that practically shouted "old money." Dillon had just rung the doorbell. They were here to confirm Gina's story.

He looked at Callie again. She had traded her contacts for eyeglasses, and she wore her hair pulled back into a tight chignon. The beige linen suit she wore emphasized her slim hips and long legs.

Dillon's pulse picked up as he drawled, "No, but then, I've seen you naked."

She socked him playfully with the briefcase she had borrowed from the hotel manager.

Seconds later, the massive front door opened. A slim, middle-aged woman with cold blue eyes regarded them warily.

Beside him, he heard Callie take a deep breath. He silently cheered her on.

"Hello, I'm Attorney LaVonda Wallace, Jackie's sister, and this is my assistant, Dillon Kramer. Are you Jackie's mother-in-law?"

The woman recoiled in shock, but recovered quickly, her instant acceptance that Callie was who she said she was confirming what Gina had told them about her stepgrandmother; she had never seen her aunt LaVonda.

So far, so good.

Still clutching a beringed hand to her flat chest, the woman stuttered, "Yes, yes. I'm Jackie's mother-in-law, Becky Monroe. Or was. She's—"

"I know," Callie inserted with genuine sorrow. "I got a letter from Gina a few days ago, telling me what happened. I came as fast as I could."

"Gina?"

From the corner of his eye, Dillon saw Callie lift a

questioning brow. She was good. She was very good. But then, he wasn't surprised. He'd already discovered that Callie possessed many hidden talents. He sternly steered his thoughts in a different direction.

"Yes, Gina. My niece?" Callie injected just the right amount of puzzlement into her voice. "They *were* living with Jackie at the time of her . . . death?"

"Of course. Your niece." Becky Monroe swallowed visibly. "You'll have to excuse me. I'm a little shocked to find out that Jackie's sister is . . . is a lawyer."

Callie frowned. "I'm not following you."

"Um, never mind. Is there something I can do for you? I have Jackie's personal belongings packed in a box—"

"I'm here for the children," Callie interrupted.

Becky's jaw went slack with dismay. Dillon didn't know about Callie, but he was growing sicker by the moment.

"The . . . the children?" Becky parroted, obviously stalling while she brainstormed an acceptable story.

Dillon didn't want Callie to give her time. She didn't deserve it.

Callie apparently agreed. "I realize that you'll probably want to keep Adrienne, since she's your biological granddaughter, but I'm here to take Gina, Matt, and Caleb back to California with me."

Faced with the unavoidable, Becky looked positively green around the gills. "I . . . they . . . they aren't here."

When she didn't elaborate, Callie checked her watch, frowned at Dillon, then at Becky. "When will they be back?"

"I . . . don't know."

"What do you mean, you don't know?" Callie asked sharply.

Becky backed up a step, grabbing the door as if she intended to slam it shut any second.

Just in case, Dillon was prepared to sacrifice his foot to ensure that she didn't succeed.

"They ran away."

Callie looked convincingly alarmed. "What? Well, they couldn't have gone far, could they? The didn't have a car, right?"

The woman shook her head vigorously. "No, they didn't."

"How long have they been gone? Have you notified the police?" Callie rubbed her temples as if she were truly distraught. "I can't believe Gina would leave her baby sister. She loved her very much."

If possible, Becky turned even whiter. "Um, yes, it is hard to believe, isn't it? As for calling the police, we didn't want to get Gina into trouble. We hoped she'd come back on her own."

"How long have they been gone?" Callie asked again.

"Since . . . since last Tuesday."

"Oh, God," Callie whispered. "Anything could have happened to them in that length of time. They could be living in a Dumpster. May we come in? I need to call the police, and I'd like to see Adrienne while I'm here."

"She's asleep," Becky lied quickly, making no move to let them inside. "Maybe you can contact the police from your hotel room? Adrienne is a light sleeper, and she's cranky when she doesn't get her nap." She started to ease the door shut, even as she spoke. "Good luck finding them, and please let me know. I've been worried sick about them."

Because Dillon didn't trust himself, he let the lying,

coldhearted woman shut the door. But Callie, apparently, had other ideas. She reached for the doorknob, cursing beneath her breath.

So much for her acting abilities. Apparently there was a time limit.

Dillon hooked an arm around her waist and swung her from the porch. She struggled, cursing like a sailor. It was obvious she wanted to draw blood.

"Can you believe that bitch?" she snarled. "She didn't care; she was just glad they'd disappeared!"

Still carrying her, Dillon headed for his Jeep.

"And she had the nerve to lie and pretend she had Adrienne! How could anyone be that . . . that . . ."

"Heartless? Selfish?" Dillon opened the passenger door and deposited her gently onto the seat. He placed a hard, meant-to-shock kiss on her mouth, momentarily silencing her. When he drew back, tears were swimming in her gorgeous dark blue eyes.

"What was that for?" she whispered.

"That was for wanting to beat the snot out of Becky Monroe."

"You should have let me." Her bottom lip trembled. A tear broke free and trailed down her face. "Gina didn't lie to us, Dillon. They really are monsters."

Grimly, he said, "I know, baby. I know." This time when he kissed her, he was tender and loving. She tasted of salt and sorrow, and he wanted badly to haul her into his arms and hold her until she smiled again. Because it wasn't the right time or place for comforting, he shut the door and went around to the driver's side.

When he got in, Callie said, "If Gina's aunt doesn't call, I want to help her get custody of her siblings." She wiped at her face and took a shuddering breath as Dillon backed out of the driveway. "In fact, even if LaVonda *does* call and wants them, she'll need some financial help, and I've got a divorce settlement I'll never touch."

As he listened to her passionate speech, a revelation hit Dillon, sending his heart into a wild spasm of panic and joy.

He was in love with Callie Spencer.

Mrs. Scuttle possessed a twisted sense of humor, Callie thought ruefully as she sat across from Wyatt in one of Atlanta's finest restaurants. She wouldn't give Callie Dillon, but she would give her Dillon's mirror image.

The secretary was either punishing Callie for tempting one of her "boys," or she was attempting to be sympathetic to her cause.

"You look preoccupied about something," Callie said to Wyatt. They had both ordered a Cobb salad to complement the lamb chops the waiter would be bringing shortly. So far the service and the food had been top-notch. "Want to share?"

Wyatt rewarded her with a faint smile, but his frown remained. "I'd love to, but . . . what the hell. Dillon doesn't think we can trust you, but that doesn't mean I have to agree. Mom's seeing Will Tallfeather behind our backs. She's stayed over at his place two nights this week."

Callie calmly laid her fork aside. The fact that Dillon didn't trust her stung a little. "Are you certain? I mean, not that I think there's anything wrong with her dating a younger man. She just doesn't seem the type."

"I know what you mean." He sighed and dropped his fork into his half-eaten salad. "I want her to be happy, and I know that Dillon does, too. I think we're both afraid she'll get hurt."

It was on the tip of Callie's tongue to blurt out that her sister felt the same way about *her*, but she wisely held back. "Why don't you and Dillon talk to her about it? Mary doesn't strike me as the kind of person who would get angry because her children are worried about her." Wyatt's sudden flush intrigued her.

"Maybe not, but I'm certain she won't like the fact that I've been following her. Since she hasn't mentioned Will to us, she'd know in a heartbeat."

"Ah. I see your dilemma. Until she gets ready to tell you, you can't let on that you know."

"Exactly."

She picked up her fork again and stabbed a cherry tomato. "And Dillon didn't trust me because he thought I would tell Mary that her sons are stalking her."

"He said you and Mom hit it off."

"We did." When Wyatt merely lifted a brow, Callie went on. "But that doesn't mean I would feel comfortable meddling in her business. She seems like a sensible woman to me." There was absolutely nothing she could do about the blush that crept into her face at the mention of the word *sensible*. She knew that as long as she lived, she would never be able to speak or hear that word without thinking of Dillon.

In the Jaccuzzi.

In the shower.

On the bed.

"So you think we should just chill and see what happens?"

Callie shrugged. "Depends. How well do you know Will?"

"Well . . . that's the kicker. I don't really know him that well. He got hired about six months ago, and Luke's being pretty close-mouthed about his background."

She couldn't resist a chuckle as she said, "And that's driving you guys a bit crazy, right?" She laughed out loud at Wyatt's guilty blush. "Just because he doesn't talk about himself doesn't mean he has something to hide."

"Maybe. But that doesn't mean that he *doesn't* have something to hide, either. We tell *him* everything," Wyatt grumbled.

The waiter arrived with their lamb chops. Callie waited until he'd gone before she ventured, "Can we go dancing after dinner?"

Wyatt cut into one of his lamb chops, pausing with his fork in midair to reply, "Sure, as long as we're not out too late. I've got Operation Aunt LaVonda starting at seven in the morning."

He didn't have to elaborate. Callie knew that he meant he would be taking a shift at the Laundromat in case Gina's aunt LaVonda called. "Okay. I thought we might drop in at the Love Nest. Dillon and I have been trying to get there, but every time we plan it, something goes . . ." Callie stared at Wyatt's reddening face in alarm. "Wyatt? Are you okay? My God, are you choking?" When he flapped his hand in front of his face and nodded, Callie shot out of her chair and hurried to him.

It wasn't easy getting her arms around his broad chest from behind him, but she managed.

The bite of lamb chop popped out at her first attempt to squeeze the life out of him. She heard him suck desperately for air, and felt his lungs expand. On legs that trembled from the adrenaline surging through her, Callie stumbled back to her chair. It had all happened so fast.

Wyatt remained standing, taking a hasty sip of his water. "Thanks for saving my life," he said in a croaky voice. "I, um, need to visit the little boy's room."

"Wait! Are you sure you're okay, Wyatt?" She thought he looked pale, but then, she probably was, too, after that harrowing experience. It was the first time she had saved someone from choking, and she hoped it would be the last.

"I'm fine, fine." Wyatt slammed his water glass onto the table and headed in the direction of the restrooms.

Callie took the opportunity to take notes about the restaurant while Wyatt was gone, using a small notebook she'd gotten from the hotel manager. When she saw Wyatt returning, she put it away, uncomfortable playing judge and jury with someone watching. Not that she had anything bad to say about the restaurant, which would probably not make Fontaine happy.

The second Wyatt's butt hit the chair, his cell phone rang.

With a definite feeling of premonition, Callie watched Wyatt answer it. She saw his expression go from polite interest to frowning worry. By the time he hung up the phone, Callie's instincts were on red alert.

"You're never going to believe this," Wyatt began.

"Let me guess." Callie smiled sweetly at his non-plused expression. "One of the 'boys' is having a crisis, and you've just got to help out."

Wyatt looked dumbfounded. "How did you know?"

"Because Dillon has pulled this stunt on me twice already, and each time it happened, I had mentioned something about going to the Love Nest." She stared at her fidgeting escort long and hard. "It doesn't take a rocket scientist to figure out that you and Dillon don't want me going to this nightclub. The *big* question is . . . why?"

"I . . . you . . ."

When Wyatt floundered, Callie leaned back and folded her arms. "I'm waiting."

Looking trapped, Wyatt finally burst out, "Okay, okay! The truth is . . . the Love Nest is a gay bar."

"Nice try, but that doesn't make sense. Why wouldn't you—or Dillon—just tell me that instead of going to extremes to keep me away from there?"

"Well, because . . . well, because we were afraid you'd give it a bad review. A good friend of Greg's owns the bar." Wyatt spread his hands in a helpless gesture. "There you have it."

Callie supposed it made sense . . . but there were a few holes in his story. "I was there, remember? It didn't look like a gay bar to me. In fact, a couple nearly ran me over as I was going in."

"Are you *positive* it was a man and a woman?" Wyatt challenged.

"Well, I . . ." Callie realized that she couldn't be absolutely certain. Besides, that wasn't really the point, was it? "Have I given you or Dillon any reason to believe I'm homophobic?"

Wyatt shook his head. "No, you haven't."

"Good, because I'm not the least bit homophobic, and I wouldn't give the nightclub a bad review because of its sexual orientation. In fact"—she didn't have to fake the hurt in her tone—"I'm upset that you and Dillon would think I was that narrow-minded."

"I'm sorry. You're so right. We were being thoughtless."

"Apology accepted." Callie picked up her knife and

fork and began to eat her cold lamb chops. "Then it's settled? We go to the Love Nest after dinner?"

"No."

Callie froze and looked at him, exasperated. "Why not?"

"Because I think Greg should take you. In fact, I think you would hurt his feelings if you didn't go with him. He'll want to introduce you to his friends."

"Fine," Callie said, exhausted by the entire conversation. "I'll ask Greg to take me."

"This Saturday night."

She started to ask him what was so special about Saturday night, but decided she'd had enough confusion for one night.

"Oh, and one other thing," Wyatt said. "Could we keep this conversation between us? Dillon was eventually going to tell you about the Love Nest himself. He was, um, trying to work up the nerve. He really hates it when I jump the gun on him."

Callie waved a careless fork at him. "Mum's the word, although I still don't know what the big deal is."

Chapter Twenty-two

"Twenty bucks says he's a wrestler, probably local."

Dillon studied the huge, bald, tattooed man talking on the one and only working pay phone in the Laundromat for a moment longer before he said, "You're on. I think he's a member of the Hell's Angels. Did you see that souped-up Harley outside?"

Wyatt, who was leaning against the washing machine next to Dillon, snorted. "Circumstantial evidence. I owned a Harley, and I wasn't a member of the Hell's Angels."

"Yeah, but look at those tattoos. Skulls and crossbones . . . an angel with horns. Could he be more obvious?"

"Maybe he just wants everyone to think he's a member. What do you *think* he weighs, three-fifty? Four hundred?"

"At least. Most of it muscle. Probably bench-lifts six hundred. How long did you say he's been on the phone?" Dillon had arrived thirty minutes earlier to relieve Wyatt of Operation Aunt LaVonda, and the biker/wrestler had been on the phone then.

Checking his watch, Wyatt said, "An hour and twenty minutes. He called collect. Whoever he's talking to is going to have one hell of a phone bill."

"In the meantime, Aunt LaVonda could be trying to call Gina."

"Think we could take him?"

Dillon gave it a nanosecond's thought before he shook his head. "Don't be an idiot. Even if we could, what would we do with him? Stuff him in a dryer?"

"I guess you have a point." Wyatt looked at Dillon. "Why don't you ask him to get off the phone?"

"Why don't *you?*" Dillon countered.

"I've got a better idea. Let's get Fish."

"I've got an even better idea. Why don't we just wait until he gets off the phone? If Aunt LaVonda got Gina's letter and tries to call, she won't give up just because she gets a busy signal." Dillon elbowed his twin. "Don't you have something better to do? I came to relieve you."

"Yeah, I do have better things to do, but I wanted to talk to you about Mom first. I have a plan involving two birds and one stone."

Nudging the laundry sack full of dirty socks with his toe, Dillon sighed. "I'm probably going to regret this . . . but here goes. What's your plan?"

"The two birds are Mom and these poor kids. The stone is a fund-raiser at Mom's house for Gina and her siblings. We'll invite all of the escorts and their families, of course."

"Including Will," Dillon muttered darkly.

"Including Will," Wyatt agreed. "Watch them together. Maybe we'll get some idea of what's going on between the two of them."

"Not a bad idea, for a brat."

"Is that a compliment?" Wyatt asked. "Because if that's a compliment, you could have left off the 'brat' part."

"Then your head would swell . . . and you'd wind up looking like the Jolly Green Giant over there." Dillon laughed at Wyatt's chagrined expression before he said, "What makes you think Mom will go for a fund-raiser, anyway?"

"Are you kidding? You know Mom. When we tell her Gina's story, she'll be putty in our hands. It could be a potluck sort of fund-raiser. Everyone could donate whatever they feel comfortable donating."

Dillon thought about Callie and her vow to help Gina, one way or the other. "Sounds like a plan. Who's going to work on Mom?"

Wyatt grinned. "I thought we'd send Callie in first. You said she and Mom had bonded."

Mentioning Callie reminded Dillon of something very important. "I don't know, Wyatt. Everyone managed to keep their mouths shut about the nightclub the day of the barbecue at Ivan's house. I don't know if we could get so lucky a second time."

"Sure we could. I'll remind everyone personally. They know what's at stake. Besides, like I told you, the unveiling is this Saturday night. Greg's escorting her. You're going to lurk in the kitchen making sure everything runs smoothly there, and I'm going to be 'helping' Lou at the bar. By Sunday, Callie will have written her review and it won't matter if she finds out."

Could his brother possibly be that naive? Dillon wondered. *He* broke out in a cold sweat just thinking about her reaction. No, if Dillon knew Callie—and he believed that he did—she was not going to be happy to discover that he had lied to her about the nightclub. "I don't want her hearing the news from someone else," Dillon said. "It has to come from me." And even then he was going to have to use a crowbar to pry it from his own jaws.

"Got it."

"When do you want to throw this fund-raiser?"

"I was thinking Sunday would be a good day. The nightclub is closed, and most of the escorts are free." Wyatt pointed a finger at Dillon. "And *you* can make sure Will isn't working. We definitely want that mother-stealing weasel to be there."

"And Mrs. Scuttle? Do we invite her?" Dillon rubbed his jaw ruefully. "I'm not sure it would be safe."

"Are you kidding? I'm putting Mrs. Scuttle in charge of collecting donations." Wyatt's grin was smug. "That pretty much guarantees nobody will hand her anything smaller than a fifty."

Dillon burst out laughing. "Yeah, that pretty much guarantees it." He caught a movement from the corner of his eye and straightened abruptly. "Hey, Bigfoot's off the phone."

Beside him, Wyatt stiffened. "Yeah, and he's heading our way."

The big guy reached them. He was scowling. "You guys happen to have change for a dollar? I gotta get some fabric softener out of the machine. My old lady says I gotta do the whole damned basket of laundry over."

Dillon and Wyatt gaped at him.

Wyatt, of course, couldn't resist. He fished out four quarters and exchanged it for the dollar bill the man was holding out. "You've been talking to your wife for an hour and a half about *laundry?*"

The man's scowl deepened. He ran a distracted hand over his clean-shaven head and heaved a weary sigh. "Yeah. We just had a baby a couple of weeks ago. The first hour of our conversation was her telling me how to pretreat the stains—which I also forgot to do the first time around." He stomped to a folding table and grabbed up a basket of laundry, still muttering. "I get the stains, but I don't get why I have to use fabric softener. They didn't have fabric softener back in my grandmama's day, and we managed just fine."

When he was out of earshot, Dillon looked at Wyatt, who stared back at him, his eyes laughing. "You know what Mom would say, don't you?" Dillon asked.

His twin nodded. "She'd say, 'Don't judge a man by his tattoos.'"

"Exactly."

An hour and four root beers later, Wyatt was still staring at his gloomy face in the gleaming new mirrors they had installed on the dance floor wall. Lou and Fish were already bitching about how hard they were to keep clean.

He was no closer to solving his immediate problem of what to do about Callie and Saturday night. When she'd caught on to his game—which, apparently, his dear brother had run into the ground—he'd had no choice but to improvise.

So he'd told her the Love Nest was a gay bar.

Big mistake.

He'd tried to work up the courage to tell Dillon what he'd done, but he'd chickened out. To prevent Dillon from going into cardiac arrest, he also would have had to tell him that he was fairly certain Callie wasn't a reviewer. To do that, he'd have to admit that he'd suspected all along, but had been enjoying watching Dillon face a challenge for a change.

Three big reasons for Dillon to go ahead and kill him, or worse, never speak to him again. He'd carried the game too far for it to be funny any longer. Before he'd really known Callie, he hadn't thought it would be a big deal to her to find out that Dillon had been charming the pants off her so that she'd go easy on Atlanta in her reviews.

But now that Wyatt knew Callie, knew about her past and how badly she'd been hurt, he wasn't at all certain she would find the truth funny, especially if she didn't believe that Dillon had actually fallen in love with her.

Wyatt took a drink of his root beer and sighed. What to do, what to do?

He could go to Callie and tell her the truth about everything.

In which case he would die a slow and torturous death at the hands of his brother.

He could go to Dillon and confess everything.

In which case he would die a slow and torturous death at the hands of his brother.

Or . . . he could find a way to fool Callie into believing the Love Nest really was a gay bar, keep Dillon in the kitchen so he wouldn't know until after she'd gone, then lock Dillon in the cooler and explain everything with three inches of cold steel between them. He'd explain how it had started out as a joke, but had become so complicated Wyatt hadn't known how to come clean without possibly mucking up Dillon's budding romance with Callie.

Once he told Dillon that Callie wasn't a reviewer, his brother wouldn't have any reason to be mad, right? And surely he would understand how irresistible it had been for Wyatt not to tell Dillon when he realized Callie wasn't who she claimed to be? If Dillon had been in *his* shoes . . . okay, scratch that. Dillon wasn't and never had been the practical joker in the family.

But that was beside the point. The point was, it wasn't *his* fault Dillon had been too much in lust to see for himself that Callie was lying about her reasons for being in Atlanta. And it wasn't *his* fault that Dillon was too stubborn to see that even if Callie *was* a bona fide reviewer, she would be fair and honest because that was who she was.

So he was back to three not-so-very-good choices.

Blow the whole thing wide-open with Callie.

Tell all to Dillon and beg his forgiveness.

Or continue mucking things up in the name of love and laughter.

Not entirely certain he was making the right choice, Wyatt took out his cell phone and dialed Greg's number. When Greg answered, Wyatt muttered a quick prayer and said, "Greg, how many gay people do you know and what would it take to get them to come to the Love Nest Saturday night?"

After a moment of thoughtful silence, Greg told him. Wyatt felt the color drain from his face.

Without a twinge of guilt, Dillon admired Callie's wiggling butt as she leaned over the laundry basket, buried up to her elbows in clean socks. She emerged seconds later, triumphantly holding up two matching socks.

Her cheeks were flushed, her hair mussed in a sexy way that had Dillon hyperventilating, and she had a definite gleam in her eyes that told Dillon she knew it.

"Got it! Now it's your turn."

Sorting and folding socks. Who would have guessed Callie could turn such a mundane chore into something naughty and fun? Dillon shook his head, smiling ruefully as he took his turn at the basket. He could feel Callie watching him every bit as unabashedly as he had watched her.

"Your butt is the bomb," Callie murmured, making him chuckle and blush.

Just for kicks, he took a little longer than necessary to find a match among the three dozen socks in the basket. By the time he turned around, Callie was breathing hard. Dressed in a short skirt and a matching cropped top in some type of clingy T-shirt material, she looked carefree and sexy as hell.

Because they weren't alone in the Laundromat, Dillon did his best to take his mind off the fact that he wanted to hoist her onto a washing machine and have his way with her. "I can't believe you prefer to spend your afternoons in a hot Laundromat when you could be enjoying the hotel pool or spa."

She shrugged, making the cropped top rise and giving him a glimpse of her belly button. Hopping onto a spinning washer to level the machine out, she eyed him speculatively for a long moment before she spoke. "I guess I can tell you, now that I really am doing the reviews."

Dillon's face froze with shock. He struggled to sound casual as he said, "Tell me . . . what?"

"Don't get your feelings hurt. I would have told you before, but I swore to Fontaine that I wouldn't let anyone know. The whole point of my being a decoy was so people would think I was here to review."

The basket of unfolded socks was forgotten. Dillon felt a swirling sensation in his gut, and it wasn't pleasant. "A decoy? You aren't here to do the reviews?"

She laughed. "Well, yeah, I am now. Someone's been calling ahead wherever Fontaine goes, alerting the businesses, so she sent me in as a decoy. She was going to come later . . . when everyone thought the reviews were over. But she broke her ankle, so I have to do them for real." Callie cast him a coy smile and crooked her finger.

Like a puppet, Dillon obeyed. He was too dazed to do anything else.

"The problem is, she says I'm too easy to please." Her eyes darkened, her lids drooping as she tugged at him until he was standing between her legs. "What do *you* think, Dillon? Am I too easy to please?"

He was absolutely certain she wasn't talking about restaurants, nightclubs, or hotels. For the first time since he'd met her, Dillon had trouble concentrating on sex or how not to have it. "Maybe the service is just unbeatable," he finally managed, trying to sort out the facts in his head. What she'd told him made sense. The manager at Marie's had said she'd gotten a warning the week before Callie arrived.

The news was still a shock.

Callie hadn't been a reviewer when she first came to Atlanta, but now she was. All this time he'd been worried about his business and others in the city, she'd been nothing but a very pretty, very distracting decoy.

Now she was a very pretty, very distracting *reviewer*.

Her thighs tightened against his hips. "So I thought maybe you could help me be more . . . impartial. You *live* in Atlanta. Who would know better than someone who regularly goes to the local restaurants and nightclubs? Naturally, I'll have to be on my own when it comes to the hotels, but I think I can handle that part. Think you could help me?"

He couldn't help her, of course. When she found out

that he owned the Love Nest, she would never believe that he could be impartial about any of it.

"Greg's taking me to the Love Nest Saturday night," Callie said, startling Dillon. "Maybe afterward you and I could get together in my hotel room and um, debate the pros and cons." She licked her lips, making them glisten. "I want to be fair, and it's like you said before, how can I be fair if I've been to a place only one time?"

Dillon was literally saved by the bell. "The phone! It's ringing!" He raced to it, Callie fast on his heels. Breathlessly, he snatched it from the hook and said, "Hello?" Callie pressed her ear as close to his as she could get.

There was an alarming silence before a female voice said, "I'm trying to reach my niece, Gina Stone. This is the number she gave me—"

Callie yanked the phone from his ear, her excitement over the top. "Yes! Yes! Aunt LaVonda? I mean, LaVonda Wallace?"

"Gina?"

Laughing and crying at the same time, Callie said, "No, I'm not Gina, but we know her. We're taking turns staying at the Laundromat for Gina so we wouldn't miss your call."

"Is she okay? Are the kids okay?"

"Yes, yes. They're fine. They're staying at a homeless—"

"Oh, my God!"

"No, no," Callie hastened to assure her. "It's a very nice place, I promise. It's a beautifully restored plantation—"

Dillon gently plucked the phone from Callie's hand. "Mrs. Wallace? This is Dillon Love. We're sorry about your sister."

"Thanks." The woman's voice broke. "I wish I could

have been there for the funeral, but I just today got Gina's letter. It was forwarded to me from my old address. Why . . . why aren't they staying with Jackie's in-laws?"

"We found them in a Dumpster—"

"Oh, my God!"

Callie snatched the phone back, casting Dillon a chiding look. "They hadn't been there long, and it was a new Dumpster, very nice, actually. They had a couch, and an end table—"

Once again Dillon retrieved the phone, looking exasperated. "We took them for pizza and got the story from Gina. Apparently the in-laws were talking about calling social services, since they didn't know how to contact you."

Glaring at Dillon, Callie leaned close and shouted into the receiver, "I highly doubt they would have tried!"

"She does have a point," Dillon conceded. "We wanted to verify Gina's story, so Callie and I—"

"Who's Callie?" LaVonda broke in to ask with bewilderment.

"She's a reviewer from California, and I was escorting her at the time my twin brother heard the baby crying—"

"Oh, my God!"

This time Dillon just handed Callie the phone before she could yank it from his hands. Apparently neither of them could tell the story without alarming LaVonda.

"Listen, LaVonda. What you have to keep in mind is that they are all okay. Yes, Adrienne was with them in the Dumpster. Gina said that his parents didn't believe Adrienne belonged to Donny—"

"That's bullshit!" LaVonda cried angrily. "My sister

might have been gullible about men, but she wasn't a tramp. I *knew* she was making a mistake marrying into that snotty family! If I hadn't been in the middle of taking the bar exams—"

Callie dropped the phone. It dangled for a moment before Dillon reached for it. "She's a lawyer," Callie whispered, looking dazed by the revelation. "She's really a lawyer!"

"Sorry," Dillon said, feeling dazed himself. "You gave us a shock by telling us you're a lawyer."

"I'm not following you," LaVonda replied a little haughtily, and *Dillon* nearly dropped the phone.

He shook his head, deciding some things were better left unanswered. "We'll explain later," he said. "Right now we need—Gina needs—to know if you want the children to come live with you. If not, she's prepared to go to a judge and beg for custody of her siblings."

LaVonda's voice broke again as she said, "Of course I want them to come live with me!"

Dillon swallowed a suspicious lump in his throat. "Let me give you the number at Hope House, where they're staying." He gave her the number, then the number of his cell phone, promising to pick her up at the airport when her flight arrived. Finally he hung up.

He gathered a sobbing Callie against him and struggled with his own tears. "She can't make it until Sunday, but she's coming."

Callie didn't answer; Dillon suspected that she couldn't.

Chapter Twenty-three

Mary brushed dirt from her gloved hands and sat back on her heels. Tears glistened in her eyes. "And Dillon was actually *rocking* the baby to sleep? Holding it, with his own two hands?"

Callie nodded. "There's more."

Slapping a hand to her chest, Mary waited, wide-eyed with wonder.

"After he rocked Adrienne to sleep, he carried her up two flights of stairs to put her to bed." Callie sifted dirt through her fingers, loving the cool feel of the soil. It was a beautiful, bright afternoon, and she and Mary were planting tulip bulbs along the walkway in Mary's beautiful backyard. "Then he read Caleb a bedtime story."

By this time Mary had heard the whole story and knew that Caleb hadn't spoken since his mother's death. A tear rolled down her cheek. When she swiped at it, she left a streak of dirt behind. "Those poor children. Thank God they have Aunt LaVonda."

Feeling slightly ashamed for taking advantage of

Mary's emotions, Callie took the opportunity to launch Operation Help Gina and the Kids. "Um, we were wondering if we could have a little fund-raiser here, at your house, to raise money for Gina and her siblings. Taking on four kids will be expensive, so we wanted to give LaVonda a little head start."

Mary was nobody's fool. "Dillon's idea?"

Callie blushed. "Actually, I think it was Wyatt's idea." Before Mary could think of rejecting the plan, Callie rushed on. "I could help you, of course, and I'm sure some of the other women will want to pitch in. It could be a potluck fund-raiser, so you wouldn't have to do all the cooking."

"Hmm. When?"

"This Sunday. That also happens to be the day Aunt LaVonda is arriving to get the kids, so the timing couldn't be better. We could all meet her, make sure she's everything that Gina says she is. The last thing those kids need is another relative who doesn't really want them."

"I agree."

"Then you'll do it?" Callie held her breath.

"As if you ever believed I wouldn't," Mary chided. She took her spade and began chopping the dirt in preparation for the next bulb. "By the way," she asked casually, "have you told my son that you're in love with him?" Without missing a beat, she added, "There. This hole's ready. Hand me a bulb from that basket, would you?"

It took a moment for her words to sink in. When they did, Callie's heart did a triple somersault. "W-what?" Was it that obvious? The thought threw Callie into a panic.

"Calm down. I'm not only Dillon's mother; I'm a

woman." Mary patted Callie's knee, leaving a handprint on her denim capri pants. "I seriously doubt my bullheaded son has realized it yet, just as he probably hasn't realized that he's in love with *you*."

This time Callie's jaw dropped. She sputtered. "He's not . . . we're not . . . I mean, he's not in love with me." If only he were!

"Oh, really?" Sounding smug, Mary covered up the bulb and dusted her hands again. She looked at Callie. "I'm not going to lie to you. Dillon's had lots of women since he hit puberty. Women just seem to fall all over themselves when he's around."

Heat rushed into Callie's face. *She* was one of those women.

"But I could tell that he never took them seriously. Until you. For the first time, he's doing the pursuing."

In all honesty, Callie had to say, "I think it's mutual."

Instead of arguing, Mary smiled slyly. "Even better. You know, Wyatt knew before I did that you were Dillon's soul mate. He knew after that first meeting you and Dillon had at the hotel bar, when Dillon didn't realize you were a client."

Callie covered her hot face. "Oh, my God. I remember Wyatt—when I thought he was Dillon—telling me that he thought his brother was in love. He was laughing about it." Could Wyatt have known? *Was* Dillon in love with her? Did she dare hope he felt the same way she did?

"Don't worry. Your secret's safe with me. I know you'll tell him in your own good time."

Tell him? Callie swallowed hard. How could she tell Dillon she was in love with him when she couldn't even *think* it without hyperventilating? True, she was no longer in mourning for her lost marriage, but that didn't mean she was ready to jump right back into the fire. What if Wyatt and his mother were wrong?

Worse . . . what if they were right, and Callie found the courage to take the risk? Would she ever feel truly secure being with a hunk like Dillon? It was his *job* to be in the company of women day in and day out. He was bending the rules dangerously with her. What would stop him from bending the rules with someone else? What if she was just another "good time"?

"Looks like you've got some thinking to do," Mary startled her by saying. She placed a spade in Callie's hand. "Dig. You'll be amazed at how much thinking your brain can do while you're working with the soil."

But Mary was wrong. An hour of planting tulips brought Callie no closer to finding an answer. What she *did* discover, however, was that she didn't have to visit yet another steakhouse to do a review. Mary was more than willing to tell her everything she needed to know about the Angus Feedlot, the next business on her list. The woman was thorough and impartial, impressing Callie by also pointing out the negative aspects of the restaurant, such as the long wait for a table on weekend nights, and the feeling of being rushed when you finally did get a table.

She spent the evening with Mary instead, whipping up western omelettes in Mary's homey kitchen and planning the fund-raiser . . . and listening avidly as Mary regaled her with the childhood escapades of Wyatt, Dillon, and Isabelle.

After dinner, they took their coffee onto Mary's deck overlooking the spacious backyard. Mary shocked Callie by lighting a pipe. The sweet-smelling aroma of vanilla bean drifted on the breeze.

Mary flushed when she caught Callie staring at her.

"Please don't tell the boys. They'd have a fit." She puffed thoughtfully on the pipe for a moment before she continued. "Their father used to smoke this pipe after dinner. Since he died, I've sort of carried on. It makes me feel close to him."

Callie's eyes watered. "You must have loved him very much," she said softly. She was reminded of the expression, "better to have loved and lost, than not to have loved at all." Did she agree? She discovered that she didn't know . . . yet.

No, that wasn't true, she decided. Even if it turned out that Dillon didn't want a future with her, she still wouldn't wish they had never met. The times she'd had with him so far were already shaping up to be the best times of her life. She wanted them to continue, but she was deathly afraid that she was asking for too much.

Mary sighed. "I did love him, but I can't say it was always a bed of roses. He worked too much, and I resented him for that, resented him on my kids' behalf. I know *why* he worked too much; I just didn't agree with his reasoning. He thought it was more important that our kids have nice clothes and a nice house. I believed it was more important they have their father's time."

A zealous June bug flew into the patio doors and fell onto the patio table, flopping around. Callie and Mary simultaneously covered their coffee mugs with their hands, laughing. The June bug finally recovered from his dive and took off again, weaving drunkenly into the night.

"Is Isabelle anything like her brothers?" Callie asked, amazed at the contentment she felt just sitting with Mary and listening to the crickets. Before Atlanta and Dillon, she would have been blind to the beautiful simplicity of the moment.

Laughing, Mary put the pipe aside and folded her hands across her lap. "They say your last child is always the most rotten. Well, Isabelle's no exception. The boys did their share of tormenting her, but it was mostly for show. They spoiled her every bit as much as I did. Still, I think she turned out pretty okay despite our best efforts to ruin her. Naturally, they're ridiculously overprotective of her, and she hates it. I've had to lie to my sons on her behalf more times than I can count, just to give her a chance to live a normal life."

Remembering Wyatt's concern over Mary seeing Will, Callie had no trouble believing Dillon and Wyatt could fast become pains in the butt. Throwing caution to the wind, Callie said, "They seem to be equally protective of you. I think it's sweet."

Mary shot her a dry, are-you-serious look and rolled her eyes. "Yeah, it's sweet . . . unless you're the mother or the sister of my two boys." She gave her head a rueful shake. "If I ever meet anyone special, I'll have to sneak around just to keep Dillon and Wyatt from scaring him away, or worse, putting him in traction."

"I'm sure they'd want you to be happy," Callie murmured, feeling unaccountably guilty knowing what she knew, that Mary's sons were stalking her.

"I have no doubt they would want me to be happy, but *believing* any man was good enough for me would be the problem. In some ways they are hopelessly narrow-minded."

But Callie noted the affection that laced her voice when she spoke of her children, and suspected that Mary wouldn't change a hair on their heads if she had the chance.

When Mary touched her hand to gain her attention, Callie jumped. The other woman looked suddenly anxious.

"You don't believe in perfection, do you, Callie? I mean, you do realize that even people with the best intentions make mistakes?"

This wasn't a random question, Callie thought. She licked her dry lips. "What do you mean?"

Mary stared at her hard for a long moment, as if she were on the verge of revealing something important. But in the end she sighed and looked away. "Nothing. I just wanted you to know that sometimes people get their priorities a little screwed up, and don't realize it until they've made a mess of things."

Callie's heart skipped a beat. Mary was definitely trying to tell her something. "Is this about Dillon? Do you know something that I should know? Does he . . . does he have a girlfriend?"

"No! No, no." Mary laughed, but not unkindly. "Despite my devotion to my sons, I would never go along with something like that, even if I *didn't* think you'd make the best daughter-in-law a mother-in-law could have."

As Callie blushed furiously, Mary picked up her coffee mug, peered cautiously into it in search of bugs, then took a sip. Callie suspected the woman was giving her time to recover from the compliment, and she was grateful.

Because the compliment also brought back the dismal reminder that Dillon had mentioned nothing of love.

The first thing Dillon noticed when he let his weary body into his apartment was that the basket of folded socks he'd left on the sofa was gone.

For a second he savored the memory of Callie's pert little bottom wiggling around. "Mom?" he called out. Aside from his mother, Wyatt was the only other person with a key to his apartment, and he knew his brother had not put away his laundry.

"I'm in the kitchen!"

He kicked off his shoes and joined his mother in the kitchen. She was wearing a jogging suit and a pair of neon-green flip-flops, and she was making hot cocoa.

A jolt of alarm chased the weariness away. "What's wrong?" he asked, eyeing the steaming pan of cocoa suspiciously.

Mary shot him a chiding look over her shoulder. "You really should work on that paranoia, son."

Dillon grunted. He pulled out a chair, turned it around, and straddled it. "You fixed hot cocoa the day you told us Daddy died."

His mother's shoulders stiffened. She kept stirring.

"You also fixed hot cocoa the day you told us our cat had gotten hit by a car."

Still Mary didn't turn around, but she said, "A coincidence, plain and simple."

"You fixed hot cocoa the day you found out that all of our fish had died from ick."

"Another coincidence," Mary declared staunchly.

"And was it a coincidence the day you fixed hot cocoa and told us that Isabelle was moving away to go to college?"

"Oh, for heaven's sake!" Exasperated, Mary slapped the spoon she'd been using onto the stovetop and turned around. She propped a hand on her hip and glared at her firstborn. "I'm fixing hot cocoa because I've got a craving for it . . . and because I wanted to tell you that I think you're making a mistake by not telling Callie you own the Love Nest."

"Aha!" Dillon said smugly. "I knew you didn't come over to put away my socks."

"No, I didn't." She turned abruptly to pour the cocoa into mugs and bring them to the table. "Well? Are you going to sit there and tell me you don't have feelings for Callie?"

"You know I'd be lying if I said that." Dillon pulled his mug forward. His mother took hers and sat across from him. He recognized the militant gleam in her eyes and accurately guessed the cause. "You've been spending time with Callie."

Mary's chin went up and out. "As a matter of fact, I have. We spent the whole afternoon and most of the evening together. She's a rare, wonderful person."

"Yes, she is."

"At least you realize *that* much," Mary said. "Do you love her?"

"Yes, I do." Dillon chuckled at her stunned expression. "Why so shocked? You already knew, didn't you? Mothers not only have eyes in the back of their heads, they're mind readers as well. Right?"

"Well, I . . ." Mary frowned. "If you know you love her, why aren't you telling her the truth?"

Is was a damned good question, one Dillon had been asking himself all night. He sighed. "I've been lying to her for two weeks. Tomorrow night Greg's taking her to the club. If I come clean now, I'm afraid she'll be too angry to see my confession as anything other than a clever manipulation on my part. So . . . I've decided to wait until she's been to the club, then sit her down and spill my guts before she can write her review. This way she'll know that I'm sincere. In fact, I'm going to take down those silly mirrors, give the waitresses back their old uniforms, and show her the real thing."

"I can't believe it took you this long to figure it out."

Dillon tried to explain. "It wasn't just my business at stake. Would it have been fair for me to risk mucking it up for everyone else?"

"That depends. Are these people—most of whom you don't even know—more important to you than Callie?"

"I thought they were at first. I know they aren't now."

"What are you going to do if Callie doesn't forgive you?"

Shit. His mother always asked the *scary* questions. The kind that made his gut clench with fear. "I don't know."

Mary grimaced. "Is that the best you can do?"

Unfortunately, Dillon mused with a heavy heart, it was.

After typing the last sentence of the review on the Angus Feedlot steakhouse, Callie sent the e-mail to Fontaine and sat back in her chair. She stretched and groaned, placing a hand on her aching back. She wasn't used to gardening, or sitting in a chair typing for two solid hours.

When the phone rang a few moments later, Callie wasn't surprised. She knew it would be her sister. She picked up the phone and stretched out on her bed before she said hello.

"Who are you and what did you do with my sister?" Fontaine demanded.

Callie rolled her eyes. "I'm an exchange student from the planet Sarcasm. Don't worry; your sister's brain is on ice." A more accurate description, Callie mused, would be on *fire*, but she didn't think her sister would appreciate her humor.

"You know, I'm very close to believing you. You actually said bad things about this Angus Feedlot place. God, it sounds like the name of a slaughterhouse. No wonder you didn't like it."

After slowly counting to ten, Callie said with exaggerated patience, "Fontaine, is it possible you overlooked all the *good* things I said about the restaurant? The food is great, superb, and they've got a fantastic salad bar. The prices are very reasonable, too. Kids under three eat free."

"Yeah, yeah, but when you're hungry, who wants to stand in line for an hour? Especially with kids? And who wants to be rushed when you finally do get a table?"

"As a matter of fact," Callie said, feeling just a tad guilty for quoting Mary verbatim, "if the food was worth it, then I wouldn't mind standing in line."

Fontaine caught her slip just seconds after Callie did. "*If* the food was worth it? You mean you *know* the food was worth it, right?"

Reminding herself that she had warned Fontaine she wouldn't be good at this, Callie came clean. "Okay, I didn't actually go to the restaurant, but I heard it on good authority—from someone local—that it's worth the wait, and even the rush once you get a table. Mary said—"

"Who's Mary?"

"Dillon's mother. She said you can always ignore the waiter or waitress if they start hinting for you to hurry it up. I mean, they can't actually *make* you leave if you're not ready."

"Callie! You can't trust the opinion of a local! Of

course they're going to be biased about restaurants in their own town."

"I trust Mary," Callie said sharply. "She told me the bad with the good, didn't she?"

Fontaine huffed a sigh. "Maybe, but do you think she would have told you if she'd ever found a roach in her soup, or a hair in her salad? Or what about how clean the silverware is, or the plates? She's not a reviewer, sis."

"And neither are the people reading *Next Stop*, Fontaine, and yes, I think Mary would tell me. She's a very honest person."

"Sounds like you're in love."

"And *you* sound like you're jealous!"

"I'm not jealous. I just want my readers to know the truth. The majority of them do a lot of scrimping and saving to take that vacation, and the last thing they want to do is waste their money on bad hotels, restaurants, or entertainment. Have you ever paid five bucks to rent a movie, only to discover it's so horrible you can't sit through it?"

"Yes," Callie snapped. "It's a risk we all take. If we were never disappointed in the bad, how would we know to appreciate the good?"

"I can see that you're beyond reasoning with." There was a deliberate pause before she added, "Maybe I should send Faith to finish the reviews."

Callie decided she'd rather take a bullet than let Fontaine know her words had hurt. "Maybe you should. That way I can continue enjoying my vacation . . . a vacation *you* decided I needed."

"Fine. Enjoy your vacation."

It wasn't hard to imagine Fontaine gritting her teeth. Callie did the same. "Fine. I will."

Although Callie hung up first, she derived no joy

from the gesture. She hated fighting with her sister. What she hated even more was the feeling that she'd let Fontaine down. Maybe it was time she found another job before their relationship deteriorated further.

Or maybe she could just move to Atlanta and start over.

The more Callie thought about it, the more the idea appealed to her. She loved the city. She loved the people.

And she loved Dillon Love.

Chapter Twenty-four

Tyler slipped the mask over his eyes and clamped a dusty black hat onto his head. He folded his arms and glared at Wyatt. "I've changed my mind. No way am I going out on that stage looking like this."

"Not even for *three* full nights of free babysitting?" Wyatt pleaded. "Besides, you look mysterious in that black raincoat. You'll knock 'em dead."

Apparently giving it some serious thought, Tyler finally narrowed his eyes. "Three full nights of babysitting *and* you have to help me lay the new carpet in the den next week."

"Done."

Jet, dressed similarly and standing next to his wife, singer Cameron Rose, voiced his own misgivings. "Are you sure there aren't any regular customers out there? I'm not in the mood to deal with hecklers."

Wyatt shook his head. "Fish hasn't left the door. The only time he took the sign down that announces we're closed till ten for a private party is when I called to tell him Dillon was on his way. He'll take it down again—

for just a moment—when Callie and Greg arrive so that Callie won't see it. The only people out there are people we handpicked—mostly friends of Greg's."

"I don't know," Jet said slowly. He opened his coat and glanced at the black bikini briefs he wore beneath, then grimaced at Wyatt. "I think I might have to ask for more than your baseball autographed by Mark McGuire."

"Name your price," Wyatt told him without hesitation. If Callie found out that Dillon owned the Love Nest, he was determined the information wouldn't come from him. If everyone played his part, she would leave believing the Love Nest was a gay bar, and he would be in the clear. Dillon could explain later . . . if his brother ever got around to telling her the truth.

Jet stroked his chin. "Do you still have that Bob Seger poster?"

Dismay flooded Wyatt. Reluctantly, he nodded. "You're talking about the one he signed? Yeah, I still got it." He swallowed hard and forced the words from his throat. "It's yours." Pointing at Ivan and Will, he said, "Name your price, boys. Do you want more than what I've already promised you? We don't have much time, and there's not much left to choose from."

Ivan grinned, clearly enjoying Wyatt's predicament. "Well, in addition to mowing the lawn two Saturdays in a row, our hedges could use trimming."

"It's done." Grimly, Wyatt turned to Will. As usual, Will regarded him with a deadpan expression. "Will? Anything besides that oil change and truck detailing?"

A slow, surprising grin spread across Will's mouth. "Yeah, there is. I want to be there when Dillon finds out what you've done."

The others laughed. Wyatt was hard-pressed to smile. "Very funny," he said, feeling nauseous just thinking about it. Thank God the waitresses had only asked for money. He'd lost an expensive set of weights to Fish, and his favorite fishing rod to Lou. His apartment was practically bare.

Although there was humor in Cameron's voice when she spoke, there was sympathy as well. "Don't mind them, Wyatt. When you explain to Dillon, he'll have to understand that you didn't have a choice. You were trying to save *his* butt when you told Callie this was a gay bar, weren't you?"

"Yeah," Wyatt grumbled. "Unfortunately, I don't think Dillon's gonna see it that way."

"I can't believe I'm finally here," Callie told Greg after they found an empty table near the stage in the dimly lit, comfortable-feeling nightclub. It was the kind of relaxed atmosphere that made her feel instantly at ease, with its scarred pine walls, mismatched tables and chairs, and down-home decor.

The waitresses, she noted, were dressed in short shorts and skimpy tops, but they looked at ease and happy with their attire. She caught Lou's eye at the bar and waved to him. He waved back.

After giving the waitress her drink order, Callie sighed and looked at Greg. "I don't know why Dillon didn't just tell me this was a gay bar instead of making excuses not to bring me." She leaned closer and lowered her voice as she asked earnestly, "Tell me the truth, Greg. Have I given you the impression I'm not comfortable around gay people?"

Greg shook his head. "Nope." He smiled and waved to someone at a nearby table before he focused on her again. "Did I tell you that Cameron is singing tonight?"

"No! You didn't! That's great. She's a wonderful

singer. I have several of her CDs. Does she sing here often?"

"Whenever Dil—um, my friend can get her."

The waitress came back with their drinks and asked them if they wanted to order anything to eat. Greg asked for menus. She grabbed some from a nearby table and handed them to him before leaving them alone again.

Callie looked at the menu, pleased to find many of her favorite foods listed. The nightclub boasted the good stuff, like baby back ribs and fiery buffalo wings, mozzarella cheese sticks and fried mushrooms. She glanced at Greg. "How's the food here?"

"Depends." Greg darted a mischievous look at her over the top of his menu. He grinned. "If you're not drunk, it's great. If you're looped, it's fantastic." He tapped his menu. "I can't come in here without ordering the buffalo wings. They're addictive, but be warned—they'll make you sweat."

His grin was contagious. "That's the way I like them," Callie said, accepting his challenge. When the waitress returned, she ordered the buffalo wings and fried mushrooms as appetizers, and the baby back ribs for the main course. She smiled at the waitress as she handed her the menu. "Thanks, and please bring lots of napkins."

"Will do," said the waitress, who'd told them her name was Debra.

Greg ordered the wings and barbecued shrimp. When the waitress disappeared, he picked up his heavy frosted mug of draft beer and sucked off the foam. "So . . . what do you think of the place so far?"

Callie's lips twitched. She debated whether she should tell Greg he was sporting a thick foam mustache. Feeling rotten to the core, she decided against it. "Um, actually, I'm not here as a reviewer tonight. I sort of got fired."

COMPLETELY YOURS

The mug of beer in Greg's hand jerked, sloshing beer over the rim. It ran all over his hand. Muttering a curse, he reached for his napkin and began to sop it up.

"Was it something I said?" Callie inquired, puzzled by Greg's sudden clumsiness. "Greg?"

"What?" Greg blinked at her, then looked suddenly relieved as he said, "I think Cameron's on."

Getting the distinct impression she had missed something important, Callie finally shook her head and focused on the stage. Cameron walked out onstage wearing a shimmering silver gown that flattered her curvy figure and made her dark brown eyes sparkle.

The singer took the mike from the stand, smiling at her audience. "Folks, we've got a special treat for you tonight."

The two dozen or so men and women listening whistled and clapped.

"Enjoy yourselves," Cameron said before launching into the rather raunchy song, "You Can Leave Your Hat On." As she sang, four men wearing eye masks and dressed in black trench coats and black hats walked slowly onto the stage. They parted, two standing on one side of Cameron, and two on the other. One by one they swiveled their hips and took off their hats. The cheers and catcalls were ear-piercing.

Callie, who was thoroughly enjoying the show and the audience's reaction, laughed and clapped her hands. She found herself waiting expectantly to see what the performers would do next. As Cameron continued with the song, the men, one by one, sailed their hats into the audience. There was a mad scramble as one of the hats landed between two men on the table next to theirs.

The scramble for the hat ended without a fight, and Callie watched as the four strippers began to slowly

281

unbutton their trench coats, hips swaying to the beat of the song Cameron belted out. When the last buttons were unfastened, they all turned their backs to the audience, much to the audience's verbal disappointment. But before the grumbling could gather volume, the men began to slide the coats slowly from their shoulders. Inch by inch, beat by raunchy beat.

Now the audience appeared to be holding its collective breath.

Finding herself no exception, Callie glanced at Greg, then did a double take to find him staring at the table instead of the stage. He looked positively embarrassed. She hadn't realized he was so shy. She frowned as another possibility occurred to her. Was he embarrassed because of her?

Kicking herself for not realizing it sooner, Callie scooted her chair close so that she could talk to him without interrupting Cameron's song. "We can leave if you'd prefer," she said into his ear. When he frowned and shook his head, she sighed and moved her chair back. It had been Wyatt's idea for Greg to bring her, she recalled. Obviously Wyatt hadn't considered that Greg might not want to be seen with a woman in a gay bar, especially when men were stripping onstage.

The coats were now midway down the strippers' broad, muscled backs, and the crowd grew louder, clamoring for them to take it off, take it all off.

Giving in to the urge to join them, Callie began to chant and clap her hands, wishing Greg would relax and enjoy the show. It was entertainment, pure and simple.

Onstage, the men shot the audience coy looks over broad shoulders before inching the coats down lower. The coats were waist high now, exposing backs that gleamed and rippled with muscles, yet hiding their swiveling hips and taut butts. Callie could almost feel the anticipation in air as the crowd waited for the strippers to drop their coats.

Well, everyone was waiting but Greg, Callie thought wryly, glancing at him to find he'd covered his face with his hands.

The floor literally shook beneath Dillon's feet.

In the restaurant kitchen tucked away discreetly behind the bar, Dillon paused in the act of stacking dirty beer mugs in a tray.

He was accustomed to a loud, appreciative audience whenever Cameron took the stage, which wasn't often. But this . . . He frowned and craned his head, trying to make out the exact words the audience was chanting. This was different because they *were* chanting, which didn't make sense. Singing along with her would make sense.

Not chanting, and especially not while Cameron was singing that raunchy song, "You Can Leave Your Hat On," a song he'd never heard her sing before.

Dillon froze. That was it. The audience was chanting, "Take it off." He scratched his head, his frown deepening as he tried to make sense of his discovery. He knew that Callie was out there with Greg, which was why he'd been keeping a very low profile in the kitchen.

He hadn't so much as peeked through the kitchen door to see if he could spot her since she had arrived. When the dishwasher had failed to show, Dillon had almost jumped at the opportunity to take his mind off the evening ahead. He dreaded telling Callie the truth about his deception.

The noise from the crowd rose to an earth-rumbling crescendo, alarming Dillon.

He could stand the suspense no longer.

Shoving the rack of beer mugs into the dishwasher, he jogged to the swinging door leading into the bar area. With all the mysterious commotion going on, he reasoned, it was unlikely Callie would notice him.

Most of his customers were standing as they stomped and shouted, so Dillon had to stand on tiptoe to see the stage. Cameron was there, center stage, singing her beautiful heart out.

His jaw dropped.

Surrounding her were four men wearing ridiculous-looking Zorro masks . . . and little else.

The men were dancing, strutting around in tight bikini underwear, to the complete rapture of the crowd.

Dillon pulled his jaw closed, wondering what the hell was going on in his nightclub as he searched for Callie and Greg.

It dropped again when he realized that the majority of the chanting crowd were men.

Wyatt shook his head to clear the sweat from his eyes. He kept his full weight and strength braced against the walk-in cooler door to keep his raging twin safely *inside*.

Until he listened to reason, or froze to death. Whichever came first.

At this point Wyatt wasn't particular.

"Sooner or later you're going to have to let me out!" Dillon shouted through three inches of steel. "And when you do, I'm going to tear you limb from limb!"

"You haven't even let me explain!" Wyatt shouted back. Dillon threw his weight against the door, and Wyatt grunted from the strain of holding him back. He knew that Fish, Lou, and Will were gathered at the far end of the kitchen, watching the scene as if they had front row seats to a women's mud-wrestling match. His life was in danger, and they were absolutely no help at all.

"There's nothing you can say that's going to make me get over this!"

Unfortunately, Wyatt feared his twin was right. Still, he had to try. "You don't understand, bro."

"What?"

"I said, 'You don't understand!'" Wyatt yelled. "She wanted me to bring her to the club, and when I called in a code red to the guys to get out of bringing her, she figured out what I was doing. I had to think quick to save *your* butt."

There was a short silence.

Then Dillon banged an angry fist on the door. "And that's the best you could do? Telling Callie the Love Nest was a *gay* bar?"

Wyatt felt a surge of righteousness. "As a matter of fact, it was! Can you think of a better excuse in thirty seconds?" Because his watch happened to be at eye level, Wyatt counted off the seconds to prove his point. When thirty seconds had gone by, Wyatt beat *his* fist on the door. "Time's up, Einstein!"

"Go to hell!"

Growing desperate to make Dillon understand, Wyatt played his dubious trump card. "Listen, Dillon. I don't think Callie came to Atlanta as a reviewer, so there's probably nothing to worry about." He put his ear to the door so he wouldn't miss Dillon's response.

"You idiot!" Dillon said, loud and clear. "I know that. She didn't come here as a reviewer, but her sister broke her ankle and ask Callie to go ahead and do the reviews for real."

"Oh, shit," Wyatt whispered. Behind him, their audience burst out laughing, the skunks. He ignored them. He raised his voice. "How was I supposed to know that? Huh? Come on, Dillon. Give me a break. I was trying to help you when I lied to her. I swear it." Wyatt was waiting for Dillon to answer when a thought occurred to him. "Hey, what difference does it make if she thinks the Love Nest is a gay bar? If she gives it a good review—"

The force of Dillon's lunge against the door not only caught Wyatt by surprise, it knocked the breath from his lungs. He flew backward, landed on his butt, and skidded across the floor before coming to a stop.

A frostbitten, red-faced Dillon emerged from the cooler. He stared down at Wyatt, his fists clenched, his chest heaving. "None of it matters," Dillon said. "Because I'm going to tell her the truth. Only now, thanks to you, I've got another lie to unravel." After a long pause, he held out his hand to Wyatt.

Wyatt eyed Dillon's offer of help warily before taking his hand. He knew he probably deserved a good sock on the jaw, so he figured he would take it like a man.

As Dillon drew Wyatt up to eye level, he kept a hard grip on Wyatt's hand. His voice was soft as he asked, "I suppose you've got a good reason for not telling me your suspicions about Callie when you found out?"

Suspecting Dillon would see through anything but the truth, Wyatt braced himself and said, "Not any reason you would like. Besides, I was never absolutely certain."

But Dillon didn't hit him. He just stared at Wyatt a moment longer, then dropped his hand and walked away.

As far as Wyatt was concerned, he would have preferred a punch in the nose.

Chapter Twenty-five

Callie was ready, willing, and nearly naked.

Dillon swallowed hard. Sweat popped out on his brow as he tried not to ogle the negligee-clad woman posing in the doorway of her hotel room.

She flashed him a slow, sexy smile, unaware of the turbulence boiling inside him. "I've thought of another way to not have intercourse. You interested?"

He was, but he doubted *she* would be after he told her what he'd come to tell her. Discovering his mouth had gone bone dry, he marched past the alluring woman offering herself to him and grabbed an orange juice from the minibar. He uncapped the lid and downed the entire bottle.

When he lowered it, Callie lifted a questioning brow. She was still smiling that knee-weakening sex-kitten smile, though. Dillon wished she would stop, then remembered that all he had to do was open his mouth and she probably would. In fact, she would probably take the bottle from him and clobber him over the head with it.

Sheridon Smythe

"You forgot the vodka...lover boy," she purred, shutting the door and sashaying toward him.

Dillon held out a desperate hand before she could touch him. "Stop! We need to talk."

"Talk?" Still clueless, she started to reach for his shirt. "If that's what you want to call it . . ."

With a groan, Dillon grabbed her wrist and held her still. "I want you," he said gruffly. "You don't know how badly I want you . . . want all of you, want to bury myself inside of you."

Now both dark brows rose in slight amusement. "My, aren't we intense tonight." Holding his gaze, she let the outer see-through part of her negligee slip to the floor. "Go for it. You won't get a fight out of me . . . unless you *want* one."

Dillon clenched his teeth hard. He'd never known another woman as erotic, yet as innocent as Callie.

He was afraid he never would again.

Was it any wonder that he considered—briefly—taking advantage of her offer before he told her the truth? He was a man, after all, and she was all woman. The thought of going through life having never known what it felt like to plunge himself into her hot, tight sheath seemed a fate worse than death.

But no, he couldn't. He loved her too much. The *love* factor, he realized, made all the difference. It was the reason he wanted her so badly. It was the reason he felt that he couldn't breathe right now because of his fear.

"Callie . . . I need to tell you something." His voice was hoarse. Regretful. Full of pain and need.

He finally got through to her. The sexy light in her eyes dimmed. Her expression then turned wary . . . fearful, then finally resigned.

She tried to be flippant, and failed. "Is this the other

proverbial 'shoe,' Dillon?" As if she hadn't a care in the world—or worse, expected it—she waltzed to the bed and sat down. She swung her legs and looked at him, waiting.

Outwardly calm, yet vulnerable.

Dillon had a cowardly moment as he looked at her face and saw once again the wary, vulnerable look of the woman Callie had once been before she'd met him.

Before she met him.

He licked his dry lips. "I want you to know . . . first . . . that I've come to care about you a lot." The *love* word stuck in his throat, but only because he feared she'd laugh at him when it was all said and done.

She swung her legs and looked at him. "But?"

Because he hated cowards, Dillon forced himself to stop being one. He blurted out, "I own the Love Nest."

It took a long, long moment for the words to register. Finally her astonishment was replaced by sheer shock. "Are you . . . are you trying to tell me that you're *gay?*"

How could she possibly come to that conclusion after what they'd done? It boggled Dillon's mind. "Of course I'm not gay. And the Love Nest isn't a gay bar. Wyatt lied to you."

She frowned. "Why would he tell me that?"

"Because *I* own the bar, and I don't really work for Mr. Complete." Dillon hurried on before he lost his courage. There was no turning back now. "I'm a good friend of Luke's. I agreed to fill in for him while he was on his honeymoon, and because I needed a break from running the nightclub."

She had stopped swinging her legs, but her puzzled expression remained. "I still don't get it."

"*Next Stop* gave me a bad review last year. It nearly sent me under. When I saw that Luke had agreed to trade escort services for an ad in your sister's magazine, I . . . um, decided to take advantage of the opportunity and, um, escort you myself."

Dillon saw the moment she got it. The dawning realization in her eyes tempted him to fall to his knees and start begging her forgiveness. And just as he'd feared, the realization slowly but surely turned to frigid awareness.

He didn't have to tell her his motives for seeking her out. She knew.

Because he knew Callie—and loved her—Dillon also knew that behind that frigid awareness her newly healed and very fragile heart had been dealt a devastating blow.

"You played me."

The words fell into the air like shards of ice. Dillon almost fancied he could hear those shards shattering on impact. Silently willing her to believe him, Dillon said, "I can't deny that at first my only thought was to distract you, woo you, soften you up in the hope you'd go easy on the review. Then I bumped into you in the bar, not knowing who you were, and felt a connection to you I've never felt before."

Her expression hadn't changed. She was stone and ice. "Obviously the connection wasn't deep enough to warrant the truth."

He knew she was right, so there wasn't any point in lying. "Once I started the ball rolling, I couldn't seem to stop. There was the welfare of the other businesses to consider. What if we had an affair, and it ended badly? What if it colored your entire outlook on Atlanta, and it showed in your reviews?"

Her gaze dropped for a moment, and color rushed to her cheeks. "That's why you didn't want to go all the way with me?" She glanced up and saw the answer on his face, and she laughed, a shrill, humorless sound that made Dillon wince. "Men! They think intercourse means making love. For a woman, there are dozens of ways to make love without having intercourse." She stood up abruptly and stalked to the wrapper she'd left on the floor at his feet. She snatched it up and shoved her arms into it. Her eyes flashed lethal daggers at him. "I'm sorry you wasted your time, Dillon, since I was only a decoy all along."

"It wasn't a waste of time," Dillon said with all his heart and soul.

She laughed again, and the sound was ragged. "Poor Dillon. First I'm a dreaded reviewer; then I'm not; then I am. Well, here's another news flash for you. I got fired last night from the job I wasn't supposed to have in the first place, so all your efforts tonight at the Love Nest were a waste of everyone's time." She shot him a venomous look rife with pain as she added, "Although I *did* enjoy the show!"

Dillon grabbed her arm as she started to march past him to the door. "That wasn't supposed to happen. Wyatt didn't want you to find out about my owning the nightclub from anyone but me."

She bared her teeth in a parody of a smile. "Wasn't that sweet of your twin? You must be proud that your brother is just as devious and deceitful as *you* are! And it worked! How lovely for both of you."

"Callie, I've fallen in love with you." Dillon said the words softly, with an ache she couldn't fail to hear.

Jerking her arm free, she stalked to the door and opened it. Her eyes glittered with suppressed tears as she said, "Don't worry, Dillon. Apparently you were too busy scheming to get a good review to realize that I don't have an ounce of spite in me. Your precious *Atlanta* is safe. You don't have to keep up the charade of caring about me."

"Dammit! I'm not keeping up a charade!" When she merely lifted an arm and pointed at the open door, Dillon swallowed his frustration and stomped to it. He paused, furious with himself and knowing she had every right to be angry and disbelieving. His voice was low and compelling as he gave it one last shot. "When Wyatt told me that he knew all along you weren't here as a reviewer, I was so mad I wanted to kill him. Now I understand why he didn't tell me. If he had, the last two weeks we've spent together, the crazy, bizarre adventures we've had, might not have happened. For that reason alone I can't be mad at him, because I wouldn't take back one single moment." His intense gaze bore into hers. "Not . . . one . . . single . . . moment. Think about that, Callie. Think about it hard before you throw our love away."

And with that, he left. The door slammed hard behind him, sending his heart to his feet. It was such a terrible, final sound.

Had he lost her for good? Were his stubborn, blind, bullheaded ways going to cost him the love of a lifetime?

As Dillon waited for the elevator, he realized nothing else mattered the way Callie mattered. With more than a little surprise, he suddenly knew that he would give up his nightclub, Atlanta, and all his possessions just to have her forgiveness and her love. He could no longer imagine life without Callie.

Which meant he had to get her back.

* * *

Callie stared without blinking at the closed door, a rush of recent memories tumbling through her brain at a speed that left her breathless and numb.

Mary, asking her if she believed that nobody was perfect.

Dillon's mother had known, too, and that hurt.

Wyatt, filling in for Dillon after their first meeting. Obviously *he* had known as well, but Callie was unclear about his motives. Had he truly believed Dillon had fallen in love? Or was Wyatt merely being loyal to his twin by aiding him in his deception? She didn't know. Couldn't decide. Didn't dare trust her heart. It was obviously incapable of sorting the wolves from the sheep.

How about the rest of the gang? Mrs. Scuttle? Cameron? Casey and Diane? Callie felt hot color rush into her cheeks as she remembered the backyard barbecue and how everyone had carefully avoided talking about Dillon. Yes, they had all known and had gone along with Dillon's deception.

Even Mrs. Scuttle, because Callie couldn't believe a deception that big could have gone on without the shrewd woman knowing.

And that hurt as well.

She had come to Atlanta as a scared, mistrustful, introverted woman who badly needed to get over her broken heart and get a life.

She thought she had found one. She believed she had found true friends she could trust and depend on and care for. She was convinced she had found a man she could love, even if she couldn't have him for eternity.

Even if he couldn't be completely hers.

Deep inside her bruised, hopeless heart, she had convinced herself she would have to take her precious memories and walk away with them, that she either didn't deserve Dillon's loyalty and love, or wasn't lucky enough to have it.

One more week, Callie thought, trudging slowly to her bed. One more week and she could have left Atlanta after experiencing the time of her life, taking with her wonderful, awesome, unforgettable memories of her time spent with Dillon and his family and friends.

She loved him, but she had resigned—no, convinced—herself that she couldn't be that lucky. If tonight hadn't happened, she would have left Atlanta with her memories and with a confidence she desperately needed to go on with her life.

Callie fell back onto the bed and stared at the ceiling. Her brief bark of laughter held a wealth of self-contempt. Who was she fooling? She might have left Atlanta, and she might have carried on with more confidence, but she would never have forgotten Dillon.

She *loved* him. Totally. Thoroughly. Heartbreakingly. In an all-consuming way she had never loved Lanny.

Her bottom lip trembled. She bit down on it hard. She was a coward.

The realization wasn't easy, and it was painful. Gut-wrenchingly, jaw-clenchingly painful.

She was a coward, because she would have left Atlanta and Dillon just to avoid the pain she was feeling now. Just gone on her merry way, loving him and living without him because she was too afraid of *this* ever happening. Convincing herself that her memories of their time together would be enough, that they would sustain her.

It would have been the *safe* way to go.

Her laughter now held a hint of hysteria. Oh, she'd

gotten exactly what she deserved, being such a coward! She could leave Atlanta, but she would have to take her pain with her.

She turned her head, staring at the phone, her heart yearning to call Fontaine and spill her guts. She owed her sister an apology, she knew. Who was she to judge Fontaine? Until she walked a mile in her sister's shoes, she couldn't possibly know.

Decisively, Callie picked up the phone and dialed her sister's number. When Fontaine answered, sounding surprisingly cheerful and slightly tipsy, Callie was speechless for a full moment. Finally she sputtered, "Fontaine?" as if she wasn't entirely certain she had the right number.

Fontaine continued to shock her by laughing happily into the phone. "Callie! How are you? Sis, I am *so* sorry about our argument!"

Once again Callie had to struggle to think beyond her shock. "Are you okay, Fontaine? You sound . . ." How did she sound? Callie couldn't find the correct word.

"Happy?" Fontaine supplied with another one of those mind-boggling, bubbly, happy laughs so uncharacteristic of her business-oriented sister. "I owe part of it to you, darling sister."

"You . . . you do?"

"Yes! You said I kept dumping great guys because I was afraid of commitment. When I hung up the phone, I started thinking about what you said and I realized that you were right. So I called Juan."

Callie nearly dropped the phone. "Juan? The limo driver you had sex with when you got stranded on that bridge?"

Fontaine laughed again. "You remember! Well, what I didn't tell you was that it was love at first sight."

"He's there with you now," Callie guessed.

"Yes, he is. He's been taking great care of me."

"Well." Callie was overwhelmed with envy for a moment. Then she quashed her selfish thought and grinned. "Good for you!" she said sincerely.

"Thanks. I don't know if I would have done it if you hadn't been so brutally honest with me." There was a pregnant pause, and then Fontaine said, "The other news is a combination of good and bad. I discovered that Faith is our sneaky little mole!"

"No!" Callie was truly shocked. Faith had been with the company since its birth. "Are you certain?"

"Unfortunately, yes. She came to the house yesterday morning to go over some things, and when she excused herself to go to the bathroom, I realized I was missing a page of the layout I was holding. I was looking for it in her briefcase when I came across a list of the establishments I had planned to review in Atlanta—the same list I gave you."

Callie frowned. "She's your assistant. Is it so unusual that she would have the list?"

"You're darned right it is! I purposely didn't give her one, although truthfully I wasn't thinking that she could be the snitch. The clincher was that she had marked most of the businesses with a highlighter."

"Ouch!"

"Yes, ouch. When I confronted Faith, she admitted that she'd been alerting them. Well, I mean she could hardly deny it with the evidence right there in front of her."

"And her reasons?"

"For the perks," Fontaine said with a huff. "She has some vacation time coming up and she was planning to travel a lot. The very grateful establishments she was

alerting showed their appreciation by offering her hotel rooms, free meals at restaurants, and even free
drinks at some of the nightspots. It's disgusting."

Callie couldn't help smiling at Fontaine's outraged
tone. "Well, I'm sorry you lost a good assistant, but
glad you found out before she decided to dip into the
petty cash to fund her vacation."

Fontaine gasped. "I hadn't thought of that! I should
check first thing in the morning. What would I do
without you?"

"Get your own life?" Callie suggested in a teasing
tone. And then, before her sister could get sappy, she
said, "Hey, let me talk to Juan."

When Fontaine put Juan on the phone, Callie said
quickly, "She keeps a stash of Twinkies under her bed."

She hung up to the sound of Juan chuckling and
Fontaine feigning outrage in the background.
Fontaine sounded happy and carefree, and Callie was
glad for her sister; she really was.

That didn't stop her from wishing *she* could be
happy, as well.

Relaxing against the pillows, Callie sighed and allowed her battered heart to consider hope for a moment. What if Dillon had told the truth about loving
her? What if his declaration had nothing to do with
the fact that he believed she had influence over
Fontaine in regard to the reviews? Had Lanny's un-
faithfulness destroyed her faith, as well?

Callie's eyes narrowed at the ceiling. If Lanny truly
had destroyed her ability to hope, then it meant he'd
taken more from her than anyone could have dreamed.

The fund-raiser was tomorrow. She had to go. She
had promised Mary that she would help, and she
wouldn't let her down. Besides, Gina and her siblings

were the only ones Callie knew for certain hadn't been part of Dillon's deception. She wanted to see them before she left, and she wanted to meet Aunt LaVonda.

Was there any harm in watching Dillon and judging—without Lanny's ghostly influence—for herself whether he was sincere in loving her?

She turned onto her side and tucked her hand beneath her cheek. What did she have to lose?

Her heart was already breaking.

Chapter Twenty-six

Because Callie knew that if she had to spend one more moment in her hotel room staring at the walls she would scream, she arrived at Mary's an hour before schedule.

She found Mary in the backyard, trying to hold down a paper tablecloth and tape it to the table at the same time. The warm breeze was making the task nearly impossible to do single-handedly.

At the sound of Mary's frustrated curse, some of Callie's tension and heartache eased. Even if Dillon didn't love her, she knew she would not walk away from Atlanta empty-handed. She had found a wonderful friend in Mary, as well as several others.

"Looks like you could use a hand," Callie said, approaching the table and grabbing a billowing corner of the tablecloth. She held it down as Mary taped it to the weathered wood of the table.

When the task was done, Mary stood back and looked at Callie. "You look beautiful. Love the dress.

That powder-blue color lightens your eyes, and the matching hat makes you look like a model."

Callie blushed. "Thank you."

Mary waved a careless hand at her. "Wasn't anything but the truth. Did you read the review your magazine gave Dillon's nightclub last year?"

By this time Callie was accustomed to the way Mary leaped from subject to subject. She was also growing accustomed to the woman's uncanny perception. Mary had known Callie would read the review. "Yes, I did. It was awful." She hesitated, then said slowly, "My sister can be brutal. I'm sorry."

"Don't be. It wasn't your fault, and to tell you the truth . . ." Mary glanced at the patio doors leading into the house before she stepped closer. "Just between you and me, Dillon doesn't have a very good sense of style. Gets it from his father's side of the family. I mean, really, the Love Nest? Would *you* name a nightclub that?"

A giggle escaped Callie. "No, I wouldn't. I wondered who had come up with the name."

"I'm sorry to say it was Dillon." Mary's eyes twinkled. "Good thing he's drop-dead gorgeous, huh?" When Callie nodded, Mary laughed. She quickly sobered. "So . . . did you two settle anything? Or is this going to be one of those tension-fraught parties where you and Dillon spend the entire time trying to avoid each other, and everyone else pretends not to notice?"

Callie sat down on the picnic table bench and heaved a great sigh. "I don't know, Mary. He lied to me, and tricked me. How can I trust him?"

Joining her on the bench, Mary slipped an arm around her shoulders. "Listen, Callie. I'm his mother, so you probably wouldn't be surprised if I tried to talk you into handing Dillon your poor bruised heart on a silver platter, with a bottle of Tabasco on the side. But you probably *will* be surprised when I tell you that deciding to trust someone with your heart is a decision only *you* can make. This way you can't blame the outcome on anyone but yourself."

"But you said yesterday that you believe Dillon loves me," Callie persisted, shamelessly seeking reassurance.

"That was my gut feeling, not a psychic vision."

"But you're his *mother.*"

"And *you're* the woman who helped Dillon get over his fear of children, and prompted him to do something he's never, ever done before in his life."

"I . . . I have?" Callie's voice rose in a nervous squeak at Mary's grave tone, which gave her no indication whether it was a good thing or a bad thing. When Callie thought of all the ways she and Dillon had avoided having actual intercourse, heat rose into her face. Was this the prompting Mary spoke of? But no, it couldn't be, because Dillon had admitted that he wasn't actually working for Mr. Complete, so his ethics hadn't been compromised.

Mary nodded somberly, but her eyes had begun to twinkle. "Yes, you have. For the first time in his twenty-nine years of life, Dillon not only picked up his dirty socks; he washed and folded them."

It took a moment for Callie to realize what Mary had said. When the words sank in, Callie let out a shaky laugh. Then she had a vivid mental image of Dillon bending over the sock basket, teasing her with his buns of steel.

She colored all over again, and this time Mary burst out laughing, as if she knew exactly what Callie was thinking. Callie joined her. When she finally caught

Sheridon Smythe

her breath, she said, "Let me get this straight. Dillon picks up his dirty socks, washes and folds them, and you believe this is proof that he loves me."

"He's never done it for anyone else," Mary said with conviction. "I'll tell you something else, too. If I hadn't found that basket of folded socks on his couch and put them away, I think *he* would have."

She sounded so astonished by the possibility, Callie found herself giggling again. "You're really serious about this, aren't you?"

"Definitely! Sometimes people are so intent on looking for deep, meaningful signs of love, they forget to look right beneath their noses."

"Or in laundry baskets," Callie said with a straight face, although she could do nothing about her twitching lips.

"Exactly." Mary patted Callie's knee as if she were a teacher praising a smart student. "Come on. Let's go ice the cupcakes. I've got the cutest little candy-animal decorations for the children to put on afterward. . . ."

Anticipation warred with trepidation as Callie followed Mary inside.

Could she really put all her faith in a laundry basket full of socks?

Dillon hated losing.

If the "boys" loved Mrs. Scuttle so much, why did they insist on drawing names just to decide who would pick her up and bring her to the fund-raiser?

And why did he have the gut feeling that every name on those scraps of paper had read, *Dillon?*

"Are you paying attention, Dillon?" Mrs. Scuttle asked from her position in the passenger seat of his

Jeep. "Because I don't fancy dying today just because you can't keep your mind on your driving."

When he didn't immediately answer, she ground a bony elbow into his ribs. Dillon gasped and hastily said, "I'm paying attention, I'm paying attention!"

"Good. Because I'm—Eek!" she screeched suddenly, slamming her purse into his shoulder and jarring his teeth from the impact. "Watch out!"

With his heart pounding and his shoulder throbbing—*what the hell did she keep in her purse, anyway? The kitchen sink?*—Dillon pulled the Jeep onto the shoulder and brought it to a shuddering halt. "What is it?" he barked, looking wildly all around him.

There was no traffic. No animals in the road. No kids playing, no bikes, joggers, or hitchhikers.

It was clear in either direction.

When he looked at Mrs. Scuttle for an answer, he found her big owlish eyes narrowed murderously on him. Her lips, pressed tightly together, had all but disappeared.

Was he the only person who recognized insanity? he wondered, breaking out into a cold sweat while she continued to look at him as if he'd mowed down a litter of kittens crossing the road.

Barely holding on to his patience—and his courage—he asked again, "What is it?"

"It was a frog, Dillon," the secretary announced, with about as much emotion as a sane person would use if they were talking about a group of preschoolers. "You ran over a poor helpless frog. Aren't you ashamed? Do you need glasses?"

The reason for the name drawing became crystal-clear at that precise moment. Dillon opened his mouth, then prudently closed it. She was too close and her purse was too damned heavy for him to say what he really wanted to say.

Not to mention the gallon-sized coffee can she clutched in her other arm. On the front she had taped a sign with letters in big, bold neon-green. It read, "Give me your money or your life." Dillon had no doubt whatsoever that Mrs. Scuttle would take in the haul of the century before the fund-raiser ended, and woe to those who didn't know her well enough to be frightened.

As far as he knew, the can was empty, but he wasn't taking any chances.

Striving to sound sincere instead of sarcastic, Dillon said, "I'm sorry, Mrs. Scuttle. I didn't see the frog."

"Don't apologize to me!" she bawled, nearly deafening Dillon. "Apologize to that frog's poor family!"

It would be useless, he decided as he pulled back onto the road and continued at a snail's pace, his eyes glued to the blacktop, to explain to Mrs. Scuttle that frogs didn't have families, that they laid their eggs and swam away.

Useless and dangerous.

Mentally cursing his mischievous friends for putting him into this position, Dillon kept his eyes peeled for anything that might prompt the secretary into another life-threatening outbreak.

Life-threatening to him, that is.

By the time they crept onto the shady street where his mother lived, Dillon was certain they would be the last ones to arrive. "Do you want me to drop you off at the house before I park?" he asked, inwardly congratulating himself for his infinite patience.

Mrs. Scuttle promptly squashed his fragile ego.

"No, I want you to make me drag this poor old frail body two blocks because you don't have any brains."

Was he just being paranoid and overly sensitive? Dillon wondered, or was Mrs. Scuttle more vicious than usual? Though he knew better, he heard himself asking, "Are you mad at me about something?"

She turned to look at him as he stopped the Jeep in front of his childhood home. "Mad at you?" She blinked a dozen times in rapid succession. "Why would I be mad at you, Mr. Frog Killer? You nearly wrecked Luke's business because you couldn't keep your horse in the corral—"

Dillon choked. His *horse?*

"—you broke Callie's heart just when she was beginning to trust men again, and you lied to a poor old helpless widow woman about being diabetic." She eyed the can in her lap wistfully for a long moment.

Long enough for Dillon to casually place his hand on the door latch for a quick getaway if she started swinging.

Finally she tore her gaze from the weapon and looked at him again with a feigned innocence she'd had seventy-nine years to perfect. "Why would I be mad at you?"

Feeling reckless—and obviously suicidal—Dillon leaped headfirst into the frying pan.

But he wisely kept his hand on the door latch.

"I'm going to tell you why you shouldn't be mad at me." There was a split second of hesitation when he saw Mrs. Scuttle's magnified pupils dilate. He wasn't going to begin to guess what it meant, because if he did, he suspected he'd lose his courage. "In the first place, I wasn't working for Luke, so I wasn't getting

305

paid, which meant that I wasn't breaking any rules by, um, *being* with Callie. In the second place, I happen to love Callie and intend to convince her of that fact if it takes the rest of my life."

Mrs. Scuttle started blinking again, but she kept quiet.

"Lastly, I lied to you about being a diabetic because I didn't want you to eat that Danish." He paused, his fingers tightening on the door latch before he added, "Because that Danish was covered in rat droppings. *Not* raisins."

The secretary appeared to be speechless with shock. It was a great moment for Dillon. A fine moment. A moment he knew would live on in his memory forever.

He couldn't wait to tell the boys.

After opening and closing her mouth several times, Mrs. Scuttle finally whispered, "You ate that nasty Danish for *me?*"

Hmm. Dillon gave the question all of two seconds before lying through his teeth. "Yes." Feeling almost giddy, he watched the dislike in her eyes give way to something akin to hero worship. She placed a cold, gnarled hand on either side of his face and smiled at him.

Then she inched forward, lips pursed.

Dillon sighed blissfully and turned his cheek for the much-earned victory kiss. He even closed his eyes to savor the moment. He couldn't wait to tell the guys that Mrs. Scuttle had actually given him a chaste kiss on the cheek. He was certain she'd never expressed gratitude to the other guys.

Only it wasn't his cheek her thin lips settled on.

It was his mouth, and it wasn't a chaste kiss, but a full-blown man-woman kiss with a touch of tongue.

Her tongue, that is, because the Jaws of Life couldn't have opened Dillon's lips at that moment.

His warm fuzzies vanished in a burst of horror. Before he could seal his fate by jerking away, she ended the kiss and leaned back in her seat. He stared at her dreamy expression, dismayed and embarrassed beyond belief.

She didn't seem to notice. "Poor Dill," she cooed. "I know it hurts, but you'll be happier with Callie. She's young." Her ample bosom rose in a deep, regretful sigh. "I'm too old to have kids."

He tried not to jerk back when she reached out and gave his cheek a solicitous pat. He succeeded . . . just.

"Now, I know it's going to be hard, but you're going to have to forget that kiss. It never happened, understand? I wouldn't hurt Callie for the world."

Dillon swallowed three times before he could manage to speak. Nevertheless, his voice came out hoarse. "Um, I'll try to forget." A fifth of Jack Daniel's ought to do it. "Thank . . . thank you for being strong for both of us."

"It was my pleasure, Dill. My pleasure."

"Something's wrong with Dillon," Casey announced, relieving Mary of the plate of deviled eggs she was holding. One by one she started popping them into her mouth. She spoke around the food to Mary and Callie, who had returned to the kitchen for more appetizers. "He keeps asking people if they brought any liquor, and he's not being picky about what kind."

Mary's eyebrows rose. She shot Callie a pointed look as she said, "Laundry basket."

"Laundry basket?" Casey parroted.

Callie frowned, ignoring Casey's bewildered look.

307

"I've seen Dillon drink. How can that be a laundry basket?"

"He drinks beer and wine occasionally, but he never gets drunk." Mary opened a plastic bowl and filled a tray with cold shrimp. "In Dillon's case, once was enough. He puked blue margaritas for a week."

Casey snatched a big prawn from the tray and shoved it into her mouth. "Will someone please tell me what you two are talking about?"

"We're talking about Dillon, and how odd it is that he wants to get drunk," Mary said, adding a bowl of cocktail sauce to the tray.

"But I don't understand what that has to do with a laundry basket." Casey took another shrimp, dipped it, and inhaled it. She swallowed it after three chews. "You guys are making me feel dizzy."

"Sorry." Callie handed Casey a much-needed napkin. "The laundry basket is a metaphor."

"God," Casey said, sounding disgusted. "Can you speak English? I'm not Einstein!"

Mary took pity on Casey. "What we really mean is, we're looking for clues that prove Dillon's in love with Callie."

Casey's eyes bulged. She nearly choked on her shrimp. "Are you serious? You guys are just now figuring out that Dillon loves Callie?"

"No, *I* knew it," Mary said. She pointed the shrimp tray at Callie. "But you know how it is. The woman's always the last to know, or in this case, the last to be convinced."

"Well," Casey said, apparently giving up on the mystery of the laundry basket, "all I can say is that Dillon looks as if he saw Mrs. Scuttle naked or something.

308

Kind of green around the gills, if you know what I mean."

Mary glanced at her watched and frowned. "Wasn't he supposed to pick up Aunt LaVonda at the airport?"

"Yeah, but he sent Will, said he didn't think he could drive." Casey emphasized her point by lifting her brows until they disappeared beneath her bangs. "Hint, hint. Something's *wrong* with him."

Switching the empty tray in her hand for the one that Mary held, Casey waddled through the patio doors. She didn't have the look of a woman ready to share, either, Callie noted with deep affection and more than a little envy.

"Poor Dillon," Mary said in a neutral tone. "He's obviously scared to death that he blew it with you."

"I guess I should talk to him." Callie put a hand over her quivering stomach to still the butterflies there. She'd been trying to gather her courage from the moment Dillon arrived, but each time she chickened out.

What if he'd changed his mind?

What if he didn't love her?

What if he was scared to death because he knew he had to tell her that he didn't love her after all?

"Go." Mary gave her a slight push. "Get it over with before you both get sick."

Callie took a deep breath, nodded, and went to find Dillon.

She ran into Mrs. Scuttle on the patio. The elderly secretary was clutching a big coffee can and beaming.

"He's grilling hot dogs for the kids," Mrs. Scuttle told her before Callie could ask. She patted Callie's arm. "You take good care of him, you hear? You're a lucky woman."

With that mysterious comment ringing in her ears, Callie spotted Dillon and moved slowly through the clusters of people chatting and eating. She estimated there were around fifty-five people, most of whom she didn't know. One man, dressed in an expensive suit, held a Ziploc bag of ice to his jaw. When he saw her staring, he lowered the bag and shot her a rueful smile.

"Mrs. Scuttle accidentally hit me in the jaw with her money can," he explained.

"Oh." Callie moved on hastily, fearing it hadn't been an accident at all.

With her gaze intent on Dillon, she bumped into a hard wall and bounced backward.

An arm shot out to steady her. Callie mumbled her thanks, but she did a double take when she saw the raw steak the guy was holding in his other hand.

And then she saw the man's black eye. "Oh." She gasped, staring at his injury. "I'm afraid to ask you what happened."

"Just an accident. Mrs. Scuttle dropped my donation money, and when I bent down to pick it up, she accidentally elbowed me in the eye."

"Yeah, okay." Callie swallowed a groan. She needed to get to Dillon, but now she had a new quest. They had to stop Mrs. Scuttle from outright killing someone who didn't donate what she thought they could easily afford.

Her alarm grew when she passed a woman limping and another man rubbing a bump on his forehead as if he'd run into a wall.

Or a coffee can filled with money.

She stopped at a picnic table to question a guest who was soaking his hand in a bowl of ice water.

Thank God he'd injured himself by grabbing a hot spatula from one of the outdoor grills.

By the time she reached Dillon, she was sweating bullets. "Dillon!"

He turned at the sound of her voice, flashing her a pained smile.

The butterflies in Callie's stomach turned into angry bees. Dillon looked as if he'd bitten into a rotten apple; definitely not the look of a man greeting the woman he supposedly loved. Her lips were dry; she had to lick them twice them before she said, "You've got to be firm with Mrs. Scuttle about this."

Dillon's pained expression turned to outright dismay. "What? I do? How did you . . ." He shook his head as if dazed. "It's terrible, isn't it? I never thought she would do something like that."

Callie blinked, wondering if she'd heard Dillon correctly. "You didn't? I mean, she's done this before, hasn't she?" Her confusion deepened when Dillon jerked back as if she'd slapped him.

"No! Never!" He emphatically shook his head. "It just came out of nowhere, and I did *not* encourage her!"

"Well, that's a relief. It sounds just like something you or Wyatt might encourage her to do, especially if it involves money."

Dillon's jaw dropped. His face flushed a dull red. "You think that I . . . that we . . . that we . . . would encourage her to do it for money?"

When his normally deep voice ended on a high, squeaky note, Callie attempted to calm him. He was genuinely upset, she realized, feeling guilty. "I'm sorry, Dillon. It's just that I'm afraid she's really going to hurt

311

someone when she goes after them like that." To her mystification, Dillon's Adam's apple bobbed up and down as he swallowed nervously.

"I know exactly what you mean," he said hoarsely. "She could cause someone to have a heart attack." He swallowed again. "Not to mention nightmares."

Callie blew out a relieved breath. "Whew! I'm glad you agree with me. For a moment there I thought we were talking about two different things. So you'll find her and tell her it's got to stop before it goes too far?"

"Yes, yes, if you're that concerned about it, although I can't imagine why you'd be jealous of an old lady."

"Jealous?" Callie narrowed her eyes. "Did you find some alcohol? Are you drunk?"

"I wish," Dillon mumbled.

"Why would I be jealous of Mrs. Scuttle abusing the guests to get bigger donations out of them? Am I missing something here?" When Dillon closed his eyes and let out a dry, helpless laugh, Callie realized she *had* missed something. Unfortunately, she didn't know what. "Dillon?"

Instead of answering, Dillon pulled her into his arms and nearly crushed her. She could feel him trembling all over. His breath was hot near her ear as he whispered, "Let's go upstairs. I want to show you my bedroom."

Callie melted against him, more than willing to see it.

Chapter Twenty-seven

"We shouldn't stay long. Aunt LaVonda will be here shortly."

Dillon closed the door and locked it. He leaned against it and looked at Callie, who stood in the middle of his childhood bedroom with something akin to panic darkening her blue eyes to violet.

He knew what panic felt like, and sympathized. He was hard-pressed to blot the memory of Mrs. Scuttle from his mind. But he knew that if anyone could do it, Callie could. He let his gaze drift lazily over her until he was rewarded by her quickened breathing. Now *that* was the Callie he knew and loved.

Panting for him. Breathless and aching.

Speaking of aching . . . He pushed away from the door and walked slowly to her, his voice a lazy drawl as he said, "Her plane doesn't land for another hour. I sent Will early because he and Mom couldn't seem to spend five minutes apart."

She stood her ground. Shoulders straight. Gorgeous, sexy blue eyes riveted to his face. Her lips parted. He grew hard just watching her little pink tongue dart out to moisten them.

"Would it be so bad if Mary fell in love again?" she asked huskily.

But Dillon didn't want to talk about his mother. He wanted to talk about Callie, and whether she had the capacity to forgive a foolish man for taking so long to see that Atlanta meant nothing to him if Callie wasn't a part of it. "We need to talk, Callie. You and I. I have to tell you that—" Before he could finish, Callie stepped brazenly forward and placed a shushing finger to his lips. He resisted the urge to suck her finger into his mouth.

"Don't," she warned, her eyes big and blue and filled with a sharp, searing need that Dillon recognized. "Don't say anything just yet. Let's just do it."

Dillon's throat went dry. "Do it?" he croaked.

She nodded, slowly dropping her finger. The tips of her breasts hovered scant centimeters away from his chest. "Yes, do it. Have intercourse. Make love. Have sex. Go all the way." She took a tiny step forward, just enough to make him suck in a sharp breath as her hard nipples touched his chest. "I don't want you to talk, unless it's R-rated."

Her eyes grew liquid, and the sight went straight to Dillon's knees, turning them to jelly. What happened to the panic? He wondered. He kept his mouth closed, afraid to break the spell.

"No matter what you say or do afterward, I want this moment. Right here, right now. I want you inside of me, fulfilling all those delicious, erotic promises you've been making." Her jaw hardened. The sensuous light in her eyes darkened with determination.

When the tips of her fingers touched his chest lightly, Dillon had to stifle a moan.

"I'm not going to spend the rest of my life wondering what I missed, Dillon." She glanced behind her to the single bed where Dillon had dreamed and slept during his childhood. She looked back at him, her eyes blazing with lust and fear and need. "I want you to take me to that bed and give me what you promised. Then if you want to talk, we'll talk."

"Are . . . are you sure?" he asked in a croak. He was afraid, deathly afraid Callie wasn't thinking straight. That she'd regret her demand afterward, when it was too late. "Because I really want to tell you that I—"

That finger again. Closing his mouth and making him swallow words of love and adoration and commitment.

The realization made him stiffen in alarm. Was that it? Was Callie trying to tell him that she was not in love with him, but in lust? Was she attempting to have sex with him before she gave him the bad news? Dillon struggled with his libido as he analyzed his ego.

Yes, they had teased each another, brought each other to many fabulous orgasms without the benefit of intercourse. Did Callie feel as if he *owed* her the whole enchilada before she packed her suitcase and caught a plane?

Dillon was torn. The man in him wanted to sink into her, find out if she was as tight as he suspected she was. Wanted to plunge into her hot sheath and watch her face, watch it grow taut with sexual tension as she grew closer and closer to her release. Watch her blue eyes darken to black.

He wasn't a hypocrite. He *wanted* to be the first man to fill her in three long years.

But he wanted to be the *only* man, from this moment on until death did they part.

"I can't," he blurted out. Sweat popped out onto his

brow and on his upper lip. What was he doing? His jeans felt as if they would burst, and he was telling her he couldn't? It was almost comical, considering the fact that the mere touch of her hands could set him off.

Her brows lifted, then fell, clearly conveying how little she believed him. With a confident smile playing about her moist, full lips, she traced the hard outline of his erection through his jeans. Her fingers felt like hot pokers through the denim.

He wouldn't have been surprised to find sparks flying from his zipper.

"The *hell* you can't," she said in a low, gut-punching voice. "I think you want to as much as *I* want to. In fact, I think you're going to start taking my panties off right now."

Before she finished the sentence, Dillon discovered his hands were under her God-she's-hot dress, as if he were a puppet and she the puppet master. The tips of his fingers brushed the top elastic of her panties, then hooked and tugged them down.

Just like a good little puppet.

Down along her firm thighs, past her knees until they pooled around her ankles.

He watched, dazed and mesmerized as she stepped out of them, her hot, erotic gaze never wavering from his face.

She was now naked beneath a dress he'd been wanting to tear off of her from the moment he saw her bending over his mother's oven to check on the stuffed mushrooms.

There was no bra. He knew it because he knew Callie. Had explored every inch of her body. Had tasted, touched, and invaded every part of her that could be tasted, touched, or invaded.

With the exception of the ultimate.

She was offering that to him now. Demanding it, if he wanted to face the truth. Whatever her motives, he knew he was beyond denial, beyond redemption.

He wanted Callie.

And she wanted him.

Yes, they could damn well talk later.

It wasn't a coincidence, Callie decided, sucking in a sharp breath as Dillon lifted her dress over her head, that the song drifting up from the party below was "Black Velvet," a sultry, sexy song that made her blood throb in her veins.

As if she weren't already throbbing enough.

She was now naked, standing in the stream of evening light coming through the window. They were at the front of the house, upstairs, away from people and the party going on in Mary's backyard.

They were shameless—*she* was shameless. Their absence would be noticed; people would start to speculate. Will would be returning with Aunt LaVonda.

"If they notice, they won't care," Dillon said, clearly reading her expression. "But if you want to postpone—"

"No!" Callie flushed. She hadn't meant to yell at him. When he flashed her a wicked, knee-weakening smile, the last of her reservations fell away. She reached for his jeans button and flipped it open, then drew down the zipper, freeing his erection for her eager little hands.

She couldn't wait to feel him inside her, claiming her, branding her.

Dominating her.

Loving her.

"Please, Dillon," she heard herself whisper. "Before

something or someone interrupts us." She closed her hand around him, heard him suck in a raw breath.

"You want it fast and hard?" Dillon growled, pushing her slowly toward the bed. "Because I don't know if I can do it any other way right now."

"Yes, that's the way I want it." She pushed his jeans over his hips and helped him step out of them, then went to work on his shirt as he tore open a condom and sheathed himself. In moments he was naked.

In seconds she was on her back and Dillon loomed over her, his face a taut mask of tenderness, anticipation, and passion.

"I don't want to hurt you," he whispered, gazing into her eyes.

Callie opened her legs and thrust her hips upward until she felt the hot tip of his erection at her entrance. "You won't," she said with more confidence than she felt. "I'm ready." It wasn't a lie. She'd never been more ready in her life.

He sank slowly into her, inch by incredible inch, stretching her. Filling her. Callie felt tears spring to her eyes. She bit her lip, not from pain, but from sheer emotion. God, she loved him.

Her heart thundered as she watched his expression. He continued to ease into her, jaw clenched as he fought the urge to do it fast and hard, the way they both wanted. As he buried himself to the hilt, he threw back his head.

"God, Callie. You're so tight I can barely hang on!" The cords in his neck bulged.

"Then don't. Don't hang on." She was panting, burning up inside. She'd never felt anything more incredible in her life. Taking his face in her hands, she forced him to look at her. "You won't leave me behind,

Dillon." Her smile was slow and full of promise. "In fact, I think I might leave *you* behind."

She wasn't kidding. The moment he began to withdraw, she felt her muscles start to contract wildly around him, as if her body feared he'd leave her for good.

But Dillon wasn't leaving her. He began to stroke her, his pace increasing with each thrust. She clutched his arms, trying to wait for him, trying to hang on.

She couldn't. Digging her nails into him, she arched her hips and tumbled over the edge. A cry escaped her. Dillon caught it with his mouth, his tongue thrusting deep as he followed her over the edge, their explosion all the more pleasurable as they came together, feeding from each other to experience the ultimate orgasm.

As the waves of pleasure slowly receded, Callie struggled to catch her breath. She smiled up at Dillon, her heart feeling as if it would burst. "That was indescribable." His lazy, answering grin made her madly pounding heart somersault.

"I agree," he said, placing a tender, lingering kiss on her mouth. He pulled back, supporting himself on his arms to keep his weight from crushing her. His expression turned serious. "Callie . . . I—"

The expectant moment was shattered by an ear-piercing scream. It was a child's scream, a wail filled with grief and terror.

Dillon didn't take time to button his shirt, or mention to Callie that she'd put her dress on inside out. He thundered downstairs with Callie at his heels, his imagination escalating as the horrible screams continued.

They burst from the patio doors into the backyard, pushing through the crowd of people blocking their view.

He stopped dead in his tracks, vaguely aware that Callie literally bounced off his back before she clutched his waist to hold herself steady.

It was Caleb who was screaming. Standing helplessly before him was a striking, dark-haired woman dressed in a slightly wrinkled business suit.

"What is it?" Dillon demanded, instinctively looking to Gina for an answer. His heart lurched at the sight of her grief-stricken face. She was balancing a clueless Adrienne on her slim hip. Matt, standing on the other side of the screaming Caleb, looking equally shocked and grief-stricken.

Before Dillon could question what drove him, he scooped Caleb into his arms and pressed the child's face to his shoulder. "Shh, little one. It's okay. I've got you." He rocked him back and forth, holding him tightly.

Caleb's screams stopped abruptly. Harsh sobs began to rack his body. Dillon heard him utter his first words since losing his mother. His voice was pitiful, gut-wenching. "Mommy. My mommy."

Over his shoulder, Dillon shot Gina another bewildered, questioning look.

The teenager wiped at her eyes and took a shuddering breath—ever the warrior—before she said, "It's Aunt LaVonda. I'd forgotten how much she looks like Mama. Caleb thought it *was* Mama. When Aunt LaVonda told him who she was, he started screaming. I couldn't get him to stop."

LaVonda was crying openly as well. She reached out and stroked Caleb's back. "I'm sorry, Caleb. I miss her, too, but you've got me now. You're all going to come live with me in California. Would you like that? It'll be fun."

In his arms, Dillon felt Caleb stiffen. His sobs subsided to sniffles. He lifted his head and peeped at his aunt through tear-spiked lashes. His bottom lip shot out as he said peevishly, "I want my mommy."

"I know, sweetie." LaVonda summoned a smile through her tears and held out her arms. "I do, too, but she's gone to heaven to live with the angels."

Caleb eyed her outstretched arms for a long moment, then slowly shifted his weight in that direction. LaVonda took him and hugged him tight. She held out her arm to wave the other children to her.

They didn't need much prompting. Soon LaVonda was clutching them all to her, crying and laughing at the same time.

Dillon looked around, noticing that there wasn't a dry eye in the group. When his gaze landed on Will, he felt a jolt of surprise.

Will was staring at LaVonda, his expression shell-shocked, dazed. Dillon recognized that look . . . and his confusion deepened. He glanced at his mother, who was watching LaVonda and wiping her face as tears continued to roll down her cheeks.

His protective instincts prompted a wave of anger. Though he might not approve of the romance between Will and Mary, he didn't want his mother hurt, and if he was guessing correctly, Will would soon be breaking her heart in favor of LaVonda.

Catching Wyatt's eye—which was suspiciously wet—Dillon jerked his head at Will, sending Wyatt a silent message. He skirted the crowd and caught Will by the arm just as Wyatt caught Will's other arm.

"We need to talk to you," Dillon said in a low voice. "Come with us."

Sheridon Smythe

Not really having a choice, Will went with them into the kitchen. He leaned against the counter, clearly confused by the menacing faces of his friends. "What's up? Why are you two looking at me as if I'm the lowest form of life?"

"We know you've been seeing Mom behind our backs," Dillon said without preamble. "And I saw how you were looking at LaVonda."

Wyatt gasped, apparently having missed Will's infatuated look. "What the hell?" He clenched his fists and started toward Will.

Dillon caught his rock-hard arm, having seen Will's confusion give way to amusement. "Wait. Let's give him a chance to explain."

"I have been seeing your mom behind your backs," Will confirmed, actually smiling. "But it's not what you two paranoid, overprotective slugs think." He paused to give them time to anticipate his next words. "I've been helping Mary study."

"Study?" Dillon echoed, disbelief mixing with righteous anger.

Will nodded. "I'm a teacher . . . or was."

"Why in the hell didn't you tell us?" Wyatt demanded.

"There's a reason." Will's amusement became a thing of the past. He sighed. "It's embarrassing and humiliating. I guess I wanted to give you guys a chance to get to know me before you passed judgment."

"Okay," Dillon said. "We know you, so spill."

"As you know, I'm from North Dakota. I was a high school teacher there. There was this girl I taught. . . ." Will paused to rub a hand over his chin. He looked from one twin to the other, as if trying to gauge their reactions ahead of time. "She became infatuated with me, and when I repeatedly rejected her advances, she went to the school nurse and told her that we'd been having an affair."

"They believed her," Wyatt guessed, sounding disgusted on Will's behalf.

Will shrugged, but his dark eyes sparked with remembered pain. "Some did ... and some didn't. It didn't really matter at that point. The school had to let me go. The girl dropped the charges, but the damage was already done."

"Man, that sucks." Wyatt went to the refrigerator and grabbed a bottle of root beer. He offered one to Will and took one for himself. "So can't you get a teaching job here?"

"Maybe, but I think it's going to take some time before I even *want* to teach again." Will shook his head as if to shake off the unpleasantness of his thoughts. He looked at Dillon, and his smile returned. "Enough about me." His gaze dipped to Dillon's crotch, then up again. His dark brows lifted. "Did you know your fly's open?"

As Dillon gave a start, then hurriedly zipped his pants, Wyatt and Will burst out laughing. He glowered at them. "What do you guys do for entertainment when I'm not around?"

"Well," Wyatt said, looking over Dillon's shoulder as he lifted his soft drink in a mock toast. "There's always Callie. I'm sure I'm not the only one who would like to know why she's wearing her dress turned inside out."

At Callie's embarrassed shriek, Dillon swung around. He caught her before she could dart away, pressing her flaming face into his shoulder. He continued to glower at Will and Wyatt, but he was inwardly laughing as he silently waved them from the room. He and Callie had unfinished business, and come hell or high water, he was going to get on with it.

When they were alone again, he hooked a finger beneath her chin and lifted her flushed face. He kissed her, slowly and thoroughly, until they were both trembling and weak-kneed. Finally he reluctantly put her from him.

He looked deeply into her eyes until he was satisfied with what he saw. "Do you trust me?" he asked huskily.

She nodded.

"Close your eyes." When she'd closed them, Dillon poured a glass of milk and took her hand, curling her fingers around it. "Keep your eyes closed, and drink this." He helped guide the glass to her mouth.

She took a cautious sip, then a bigger one. Dillon let go, watching her drain the entire glass of milk with obvious enjoyment. When she'd finished, she opened her eyes and looked at him.

Her adoring expression spoke a thousand words.

"Thank you," she whispered, just before she kissed him.

Dillon finished the kiss by licking the milk mustache from her upper lip. Now was the time, he thought to himself. He was going to pop the question before another emergency arose. "Callie, will you—"

"Callie?"

He bit off an oath and turned with Callie in his arms. Was there a big conspiracy to keep him from declaring his love and proposing to Callie?

Casey stood braced in the kitchen doorway. Her face was ashen, her eyes huge pools of fear.

"I . . . I think my water just broke," Casey whispered. "In the bathroom. All over Mary's pretty bathroom rug."

"Are you having labor pains?" Callie demanded, racing to Casey. She waved Dillon over to help support her as they led her to a chair.

"My . . . my back's been hurting since yesterday, but I just thought it was because I've gained so much weight."

"Is it hurting now?"

"Yes."

"Does it come and go?"

"No. It's just one big long pain right now." She caught her breath, and Dillon caught his as well. "I feel a lot of pressure between—"

"I'll go find Brett," Dillon said hastily, feeling a familiar panic creep over him.

Casey caught his arm, her fingers digging in painfully. "He left about thirty minutes ago."

"I'll call him on his cell." Dillon's hands were shaking as he pulled out his cell phone and flipped it open. When would the madness end? he wondered. And how could a woman of Casey's intelligence not realize she was in labor?

"Don't bother," Casey said breathlessly, as if something or someone were attempting to squeeze the life out of her. "He's on his way to Chicago, and if he's boarded the plane he'll have his cell turned off."

"What the hell is he doing going to Chicago when his wife is about to have a baby?" Dillon demanded almost shrilly.

"The baby wasn't due for another two weeks," Casey explained.

"Then I'll call an ambulance." He looked up and caught Callie's chiding expression. With an inward sigh, he heard himself saying, "Or we could take you to the hospital in my Jeep."

Callie helped Casey to her feet. "I'll drive. Dillon, you can sit in the back with Casey in case she needs you."

In case she needed him? Dillon didn't like the sound of that. In fact, the implications turned his legs to jelly. "I want to drive," he said, and even to his own ears he sounded like a belligerent child.

"I don't *think* so," Callie said. "If this baby comes before we get to the hospital, I don't want you to be behind the wheel."

Dillon's jaw dropped. "You think it would be safer for me to be . . . be . . ." He shuddered, unable to finish. Callie knew about his irrational fear of children—babies in particular—even if he had managed to make great strides to overcome his phobia. Why would she torture him this way?

As if she had read his mind, Callie placed a brief, tender kiss on his open mouth. "Think of it as practice, darling."

He closed his mouth, attempting to glare at her. Oh, she was good. She was very good.

God, he loved her.

Chapter Twenty-eight

"She's squeezing the life out of my hand again," Dillon said for the fourth time since leaving his mother's house.

Callie bit back a smile, glancing in the rearview mirror at Dillon's tense expression. "She's having contractions, Dillon. It's normal. Keep timing them."

"*She* happens to be in labor, not deaf," Casey grated out. "God, this hurts! I want drugs. Give me drugs."

"She wants drugs," Dillon said, as if he believed Callie could produce them on command. "What should I do?"

"Keep holding her hand. Talk to her." Callie pressed the accelerator a little harder. If her calculations were right, Casey was progressing fast for a first-timer. As much as she wanted to desensitize Dillon, she didn't think he could handle delivering a baby in the back of his Jeep.

"Talk to her? I . . . I . . . okay. I remember when Mom went into labor with Isabelle. We were putting up an aboveground pool in the backyard—not one of those easy, pop-up kind they sell now. Wyatt and I were so excited we didn't even mind having to clear the ground. In fact, a couple of our friends were help-ing us—"

"Get to the damned point!" Casey snarled.

Callie heard Dillon hiss and knew that Casey was having another powerful contraction. She glanced in the side mirror at the traffic behind her, then did a double take. There was a convoy of cars following them, most of them familiar. Casey hadn't wanted to ruin the party, so they had attempted to sneak away. Mary had caught them but had promised to keep quiet.

So much for promises, Callie mused ruefully. From the looks of it, the entire party was behind them. When Dillon started talking again, she tried to focus on her driving, but it was impossible not to respond to the rough, nervous timbre of his voice.

It was a sound she hoped to hear every day for the rest of her life. Did Dillon feel the same way? Did he really love her? Did he want to marry her?

"The whole time we were putting the pool together, she was in labor, but she wouldn't tell us. When she fi-nally did go to the hospital, she barely made it before Isabelle was born."

"So your mother is a freakin' saint!" Casey said with uncharacteristic vehemence. "Got any other stupid stories rattling around in that gourd you call a brain?"

Callie caught Dillon's bewildered expression in the mirror and gave her head a slight shake. "How about you and Wyatt? Has your mother ever told you what it was like having twins?"

Dillon's expression brightened. He even managed a chuckle or two. "She's only thrown it in our faces about a million times. She was in labor for about eighteen hours before I was finally born. Wyatt wasn't ready to come out, so the doctor had to reach in and pull him out, kicking and screaming. He's been a mama's boy ever since."

"Eighteen hours?" Casey echoed in horror.

Callie and Dillon groaned simultaneously. She felt compelled to defend Dillon. "Casey, Dillon's just trying to distract you from the pain. He's not intentionally torturing you."

Sounding resigned, Dillon said, "I take it eighteen hours is a long time to be in labor?"

"Yes," both women said. Before Casey could dwell on it, Callie hastened on. "Casey, do you want us to call someone for you?"

She was silent a long moment before she said in a subdued voice, "Mom and Dad went to Florida to visit my brother and his family. She was supposed to be in the delivery room with me, too. We thought we had two more weeks." Casey's shaky sigh was audible. "Looks like I'm going to have to do this alone."

Before Callie opened her mouth, Dillon was shaking his head. She ignored him. "You won't be alone. Dillon and I will stand in for Brett and your mother. Won't we, Dillon?"

"But doesn't Dillon have this phobia about babies?" Casey asked.

"Which is exactly why he should do this." The more Callie thought about it, the more excited she became.

"*He's* not deaf, and he's sitting in the backseat," Dillon said. "And I am *not* going to stand in for Brett. Holding her hand while she breaks my fingers is one thing; watching her give birth is quite another. Nope. I won't do it."

* * *

"Are you her husband?"

"No," Dillon said as yet another nurse came into the room to check on Casey. He glared at Callie, who stood on Casey's right side. She was calmly feeding Casey ice chips while *he* continued to sacrifice his hand to the strongest woman he'd ever known.

Brett was so going to owe him for this one. Big-time.

"My husband's on his way back from the airport," Casey panted. Fortunately, they had been able to reach him before he boarded his flight. "Do you think he'll have time to get here?"

The nurse removed her hand from a place Dillon didn't want to think about, popped off her gloves, and pitched them in the wastebasket. "How long will it take him to get here?"

"Um, that depends on traffic."

Casey wasn't the only one who didn't think it was funny when the nurse laughed. Dillon scowled at the nurse as Casey proceeded to tell her exactly what she thought of her dark humor.

When she'd finished, the nurse smiled, patted her knee, and left the room. Dillon had the distinct impression it wasn't the first time the nurse had been told off by a patient.

Callie, ever the diplomat, said, "I don't think she meant—"

"Oh, shut up," Casey snapped. "Stop taking up for morons, would you? That nurse needs an attitude adjustment, and I'm just the person to give it to her."

"Amen," Dillon muttered, earning a chiding look from Callie. He started to wow her with a sexy smile before he remembered that *she* was the reason he was standing in a delivery room about to witness a gruesome event no single man should have to see.

The minutes seemed to crawl by. Dillon's stomach hurt from clenching and unclenching each time Casey struggled through a contraction. He'd lost the feeling in his fingers a long time ago, but he suspected it was nothing compared to what Casey was going through.

Finally the doctor came into the room. She was a thin woman in her early forties, with long, gray-streaked hair she wore in a casual ponytail down her back. She graced them with a smile as she slipped on the latex gloves a nurse handed her. "How are we doing?" she asked, focusing on Casey.

"Just peachy." Casey gasped, gritting her teeth against another contraction. "Dr. Martin, this wasn't supposed to happen for another two weeks."

"Yes, well, babies don't always follow our schedule, I'm afraid." The doctor's arm disappeared beneath the sheet that was shielding Casey from Dillon's view. He braced himself, knowing from experience that Casey was about to squeeze his hand. Not that he was feeling much in that area.

"Hmm. Well, looks like you're about ready to deliver. I'll alert the nurses and be right back. Don't push just yet, okay, Casey?"

Dillon's mouth went dry as he watched Dr. Martin push the rolling chair away and stand to strip off her gloves. He almost didn't recognize his own voice as he asked the doctor, "What . . . what happens if she pushes?"

Dr. Martin seemed to notice him for the first time. "Are you the husband?"

"No!" Dillon nearly shouted. He made an effort to calm himself. "I'm just a . . . a friend."

"Her husband's on his way back from the airport," Callie explained.

"Oh, I'm sorry. Unless he gets here in the next thirty minutes, he's going to miss it."

"You didn't answer my question," Dillon reminded her. "What happens if she pushes?"

"Just make sure she doesn't until I get back."

The doctor disappeared. Dillon felt icy cold sweat trickle down his spine. He looked at Callie, wondering how she could remain so calm. "I can't do this," he blurted out. "Maybe Wyatt or Greg or somebody would be willing to—Yow!" He looked down at his hand. The tips of his fingers had turned an interesting shade of purple.

"I don't want Wyatt, or Greg, or anybody else," Casey said distinctly. "I want you and Callie."

"Why me?" Dillon asked, helpless to look away from the intensity of Casey's gaze. He knew why Callie wanted him to participate, but he didn't understand Casey's reasoning.

"Because Wyatt would drive me crazy with his off-color jokes, and Greg would probably faint." She stared at the big hand she was crushing. Her voice softened. "And because you're just as scared as I am, and for some reason that makes me feel okay to be scared." She cast Callie an apologetic glance. "No offense, Callie. I'm very glad you're here, too, for the opposite reason. I've got fear on one side, and strength and calmness on the other." She brought both their hands to her cheeks. "If I can't have Mom and Brett, I can't think of anyone else I'd rather have beside me."

Dillon swallowed a suspicious lump in his throat. "Okay, I'll stay." He caught Callie's tender expression just as the door burst open and a group of nurses swept in with the doctor in the lead.

Dr. Martin stood back as the nurses bustled around

Casey, adjusting the stirrups and arranging themselves around her. Dillon kept his gaze glued to Casey's flushed, perspiring face.

"Now you can push, Casey," Dr. Martin said. She seated herself on the rolling stool and positioned herself between Casey's legs.

The next fifteen minutes were the longest minutes of Dillon's life. The nurses worked in harmony, coaxing, pleading, and sometimes bullying Casey into pushing. Caught up in the excitement, Dillon found himself chanting with the rest of the group as Casey strained time after time.

A woman should get a medal for this, Dillon thought, wiping his forehead before the sweat could sting his eyes.

Suddenly a familiar voice rose above the others, catching Dillon's attention. He stared at the crowd of nurses, zeroing in on one particular nurse standing near the back of the room. She wore a mask and a cap, but he'd recognize those big owlish eyes anywhere.

He'd seen those eyes up close and personal.

"Come on, girl!" the woman bawled, unaware that Dillon had spotted her. "Put some elbow grease into it!"

Mrs. Scuttle, masquerading as a nurse.

He tried to signal to Callie, but she was focused entirely on Casey.

And then it happened, and Dillon forgot all about Mrs. Scuttle and her bizarre presence in the delivery room.

With one giant push, Casey delivered her baby girl into Dr. Martin's waiting hands. The doctor smiled and held the baby aloft for all to see.

Then she waved for Dillon to move closer.

His feet felt like lead as he obeyed. She handed him

the scissors and pointed to where he should cut the umbilical cord. Dillon saw that his hand was surprisingly steady as he cut the cord and handed a nurse the scissors.

"Do you want to take her to her mother?" the doctor asked.

Dillon hesitated. The baby looked slippery, and his hands were sweaty. But he reached for her anyway, staring down at the tiny fingers and toes and her cute little rosebud mouth.

His heart melted.

An elbow in the ribs jolted him out of his dazed state.

"Well, don't just stand there gawkin' like you did all the work!" Mrs. Scuttle said. "Give that precious little lamb to her mother before she catches a cold."

He did, surprised at his reluctance to give her up into Casey's eager but exhausted arms.

After witnessing the miracle of birth with Dillon, Callie took his sweaty hand and pulled him into the hall. Mrs. Scuttle stayed behind, cooing over the baby and ignoring the sharp, speculative looks from the other nurses.

"You were wonderful," Callie told him. She couldn't resist smiling at his dazed expression. "That wasn't so bad, was it?" Dillon attempted to glower, but Callie saw through his facade.

"It wasn't exactly a picnic, watching a woman suffer like that."

"Yeah, but look at the reward," Callie pointed out. "That makes it all worth it."

Dillon jerked his head in the direction of the delivery room. "I take it you want a couple of those someday?"

Callie's heart did a flip in her chest. She licked her lips, suddenly nervous. She couldn't quite decipher Dillon's expression. "Um, yeah. A couple, maybe three." Her breath caught in her throat as Dillon moved closer. His eyes darkened with emotion. He hooked a finger beneath her chin.

"You realize that twins run in our family?" he asked softly.

She swallowed hard. "Yes, I know. I could handle it. I think the big question is, could you?"

Bringing his mouth within a hairbreadth of hers, Dillon whispered, "Yes. Thanks to you, I've had a lot of practice. Callie, will you—"

"There they are!" a voice shouted loud enough to draw several frowns from the nursing staff.

"Did she have her baby?"

"Is she okay?"

Callie caught Dillon's disgruntled expression just before he turned to face the group rushing along the hall in their direction. Although she was fairly certain he'd been about to propose, she would have liked to have heard the actual words.

Among the group of party guests she saw Mary and several escorts, along with LaVonda and the kids. A couple she didn't recognize was in the lead. The woman was breathtakingly beautiful, with a tall, full figure and a friendly twinkle in her eyes. The man beside her was just as striking. Close behind the couple was the whole gang, including Brett, who pushed through them like a madman.

He stumbled to the front, gasping for air, his hair standing on end and his suit a rumpled mess. "Am I too late?"

"You're damned right you are," Dillon growled,

then spoiled the effect by reaching out and clasping Brett's shoulder. He grinned. "You've got yourself a little beauty in there. Congratulations!"

But Brett groaned and covered his face. "Oh, no! She had to go through it alone!"

"No, she didn't," Mrs. Scuttle said from behind Callie and Dillon. "Dill and Callie were with her the whole time." She gazed at Dillon with an adoring expression that had the entire group gawking. "Dill was wonderful."

Callie was amazed to see him blush at the secretary's praise. To cover the awkward moment, she stuck out her hand to the tall woman. "I'm guessing by your gorgeous tan that you must be Lydia. I've heard a lot about you."

Lydia laughed. "Same here. We came straight from the airport. This is my husband, Luke. Luke, meet Callie."

Luke shot her a wicked smile as he shook her hand. "So this is what all the fuss is about." He glanced at Dillon and lifted an eyebrow. "You didn't mention that she was stunning," he chided.

"I don't remember mentioning her at all," Dillon shot back, but he was smiling as well. "I'm sure Mrs. Scuttle kept you informed."

"Mrs. Scuttle . . . and a few others," he drawled with a laugh. "Welcome to the family."

"Yeah, well, payback is a bitch, as you'll soon find out when you stand in for me while Callie and I are on our honeymoon."

"Hey!" Wyatt protested. "What about me? I can run that nightclub with one eye closed." And then it dawned on Wyatt what Dillon had said. "Wait! You guys are getting married?"

Callie caught Dillon's hopeful, questioning look and nodded. It wasn't exactly the proposal of her dreams, but with Dillon, things tended to lean toward the bizarre.

Before any further questions could be asked, the curtains to the nursery opened. A smiling nurse held the new baby aloft, and the group crowded around the window.

Dillon took the opportunity to kiss his fiancée. When he finished, Callie had to struggle to remember her own name.

"Callie, will you—" Dillon began.

"Hey, Dillon! What did she name the baby?"

"Do you know how much she weighed?"

Without losing focus, Dillon ignored the hecklers and finished what he'd started to say a dozen times. "—marry me, have my babies, and grow old with me?"

"Yes to all three, Dillon." With a blissful sigh, she rested her head against his wildly beating heart. Now, *that* was a proposal, she thought.

Epilogue

Dillon glanced at the speedometer for the fourth time in four minutes. He didn't dare take his eyes from the road as he said, "Tell me what they're doing now."

"Jada is drooling, and Kaden is sleeping. I know this makes you nervous, Dillon, but we've tried everything else. Driving them around is the only thing that seems to help their colic. Some birthday, huh?"

He felt Callie's patient stare and tried to ease his impossible grip on the steering wheel. As for the beads of sweat on his upper lip and forehead, he could only hope and pray that it was too dark for her to notice.

The words slipped out before he could stop himself. "Are you absolutely certain they're buckled in correctly?"

She sighed before she said with studied patience, "Absolutely one hundred percent certain. We both checked the restraints a dozen times." She reached out and touched his arm in a loving gesture that should have relaxed Dillon.

It didn't.

"Sweetheart, I thought you'd gotten over your fear of children."

Dillon checked the speedometer again and wished he could see the little mirror in the back window that allowed Callie to see the babies' reflections. "That was before," he said.

"Dillon—"

"I know, I know. I'm being paranoid and overprotective and silly."

"No, I—"

"But better safe than sorry, right?" He dared to take his eyes from the road for two seconds to cast her a weak, apologetic grin. His eyes widened at the expression on her face.

He jerked the wheel, making the new SUV swerve. "What is it? Is something wrong? Did they stop breath—"

"Calm down, and look in your side mirror." There was the barest hint of laughter in her voice as she added, "Does anything look familiar?"

"Damn!" Dillon bit off another curse at the sight of flashing lights closing in fast behind them. No way, he muttered to himself as he pulled onto the shoulder and set the brake, could they be unlucky enough to get Super Trooper again. Atlanta was a big city. The odds had to be against—

He was reaching for his wallet when he heard a familiar tapping on the window.

Along with a familiar voice.

"Step out of the vehicle, sir."

He and Callie groaned simultaneously, although her groan sounded like more of a smothered laugh. "I do not believe this," he said as he released his seat belt. "Where is Mrs. Scuttle when you really need her?"

"Try not to lose your temper, darling," Callie called after him sweetly.

"There's no reason to lose it," Dillon said loud enough for Officer Witless to hear. "I wasn't speeding and we haven't stopped anywhere since we left the house, which rules out robbery. We were *both* wearing our seat belts, and I have my headlights on." He folded his arms and glared at Officer Gorden. "I'm real curious to know why you stopped me."

Officer Dum-Dum put his hands on his hips. "You were driving too slow," he announced. "Thought you might be trying to conceal your intoxication."

Dillon narrowed his eyes and counted to ten. Slowly. "I haven't been drinking. I would never drink and drive, and I certainly wouldn't with my kids in the car."

"*Your* kids?" Gorden looked around Dillon's broad shoulders into the backseat of the SUV. "You had two kids? At the same time?"

Through gritted teeth, Dillon said, "They're twins. Surely you've heard of twins?"

"And I supposed you're going to tell me that Ms. Spencer is now Mrs. Love?"

"As a matter of fact . . . she is." Dillon kept his arms folded tightly to keep from lunging at the stupid cop. "Are you going to give me a ticket for driving too slow? Because if you are, you need to do it. Jada and Kaden have colic, and in about five seconds they're going to realize the vehicle isn't moving." He managed to inject a little false concern into his voice as he added, "And believe me, you do *not* want to know what it sounds like when twins wail at the same time."

Officer Gorden sighed and shook his head, as if he regretted what he was about to do. He pulled a folded piece of paper from his front pocket and opened it.

"I'm afraid there's been a warrant issued for your arrest, Mr. Love."

Dillon's jaw dropped. "What the hell?" Surely his ears were playing tricks on him? Because he could have sworn he'd heard his wife snicker.

"Yes," the cop told him gravely. "It's a warrant for your arrest . . . for the violation of driving on your birthday."

The words were so ludicrous, Dillon took a moment to digest them. When he did, he let out a string of curses that caused Officer Gorden to take a wise step back. "How much?" he bellowed at the cop. "How much did my brother pay you to do this?"

Behind him in the SUV, Callie burst out laughing.

Unrepentant, Gorden grinned. "I owed him one. He gave me some good advice on how to get my wife to take me back. We had a fight."

"Well," Dillon drawled sarcastically, already thinking of ways he was going to torture good ol' Uncle Wyatt. "That's just too sweet of him."

Without another word, he got back into the SUV and started the engine. Callie was still laughing, and he could hear Officer Gorden laughing all the way back to his patrol car.

He sat there a long moment, gripping the wheel. Slowly the tension drained out of him as he realized how ridiculously uptight he was being. Becoming a father—twice—was a wondrous thing, but sometimes it scared the shit out of him.

He felt a bubble of laughter rise in his throat, followed by another, and another . . . until he was helpless with it.

"Happy birthday, *Dill*," Callie managed to gasp out.

Dillon retaliated by reaching over and pulling her in

for a lusty kiss that left her breathless . . . and no longer laughing.

They didn't surface for air until one of the twins let out a halfhearted cry of protest. This time Dillon didn't panic. He calmly released the emergency brake, checked his mirrors, and pulled out onto the road.

Dear Readers:

A popular question I'm often asked is "where do you get your ideas?" I'd have to say about eighty percent of the time I truly don't know, but in the case of *Completely Yours*, I do have an interesting story to share.

Sometime in the spring of 2003, I received a flattering fan letter from a woman in Wisconsin regarding one of my previous titles. We began to converse back and forth through email and I soon discovered she was going to have twin boys in December. Well, everyone knows that twins inspire awe in most of us, almost as if they're magic. I was no exception! I instantly became an excited cyber aunt to those twins. When they're grown, they probably won't thank me for sending Tammy matching elf outfits to her baby shower. (Please don't hate me, boys. After all, it was Christmas!)

The day Tammy Haverkampf sent me an email telling me she and her husband Tom had decided on the names Dillon and Wyatt for the twins, I was struck with an idea for a spin-off to my romantic comedy, *Mr. Complete*, involving twin hunks named Dillon and Wyatt Love. With strong hero names like Dillon and Wyatt, how could I go wrong?

In this rare instance (for me, at least), a work of pure fiction *was* inspired in part by the arrival of twins in Rhinelander, Wisconsin. Thank you, Tammy, Tom, sister Isabelle, and, of course, Dillon and Wyatt.